Christopher Fowler is a director of The Creative Partnership, a film promotion company based in Soho, and is the author of the novels *Roofworld, Rune, Red Bride, Darkest Day, Spanky, Psychoville, Disturbia* and *Soho Black*, and of the short story collections *City Jitters, The Bureau of Lost Souls, Sharper Knives, Flesh Wounds* and *Personal Demons*.

Also by Christopher Fowler

ROOFWORLD
RUNE
RED BRIDE
DARKEST DAY
CITY JITTERS
THE BUREAU OF LOST SOULS
SHARPER KNIVES
SPANKY
PSYCHOVILLE
FLESH WOUNDS
DISTURBIA
PERSONAL DEMONS
SOHO BLACK

UNCUT
UNCUT
UNCUT
UNCUT
UNCUT
UNCUT

Twenty-one Short Stories by
CHRISTOPHER FOWLER

WARNER BOOKS

A *Warner* Book

First published in Great Britain by Warner Books 1999

Collection Copyright © Christopher Fowler 1999
Introduction Copyright © Christopher Fowler 1999

All stories copyrighted to Christopher Fowler. 'Jumbo Portions' © 1988;
'The Master Builder' © 1989; 'On Edge', 'Norman Wisdom and the Angel of
Death', 'Dale and Wayne Go Shopping', 'Last Call for Passenger Paul',
'In Persia', 'Black Day at Bad Rock' and 'Chang-Siu and the Blade of Grass'
all © 1992; 'The Laundry Imp', 'Night After Night of the Living Dead',
'Tales of Britannica Castle', 'Perfect Casting', 'The Most Boring Woman
in the World', 'The Unreliable History of Plaster City', '*Jouissance de la Mort*',
'Mother of the City' all © 1995; 'The Human Element' © 1998, 1999;
'The *Trafalgar* Lockdown', 'Thirteen Places of Interest in Kentish Town'
and 'Two Murderers' all © 1999.

A CIP catalogue record for this book
is available from the British Library.

ISBN 0 7515 2644 4

Typeset by Solidus (Bristol) Limited
Printed and bound in Great Britain by
Clays Ltd, St Ives plc

Warner Books
A Division of
Little, Brown and Company (UK)
Brettenham House
Lancaster Place
London WC2E 7EN

For everyone at The Creative Partnership.
Thank you for twenty fantastic years.

Contents

Introduction: Anti-Bob

Recently I was invited to a signing in a Medway town as part of a literary festival. A bout of 'flu had forced me to cancel an earlier appearance, and this time I was determined to go. Upon reflection, it had probably not been a good idea to cane it at a party the night before I made the trip. I arrived in Rochester looking and feeling like a recently exhumed corpse. I was dimly aware that my perceptions were still being affected by the previous night's chemical indulgences.

Rochester was once filled with the kind of naval trades that pertained to the processing of cargo. Now it has become an 'English Heritage' centre, its buildings tarted up for tourists, its high street pedestrianised, its traditional businesses replaced with 'Olde Worlde' antique shoppes filled with house-clearance trash. I watched appalled European visitors passing tea-shop displays of inedible factory-produced cakes, and wandered through horrible mock-Victorian shops stickered with 'Do Not Touch' signs, wondering what the hell an urban writer like myself was doing here in 'Li'l England – the Disney Remix'.

The answer became clear once I arrived at the shop, whose owner introduced himself and beat a hasty retreat just as a gaunt, hyperactive man appeared between the bookshelves. Bob – let's call him – had been appointed to act as a Master of Ceremonies for the festival's various readings and signings. Within five minutes Bob had filled me in on the key moments of his life, his hobbies and interests. He wrote poetry, which he read aloud while accompanying himself on a drum. He thrust self-published volumes of appalling doggerel into my hand, told me of his adventures with the Sandinistas, his interest in middle-aged punk poets, his Shamanism, his sixth-form-style paintings and his ability to create magical realism in the form of haikus.

I tend to think haikus are poems for people who can't develop fully rounded thoughts. Bob was one of those people who could have made a trip to Neptune sound as interesting as an insurance claim. As he droned on and on, and I stared at him with a fixed rictus of a grin that hopefully hid the fact that I was speeding off my face and seeing him as only a pair of shimmering eyes on a stick, his sweet wife crept shyly down and stood waiting – as she presumably had on so many previous occasions – for him to finish. Slowly it dawned on me that this man was the reason for the festival, that he had probably persuaded the council to cough up so that he and his self-congratulating coterie of failed art-pals could inflict themselves on a bewildered local populace.

Then again, perhaps the local populace had sussed the situation; not a single person turned up for the signing, and had they done so, five minutes with Bob would have sent them fleeing back into warmth and sunlight.

The ironic part of this story is that Bob loathed Charles Dickens (who had local connections with Rochester), and by osmosis all 'traditional' literature. As Bob wittered on about vicariously fighting Thatcherism from the sidelines, I noticed that he was leaning on – and squashing – an ancient volume of Pope's poetry; that under this was a first edition of Bertrand Russell's *Satan in the Suburbs*, and beneath this in turn were collections by Dryden, Keats and a dozen others.

Blinded to the shimmering beauty of language within his reach, he had set himself to spreading the word of middle-aged mysticism through the town like a damp grey plague. One look at Rochester tells you it is a town dying on its feet. One hour spent in the company of people like Bob tells you why.

This volume is intended as an antidote to the world of Bobs.

The hardest part of choosing twenty-one tales from nearly eighty has been deciding which ones to leave out. The selection process was set partly by copyright availability, and by a desire to provide accessibility to a wide range of readers. I was drawn to tales with a sense of fun, and thought it would be a good idea to include some stories which offered more than just their literal meanings. I think I could easily have switched the ones I've chosen with the ones I left out, without affecting the tone or rhythm of the collection.

Of the included tales, 'The Master Builder' and 'On Edge' were both filmed, the former with Tippi Hedren, the latter with Charlie Boorman and Doug Bradley. The tale 'In Persia' has become the starting point for a new novel, *Calabash*.

Oddly, the two stories which receive the most critical attention couldn't be included because they don't stand up alone. Most of the ones in this collection seem to inhabit a world where the innocent suffer, the guilty go unpunished, and the only way you can be safe is by staying very, very still.

Hitting adolescence in the horrible three-day-week times between swinging London and glam-rock, I'm surprised I haven't set more stories in exotic locations. Seeing these tales grouped together for the first time I've noticed a few other points. I treat locations as characters. I never write about happy families. I am an optimist. I like setting up jokes. I like strong women. I prefer change to stasis. I love London. And I'm not as smart as I thought I was. I had hoped to find one story – just one – that I was completely happy with. But it doesn't exist and never will. The tale you care for most is always the one you'll write next.

And that, I think, tells you as much about me as anyone needs to know.

The Human Element

Waving palm fronds. Blue waters retreating on white sand.
The siren song of the islands. . . The daydream vanished as
the train doors opened. Alighting from the train, Mr Mottram
was swept along the platform and up the stairs with the rush-
hour passengers, caught in the cross-currents of the com-
muter tide and finally expelled from the subway exit like
debris being discharged from a sewage outlet into open sea.

Slowing himself to a halt in the crowded sidewalk, he
smoothed down his straggling fair hair and looked up at the
world. It had taken him a lot of courage to leave the safety of
the small Norfolk village where he had lived his entire life.
Tall glass office buildings crushed in on every side, a thin
wedge of evening sky whirling between their rooftops. All
around him secretaries, clerks, shop assistants, students, salesmen, receptionists and executives passed in slipstreams, eager
to get home. Mottram put down his travel bag and dug into
his jacket pocket, searching for the scrap of paper on which
he had written the address of the hotel. Behind him there was
a thud as somebody stumbled over his bag.

'Damned tourists,' said the man to his colleague, glaring
angrily at Mottram as he dusted down the knees of his trousers.

Good lord, is it that obvious I'm a visitor? thought Mottram. Looking at his clothes, he supposed that it was. To begin with, he was the only person on the street wearing Ocean Pacific surfer shorts and a Hawaiian shirt decorated with marlins and palm trees, an unusual choice of wardrobe bearing in mind that the temperature was around two degrees centigrade and more suited to snowboarding than sunbathing. When his holiday flight-connection had been delayed by severe weather, Mottram had decided to stay in the city overnight. But as his travel bag contained only suntan oil, a T-shirt, a pair of swimming trunks and a straw hat, he was already beginning to regret the decision. He had dozed through the captain's weather report, and received no warning about the outside temperature until he saw passengers hauling padded coats out of their luggage. Worse, he had allowed his suitcase to be forwarded to his final destination. But it was an adventure, something not preplanned in the brochure. He would buy himself a sweatshirt and a pair of jeans.

'Watch it, asshole.' Two enormous tattooed men in overalls pushed past Mottram carrying a large wooden crate into a department store. Mottram pulled his bag against a wall and rummaged through it, finally producing a crushed strip of paper. The ink had run slightly, making the lettering illegible. It looked like 'Hotel Centaur', but couldn't be, could it? 'Central', perhaps. Avenue C or D? No telephone number. The battery was flat on his mobile, anyway. He looked up at the strip of dimming sky. It would soon be dark. Which direction, though? The avenues stretched away in vertiginous perspective.

Nine hours earlier, Mottram had left his home in the quiet English village where he had grown up and caught a train to

Heathrow airport, planning to head down to a friend's apartment in the sun. But instead of arriving in time for cocktails, he now found himself in the wrong city and in the wrong part of town, thanks to the bus driver's refusal to split a hundred, let alone change a traveller's cheque.

Mottram examined the scrap of paper again. The word had to be 'Central'. Witnessing his altercation with the bus driver earlier, the lady sitting next to him had recommended a small, inexpensive hotel which she said was just a couple of stops on the subway. She had written down the address for him. She seemed normal enough. She wasn't drinking out of a paper bag and her shoes matched. Mottram had been told to watch out for certain signs in the city. He decided to trust her judgement. He pushed the note into his pocket and swung his travel bag onto his shoulder, hitting a child in the back of the head.

'I'm awfully sorry,' he called to the smartly dressed woman who grabbed her child to her, but they were already vanishing in the crowd.

'I wonder, could you tell me. . .' The man whose arm he touched stared at him as if he was a lunatic, then hurried on.

'Excuse me. . .' Mottram attempted to hail a grey-haired woman who looked as though she worked in a bank. 'Could you direct me to—' She flicked a blank glance at Mottram, but seemed to stare right through him to the other side of the street. Mottram frowned. Maybe his technique needed work. He decided to walk on. The lady on the bus had told him that the hotel was near the subway exit, so this could be the right street. Of course, there were four exits to the subway. . .

As he walked, he studied the storefronts. Jewellery shop, dry cleaner, electronics shop, Greek deli, sneaker emporium, coffee shop; their lights spilling onto the concrete as the day above them faded. As he passed a car wash, black rubber strips flipped aside to reveal a glittering white cadillac within, like the contents of a Fabergé egg. Mottram was fascinated by his surroundings. It was his first time abroad, his first time in a big city, his first time anywhere. There seemed to be so much more of everything than he had imagined. All he had ever seen of London was the railway station and the airport. He suffered from minor bouts of agoraphobia, and worked at home, planning spreadsheets on a computer that was linked to Norwich council. He spent most of his spare time on the Internet. It meant that he never needed to go anywhere. The trip had been suggested by his doctor as a means of rectifying this state of affairs. He had downloaded a picture of the city where he would have to catch his connecting flight, and it looked very nice.

Mottram walked past a large square tunnel entrance, then stopped and looked down into the darkness. What was this? Everything was new and interesting. As he stood peering in, the noise of a car engine grew until a Chrysler suddenly burst from the underground car park, nearly slamming him over the bonnet. He threw himself to one side as the vehicle lurched off into the homebound traffic with a squeal of tyres.

'Hey, mister, you lost?' The cabdriver, overweight, unshaven, layered in sweatshirts, was leaning from the window of his car calling to him. He had a half-eaten burger in his right fist. It was leaking ketchup down the car door. Deafening salsa music played on his radio.

'I'm looking for a hotel,' Mottram called back. 'I have the address here but I can't decipher it.' He brought the piece of paper over.

'Decipher. *Decipher*, eh? Here, gimme dat.' The cabbie screwed up one eye and stared hard with the other, as if trying to divine the message by psychic means. 'Oh yeah,' he said unconvincingly, 'yeah, I know dis place, get in, get in.' Despite the presence of a meter, the vehicle was a badly rear-ended Pinto, and did not look like a regular cab. *Weren't Pintos the ones that used to catch fire?* Mottram wondered as he cautiously climbed in. The back seat dipped in the middle, the ashtrays were overflowing and the driver was behind a chickenwire barrier. Mottram perched on his seat unhappily and studied the dashboard, which was covered in agonised plastic saints displaying their stigmata.

'How far away is it?' he asked.

'Couple blocks, but they're long blocks an' what wichoo carryin' that bag—' He slammed the cab noisily into gear and bounced it out of the kerb on the third try. 'Your first time in town?' he called, removing his eyes completely from the road and looking over his shoulder.

'Yes,' answered Mottram, 'is it that obvious?'

'You're dressed like you're escaped from a nuthouse if you don't mind my sayin'. The only way you could make it more obvious is to fix a fucking neon sign on your head.' The driver blew his nose on the back of his hand and the car fell down a pothole. Mottram's forehead thumped against the chickenwire, leaving an imprint on his skin. He gripped the armrest as the car tilted around a corner.

'I'm not a cabbie,' said the cabbie. 'This is not what I do.'

'Oh,' Mottram managed, discomfited.

'I don't have to do this. I'm a interior designer. I did the seats. You like the seats?'

'They're – uh—' Mottram stared disbelievingly at the lime-coloured leopardskin seat covers. 'They're very. . .' His voice trailed off.

'I had to recover 'em. Had a guy in the back, slit his wrists.

His fuckin' *wrists*. Ruined the fabric. Had nine bucks on 'im. I still can't get it outta the carpet.'

Mottram looked down between his feet at the darkly matted floor. Just then he remembered that he had no change smaller than a hundred. He tapped gingerly on the chicken-wire.

'I wonder – can you change a large bill?'

'Lessee here.' The driver rummaged inside his shirt and produced a couple of filthy crumpled notes. 'I got forty.'

'Well, I, um, don't have anything smaller than this.' He exhibited the bill against the wire.

'That ain't my problem. I got forty.'

'You mean this trip's going to cost me sixty?'

'It's your choice. We could drive around the fucking block until you've had your money's worth.'

'No, I don't think so.' Mottram slumped back with a sigh. He lifted a corner of the seat cover, peeped under it, then hastily smoothed it back down.

'Good, 'cuz we're here.' The driver slewed the cab over to a deep gutter and the far side of the vehicle dropped so much that Mottram almost rolled straight out onto the sidewalk. The cabbie glared at him, waiting. Mottram reluctantly slipped the rolled hundred through the wire and received forty back.

'Thanks, mister. You enjoy your stay.'

Mottram barely had time to close the back door before the cab belched back into life, rocked out of the gutter and pulled into the streaming traffic. He set down his bag and looked up, expecting to find himself in front of the hotel. Instead he was standing before a rundown porno cinema showing a movie called *Shaving Ryan's Privates*. Next door was a massage parlour with rotating red lights attached to the windows and a bad painting of a nude woman on her knees sucking what appeared to be a whip-handle.

'There ain't nowhere you need around here, man. That driver, he taken you for a fool, 'cause of your Hallowe'en outfit.' A tall young man in a black nylon jacket and grey sweater-hood stood in the doorway of the parlour watching him. He had a set of sharpened steel bars sticking through his nasal septum. Mottram wondered how he got his jumper off and on without getting them caught. The young man waggled his fingers at the slip of paper in Mottram's hand. 'Show me that.'

A frantic jumble of radio stations blared from passing cars. Strip joints, bars and pool halls flooded the street with hard ugly light. All around them, teenagers with gold teeth and woolly hats stood huddled in corners. They appeared to be making deals of some kind. The wind was rising. Empty Coke cups and wrappers blew across the sidewalk. There was a rancid frying smell in the air.

'Can you read it?' asked Mottram.

The young man looked doubtful. 'Maybe you should go to another hotel.'

'I don't suppose you know of one around here?'

'No.'

'How far am I from this place?' Mottram took back his piece of paper. The man with the nasal piercings shook his head, clearly losing interest. 'I don't know, man. Ask the door-guy there.' He pointed to the corner of the street.

'What's that?'

'The Lucky Deuce. The bar on the corner.' Mottram peered into the gathering darkness but saw no bar. 'You just tell him you're a dumb tourist and he'll give you directions.'

'I don't see a bar.'

'Look, put your feet like this, one in front of the other, an' walk about a hundred yards. There's a big meer.'

'A what?'

'A meer. The thing you get reflected in.'

'Oh, a mirror.'

'That's what I say. He just there, he knows everywhere, he'll help you.'

'Righto. Thank you very much.'

'Yeah, no problem.' He gave a little wave as Mottram walked uncertainly away. 'Asshole,' he muttered under his breath.

When Mottram reach the mirror-windowed bar with the neon beer sign in its corner, he realised why people were treating him badly. He looked ridiculous, from the little round glasses that perched on his nose to the skinny white legs that stuck out of his baggy shorts. Even with his own limited knowledge of the world, he could tell that is was the kind of look all crazy people ended up sharing. A band of shark-like youths swaggered past him, warily eyeing their path. Against the glass exit-doors of the bar, a wasted-looking security guard leaned, cleaning his nails with his keys. He wore a grey padded jacket unzipped to reveal a sweatshirt that read: 'Your God Is Not My God'.

Mottram was beginning to feel very far from home. He set down his travel bag and looked up at the crackling neon sign. The letters 'UCK U' buzzed back at him, shining pink against the deepening blue-black of the evening sky. Despite the setbacks he was experiencing, Mottram looked upon his trip as a cultural expedition. After all, he thought, most people just visit the tourist attractions, but who gets to see real city-life like this? *Who would want to?* warned a voice in his head.

There was a surprising number of young women hanging around on the sidewalk now. They certainly didn't seem to be dressed warmly enough. Some of them leaned in shadowy doorways, talking softly to each other, breaking off to watch the cars pass. Determined to improve his social skills, Mottram approached the doorman and explained his predicament. He was starting to feel as if his search for the hotel had a greater meaning, that he had to find it or count himself a failure in some obscure way. He was determined more than ever to locate it.

'Yeah, I heard of this place.' The doorman tapped Mottram's note with his forefinger. 'Supposed to be nice.'

'Do you know where it is?'

'It's weird, I know it – it's right around here someplace. But just where . . . Go in and ask Rudy. He's the bartender, been here a thousand years, he'll remember.'

Mottram felt as if he could use a warming drink, a nice cup of tea with a shot of brandy in it. He stepped inside. It was so dark that he fell over the carpet twice before reaching the bar. A wavering, whiny voice sang on a tape that sounded as though it had stretched with overuse. Clambering onto an impossibly high stool, he realised that the chances of obtaining tea here were slim, so he ordered a brandy. A handful of red plastic booths had been filled, mostly by young women in short, tight skirts. The bartender had a nose like a piece of very old fruit. His hair was a peculiar shade of orange, and his dyed eyebrows looked like caterpillars. He coughed into a beermug and squeakily wiped it clean. Mottram leaned across the counter.

'The gentleman on the door said you could direct me to this hotel.' He held up the increasingly crumpled piece of paper. The bartender set down his mug and squinted at the address.

'Yeah,' he said finally, 'that's the Central. Yeah, I know where that is. Nice place.'

'Can you tell me how to get there?'

'Sure.' The bartender thought for a second. 'I don't do directions so good. Be easier if I draw it for you. It's not very far away. Couple of blocks, no more.' He took a pencil from the glass on the counter, drew on a paper cocktail-napkin and passed it across to Mottram. 'You go out of here, left to the next block, past the roadworks, right at the opposite corner and it's a couple of hundred yards down on the left. Big sign outside. You can't miss it.'

'Thank you,' said Mottram, pleased, 'thank you very much.'

'No problem.' He returned to cleaning the glasses. The whiny tape came to a sudden end and the place lapsed into dead silence. Somebody coughed violently, as though they'd swallowed something awful. Mottram sniffed the air.

'There's a funny smell in here,' he pointed out, 'damp.'

'Yeah,' agreed the bartender. 'It's the toilets. The girls, they jam up the bowls with their things, you know? Towels and condoms. The toilets aren't built to take stuff like that, they overflow. We put so much disinfectant down you can smell it from the street, it gets in your clothes. You can taste it sometimes. Them – you know,' he made a gesture in the air, 'them disinfectant cakes. The speed they disappear I figure the rats use 'em as breath fresheners.' He leaned forward, beckoning Mottram confidentially. 'This used to be a high-class place. We had a live jazz band. Art Blakey, he came here once. Then it was a fag disco. Every night was like a fuckin' end-of-the-world party. Then we got new owners and it became an SM joint. At the end of those evenings we used to find broads chained to the bathroom pipes. Then the brothers moved in. They taped packets under the booth tables, using the place as a drop point, so we were raided all the time. Cops really know how to drink. Now it's just a regular bar, and I spend my time stopping hookers from blowing their johns 'round the back of the stage on account of the mess. I tell you,' he sighed sadly and leaned on the bar, 'it's a fucking long way from Art Blakey.'

'Hey, honey, you in the palm-tree underwear, you looking for a good time?' *That girl can't be more than seventeen*, thought Mottram. She was dressed in a pink satin top pulled down to her nipples and a red rubber skirt as wide as a man's belt. He halted in mid-stride and looked back at her. Until now, the nearest he had ever been to holding a conversation with a prostitute was having lunch with his nephew who worked in advertising. The girl beckoned.

'My name's Betty Sue. What's the matter, old timer, you lose your surfboard? The tide's a long way out from here. You buying or just browsing?' Up close, her face looked much harder than it had from a distance. She reached out a thin white arm and grabbed the waistband of his shorts. Mottram, in turn, let out a squeak of surprise. *Old timer*, he thought, *what's she on about? I'm thirty-seven.*

'Listen, it's getting kind of cold out here. What do you have in mind?'

'Well, I don't,' explained Mottram. 'That is, I'm looking for my hotel.'

'Look, I can't say it for you, you have to tell me what you want, it's a legal thing.'

'I just want to get to a hotel. I'm very tired.'

'Call it whatever you want to, honey. Tell you what, I'll do a deal with you 'cause I feel sorry for you standing there with no pants.' Her other arm slid snakelike around his waist. She ran long red nails down the flies of his shorts. Mottram felt a long-dormant stirring. 'I can guarantee you a real white-knuckle ride with special extras, one night only,' she whispered into his ear, snapping gum and almost deafening him. Mottram's palms were starting to sweat.

'Look, you're awfully attractive,' he mumbled, 'but I really think I have to be getting along.' He pulled himself free with difficulty and readjusted the waistband of his shorts.

'Okay, but think about it. If you get lonely in the night I'll still be here, worse fucking luck.'

'Thank you,' said Mottram, straightening his hair. 'I'll try to remember that.'

'Have a good vacation,' she called as he headed down the street with the napkin still in his hand. When he reached the roadworks at the next intersection, he suddenly had a complete mental blank about which direction to continue in. Unfortunately, the bartender had failed to mark his instructions with any street names. The map could be any one of four ways up. He sighed, folded the original scrap inside the napkin and pushed it into the pocket of his shorts.

It was then that he discovered his wallet was missing.

Thinking back, he remembered taking it out in the bar. It had been in his pocket when he had walked over to the hooker. He turned around and started back.

Not only had his wallet disappeared. So had the girl.

'Bottle blond, kinda short, lot of make-up, red skirt, about thirty-five, that the one?'

'Yes,' Mottram admitted, 'that was probably her. She looked much younger from a distance.'

'No shit. Well, you better go report your credit cards missing pretty quickly, because Jessie will rack up a bill before you even find a cop. She goes nuts if you call her a hooker.'

'You mean she's not?'

'Oh sure. She's supposed to have been an actress in some soap opera, says she used to play the lead. She should be on one.'

'A soap opera?'

'No, a lead.'

The burly black man on the door of the 'She's So Fine' bar had beckoned Mottram over after watching him walk up and down the street in total confusion for fifteen minutes. The entrance to the bar was wreathed in fizzing red lightbulbs that seemed about to explode and shower them in shards of molten glass. It made the Lucky Deuce look like Claridges. The bulbs cast a saturnine glow over the doorman's face.

'So here's what you do, go find a cop.'

'I've been looking for one for the past—'

'They don't come around here. You need to go back up the street a few blocks.'

Mottram turned and looked back. Behind him, the sidewalks were brighter and busier. Had he come from that direction? Cabs bounced over the intersection where the hookers stood dipping their heads to check out passing drivers. Mottram opened his fist and uncrumpled his napkin, but the sweat from his palm had made the ink run, and it was illegible. His original piece of paper seemed to have fallen out of his pocket. He racked his brains trying to remember the name of the street.

'Look, I really need to get to a decent hotel. A bed, some warmth—'

'There are no "decent hotels" in this neighbourhood, friend.'

Mottram ignored him and continued. 'The Central, that was it, on Avenue "C", but I'm beginning to think it doesn't exist.'

'What's the intersection?' asked the doorman.

'I don't know. We don't have intersections where I come from.'

'I can tell you where "C" is.'

'You can?'

'You're standing in it.'

Mottram finally felt as though he was getting somewhere. He stood on tiptoe, peering down the street. The bitter evening air had numbed his kneecaps. His breath formed crimson clouds in the light of the club.

'I must be near the hotel, then,' he said. 'How long is this street?'

'A hundred and fifteen blocks.' The doorman grinned inanely. It looked like he was on drugs.

Mottram narrowed his eyes suspiciously. 'Are you teasing me?'

One of the club's strippers came out and stood in the bulb-encrusted doorway to light up a cigarette. 'Is fucking crazy,' she told the doorman, 'we can do anything we like in there except smoke.' She looked at Mottram. 'Isn't that fucking crazy?' She stared at Mottram's clothes, fascinated. She was wearing a blond nylon wig, a white imitation-fur bustier, purple suede hotpants and battered mock-alligator skin thigh boots. She had a huge love-bite on her throat.

'You want to come in and watch the exotic dancers?' asked the doorman. 'You look so cold.'

'No,' said Mottram, 'I really think I should find a hotel and report my wallet.'

'Is terrific show,' he added without much conviction. 'Maria here does a thing with a boa.' Mottram pictured her covered in red ostrich feathers.

Maria leaned to one side, wiggled her fingers at Mottram

18   U n c u t

and snapped her gum without losing the cigarette in the corner of her mouth. 'You know, a boa?' she said. 'It's a snake.'

'Thanks all the same,' said Mottram, drawing on his failing reserves of English politeness, 'but I really don't think I should go in a strip club.'

'This ain't a strip club,' explained Maria, 'is exotic revue. Girls and snakes.'

Mottram waved a farewell to the doorman, picked a direction and headed off on aching feet.

'Hey!' called the doorman after him. 'Have a good vacation!'

Still no sign of a policeman. It was starting to rain. At least he hadn't kept his traveller's cheques with his wallet. He could cancel the credit cards with a few quick phonecalls when he reached the hotel. It was his own fault, he thought, as he trudged on past darkened warehouses and factory outlets. He should have stayed where he was, cut his losses and aimed for the nearest half-decent hotel. He would never have dreamed of venturing into an equivalent part of town in, say, London, so why do it here? For someone employed in urban planning, he realised that he was a little naïve.

Mottram left the clip joints and dives behind, and found himself walking through a darker, more residential part of the street. The crumbling buildings sandwiched between derelict storefronts were beyond gentrification. Only the bulldozers could help now. The interiors of the wholesale stores he passed were filled with litter, old mattresses and broken panels of wood, awaiting demolition. This was probably a beautiful neighbourhood once, he thought. Could it ever be again? An answer to this question appeared as he passed a pitted intersection and found himself on a block consisting of rubble-strewn lots and half-destroyed facades. Six or seven ragged-coated tramps stood warming their hands around a blazing oil-drum. As Mottram stared into the darkness of the lot he could make out many more figures slumped in the remaining corners of the building nursing bottles to their chests.

Suddenly a tramp popped up from a wall in front of him. Mottram gave a yelp of alarm, but with typical indecision, he remained rooted to the spot as the filthy old man loomed close.

'Hey, buddy, you got a couple of notes to spare for an old soldier?' he whistled through broken brown teeth. He scratched the stubble on his face and stared at Mottram's clothes. 'Say, what happened to you? Somebody steal your pants? Those bastards. Those *bastards*!'

'No,' said Mottram, 'but someone stole my wallet, so I can't give you any money.'

'Stole your wallet too? Jeez, that's terrible! You wanna hit?' He wiped the top of his whisky bottle on his coat and proffered it.

'No, thank you. I have to find the Central Hotel.'

'Oh, that's just along here a couple of blocks. Or is that the Central Mission? Shit.' He pulled off his woollen cap and clawed at his grey hair. Mottram began to scratch sympathetically. 'That's the trouble see, mister. I can't remember nothing.'

'Why's that?'

'I'm a bum,' shrugged the tramp. 'What's to remember?'

'Well, I'm sorry,' said Mottram, 'but I have to be getting along.'

'I wasn't always a bum,' the tramp continued, regardless. 'Believe it or not, I used to have a regular job. I was a movie

producer! Hard to imagine, huh? Or was I – an airline pilot?
Anyways, now I'm living in derelict buildings. Guess the city
got the last laugh on me.'

Mottram had no idea what to say. He looked at the
tattered man balancing before him and tried to imagine himself in the same position. Suddenly the tramp brightened up.
'Say, you're welcome to stay for something to eat.'

'Thanks, that's very kind of you but no, I have to be getting
along.' He swung his travel bag onto his frozen shoulder.

'Okay, but if you change your mind you know where we
are.' He pointed over at the others gathered around their fire.
'These guys ain't so hot on intellectual conversation, but they
really know how to party.'

The tramp turned away and began picking his path across
piles of shattered brickwork. A platoon of brown rats scam-
pered out of his way. His shadow danced in the light of the
crackling oil-drum. He turned around and called back to
Mottram. 'Some nights when there's nobody around, we sing.
We're pretty good, for bums. It's a free life.'

Mottram watched until the tramp had rejoined his colleagues, then walked briskly away down the avenue of derelict
warehouses.

Ten minutes later, two streets over and back in bright light,
he found himself standing at the bottom of the steps of the
Central Hotel. He looked up and released a low growl. It was
something he always did when he was angry or frustrated. He
studied the smart facade, the tall white marble columns, the
polished brass of the revolving doors. The hotel was everything he had hoped it would be, barring one thing.

It was shut.

Once again he read the sign hanging behind the glass of the
entrance doors.

CLOSED FOR REFURBISHMENT UNTIL MAY! VISIT
OUR WEBSITE!

Hopelessly he looked around, praying he'd find another hotel in the area, but the streets here were devoid of life. He brushed back his thinning fair hair and sighed. He had to find a working telephone and call a cab. He would ask to be taken to the nearest hotel in the neighbourhood. He was dead on his feet. All he wanted was a wash in hot water and a soft bed.

He sat down on a low wall between two hedges cut into neat oblongs, and massaged his aching feet. The rain began to fall harder. He watched it bouncing up on the sidewalk in front of him. He had not found a telephone box, a patrolman, a police car or even another human being. He looked at his watch. It was nearly 11 pm. He gently slid his sore toes back in his sandals and stood. For the past few minutes he had been considering the possibility of flagging down a car, but since that time he had not seen another vehicle. Perhaps, he thought, he had died and been consigned to some kind of purgatory. His travel bag had chafed a red stripe on his shoulder. He switched it over to the other side and struck on up the road once more. All around him, tall walls concealed houses with darkened windows.

Mottram reached a wide, deserted intersection and decided to flip a coin to choose his next direction. Unfortunately he threw the coin too high, failed to catch it and watched miserably as it rolled between the bars of a storm drain. He bent over and peered down into the depths of the sewer.

'Are you all right?'

He rose quickly and turned around. An attractive, expensively dressed woman of about forty-five stood beneath a black umbrella. She was swaying slightly and watching him. In one gloved hand she held a lead to which was attached a small hairy dog of indeterminate pedigree.

'Oh, I'm fine thank you,' said Mottram automatically, then realised that he wasn't.

'I thought you were being sick.'

'No, I'm English.'

'So what's the problem.'

'I'm, er, lost, actually.'

'Been swimming?' She glanced at his shorts, amusement in her eyes.

'Um, no.' By now he was rather tired of repeating the story. 'I need to find a hotel for the night.'

'My God,' laughed the woman, 'you're miles from one, except the Central, and that's closed. Coco-Beware, no!' She jerked the lead just in time to prevent the odd little dog from peeing on Mottram's shoe. 'Listen, if you like I can drive you to the nearest hotel.'

'Oh no,' he protested, 'I wouldn't want to put you to any trouble.' But he prayed she would insist.

'Oh, I insist,' said the woman, holding out her glove. 'My name's Gloria. Who are you?'

'Bernard, Bernard Mottram,' said Mottram, gratefully pumping her arm.

'Well, Bernard Bernard Mottram, I'll be happy to drive you,' said Gloria. 'I like the company. I'm so goddamned bored taking this dog out every night, the drive will cheer me up.' Gloria's Audi was parked in the next road. She beeped its alarm, opened the passenger door and threw the dog in, then tossed his travel bag onto the animal. Mottram began to suspect, rightly as it turned out, that she had been drinking.

'When I was single, oh when I was single,' said Gloria. She

started the car and pulled away with a force that threw Mottram's head back and sent the dog somersaulting across the seat. 'God, I used to be so happy. I had friends, parties, a life, regular sex. The things you need.' She manoeuvred the car between two parked trucks at a speed Mottram would not have attempted sober. 'Then Harvey persuaded me to marry him. I must have been mad. He gives me little lists of things to do. He wears an apron when he cooks. Do you have any idea how depressing that is?'

Gloria rolled the car around a sharp corner. Even though it was an Audi, it had trouble making the turn. Mottram wondered if she was somehow related to the cabbie with the lime seat covers. Coco-Beware gave a yelp of pain as gravitational force threw it against the window.

'Harvey loves that dog,' Gloria muttered, reaching over to the glove box. For a moment it looked like there was no one driving the car. She reappeared with a silver hip-flask, unscrewed the cap and took a long swig, tipping her head right back. 'It's a very rare breed. Let's see if I can find a bridge on the way to your hotel and we'll throw the little fucker off it.' She wrenched the stick shift and the vehicle leapt forward.

Mottram was beginning to fear for his life. He stared out of the window but failed to find any clue to their surroundings.

'Don't ever get married, Bernard, not if you value your sanity. We had people over from his office last night. The wives spent four hours discussing drapes. I began to have these strange thoughts. I couldn't feel my legs. Then I realised the martinis were kicking in.' She revved the engine experimentally. 'They're coming over again next week, unless I can convincingly fake my own death before then.'

She swung the Audi onto a bridge and reached over into the back seat. For a moment Mottram thought she really was going to fling the dog out of the window, but she was just reaching for a cigarette. He looked out of the passenger seat and saw a black river passing far beneath.

'Take the wheel a second, will you?'

Mottram steered wide-eyed as Gloria rooted around for her cigarettes, her bottom turned towards him, her feet barely touching the pedals. Weaving back and forth over the lane lines, the car shot across the bridge into the deepening night.

'What's that noise?' asked Mottram with a start.

'What noise?' Gloria was now the right way up in the driver's seat, but the speedometer needle was hitting sixty.

'Oh my god, it's a police car. Slow down!'

'Are you kidding? Do you have *any idea* how drunk I am? Harvey would kill me.' Gloria put her foot to the floor and the Audi roared ahead. 'We can outrun them in this baby, no problem.' She caught his frightened look. 'Oh relax, I'm joking. The cops always turn off at the next junction.' She swung the wheel hard. Behind her, Coco Beware performed an involuntary backflip. The river, its oily black surface glittering in the moonlight, flashed by between the darkened buildings on their left. In the distance, the pulsing lights reappeared, accompanied by a high-pitched see-sawing sound.

Mottram grabbed Gloria's arm. 'I really don't think this is a good idea. They're bound to catch us. Please!'

'Oh for God's sake, Bernard, be a man!' cried Gloria. 'Where are all the real men?' The car mounted the kerb and caught the corner of a bale of leaflets, *Starsky and Hutch* style, bursting them across the bonnet and fountaining hundreds of sheets into the air. Several stuck themselves across the windscreen. Gloria looked over the wheel and found herself reading Scientology recruitment slogans.

'Bernard!' she shouted. 'I can't see a goddamn thing! Can't you climb out there and do something?' The car overshot the next bend in the road. Two wheels hammered up on the empty sidewalk. Behind them, the patrol car put on a burst of speed and almost rear-ended them. The police seemed to be shouting something through a loudspeaker system.

'I really think we should stop,' pleaded Mottram. He leaned out of his window and looked back at the patrol car. One of the policemen appeared to be pointing a gun at him. Gloria grabbed his shirt and pulled him back inside.

'You don't seem to understand,' he shouted at her, 'we'll both go to jail!'

'You think I'm not in jail now?' she answered, her face fighting to retain its composure.

'You'd better give me the wheel.' Mottram fought for control of the car. Gloria pushed his hands away and stamped down hard on the gas pedal. Coco Beware released a forlorn howl, and the Audi overshot the approaching curve by about a hundred and twenty feet, sliding gracefully on a pan of rainwater. When it burst through the railings, it seemed for a moment that the car had sprouted wings and would fly gracefully across the river, touching down gently on the other side. Seconds later it slammed into the water as though coming off a fairground chute. From inside the vehicle a trio of screams were heard, one of them from a dog.

Mottram sat beneath harsh neon strips on a steel bench, wrapped in an itchy grey blanket that smelled as though it had been shared by many other people that night, not all of them continent. He was shaking and covered in mud. No matter how hard he tried to flatten it, his hair remained standing on end. He had lost his travel bag when the car had sunk, just before the police launch had picked them out. Gloria had been taken downstairs to the cells after biting a cop on the hand. Nobody had even bothered to look for the dog.

Mottram stared at the clock on the wall. It was twenty to five in the morning. Back home, the people in his village would all be tucked up in their warm houses, fast asleep. He had been forced to wait several hours for the police to take his statement, because of the night rush. The place was crowded with shouting, moaning, complaining, drunk, drugged, confused, angry, mad people in various states of arrest. Mottram just wanted to be in his own bed. He just wanted to go to sleep. Was that asking too much? The man next to him had been brought in at the same time for some kind of drug offence, and he had already been released. It didn't seem fair. The sun was beginning to redden the sky beyond the wire-clad windows of the police station. The duty sergeant looked up at Mottram, smiled abstractedly and continued tapping at his computer. Finally a pair of officious-looking young cops spoke to the sergeant, who nodded in his direction. One of them held a charge sheet.

'Okay, Mr Mitcham—'

'Mottram. Bernard Mottram,' said Mottram reasonably. He was still, after all, a man of reason.

'Yeah, whatever. Well, we're talking about a pretty serious thing here.'

Mottram felt his nervous tremors start to increase. 'What are you talking about? I'm the innocent party in this.'

'You sure you're innocent?'

'Absolutely.'

One of the cops turned around to the crowd and bellowed, 'Hey, are you guys innocent or guilty?'

'Innocent!' they all shouted back.

The cops grinned and shrugged. 'Let me put it this way, Mr Mitcham,' said one, 'this city has zero tolerance for drug dealers.'

'What do you mean, drug dealers, I was trapped in a car driven by a drunk woman.'

The cops consulted the charge sheet. 'Says here you were arrested with a couple of grams of crack cocaine on you.'

'Oh don't be so stupid,' Mottram finally exploded. 'That was *him*.' He pointed to the empty space on the bench beside him. 'No wonder you let him go home. You've got the bloody charge sheets the wrong way around!'

'You don't have to be abusive, sir,' said the other cop.

'Abusive!' spluttered Mottram, turning puce above his blanket. 'Is everyone around here stark raving mad? You bloody stupid fucking morons! Can't anyone get the simplest bloody things right? Jesus H. Christ on a fucking bike!'

'That's quite enough, sir.' They grabbed him by the arms and dragged him off the bench.

'Will you let go of me, you pair of gormless dimwitted baboons!' yelled Mottram. 'Ow! You're hurting me! If you don't put me down, you braindead imbeciles, in all my life – never met such – simple common sense – lacking human decency – all mad—' Words finally failed him. He realised now how unprepared he had been for any of this. In everything he had read and seen on television, in magazines, on the Internet, there had been nothing about how utterly disorganised people could be.

The duty sergeant studied the list of charge sheets on his screen, highlighted one and hit the Return button, but couldn't help feeling he'd done something wrong. He wasn't very good with computers. *To be honest, I didn't see anything wrong with the old pen and paper system*, he thought to himself as the cops carried the screaming Mottram down to the cells. *I used to have a nice pen, I wonder what happened to it? Maybe it's in my desk.*

He could still hear Mottram hurling abuse at his officers. Cries of indignation bounced back up the stairs from the cells. *Funny*, he thought, feeling the station room warm with the light of the rising sun, *Englishmen are usually so polite.* The sergeant began pulling out the drawers of his desk as his officers started to argue about who was going for breakfast.

Norman Wisdom and the Angel of Death

Diary Entry #1 Dated 2 July

The past is safe.

The future is unknown.

The present is a bit of a bastard.

Let me explain. I always think of the past as a haven of pleasant recollections. Long ago I perfected the method of siphoning off bad memories to leave only those images I still feel comfortable with. What survives in my mind is a seamless mosaic of faces and places that fill me with warmth when I choose to consider them. Of course, it's as inaccurate as those retouched Stalinist photographs in which comrades who have become an embarrassment have been imperfectly erased so that the corner of a picture still shows a boot or a hand. But it allows me to recall times spent with dear friends in the happy England that existed in the fifties; the last era of innocence and dignity, when women offered no opinion on sexual matters and men still knew the value of a decent winter overcoat. It was a time that ended with the arrival of the Beatles, when youth replaced experience as a desirable national quality.

I am no fantasist. Quite the reverse; this process has a practical value. Remembering the things that once made me happy helps to keep me sane.

I mean that in *every* sense.

The future, however, is another kettle of fish. What can possibly be in store for us but something worse than the present? An acceleration of the ugly, tasteless, arrogant times in which we live. The Americans have already developed a lifestyle and a moral philosophy entirely modelled on the concept of shopping. What is left but to manufacture more things we don't need, more detritus to be thrown away, more vicarious thrills to be selfishly experienced? For a brief moment the national conscience flickered awake when it seemed that green politics was the only way to stop the planet from becoming a huge concrete turd. And what happened? Conversation was hijacked by the advertising industry and turned into a highly suspect sales concept.

No, it's the past that heals, not the future.

So what about the present? I mean right now.

At this moment, I'm standing in front of a full-length mirror reducing the knot of my tie and contemplating my frail, rather tired appearance. My name is Stanley Morrison, born March 1950, in East Finchley, North London. I'm a senior sales clerk for a large shoe firm, as they say on the quiz programmes. I live alone and have always done so, having never met the right girl. I have a fat cat called Hattie, named after Hattie Jacques, for whom I have a particular fondness in the role of Griselda Pugh in Series Five, Programmes One to Seven of *Hancock's Half Hour*, and a spacious but somewhat cluttered flat situated approximately one hundred and fifty yards from the house in which I was born. My hobbies include collecting old radio shows and British films, of which I have an extensive collection, as well as a nigh-inexhaustible supply of amusing, detailed anecdotes about the forgotten British stars of the past. There's nothing I enjoy more than to recount these lengthy tales to one of my ailing, lonely patients and slowly destroy his will to live.

I call them my patients, but of course they aren't. I merely bring these poor unfortunates good cheer in my capacity as an official council HVF, that's a Hospital Visiting Friend. I am fully sanctioned by Haringey Council, an organisation filled with people of such astounding narrow-minded stupidity that they cannot see beyond their lesbian support groups to keeping the streets free of dogshit.

But back to the present.

I am rather tired at the moment because I was up half the night removing the remaining precious moments of life from a seventeen-year-old boy named David Banbury who had been in a severe motorcycle accident. Apparently he jumped the lights at the top of Shepherd's Hill and vanished under a truck conveying half-price personal stereos to the Asian shops in Tottenham Court Road. His legs were completely crushed, so much so that the doctor told me they couldn't separate his cycle leathers from his bones, and his spine was broken, but facial damage had been minimal, and the helmet he was wearing at the time of the collision had protected his skull from injury.

He hasn't had much of a life, by all accounts, having spent the last eight years in care, and has no family to visit him.

Nurse Clarke informed me that he might well recover to lead a partially normal life, but would only be able to perform those activities involving a minimal amount of agonisingly slow movement, which would at least qualify him for a job in the Post Office.

Right now he could not talk, of course, but he could see and hear and feel, and I am reliably informed that he could understand every word I said, which was of great advantage as I was able to describe to him in enormous detail the entire plot of Norman Wisdom's 1965 masterpiece *The Early Bird*, his first colour film for the Rank Organisation, and I must say one of the finest examples of post-war British slapstick to be found on the face of this spinning planet we fondly call home.

On my second visit to the boy, my richly delineated account of the backstage problems involved in the production of an early Wisdom vehicle, *Trouble In Store*, in which the Little Comedian Who Won The Hearts Of The Nation co-starred for the first time with his erstwhile partner and straight-man Jerry Desmonde, was rudely interrupted by a staff nurse who chose a crucial moment in my narration to empty a urine bag that seemed to be filling with blood. Luckily I was able to exact my revenge by punctuating my description of the film's highlights featuring Moira Lister and Margaret Rutherford with little twists of the boy's drip-feed to make sure that he was paying the fullest attention.

At half past seven yesterday evening I received a visit from the mentally disorientated liaison officer in charge of appointing visitors. Miss Chisholm is the kind of woman who has pencils in her hair and 'Nuclear War – No Thanks' stickers on her briefcase. She approaches her council tasks with the dispiriting grimness of a sailor attempting to plug leaks in a fast-sinking ship.

'Mr Morrison,' she said, trying to peer around the door of

my flat, presumably in the vain hope that she might be invited in for a cup of tea, 'you are one of our most experienced Hospital Helpers' – this part she had to check in her brimming folder to verify – 'so I wonder if we could call upon you for an extracurricular visit at rather short notice.' She searched through her notes with the folder wedged under her chin and her case balanced on a raised knee. I did not offer any assistance. 'The motorcycle boy . . .' She attempted to locate his name and failed.

'David Banbury,' I said, helpfully supplying the information for her.

'He's apparently been telling the doctor that he no longer wishes to live. It's a common problem, but they think his case is particularly serious. He has no relatives.' Miss Chisholm – if she has a Christian name I am certainly not privy to it – shifted her weight from one foot to the other as several loose sheets slid from her folder to the floor.

'I understand exactly what is needed,' I said, watching as she struggled to reclaim her notes. 'An immediate visit is in order.'

As I made my way over to the hospital to comfort the poor lad, I thought of the ways in which I could free the boy from his morbid thoughts. First, I would recount all of the plot minutiae, technicalities and trivia I could muster surrounding the big-screen career and off-screen heartache of that Little Man Who Won All Our Hearts, Charlie Drake, climaxing with a detailed description of his 1966 magnum opus *The Cracksman*, in which he starred opposite a superbly erudite George Sanders, a man who had the good sense to kill himself when he grew bored with the world, and then I would encourage the boy to give up the fight, do the decent thing and die in his sleep.

As it happens, the evening turned out quite nicely.

By eleven thirty I had concluded my description of the film, and detected a distinct lack of concentration on behalf of the boy, whose only response to my description of the frankly hysterical sewer-pipe scene was to blow bubbles of saliva from the corner of his mouth. In my frustration to command his attention, I applied rather more pressure to the sutures on his legs than I intended, causing the crimson blossom of a haemorrhage to appear through the blankets covering his pitifully mangled limbs.

I embarked upon a general plot outline of the classic 1962 Norman Wisdom vehicle *On The Beat*, never shifting my attention from the boy's eyes, which were now swivelling frantically in his waxen grey face, until the ruptured vessels of his leg could no longer be reasonably ignored. Then I summoned the night nurse. David Banbury died a few moments after she arrived at the bedside.

That makes eleven in four years

Some didn't require any tampering with on my part, but simply gave up the ghost, losing the will to go on. I went home and made myself a cup of Horlicks, quietly rejoicing that another young man had gone to meet his maker with a full working knowledge of the later films of Norman Wisdom (not counting *What's Good For The Goose*, a prurient 'adult' comedy directed by Menahem Golem which I regard as an offensive, embarrassing travesty unworthy of such a superb family performer).

Now, standing before the mirror attempting to comb the last straggling wisps of hair across my prematurely balding pate, I prepare to leave the house and catch the bus to work, and I do something I imagine most people have done from time to time when faced with their own reflection. I calm myself for the day ahead by remembering the Royal Variety Performance stars of 1952. The familiar faces of Naughton & Gold, Vic Oliver, Jewel & Warriss, Ted Ray, Winifred Atwell, Reg Dixon and the Tiller Girls crowd my mind as I steel myself to confront the self-centred young scum with whom I am forced to work.

It is no secret that I have been passed over for promotion in my job on a number of occasions, but the most terrible slap-in-the-face yet performed by our new (foreign) management was administered last week, when a boy of just twenty-four was appointed as my superior! He likes people to call him Mick, walks around smiling like an idiot, travels to work wearing a Walkman, on which he plays percussive rubbish consisting of black men shouting at each other, and wears tight black jeans which seem specifically designed to reveal the contours of his genitalia. He shows precious little flair for the job, and has virtually no knowledge whatsoever of the pre-1960 British radio comedy scene. Amazingly, everyone seems to like him.

Of course, he will have to go.

Diary Entry #2 Dated 23 August

Mick is a threat no more

I simply waited until the appropriate opportunity arose, as I knew it eventually should. While I watched and listened, patiently enduring the oh-so-clever remarks he made to the office girls (most of whom resemble prostitutes from Michael Powell's excessively vulgar and unnecessary 1960 film *Peeping Tom*) about me, I comforted myself with memories of a happy, sunlit childhood, recalling a row of terraced houses patrolled by smiling policemen, uniformed milkmen and lollipop-ladies, a place in the past where Isobel Barnet was still guessing contestants' professions on *What's My Line*, Alma Cogan was singing 'Fly Me To The Moon' on the radio, cornflakes had red plastic guardsmen in their packets and everyone knew his place and damned well stayed in it. Even now when I hear the merry tickle of 'Greensleeves' heralding the arrival of an ice-cream van beset by clamouring tots I get a painful, thrilling erection.

But I digress.

Last Tuesday, while shifting a wire-meshed crate in the basement workroom, Mick dislocated his little finger, cutting it rather nastily, so naturally I offered to accompany him to the casualty ward. As my flat is conveniently situated on the route to the hospital I was able to stop by for a moment, trotting out some absurd excuse for the detour.

After waiting for over an hour to be seen, my nemesis was finally examined by Dr MacGregor, an elderly physician of passing acquaintance whose name I only remember because it is also that of John Le Mesurier's character in *The Radio Ham*. My experience as an HVF had familiarised me with basic casualty procedures, and I knew that the doctor would most likely inject an antibiotic into the boy's hand to prevent infection.

The needles for the syringes come in paper packets, and are sealed inside little plastic tubes that must be broken only by the attending physician. This is to prevent blood-carried infections from being transmitted.

It was hard to find a way around this, and indeed had taken dozens of attempts over the preceding months. The packets themselves were easy enough to open and reseal, but the tubes were a problem. After a great deal of practice, I found that I was able to melt the end of a tube closed without leaving any traced of tampering. To be on the safe side I had prepared three such needles in this fashion. (You must remember that, as well as having access to basic medical supplies – those items not actually locked away – I also possess an unlimited amount of patience, being willing to wait years if necessary to achieve my goals.)

While we waited for Dr MacGregor to put in an appearance, the boy prattled on to me about work, saying how much he 'truly valued my input'. While he was thus distracted, it was a simple matter for me to replace the loose needles lying on the doctor's tray with my specially prepared ones.

A little while ago I throttled the life out of a very sick young man whose habit of nightly injecting drugs in the toilet of my local tube station had caused him to become ravaged with terminal disease. I would like to say that he died in order to make the world a safer, cleaner place, but the truth is that we went for a drink together and I killed him in a sudden fit of rage because he had not heard of Joyce Grenfell. How the Woman Who Won The Hearts Of The Nation in her thrice-reprised role as Ruby Gates in the celebrated *St Trinians* films could have passed by him unnoticed is still a mystery to me.

Anyway, I strangled the disgusting urchin with his own scarf and removed about a cupful of blood from his arm, into which I dropped a number of needles, filling their capillaries with the poisoned fluid. I then carefully wiped each one clean and inserted it into a tube, neatly resealing the plastic.

Dr MacGregor was talking nineteen to the dozen as he inserted what he thought was a fresh needle into a vein on the back of Mick's hand. He barely even looked down to see what he was doing. Overwork and force of habit had won the day. Thank God for our decaying National Health Service, because I'd never have managed it if the boy had possessed private medical insurance. My unsuspecting adversary maintained an attitude of perky bravery as his finger was stitched up, and I laughed all the way home.

Mick has been feeling unwell for several weeks now. A few days ago he failed to turn up for work. Apparently he has developed a complex and highly dangerous form of Hepatitis B.

As they say, age and treachery will always overcome youth and enthusiasm.

Diary Entry #3 Dated 17 October

The hopeless liaison officer has returned with a new request.

Yesterday evening I opened the door of my flat to find her hovering on the landing uncertainly, as if she could not even decide where she felt comfortable standing.

'Can I help you?' I asked suddenly, knowing that my voice would make her jump. She had not caught me in a good mood. A month ago, Mick had been forced to resign through ill-health, but my promotion had still not been announced for consideration.

'Oh, Mr Morrison, I didn't know if you were in,' she said, her free hand rising to her flat chest.

'The best way to find out is by ringing the doorbell, Miss Chisholm.' I opened the door wider. 'Won't you come in?'

'Thank you.' She edged gingerly past me with briefcase and folders, taking in the surroundings. Hattie took one look at her and shot off to her basket. 'Oh, what an unusual room,' she said, studying the walnut sideboard and armchairs, the matching butter-yellow standard lamps either side of the settee. 'Do you collect art deco?'

'No,' I said tersely. 'This is my furniture. I suppose you'd like a cup of tea.' I went to put the kettle on, leaving her hovering uncomfortably in the lounge. When I returned she was still standing, her head tilted on one side as she examined the spines of my post-war *Radio Times* collection.

'Please sit down, Miss Chisholm,' I insisted. 'I won't bite.' And I really don't because teethmarks can be easily traced.

At this instigation she perched herself on the edge of the armchair and nibbled at a bourbon. She had obviously rehearsed the speech that followed.

'Mr Morrison, I'm sure you've read in the papers that the health cuts are leaving hospitals in this area with an acute shortage of beds.'

'I fear I haven't read a newspaper since they stopped printing The Flutters on the comic page of the *Daily Mirror*,' I admitted, 'but I have heard something of the sort.'

'Well, it means that some people who are required to attend hospital for tests cannot be admitted as overnight patients any more. As you have been so very helpful in the past, we wondered if you could take in one of these patients.'

'For how long?' I asked. 'And what sort of patient?'

'It would be for two weeks at the most, and the patient I have in mind for you –' she churned up the contents of her disgusting briefcase trying to locate her poor victim's folder – 'is a very nice young lady. She's a severe diabetic, and she's in a wheelchair. Apart from that, she's the same as you or I.' She gave me a warm smile, then quickly looked away, sensing perhaps that I was not like other people. She handed me a dog-eared photograph of the patient, attached to a medical history that had more pages than an average weekly script of *The Clitheroe Kid*, a popular BBC radio show which for some reason has never been reissued on audio cassette.

'Her name is Saskia,' said Miss Chisholm. 'She has no family to speak of, and lives a long way from London. Ours is one of the few hospitals with the necessary equipment to handle complex drug and therapy trials for people like her. She desperately needs a place to stay. We can arrange to have her collected each day. We'd be terribly grateful if you could help. She really has nowhere else to go.'

I studied the photograph carefully. The girl was pitifully small-boned, with sallow, almost translucent skin. But she had attractive blond hair, and well-defined features reminiscent of a young Suzy Kendall in Robert Hartford-Davies' patchy 1966 comedy portmanteau *The Sandwich Man*, in which Our Norman, playing an Irish priest, was not seen to his best advantage. What's more, she fitted in perfectly with my plans. A woman. That would certainly be different.

I returned the photograph with a smile. 'I think we can work something out,' I said.

Diary Entry #4 Dated 23 October

Saskia is here, and I must say that for someone so ill she is quite a tonic. The night she arrived, I watched as she struggled to negotiate her wheelchair around the flat without damaging the paintwork on the skirting boards, and despite many set-backs she managed it without a single protestation. Indeed, she has been here for two days now, and never seems to com-plain about anything or anyone. Apparently all of her life she has been prone to one kind of disease or another, and few doctors expected her to survive her childhood, so she is simply happy to be alive.

I have installed her in the spare room, which she insisted

on filling with flowers purchased from the stall outside the hospital. Even Hattie, never the most amenable of cats, seems to have taken to her.

As my flat is on the second floor of a large Victorian house, she is a virtual prisoner within these walls during the hours outside her hospital visits. At those times the ambulance men carry her and the folded wheelchair up and down the stairs.

On her very first night here I entered the lounge to find her going through my catalogued boxes of BBC comedy archive tapes. I was just beginning to grow annoyed when she turned to me and asked if she could play some of them. No one had ever shown the least interest in my collection before. To test her, I asked which shows she would most enjoy hearing.

'I like Leslie Phillips in *The Navy Lark*, and the Frazer Hayes Four playing on *Round The Horne*,' she said, running a slim finger across the spines of the tape boxes. 'And of course, *Hancock's Half Hour*, although I prefer the shows after Andre Melee had been replaced by Hattie Jacques.'

Suddenly I was suspicious.

This tiny girl could not be more than twenty-two years of age. How could she possibly be so familiar with radio programmes that had scarcely been heard in thirty years?

'My father was a great collector,' she explained, as if she had just read my thoughts. 'He used to play the old shows nearly every evening after dinner. It's one of the few lasting memories I have of my parents.'

Well naturally, my heart went out to the poor girl. 'I know exactly how you feel,' I said. 'I only have to hear Kenneth Williams say "*Good Evening*" and I'm reminded of home and hearth. They were such happy times for me.'

For the next hour or so I sounded her out on other favourite film and radio memories of the past, but although there seemed no other common ground between us, she remained willing to listen to my happy tales and learn. At eleven o'clock she yawned and said that she would like to go to bed, and so I let her leave the lounge.

Last night Saskia was kept late at the hospital, and I was in bed by the time the heavy tread of the ambulance man was heard upon the stair. This morning she asked me if I would like her to cook an evening meal. After some initial concern with the hygiene problems involved in allowing one's meal to be cooked by someone else, I agreed. (In restaurants I assiduously question the waitresses about their sanitary arrangements.) Furthermore, I offered to buy produce for the projected feast, but she insisted on stopping by the shops on her way home from the hospital. Although she is frail, she demands independence. I will buy a bottle of wine. After being alone with my memories for so long, it is unnerving to have someone else in the apartment.

And yet it is rather wonderful.

Diary Entry #5 Dated 24 October

What an enthralling evening!

I feel as if I am truly alive for the first time in my life. Saskia returned early tonight – looking drawn and pale, but still vulnerably beautiful, with her blond hair tied in a smart plait – and headed straight into the kitchen, where she stayed for several hours. I had arranged a ramp of planks by the cooker so that she could reach the hobs without having to rise from her chair.

Hattie, sensing that something tasty was being prepared, hung close to the base of the door, sniffing and licking her chops. To amuse Saskia while she cooked I played dialogue soundtracks which I had recorded in my local cinema as a child during performances of *Passport To Pimlico* and *The Lavender Hill Mob*, but the poor quality of the tapes (from a small reel-to-reel recorder I had smuggled into the auditorium) was such that I imagine the subtleties of these screenplays were rather lost to her, especially as she had the kitchen door shut and was banging saucepans about.

The meal was a complete delight. We had a delicious tomato and basil soup to start with, and a truly spectacular salmon en croute as the main course, followed by cheese and biscuits.

Saskia told me about herself, explaining that her parents had been killed in a car crash when she was young. This tragedy had forced her to live with a succession of distant and ancient relatives. When the one she was staying with died, she was shunted into a foster home. No one was willing to take her, though, as the complications arising from her diabetes would have made enormous demands on any foster-parent.

As she talked she ate very little, really only toying with her food. The diabetes prevents her from enjoying much of anything, but hopefully the tests she is undergoing will reveal new ways of coping with her restricted lifestyle.

The dining table is too low to comfortably incorporate Saskia's wheelchair, so I have promised to raise it for tomorrow's dinner, which I have insisted on cooking. I was rather nervous at the prospect, but then I thought: if a cripple can do it, so can I.

Saskia is so kind and attentive, such a good listener. Perhaps it is time for me to introduce my pet topic into the dinner conversation.

Diary Entry #6 Dated 25 October

Disaster has struck!

Right from the start everything went wrong – and just as we were getting along so well. Let me set it out from the beginning.

The meal. I cooked a meal tonight that was not as elaborate as the one she had prepared, and nothing like as good. This was partly because I was forced to work late (still no news of my promotion), so most of the shops were shut, and partly because I have never cooked for a woman before. The result was a microwaved dinner that was still freezing cold in the centre of the dish, but if Saskia didn't like it she certainly didn't complain. Instead she gave a charming broad smile (one which she is using ever more frequently with me) and slowly chewed as she listened to my detailed description of the indignities daily heaped upon me at the office.

I had bought another bottle of wine, and perhaps had drunk a little too much of it by myself (Saskia being unable to drink for the rest of the week), because I found myself introducing the subject of him, Our Norman, the Little Man Who Won All Our Hearts, before we had even finished the main course. Wishing to present the topic in the correct context I chose to start with a basic chronology of Norman's film appearances, beginning with his thirteen-and-a-half-second appearance in *A Date With A Dream* in 1948. I had made an early decision to omit all but the most essential stage and television appearances of the Little Man for fear of tiring her, and in my description of the films stuck mainly to the classic set pieces, notably the marvellous 'Learning To Walk' routine from *On The Beat* and the ten-minute 'Teamaking' sequence from the opening of *The Early Bird*.

I was about to mention Norman's 1956 appearance with Ruby Murray at the Palladium in *Painting The Town* when I became distinctly aware of her interest waning. She was fidgeting about in her chair as if anxious to leave the table.

'Anyone would think you didn't like Norman Wisdom,' I said, by way of a joke.

'Actually, I'm not much of a fan, no,' she said suddenly, then added, 'Forgive me, Stanley, but I've suddenly developed a headache.' And with that she went to her room, without even offering to do the washing up. Before I went to bed I stood outside her door listening, but could hear nothing.

I have a bad feeling about this.

Diary Entry #7 Dated 27 October

She is avoiding me.

It sounds hard to believe, I know, but there can be no other explanation. Last night she returned to the flat and headed directly to her room. When I put my head around the door to see if she wanted a late-night cup of cocoa (I admit this was at three o'clock in the morning, but I could not sleep for worrying about her), it seemed that she could barely bring herself to be polite. As I stepped into the room, her eyes widened and she pulled the blankets around her in a defensive gesture, which seemed to suggest a fear of my presence. I must confess I am at a loss to understand her.

Could she have led me on, only pretending to share my interests for some secret purpose of her own?

At work today we were informed that Mick had died. Complications from the hepatitis, annoyingly unspecified, but I gained the distinct impression that they were unpleasant. When one of the secretaries started crying I made a passing flippant remark that was, I fear, misconstrued, and the girl gave me a look of utter horror. She's a scruffy little tart who was sweet on Mick, and much given to conspiring with him about me. I felt like giving her something to be horrified about, and briefly wondered how she would look tied up with baling wire, hanging in a storm drain. The things we think about to get us through the day.

At home the situation has worsened. Saskia arrived tonight with a male friend, a doctor whom she had invited back for tea. While she was in the kitchen the two of us were left alone in the lounge, and I noticed that he seemed to be studying me from the corner of his eye. It was probably just an occupational habit, but it prompted me to wonder if Saskia had somehow voiced her suspicions to him (assuming she has any, which I consider unlikely).

After he had gone, I explained that it was not at all permissible for her to bring men into the house no matter how well she knew them, and she had the nerve to turn in her chair and accuse me of being old-fashioned!

'What on earth do you mean?' I asked her.

'It's not healthy, Stanley, surrounding yourself with all this,' she explained, indicating the alphabetised film and tape cassettes that filled the shelves on the wall behind us. 'Most of these people have been dead for years.'

'Shakespeare has been dead for years,' I replied, 'and people still appreciate him.'

'But he wrote plays and sonnets of lasting beauty,' she persisted. 'These people you listen to were just working comics. It's lovely to collect things, Stanley, but this stuff was never meant to be taken so seriously. You can't base your life around it.' There was an irritating timbre in her voice that I had not noticed before. She sat smugly back in her wheelchair, and for a moment I wanted to smother her. I could feel my face growing steadily redder with the thought.

'Why shouldn't these people still be admired?' I cried, running to the shelves and pulling out several of my finest tapes. 'Most of them had dreary lives filled with hardship and pain, but they made people laugh, right through the war and the years of austerity that followed. They carried on through poverty and ill-health and misery. Everyone turned on the radio to hear them. Everyone went to the pictures to see them. It was something to look forward to. They kept people alive. They gave the country happy memories. Why shouldn't someone remember them for what they did?'

'All right, Stanley. I'm sorry – I didn't mean to upset you,' she said, reaching out her hand, but I pushed it away. It was then that I realised my cheeks were wet, and I turned aside in shame. To think that I had been brought to this state, forced to defend myself in my own home, by a woman, and a wheelchair-bound one at that.

'This is probably a bad time to mention it,' said Saskia, 'but I'm going to be leaving London earlier than I first anticipated. In fact, I'll be going home tomorrow. The tests haven't taken as long as the doctors thought.'

'But what about the results?' I asked.

'They've already made arrangements to send them to my local GP. He'll decide whether further treatment is necessary.'

I hastily pulled myself together and made appropriate

polite sounds of disappointment at the idea of her departure, but inside a part of me was rejoicing. You see, I had been watching her hands as they rested on the arms of her wheelchair. They were trembling.

And she was lying.

Diary Entry #9 Dated 2 November

I have much to relate.

After our altercation last night, both of us knew that a new level in our relationship had been reached. The game had begun. Saskia refused my conciliatory offer of tea and went straight to her bedroom, quietly locking the door behind her. I know because I tried to open it at two o'clock this morning, and I heard her breath catch in the darkness as I twisted the knob from side to side.

I returned to my room and forced myself to stay there. The night passed slowly, with both of us remaining uncomfortably awake on our respective beds. In the morning, I left the house early so that I would not be forced to trade insincere pleasantries with her over breakfast. I knew she would be gone by the time I returned, and that, I think, suited both of us. I was under no illusions – she was a dangerous woman, too independent, too free-minded to ever become my friend. We could only be adversaries. And I was dangerous to her. I had enjoyed her company, but now she would only be safe far away from me. Luckily, I would never see her again. Or so I thought. For, fast as the future, everything changed between us.

Oh, how it changed.

This morning, I arrived at work to find a terse note summoning me to my supervisor's office. Naturally I assumed that I was finally being notified of my promotion. You may imagine my shock when, in the five-minute interview that followed, it emerged that far from receiving advancement within the company, I was being fired! I did not 'fit in' with the new personnel, and as the department was being 'streamlined' they were 'letting me go'. Depending on my attitude to this news, they were prepared to make me a generous cash settlement if I left at once, so that they could immediately begin 'implementing procedural changes'.

I did not complain. This sort of thing has happened many times before. I do not fit in. I say this not to gain sympathy, but as a simple statement of fact. Intellect always impedes popularity. I accepted the cash offer. Disheartened, but also glad to be rid of my vile 'colleagues', I returned home.

It was raining hard when I arrived at the front gate. I looked up through the dark sycamores and was surprised to find a light burning in the front room. Then I realised that Saskia was reliant on the council for arranging her transport, and as they were never able to specify an exact collection time, she was still in the house. I knew I would have to use every ounce of my control to continue behaving in a correct and civilised manner.

As I turned the key in the lock I heard a sudden scuffle of movement inside the flat. Throwing the door wide, I entered the lounge and found it empty. The sound was coming from my bedroom. A terrible deadness flooded through my chest as I tiptoed along the corridor, carefully avoiding the boards that squeaked.

Slowly, I moved into the doorway. She was on the other side of the room with her back to me. The panels of the wardrobe were folded open, and she had managed to pull one of the heavy-duty bin-liners out on the floor. Somehow she sensed that I was behind her, and the wheelchair spun around. The look on her face was one of profound disturbance.

'What have you done with the rest of them?' she said softly, her voice waving. She had dislodged a number of air fresheners from the sacks and the room stank of lavender.

'You're not supposed to be in here,' I explained as reasonably as possible. 'This is my private room.'

I stepped inside and closed the door behind me. She looked up at the pinned pictures surrounding her. The bleak monochrome of a thousand celebrity photographs seemed to absorb the light within the room.

'Saskia. You're an intelligent girl. You're modern. But you have no respect for the past.'

'The past?' Her lank hair was falling in her eyes, as she flicked it aside I could see she was close to tears. 'What has the past to do with this?' She kicked out uselessly at the plastic sack and it fell to one side, spilling its rotting human contents onto the carpet.

'Everything,' I replied, moving forward. I was not advancing on her, I just needed to get to the bedside cabinet. 'The past is where everything has its rightful place.'

'I know about your past, Stanley,' she cried, pushing at the wheels of her chair, backing herself up against the wardrobe, turning her face from the stinking mess. 'Nurse Clarke told me all about you.'

'What did she say?' I asked, coming to a halt. I was genuinely curious. Nurse Clarke had hardly ever said more than two words to me.

'I know what happened to you. That's why I came here.' She started to cry now, and wiped her nose with the back of her hand. Something plopped obscenely onto the floor as the sack settled. 'She says you had the worst childhood a boy could ever have. Sexual abuse, violence. You lived in terror every day. Your father nearly killed you before the authorities took charge. Don't you see? That's why you're so obsessed with this stuff, this trivia, it's like a disease. You're just trying to make things all right again.'

'That's a damn lie!' I shouted at her. 'My childhood was perfect. You're making it up!'

'No,' she said, shaking her head, snot flying from her nose. 'I saw the marks when you were in the kitchen that first night. Cigarette burns on your arms. Cuts too deep to ever heal. I thought I knew how you must have felt. Like me, always shoved around, always towered over, always scared. I didn't expect anything like this. What were you thinking of?'

'Are you sure you don't know?' I asked, advancing towards the cabinet. 'I'm the kind of person nobody notices. I'm invisible until I'm pointed out. I'm in a private world. I'm not even ordinary. I'm somewhere below that.'

I had reached the cabinet, and now slowly pulled open the drawer, groping inside as she tried to conceal her panic, tried to find somewhere to wheel the chair.

'But I'm not alone,' I explained. 'There are many like me. I see them begging on the streets, soliciting in pubs, injecting themselves in alleyways. For them childhood is a scar that never heals, but still they try to stumble on. I end their stumbling, Saskia. Miss Chisholm says I'm an angel.'

My fingers closed around the handle of the carving knife, but the point was stuck in the rear wall of the drawer. I gave it my attention and pulled it free, lowering the blade until it was flat against my leg. A sound from behind made me turn. With a dexterity that amazed me, the infuriating girl had opened the door and slipped through.

I ran into the lounge to find her wheelchair poised before

Uncut

the tape archives and Saskia half out of the seat, one hand pincering a stack of irreplaceable 78s featuring the vocal talents of Flanagan and Allen.

'Leave those alone!' I cried. 'You don't understand.'

She turned to me with what I felt as a look of deliberate malice on her face and raised the records high above her head. If I attacked her now, she would surely drop them.

'Why did you kill those people?' she asked simply. For a moment I was quite at a loss. She deserved an explanation. I ran my left thumb along the blade of the knife, drawing in my breath as the flesh slowly parted and the pain showed itself.

'I wanted to put their pasts right,' I explained. 'To give them the things that comfort. Tony Hancock. Sunday roast. Favourites. Smiling policemen. Norman Wisdom. To give them the freedom to remember.'

I must have allowed the knife to come into view, because her grip on the records faltered and they slid from her hands to the floor. I don't think any smashed, but the wheels of her chair cracked several as she rolled forward.

'I can't give you back the past, Saskia,' I said, walking towards her, smearing the knife blade with the blood from my stinging thumb. 'I'm sorry, because I would have liked to.'

She cried out in alarm, pulling stacks of records and tapes down upon herself, scattering them across the threadbare carpet. Then she grabbed the metal frame of the entire cabinet, as if trying to shake it loose from the wall. I stood and watched, fascinated by her fear.

When I heard the familiar heavy boots quickening on the stairs, I turned the knife over and pushed the blade hard into my chest. It was a reflex action, as if I had been planning to do this all along. Just as I had suspected, there was no pain. To those like us who suffered so long, there is no more pain.

And now I am sitting here on a bench with a clean elastic bandage patching up my stomach, facing the bristling cameras and microphones, twenty enquiring faces before me, and the real probing questions have begun.

The bovine policewoman who interrogated me so unimaginatively during my initial detainment period bore an extraordinary resemblance to Shirley Abicair, the Australian zither player who performed superbly as Norman's love interest in Rank's 1954 hit comedy *One Good Turn*, although the *Evening News* critic found their sentimental scenes together an embarrassment.

I think I am going to enjoy my new role here. Newspapers are fighting for my story. They're already comparing me to Nilsen and Sutcliffe, although I would rather be compared to Christie or Crippen. Funny how everyone remembers the name of a murderer, but no one remembers the victim.

If they want to know, I will tell them everything. Just as long as I can tell them about my other pet interests.

My past is safe.

My future is known.

My present belongs to Norman.

On Edge

A brazil nut, thought Thurlow, of all the damned things. That'll teach me. He leaned back tentatively in the plastic chair and studied the posters that had been taped to the walls around him.

Confidential HIV testing.

Unwanted Pregnancies.

Mind That Child He May Be Deaf.

He thought: no wonder people avoid coming here. Sitting in the waiting room gave you a chance to consider your fate at leisure.

He checked his watch, then listened. From behind a distant door came the whine of an electric drill. Determined to blot the sound from his brain, he checked through the magazines on the table before him. Inevitably there were two battered copies of *The Tatler*, some ancient issues of *Punch* and a magazine called *British Interiors*. With the drill howling faintly at the back of his brain, he flicked idly through the lifestyle magazine. A *pied-à-terre* in Kensington decorated in onyx and gold. A Berkshire retreat with a marble bas-relief in the kitchen depicting scenes from *The Aeneid*. The people who lived in these places were presumably drug barons. Surely their children occasionally knocked over the bundles of art-fully arranged dried flowers, or vanished into priest's holes to be lost within the walls?

As he threw the magazine down in disgust the drill squealed at a higher pitch, suggesting that greater force had been used to penetrate some resistant obstacle.

A damned brazil nut. Next time he'd use the crackers instead of his teeth. God, it hurt! The entire molar had split in half. Torn skin, blood all over the place. He was sure there was still a piece of nutshell lodged between the gum and the tooth, somewhere deep near the nerve. The pain speared through his jaw like a white-hot knife every time he moved his head.

The receptionist – her name was something common that he never quite caught – had sighed when she saw him approach. She had studied her appointment book with a doubtful shake of her head. He had been forced to point out that, as a private patient, his needs surely took precedence over others. After all, what else was the system for? He had been coming here regularly for many years. Or to put it more accurately, he had arranged appointments in this manner whenever there was a problem with his teeth. Dr Samuelson was away on a seminar in Florida, apparently, so he'd be seeing someone new, and he might have to wait for a while. With the pain in his tooth driving him crazy, Thurlow didn't mind waiting at all.

There were two other people in the room. He could tell the private patient at a glance. The woman opposite, foreign-looking, too much gold, obviously had money. The skinny teenaged girl in jeans and a T-shirt had Council House written all over her. Thurlow sniffed, and the knife rocketed up into his skull, causing him to clutch at his head. When the pain had subsided to a persistent dull throb once more, he examined his watch again. He'd been sitting here for nearly forty minutes! This was ridiculous! He rose from his seat and opened the door that led to the reception desk. Finding no one there, he turned into the white-tiled corridor beyond. Somebody would have to see him if he kicked up a fuss.

In the first room he reached, a fat woman was pinned on her back with her legs thrown either side of the couch while the dentist hunched over her, reaching into her mouth like a man attempting to retrieve keys from a drain. In the second room he discovered the source of the drilling. Here, an exhausted teenaged boy gripped the armrests of the chair with bony white knuckles while his dentist checked the end of the drill and drove it back into his mouth, metal grinding into enamel with the wincing squeal of a fork on a dry plate.

'You're not supposed to be back here, you know.'

Thurlow turned around and found a lean young man in a white coat looking crossly at him.

'I've been waiting for nearly an hour,' said Thurlow, feeling he had earned the exaggeration.

'And you are . . .?'

'Mr Thurlow. Broken tooth. I was eating a brazil nut . . .'

'Let's not discuss it in the corridor. You'd better come in.'

Thurlow would have been annoyed by the brusqueness of the dentist's manner had he not heard the upper-class inflections in his voice, and noted the smart knot of his university tie. At least this way he would be dealt with by a professional.

Thurlow entered the room, removed his jacket, then waited by the red plastic couch while the dentist made an entry in his computer.

'I normally have Dr Samuelson,' he explained, looking about.

'Well, he's not here, he's—'

'I know. Florida. All right for some. You're new, I suppose. You're very young.'

'Everyone looks young when you start getting older, Mr Thurlow. I'm Dr Matthews.' He continued tapping the keyboard, then raised his eyes to the screen. 'We haven't seen you for a check-up in well over a year.'

'Not for a check-up, no,' said Thurlow, climbing onto the couch. 'I had a thing, a lump.' He waggled his fingers at his cheek. 'I thought it was a cyst.'

'When was the appointment?' Matthews was clearly unable to find the reference on his screen.

'I didn't have one. Anyway, it wasn't a cyst. It was a spot.'

'And the time before that?'

'I lost a filling. Ginger-nuts. Same thing the year before that. Peppermints.'

'So you haven't seen the hygienist for a while?'

'And I don't need to see one now,' said Thurlow. 'They always try to fob you off with dental floss and sticks with rubber prongs on. What is this anyway, going on about the check-ups? Are you on commission?'

Dr Matthews ignored his remark and approached the couch. As Thurlow made himself comfortable, the dentist slipped a paper bib around his neck and fastened it.

'Don't you have an assistant?'

'I used to, but she didn't like my methods so I murdered her,' said Matthews. 'Ha ha.' He adjusted the chair from a control pad by his foot, then switched on the water-rinse pump. 'I always make jokes. It takes the edge off. Mouth open please.' He swung a tray of dental tools over Thurlow's chest.

Thurlow opened wide, and the light from the dentist's pencil torch filled his vision. He watched as the hooked probe went in, tapping along the left side of his molars, and glimpsed the little circular mirror at the corner of his vision.

Saliva quickly began to build in his mouth. The tapping continued. He knew he would have to swallow soon. Quickly sensing his unease, Matthews placed a spit-pump in the corner of his mouth. It made a loud draining sound, like water going down a sink.

Suddenly Thurlow felt the sharp point of the probe touch down on the bare nerve in his split tooth. It was as if an electric current had been passed through his head. If it had remained in contact for a second longer he would have screamed and bitten the tool clean in half. Matthews observed the sudden twitch of his patient's body and quickly withdrew the instrument.

'I think we can safely say that we've located the problem area,' he said drily, shining the torch around, then lowering the large overhead light. 'That's pretty nasty. Wouldn't be so bad if it was an incisor. It's split all the way from the crown to the root. The gum is starting to swell and redden, so I imagine it's infected. I'll have to cut part of it away.'

Thurlow pulled the spit-pump from his mouth. 'I don't want to hear the details,' he said. 'It's making me sick.' He replaced the pump and lay back, closing his eyes.

'Fine. I'll give you a jab and we'll get started.' Matthews prepared a syringe, removed the plastic cap from the tip and cleared the air from the needle. Then he inserted it into the fleshy lower part of Thurlow's left gum. There was a tiny pop of flesh as the skin surface was broken and the cool metal slipped into his jaw, centimetre by centimetre. Thurlow felt the numbing fluid flood through his mouth, slowly removing all sensation from his infected tooth.

'As you're squeamish, I'll give you an additional valium shot. Then I can work on without upsetting you.' He rolled back Thurlow's shirt sleeve and inserted a second syringe, emptying it slowly. 'It's funny when you think of it,' he said, watching the calibrations on the side of the tube. 'Considering all the food that has to be cut and crushed by your deciduous and permanent canines, incisors and molars, it's a miracle there's anything left in your mouth at all. Of course, humans have comparatively tiny teeth. It's a sign of our superiority over the animals.'

Thurlow finally began to relax. Was it the drug that was making him feel so safe and comfortable in Matthews' hands, or merely the dentist's air of confident authority? He hummed softly as he worked, laying our instruments in familiar order while he waited for the drugs to take effect. A feeling of well-being crept over Thurlow. His arms and legs had grown too heavy for him to move. His heart was beating more slowly in his chest. The lower half of his face was completely numb. Suspended between sleep and wakefulness, he tried to identify the tune that Matthew was humming, but concentration slipped away.

The dentist had placed two other metal instruments in his mouth; when did he do that? One was definitely there to hold his jaws apart. Although the overhead light was back-reflected and diffuse, it shone through Thurlow's eyelids with a warm red glow. There was a metallic clatter on the tray.

'I'm going to cut away part of the damaged gum tissue now,' said Matthews. Hadn't he demanded to be spared the details? The long-nosed scissors glinted against the light then vanished into his mouth, to clip through flesh and gristle. His mind drifted, trying not to think of the excavation progressing below.

'I don't think there's been enough left to cap,' said Matthews. 'The one next to it is cracked pretty badly, too. What the hell was in that nut?'

When the drill started, Thurlow opened his eyes once more. Time seemed to have elapsed, for now there seemed to be several more instruments in his mouth. The drill howled on, the acrid smell of burning bone filling his nostrils. However, thanks to the effect of the valium dose, he remained unconcerned. The drill was removed, and Matthews' fingers probed the spot. There was a sharp crack, and he held up the offending tooth for Thurlow to see, first one half, then the other.

'You want this as a souvenir? I thought not. Now, to do this properly I should really clear out your root canal and drive a metal post into the gum,' he said. 'But that's a long, painful process. Let's see how we can work around it without tearing your entire jaw off. Ha ha.'

The drill started up again and entered his mouth. Thurlow could not tell which of his teeth it was touching, but by the familiar burning smell he guessed it was drilling deep into the enamel of a molar.

'That's better,' said Matthews. 'I can see daylight through the hole. Now that we have room to manoeuvre, let's bring in the big guns.' He produced a large semi-circular metal clip and attached it to the side of Thurlow's lower lip. A new instrument appeared before the light, a large curved razor-blade with a serrated tip, like a cheese-grater with teeth. The dentist placed it in his mouth and began drawing it across the stump of the damaged molar. The rasping vibrated through Thurlow's head, back and forth, back and forth, until he began to wonder if it would ever stop.

'This is no good, no good at all.' Matthews withdrew the instrument, checked the blunted tip and tossed it onto the tray in disgust. 'I need something else. Something modern, something – technological.' He vanished from view, and

Thurlow heard him thumping around at the side of the room. 'One day,' he called, 'all dentistry will be performed by laser. Just think of the fun we'll have then!' He returned with a large piece of electrical equipment that boasted a red flashing LED on top. Matthews' grinning face suddenly filled his vision.

'You're a very lucky man,' he said. 'Not many people get to have this baby in their mouths.' He patted the side of the machine, from which extended a ribbed metal tube with a tiny rotating steel saw. When he flicked it on, the noise was so great that he had to shout. 'You see, the main part of the tooth is made of a substance called dentine, but below the gumline it becomes bone-like cement, which is softer . . .'

Thurlow missed the next part as the saw entered his mouth and connected with tooth enamel. One of the pipes wedged between his lower incisors was spraying water onto the operating zone, while another was noisily sucking up saliva. His mouth had become a hardhat area. Suddenly something wet and warm began to pour down his throat. Matthews turned off the saw and hastily withdrew it. 'Shit,' he said loudly, 'that's my fault, not watching what I was doing.' He reached behind him and grabbed up a wad of tissue, which he stuffed into Thurlow's mouth and padded at the operation site, only to withdraw it red, filled and dripping. 'Sorry about that, I was busy thinking about what I fancied for tea tonight.' Now there seemed to be something lodged in Thurlow's oesophagus. Through the anaesthetic he began to experience a stinging sensation. Bile rose in his throat as he started to gag.

'Wait, wait, I know what that is.' Matthews reached in his gloved hand and withdrew something, throwing it onto the tray. 'You've been a brave boy. A hundred years ago this would have been a horribly painful experience, performed without an anaesthetic, but thanks to modern techniques I'll have you finished in just a few more hours. Ha ha. Just kidding.'

He reached back to the tray and produced another steel frame, this one constructed like the filament wire in a light-bulb. Carefully unscrewing it, he arranged the contraption at the side of his patient's mouth. Thurlow was starting to feel less calm. Perhaps the valium was wearing off. Suppose his sensations returned in the middle of the drilling? Yes, he could definitely feel his jaw now. A dull pain had begun to throb at the base of his nose. The dentist was stirring something in a small plastic dish when he saw Thurlow shifting in his chair.

'Looks like I didn't give you a large enough dose,' he said, concerned. He removed the plastic cap from another syringe and jabbed it into Thurlow's arm.

'There,' he said, cheerfully depressing the plunger. 'Drug cocktail happy hour! You want a little umbrella in this one?' Thurlow stared back at him with narrowed eyes, unamused. Matthews grew serious. 'Don't worry, when you wake up I'll have finished. I think you've been through enough for one day, so I'm giving you a temporary filling for now, and we'll do that root canal on your next appointment.'

As he began to spoon the cement into Thurlow's mouth on the end of a rubber spatula, Thurlow felt himself drifting off into an ethereal state of semi-wakefulness.

While he floated in this hazy dream-state, his imagination unfettered itself, strange visions uncoiling before him in rolling prisms of light. The humming of the dentist became a distant litany, a warm and familiar soundtrack, like the work-song of a seamstress. Colours and scents bled into one another, jasmine and disinfectant. He was home and safe, a child again. Finally these half-formed memories were replaced by the growing clarity of the present, and he realised that he was surfacing back to reality.

'Oh good,' said Matthews as his eyes flickered open. 'Back in the land of the living. For a minute I thought I'd overdosed you. Ha ha. We're just waiting for the last bit to dry.' He reached into Thurlow's mouth and probed around with a steel scraper, scratching away the last of the filler. Thurlow suddenly became aware of the restraining strap fixed across his lap, holding him in place. How long had that been there?

'You know, we had a nasty case of "tooth squeeze" in here last week, ever hear of that? Of course, you can't answer with all this junk in your mouth, can you? He was an airline pilot. His plane depressurised, and it turned out he had an air bubble trapped beneath a filling. When the cabin atmosphere decreased, the air expanded. His tooth literally blew up in his mouth. Bits were embedded in his tongue. What a mess.' Matthews peered into his mouth, one eye screwed tight. 'It happens to deep-sea divers, too, only their teeth implode. And I've seen worse. There was one patient, a kid who roller-skated face-first into a drinking fountain . . .' Mercifully, he lost his train of thought. 'Well, that last batch seems to have done the trick.'

The sensation was slowly returning to Thurlow's mouth. Something was very sore, very sore indeed. He raised his hands, hoping to see if he could locate the source of the pain, but Matthews swatted them down. 'Don't touch anything for a while. You must give it a chance to set. I still have some finishing off to do.' The pain was increasing with every passing second. It was starting to hurt very badly, far worse than when he had arrived for treatment. Something had gone wrong, he was sure of it. He could only breath through his nose, and then with difficulty. He tried to speak, but no sound came out. When he tried to pull himself upright, Matthews' arm came around the chair and pushed him back down. Now the dentist stepped fully into his view. Thurlow gasped.

It looked as if someone had exploded a blood transfusion bag in front of him. He was dripping crimson from head to foot. It was splashed across his chest and stomach, draining from his plastic apron to form a spreading pool between his feet. The white tiled floor was slick with blood. Streaks marred the walls in sweeping arcs, like rampant nosebleeds. Thurlow's head reeled back against the rest. What in God's name had happened? Pain and panic overwhelmed him as his hands clawed the air and he fought to stand, chromatic sparkles scattering before his eyes as the remnants of the drug affected his vision.

'You shouldn't be up and about yet,' said Matthews. 'I've not finished.'

'You're no dentist,' Thurlow tried to say, the white-hot knives shrieking through his brain, but his words came out as a series of hysterical rasps.

The dentist seemed to understand him. 'You're right, I'm no dentist.' He shrugged, his hands held out. *So sue me.* 'I always wanted to be one but I couldn't get my certificate. I can't pass exams. I get angry too easily. Still, it's a vocation with me, a calling. I know what I'm doing is right. I'm simply ahead of my time. Nearly finished.'

He thrust his hand into his patient's mouth and made a tightening motion. A starburst of pain detonated between Thurlow's eyes. The dentist held his head back against the rest while he pulled at something. There was a ting of metal, and he extracted a twisted spring. On one end a small silver screw was embedded in a bloody scrap of bright red gum.

'You don't need this bit,' said Matthews jovially. He picked up a Phillips screwdriver and inserted it in Thurlow's mouth, happily ratcheting away, as if he was fixing a car. 'I like to think of this as homeopathic medicine,' said the dentist, 'except that I'm more of an artist. I went to art school but I didn't pass the exam because – you guessed it –' he nodded his head dumbly, *silly old me*, 'I got angry again. They took me out of circulation for a while.' He removed the screwdriver and peered inside, smiling. 'Still, every now and again I get to try out a few of my ideas. I go to a particular area and search through the Yellow Pages, then I visit all the private dentists they list. Sometimes I find one with a vacant operating room, and then I just wait for custom. I look the part, you see, white coat, smart tie, good speaking voice. And I keep the door locked while I work. No one ever tries to stop me, and nothing would ever come out in the papers if they did, because private dentists are too scared of losing their customers. You'd never think it could be that simple, would you?'

He went to the desk beside the operating chair and detached a large circular mirror. 'But let's face it, when was the last time you asked to see a dentist's credentials? It's not like the police. Let's see how you turned out.'

Thurlow could barely breathe through the ever-increasing pain, but as the dentist tilted the mirror in his direction, the next sight that met his eyes almost threw him into a faint.

'Good, isn't it?' said Matthews. 'Art in dentistry.'

Thurlow's face was unrecognisable. His lips had been cut and peeled back in fleshy strips, then pinned to his cheeks with steel pins. Most of his teeth had been filed into angular shapes, some pointed, other merely slanting. His upper gums had been opened to expose the pale bone beneath. A number of screws had been driven into his flayed jaw, and were

Uncut

attached to cables. The last two inches of his tongue – the lump he had felt in his throat – were missing completely. He watched as the leaking stump jerked obscenely back and forth like a severed reptile. Around his mouth a contraption of polished steel had been fitted to function as an insane brace, a complex network of wires and springs, cots and filaments. The skin beneath his eyes had turned black with the pummelling his mouth had taken.

'I know what you're thinking,' whispered Matthews. 'It's special, but not spectacular. You haven't seen the best bit yet. It's not merely art, it's – kinetic dental futurism. Watch.'

Matthews reached up and turned a silver handle on the left of Thurlow's jaw. The springs and wires pulled taut. The cogs turned. Thurlow's mouth grimaced and winked, the flaps of his lips contorting back and forth as his face was twisted into a series of wide-mouthed grins and tight, sour frowns. On a separate spring, the end of his tongue flickered in and out of his own ear. The pain was unbearable. Fresh wounds tore in his gums and cheeks as the mechanism yanked his mouth into an absurd rictus of a laugh. Matthews released his grip on the silver handle and smiled, pleased with himself.

'Is there somebody in there?' The receptionist was calling through the door.

'This stuff won't catch on for years yet,' said the dentist, ignoring the rattling doorknob behind him. He tilted the mirror from side to side before Thurlow's horrified face. Finally, he set the mirror down and released the restraining strap from the operating couch. Blinkered by the heavy steel contraption that had been screwed into his jaw, Thurlow was barely able to stand. As he tipped his head forward the weight pulled him further, and blood began to pour from his mouth. He wanted to scream, but he knew it would hurt too much to pull open his mouth without the help of the contraption. The receptionist began to bang on the door.

'Don't worry,' said the dentist with a reassuring smile. 'It'll seem strange at first, but you'll gradually get used to it. I'm sure they all do eventually.' He turned around and looked out of the window. 'That's the beauty of these old buildings; there's always a fire escape.' He unclipped the security catch on the casement and pushed it open, raising his legs and sliding them through the gap. Blood smeared from his saturated trousers onto the white sill. 'I nearly forgot,' he called back as Thurlow blundered blindly into the door, spraying it with his blood. 'Whatever you do – for God's sake – don't forget to floss.'

His laughter echoed hard in Thurlow's ears as a descending crimson mist replaced his tortured sight.

The Master Builder

'**The place** I went to see on West Forty-fourth?'

'Mmm – I'm lighting a cigarette – go on.'

'It turned out to be a miniature attic with a small circular window and a sloping ceiling. The kind of room you couldn't even lock a small child up in. Although of course you could lock a small child up in almost anything.'

'You're not going to be single all your life, Laurie, then you might feel different about having children.'

'I doubt it. My favourite story is still the one about the princess in the tower.'

'Tell me the rest. There's obviously more, otherwise you wouldn't be dragging this out for so long.'

'OK . . .'

'I mean, of course you're not going to find another place in midtown Manhattan for God's sake. You should have made Jerry move out.'

'Alison, it was *his* apartment!'

'Then you guys should have stayed together. It was worth it just for the location.'

'Shut up, Allie, and let me finish. So, this was the fifth apartment I'd checked out since noon, and it was raining, and naturally there was as much chance of finding a cab as there was locating the ark of the covenant, and I find myself in Herald Square so I jump the PATH train . . .'

'Oh my God, you're moving to New Jersey.'

'Well, Hoboken. It's—'

'I know, I know, only ten minutes from town and half the rent. But you know what they say, once you move off the island you never get back on. Still, I guess it's kind of *semi*-fashionable to live there now. Go on.'

'OK, so Hoboken. Well, I was walking along a street some-where off Washington, right down by the river, and I saw a For Sale notice in this window.'

'Wait, you're gonna *buy*?'

'I figure, why pay rent all your life? The point is, I put in a bid and it's been accepted.'

'Can you afford it?'

Laurie laughed. 'No, of course not. It's on the second floor, above a Korean deli, and it needs a hell of a lot of work, but it has a View. I mean, there's the river straight ahead, then the lights of the city are spread out before you.'

'Sounds perfect. What's the catch?'

'No catch, at least I don't think so. I want you to come out and see it with me before I start alterations. You're so good with design ideas, and you know I've no sense of colour co-ordination.'

On the other end of the line, Alison sighed. 'Yeah, I guess I owe it to your future boyfriends to make sure that your apart-ment doesn't end up looking like you won it on *Wheel of Fortune*. Name a date and we'll go check it out.'

'How about Saturday?'

'Fine by me.'

* * *

The September wind which blew across from the Hudson felt humid and unhealthy. It swirled around the old ferry buildings and down into the entrance of the subway as Alison rebuttoned her coat and left the station. She checked the address on the slip of paper and headed up along Third Street, past a clutch of smart new restaurants which characterised Hoboken's reborn status as a desirable neighbourhood. She quickly located the delicatessen near the corner and looked up at the windows above. The building itself appeared to be rather nondescript, its grey brickwork fascia blending with the slight architectural variations on either side. She looked back down in time to see her friend striding along the pavement towards her. As always, Laurie looked immaculate. Glossy dark hair brushed her shoulders as she turned her head and smiled. The expensively simple black suit she wore emphasised her tiny waist. She had a figure that only a dedicated career woman could afford to keep.

'I'm not late, am I?' Laurie hiked up her coat sleeve and checked her watch, revealing a slender white wrist.

'No, I was early. Looks like you'll have all the stores you need right here.' Alison gestured along the street.

'Hey, don't knock it.' Laurie stepped into the doorway beside the deli and searched her purse for keys. 'I mean, have you seen the Stylish Modes Beauty Parlor two doors along? How could I ever think of getting my hair done anywhere else?' She unlocked the outer door and beckoned Alison inside.

'It still smells a little funky in here,' she said, wrinkling her nose. 'The old lady who had the place kept cats.'

A second door admitted them to a gloomy narrow hallway and a flight of grey-carpeted stairs. Laurie gestured dismissively at the bare walls as they ascended.

'At the moment this is just so – *hallway*. Don't look at it.'

'I guess you could brighten it up by bolting some prints to the wall.'

'Allie, this is *not* Manhattan, it's a much safer neighbourhood.' She had to fit three separate keys to the door locks before they could enter the apartment.

'Oh, sure,' said Alison, studying the burglar bolts as she passed them.

The room before them was presumably intended to be a lounge/diner. The faded purple carpets released a pungent and unmistakably feline odour. Stained brown wallpaper revealed the shapes of long-removed paintings and light fixtures. Against the farthest wall a broken-backed sofa slumped, its corduroy covering worn smooth with use.

The two women moved into the adjoining room, turning around as they did so. The cramped kitchen alcove consisted of a mustard-yellow counter and a number of cheaply finished wooden cupboards. Mouse droppings lay scattered on most of the work surfaces.

'Admittedly the place doesn't look like it's been cleaned since the fifties,' said Laurie, running a manicured finger along the top of a shelf.

'Hygiene Hell,' agreed Alison, moving gingerly between the fittings, careful not to touch anything. 'If you're serious about this, all I can say is that you must have more design vision than I gave you credit for.'

'I have more than vision,' said Laurie, 'I have a View.' She tugged on a dirty grey curtain draped across the far doorway, and there it was. A huge, spectacular room with double windows and an unspoiled view of the Hudson and the city beyond.

Any objections Alison could have raised about her friend's planned purchase were felled at a stroke. Watery sunlight streaked the sides of the distant skyscrapers which filled the room's horizons like a living fresco. Barges could be glimpsed passing between the shoreside buildings, their horns sounding in forlorn cadence against the cries of wheeling gulls.

'Can you believe the previous owner had actually boarded over the windows?' said Laurie, pointing to a stack of planks standing in a corner.

'Why would anyone do that?' asked Alison, moving to the glass.

'I don't know. I guess she must have been a little crazy. I believe she was very old.'

'So when did she move out?'

'She didn't. She died. The apartment went to her nephew, but he lives in the Midwest and just wants to sell it.'

Laurie turned from the window and led the way to a far door across the room. Beyond lay a short flight of steps leading to the first of two bedrooms. Alison took a step inside and halted. The room was dark and musty with the smell of stale blankets. Here, the windows were still nailed shut with sheets of hardboard. Laurie reached across and switched on the overhead light, a single naked bulb which illuminated the sagging bed, an unravelled wicker chair and an ancient, badly painted dresser.

'I think you're going to find yourself with a lot of structural alterations on your hands,' said Alison. 'Even the walls you keep will all need replastering. You'll never be able to live here while it's being fixed up.' She tried to avoid looking at the bed, its bare mattress stained dark, perhaps with the secretions of the old woman's dying body. She looked over at Laurie, who seemed to be reading her mind.

'She didn't die here. She was in the hospital for a long time. The bathroom's through the corridor in the far corner.'

The cheap modern tub with the cracked floor seemed almost wilfully misplaced in the large bathroom. A much older china handbasin stood against a partially tiled wall. Most of the plumbing seemed to have been connected in plain sight, with pipes jutting from every corner.

'It's going to cost a fortune to do it properly, you know that.'

'Look at the outlay in terms of long-term investment,' said Laurie. 'I'll never get another chance like this.'

'Maybe you're right. There's plenty of scope for renovation, I'll say that. And the property can only go up in value.'

Laurie led the way back to the main lounge, passing another much smaller bedroom. 'You think that's too small for a guest room?' she asked. 'Maybe it should be knocked through.'

'I don't know . . . you don't want to reduce the number of rooms too much. Suppose you decide that you want someone to live with you.'

'Oh no,' said Laurie firmly. 'I'm not living with anyone ever again. And I'm never going to get married, you know that.'

'Yeah, you say so now, but maybe in a year or two . . .'

'In a year or two we could all be dead.' Laurie gestured at the walls, anxious to change the subject. 'So, could it work? What do you think?'

'What I think is the apartment's wonderful. But you're going to need a real professional to come in and handle the renovation from start to finish.'

'How do I find someone to do that?'

Alison smiled. 'I know a master builder,' she said.

Laurie Fischer worked for a large publishing house on East Fiftieth Street. She had been employed there as a commissioning editor for nearly four years, and in that time had lived up to her reputation as a formidably bullish negotiator. Three years before, on her twenty-seventh birthday and against her better judgement, she had moved into an apartment with an advertising executive named Jerry, but her relationship with him – never once referred to by either party as a romance – had all too quickly degenerated into a series of uncomfortable powerplays.

On the surface, things had seemed perfect. If the idea of cohabiting with such a man had been presented to Laurie in the form of a business deal, she would have jumped at it.

Jerry had an inquiring mind, great plans for the future, perfect teeth and a house in the Hamptons. Unfortunately, he also had an ego the size of his real-estate holdings and a lump of rock where his heart should have been. He was a grown man of thirty-four who wanted to live with a beautiful, independent woman and still be allowed to play the field. When the strains on the relationship started to affect Laurie's work, she moved out. The final parting was recriminatory and messy.

Now she was single again, still the subject of longing glances from colleagues and friends, still the woman whose private life remained a delicious mystery to all but a few.

Alison had known her for more years than she cared to admit. The two of them had gone to high school together, had shared most secrets. The only remaining unchartered territory of their friendship was that part concerning sex. Even at school, Laurie had never dated. Her academic success had been qualified by her lack of popularity with other students, most of whom had felt threatened by such a noticeably superior combination of beauty and brains. Boys had quickly christened her 'The Icicle', and she gave them no cause to reconsider the propriety of the sobriquet.

In Alison's opinion her friend was a biological time bomb waiting to explode. Surely nobody could hold back on so much for so long. Years earlier, she had forced friendship on her glacial classmate when everyone else at school had given up trying to do so, and she had never been sorry for making the effort. Laurie, once you got to know her, was an extraordinarily kind person, a generous friend, irascible and acid-tongued at times to be sure, but always true. And although Alison considered herself to be much the less attractive of the pair, she had never felt her personality eclipsed by Laurie. After all, hadn't she been the one with all the dates, and wasn't she now still enjoying a long-term romance, albeit with a married man, while Laurie dressed for success and worked late most nights?

Alison reminded herself to call Laurie and give her the telephone number of the builder. She had never met the man personally, but friends were unable to praise him highly enough. Last year he had apparently transformed an apartment belonging to an opera singer at the Met into an award-winning *Homes & Gardens* photospread, yet his fees remained low and his daily rate was considered – by New York standards at least – to be very reasonable. But then, of course, there were other reasons for the glowing testimonials of his clients . . . Smiling to herself, Alison picked up the telephone and dialled.

After half an hour of sitting in the empty apartment with a sketchpad, Laurie gave up. She rose and smoothed out the legs of her jeans, laying the pad on a pile of screwed-up paper balls. Alison had been right. Her design sense just wasn't up to the task that faced her. The deal on the property had gone through quickly enough, and the deposit had now been paid. The escrow had been handled with almost supernatural efficiency, and she saw no reason why the completion date should not be kept. What bothered her more was that she would have to continue staying with friends until the work on the apartment was completed, and who knew just how long that would take?

She looked around the room. The day's dying sunlight glanced from the river on to the walls of the lounge in soft golden hues, investing the apartment with a hint of the grandeurs to come. Checking the ancient Bakelite telephone to see if the line was still connected, she dialled the number Alison had given her that morning, and asked to speak to the master builder.

He answered the phone himself, in a voice that was deep and slow, and gave the impression that he was weighing and judging each word before committing it to use. The job provided marvellous scope for creativity, Laurie explained, but would have to be finished this side of Christmas. Could he possibly come and take a look at the property before the weekend? He reckoned he could. She gave him the address and fixed a time for the meeting. After she had hung up, she wrote the number of Mr Ray Bellano in her Filofax under 'Service: Builder'.

'You gonna do this properly, you gotta take it back to scratch and start again.' He ran a broad hand across the lounge wall, knocked on it with his knuckle, picked at a loose edge of wallpaper which lifted away from the plaster with alarming ease. 'This here is a support wall. Reckon you could replace it with a couple of central pillars, but for what? It's a big apartment. Taking out the walls'll make the den look out of proportion to the rest of the place. Now you can do that if you want, but you're gonna be sorry you did.'

In the half-hour since Laurie had opened the door to the builder he had torn down every idea she had presented. A simple yes or no didn't seem to suffice with him; there was always an adverse comment to be made. The man was downright rude.

'Sure, I can do that if you want me to, Miss, but it'll look real ugly. We can put a window in through there, but I'm telling you it'll look kind of stupid.' *We* can put a window in, as if he and Laurie were buying the apartment together. She stepped back against the far wall with her arms folded across her chest and watched as he lumbered between the rooms, digging into the plaster with the end of a metal ruler, stooping to prise up a broken section of floorboard. He was well over six feet tall, broad-chested and ugly-handsome, clad in boots and dirty jeans, dark hair curling up from the neck of his sweatshirt. When he passed her, he trailed a smell of Brylcreem and sweat.

'Come in here a minute.' He was calling to her from the main bedroom, as familiar as if they were newlyweds. Well, she would quickly put a stop to this.

'Mr Bellano,' she began in her coldest business-voice, 'let's get one thing straight around here.' She walked to the doorway and waited for him to stand and look at her.

'Please, call me Ray,' he said, turning slowly and rising to his full height. 'All my good friends do. And as it looks like this job is gonna take some time to get right, I figure we're gonna become good friends.'

Then he smiled, a dangerous white smile that squared his jaw and ran from one side to the other of his bristle-shaded face. Laurie stopped in her tracks, suddenly aware that she was alone in the apartment with a complete stranger.

'I suppose you're right,' she said in a careful, clear voice.

'Although as I'll be staying with friends in Manhattan until the work is completed, I don't suppose we will be meeting very often.' She gestured at the bedroom walls. 'I'd like you to submit plans within ten working days, together with a quote for your time, building materials and so forth.'

'Now wait just a minute,' said the builder, raising a broad palm. 'I haven't said I'll take the job yet.'

'Why, are you fully booked up?'

'No, I just don't know if I want to do it.'

He wandered from the room, leaving Laurie to fume at the man's arrogance. Who the hell did he think he was? Okay, so he'd made a good job of some hot-shot opera singer's apartment, but that didn't make him Andy Warhol. If he was so great, how come his prices were so low? She stormed after him and was about to deliver a frank sermon on male arrogance when he strode out of the bathroom, almost bumping into her, and said, 'I'll do it.' And that was the end of that.

Or rather, the beginning.

Because two weeks later Ray Bellano delivered his plans and his estimate, and another argument developed between them. The master builder had ignored her instructions, and had designed the apartment entirely to his own specifications. Only the finest materials were to be used, but this would force the final bill to the very limit of her financial allowance.

'I cannot let you do this,' said Laurie as she studied the plans in her office. 'Why do the walls have to be so thick? And why use hardwoods when you could use pine? This is going to clean me out, Ray, and I still have to buy furniture once it's finished.'

'Look, Ms Fischer,' said Ray, 'I'm sure you're great at your job – whatever it is you do – but I guess you're gonna have to trust me a little bit. I'll tell you what I want you to do. Take down this number. I want you to call one of my previous clients and ask them about me. Check it out. Then call me back and approve the fee.'

After he had rung off, Laurie decided to call his bluff. She telephoned the number he had given her and asked to speak to Mrs Irene Bloom.

'Ray Bellano? The man's simply a genius. He changed my life. He rebuilt my duplex with a selection of the oddest materials, things I would never have dreamed of using, but it worked! Inlaid redwoods and fumed ash in the kitchen! After that I commissioned him to completely rebuild my other properties. If you'd like to see some pictures of his work I could get them over to you . . .'

'That won't be necessary, thanks,' replied Laurie.

After she had rung off, she sat by her office window and watched the teeming life in the city streets far below. It looked hot down there. Sometimes, working alone in the air-conditioned silence of her office, she felt completely cut off from the outside world. Perhaps it was just an aftereffect of leaving Jerry, but she was beginning to question the point of working so hard and sharing so little with other people. The couple she was staying with were being terrific to her, cooking almost every night and filling her spare evenings with easy conversation. Still, she knew that there would be a limit to Peter's and Fran's hospitality. At dinner she made the seating numbers odd. She was a single that others were forever trying to pair up. She knew that, despite all protestations to the contrary, there would be sighs of relief on both sides when she eventually moved into her own apartment. Without further hesitation Laurie called the master builder and gave him the order to start work immediately.

A week later she pushed open the door of the Hoboken apartment and stepped into a nightmarish explosion of brick and plaster debris. A dull thudding shook the room as she lifted her high-heeled shoes across the planks that covered gaping holes in the floor. The reverberations were coming from the bathroom, where, cocooned within a storm of plaster dust, the builder stood swinging a sledgehammer at a network of twisted pipes. Coughing, Laurie stepped back and watched from a safe distance as he lifted the hammer above his head and slammed it down into the plumbing again and again. Finally he saw her and approached, wiping rivers of sweat from his forehead and flicking it to the floor. He was stripped to the waist, and wore only his faded Levis and cowboy boots. Although it was unintentional, Laurie could not help noticing the powerfully defined pectoral muscles of his chest and the thick line of darkly curled hair which trailed across a hard, tanned stomach into his jeans.

'I wouldn't advise you to come in here, Miss,' he cautioned. 'These walls ain't too safe at the moment.'

Laurie avoided his gaze and concentrated on brushing a smudge of plaster dust from her suit. 'You don't seem to have anyone helping you, Mr Bellano,' she said stiffly. 'I felt sure that you'd employ a team. You can't possibly handle the job by yourself.'

'I think you'll find that I'm more than capable of handlin' this alone, Ma'am,' he replied, a smile playing on his lips.

Did she imagine it, or was there a hint of sexual suggestion in his voice? Could it be that she was acting the uptight New Yorker with this amiable Midwesterner whose gaze was as direct and unflinching as his attitude? Not caring to analyse her feelings any further, she left the chaotic apartment with a promise to return in a week's time. He was to call her office if he needed to pay cash for any builders' deliveries. The complexity of her current work schedule made it necessary for her to ask him to limit his calls to emergencies and requests for money. She was sure he understood.

When she returned to the office she found herself in the middle of a crisis. Her secretary had been frantically trying to contact her. Where the hell had she been? Laurie was suddenly aware that she had slipped away to the apartment without telling anyone where she was going. The motive for this course of action still proved elusive to her as she headed back to Peter's and Fran's at the end of the day.

'It's really not too soon to start thinking about dating again, you know,' said Fran as she ladled linguini on to her plate. 'You don't need to be told what a terrific catch you'd make someone.'

'God, Fran, you make me sound like a teenaged kid.' Laurie started to carefully wrap pasta around her fork. 'Dating is not a fun activity for a thirty-year-old woman, believe me. You had the taste and good grace to marry Peter when you were twenty-six. I'm past that point and moving into the Twilight Zone as far as males are concerned.'

'I think you're just being cynical,' said Peter, who had the annoying mealtime habit of holding his wife's hand under the table as he ate.

'It's not just cynicism. After a while you get to know all the types and their variations. The divorced guys who are either looking for reincarnations of their ex-wives or want to tell you about their plans for getting back custody of the kids. The ones who admit that they only beat up on their girlfriends when they step out of line or make eyes at someone in a restaurant. The late-starters, the Peter Pan Syndromers, the holistic health nuts, grown men who still go to discos, for Christ's sake . . .' She felt silent, toying with her pasta, embarrassed.

'Do you know when the apartment will be completed?' asked Peter in an attempt to change the conversation which looked exactly like an attempt to change the conversation. 'This side of Christmas, right?'

'This side of Thanksgiving, hopefully,' said Laurie. 'I have to get furniture in before Christmas, but it's going very slowly at the moment.'

'You know,' said Fran carefully, 'if you were staying on the premises you could keep a much more watchful eye on the work, and maybe speed things up.'

Laurie realised then that her friends were anxious for her to name a departure date. She finished her meal in forced good humour and retired to bed early.

When she arrived at the office the next morning, the first thing she did was speak to Mr Bellano.

'I guess I could finish one of the bedrooms in the next week or so,' he said in that infuriating half-asleep voice of his. 'You wouldn't disturb me by moving in.'

That's nice to know, thought Laurie, angrily closing a file disk on her PC. *Jeez, I'd hate to inconvenience you.* She shoved the silky black hair from her eyes and stared hard at the computer screen, not seeing the pale green paragraphs that unrolled before her.

That evening Laurie Fischer visited a newly opened night-spot called the Slum Club with a young, supposedly hot new novelist from Los Angeles, who went by the unlikely name of Dig. She picked her way home through the garment district at three thirty the next morning with little more than some business cards and a hangover to remember the evening by, although she was sure that nothing very interesting had happened.

The following Saturday afternoon she moved into the

Hoboken apartment. As Ray had promised, the bedroom was at least habitable. The room had been cleared of planks, bricks and plasterboard, and the door closed as far as a door without a lock and handle could. The light in the room was a soft yellow, the colour and smell of light pine, the walls awaiting fresh paint or clean bright wallpaper. She lay on the mattress and gazed up at the ceiling as the afternoon sun fell below the water and threw slivers of light across the ceiling.

She listened to Ray working – quietly, for once – in the next room. It sounded as if he was planing wood. She could hear the metal edge dragging lightly and then lifting as he inspected his work, running his fingers across the grain, checking the finish. The man was a fifties caricature. He probably took women to bed by throwing them over his shoulder. She wondered where he lived, who his friends were. She had forgotten that there were men like him, straight-arrow guys who worked with their hands and didn't spend their time smart-talking women around in circles. How had Alison come to meet him? The slow back-and-forth of the plane on the wood gradually lulled her into light, warm sleep.

She awoke to find the room half in darkness and the builder's backlit silhouette filling the bedroom doorway. He was standing very still and looking on, plane in hand, still stripped to the waist. She raised her hand to her forehead, shielding her eyes from the remaining light. He was watching her with a contented half smile.

'What is it?' She raised herself on one elbow and smiled back.

'You called out. I think you was dreaming.'

'Really? What did I say?' Laurie looked intrigued.

The builder looked down at his boots, embarrassed. 'Oh, nothin' much.'

'Come on, what did I say?'

'You called my name.'

'I wonder why I did that.'

Suddenly he walked to the bed and dropped down on to her, his broad, fleshy lips fitting over hers in a powerful kiss which forced her head back into the pillows. His right hand found her forearm and pinned it beside her head as he used his free hand to tear open the front of her shirt. She twisted in protest, raising her leg to find it met by his powerful thighs as he lowered himself on top of her, the heavy base of his erect penis pressing a denim-clad column into her crotch. With her free hand she tried to prevent his hairy chest from pushing down on to her breasts, but found her fingers digging into his back and sliding down into the waistband of his tattered jeans. In a single swift movement he tore open her thin silk brassiere, cupping her right breast with his broad, warm fingers, tweaking the small nipple between thumb and forefinger. Lowering his head, he ran his tongue into her cleavage, leaving a broad band of saliva between her breasts, continuing down to her flat, pale stomach. Feeling no resistance now, he freed her arm and used both hands to lift her buttocks and rip open the seam at the back of her skirt, pulling it to one side and allowing it to slide from the bed. The wide palm of his hand covered her pubic area as his fingers probed inside her pants, forcing them down around her thighs. His eyes, darkly glittering, caught hers and held them as he fumbled with the opening of his jeans, freeing himself from within. She felt his hands exploring her, forcing her open as his pelvis pressed down and the head of his organ slowly entered her. She cried out, the builder's thick shaft following the rhythm of her ragged breath as inch by inch its entire length was enclosed by her shuddering body. The weight of his torso eased as he partly withdrew, holding himself aloft for a moment before pressing down hard into her, retreating and plunging again and again, the muscles in his dark arms lifting and broadening with each stroke until she felt their powerful mutual climax reach flashpoint within her and flood out in streaming neural pulses, causing her to scream now in involuntary spasms of pain and gratification.

'It was weird.'

'Weird? *Weird?* The greatest sexual experience of your life, and all you can say is it was weird?'

'That's right.' Laurie thought for a moment, her elbows on the table, the coffee cup poised between her hands. The restaurant was almost empty, but she still spoke softly. 'Dangerous.'

Alison lit a slim gold cigarette and gestured impatiently with it. 'Explain what you mean.'

'There was no tenderness. It was sex at the most basic level. No small talk, no protection, just a fast hard . . . fuck. Afterwards, he just sat on the end of the bed refusing to even catch my eye. I was lying there with my clothes in shreds around me, feeling like I'd been in a serious car crash, and he wasn't even out of breath. He rose and walked to the mirror, flicked his hair into place, shoved the comb into the pocket of his jeans, then went straight back to work.'

'You're kidding. What did you do?'

'I guess I went a little crazy, called him a few names. He just looked up from his carpentry and smiled, so I left the apartment, took a walk around and tried to cool off. I felt so ashamed.'

'Have you seen him since?'

'Sure. The next day he turned up at the apartment, on time as usual, and began work as if nothing had happened.'

'So what are you going to do now?'

'I'm not sure. Obviously, the situation can't be allowed to repeat itself.'

'But you need him.'

'To finish the job, I guess I do.'

Alison studied the end of her cigarette, a slim smile slowly forming on her face.

Two days later, despite Laurie's promises and protestations, it happened again. Through the master builder she allowed herself to enter a world of sexual experience that she had never before encountered. She tried to understand her willingness to take part in the increasingly furious bouts of lovemaking which left her bruised and exhausted, but she knew that the explanation for her behaviour lay with first understanding her enigmatic partner. Ray Bellano rarely spoke, was barely civil to her, but made love with a passion and intensity that shocked Laurie to her core. Each performance became a display of power more violent than the last, but afterwards he always dressed and left the apartment at once, returning home to who knew where. She managed to establish that he was single, and that he originally came from a town in southern Texas. Beyond this, she knew nothing.

That week, colleagues at work began to pass comments. She had started arriving at the office less than immaculately dressed. Her hair was often out of place, her blouse not quite so well pressed. She seemed a little wilder now, a little less composed. Her attention seemed harder to hold. She explained the reason for the change to no one. Perhaps, though, some of them guessed when she was forced to use make-up to cover the bite marks which now blossomed like overripe fruit on her throat. And the apartment started to take shape.

Electrical circuits were laid, pipes were plumbed, walls were erected, then skimmed and painted. The kitchen was to become a bedroom, the bedroom a bathroom. Imported Italian tiles were to be juxtaposed with inlaid parquet blocks. And in the debris of the apartment, in the shavings and wood chips and wiring and plaster and brick dust, lay Laurie, with the builder towering above, dripping sweat on to her up-turned face as he thrust rhythmically into her, as powerful as a glistening piece of oiled machinery.

One rainy Sunday afternoon late in October, as she sat on the floor of the bare guest room watching the rain sweep in from the river and spatter against the windows, she asked him why he made love to her so fiercely.

He thought for a moment, his fingers tracing the delicate red scratches that embroidered her back. As he rose to pull on his white cotton boxer shorts, he told her that he thought it was because he wanted to possess her. It was the closest she ever got to an explanation.

Laurie decided that it was time to discuss her situation with someone she could trust. With a high-collared jacket of stiff grey linen covering the smarting welts on her shoulder blades, she left the office and went to lunch with Alison.

As she picked her way through her spinach salad she told her old schoolfriend about the strange relationship she now found herself involved in.

'What I fail to understand,' she concluded, 'is why I'm doing this. It just isn't like me.'

'Sex is a great release,' said Alison. 'Sounds to me like you're getting your ashes hauled without having to worry about any responsibility. If you were a man, you wouldn't think twice.'

'Well I'm not, and I am.' Laurie pushed the half-eaten salad aside.

'Laurie, I have a confession to make,' said Alison slowly. 'I kind of expected this to happen.'

Laurie frowned. 'You "kind of expected" what to happen?'

'Well, let me explain. A few months back there was a woman at the office whose apartment had been rebuilt by Bellano, and she kept going on about his brilliant craftsmanship. But I got the feeling that she meant something else entirely. It transpired that among her female friends he was very popular for . . . giving great decor.' Alison ground out the cigarette, colouring with embarrassment. 'Let's say that the guy has a reputation for being more than just a terrific builder.'

Laurie sat in dumbstruck silence for a moment. Then she rose to her feet, unclipped her handbag and threw some money on to the table. 'You booked me a stud?' she asked, her voice taut. 'I looked that desperate to you?'

'But I didn't mean any—'

'I'm sure you probably thought you were doing the right thing, but believe me it wasn't, Allie. It really wasn't.' She turned on her heel and left the restaurant.

That evening Laurie worked late. At nine thirty, seated on the PATH train going home, she considered her options. One, she could dismiss Ray from the job and hire someone else. But would she be able to find someone who could take over from his plans? Two, she could confront him and settle the matter out in the open. Then she would face the risk of him walking out, leaving the place unfinished. Three, she could act as if nothing was wrong and let him complete his work in peace. But what would happen when he made a move to continue their liaison? Carrying on with someone who had turned out to be little more than a male prostitute was unthinkable.

As Laurie alighted from the train she knew that the affair was over.

When she arrived back at the apartment she found the builder still there. Ray Bellano was sitting in the middle of the lounge floor surrounded by blueprints, panels of plasterboard and sawn-off lengths of plank. The room smelled of shaved wood and fresh paint.

'I'm glad you're back,' he began slowly, climbing to his feet and dusting down his jeans. 'I need to talk to you about the re-siting of the kitchen.' His unruly black hair was greased neatly back as if, in anticipation of her anger, he was now anxious to make a good impression. 'You look real good.' He gestured at her suit. 'Kind of severe, though.'

'Listen, Ray,' she said coolly, 'I have to know something. What happened between us the day before yesterday, was that all part of the service? When you decorate a place, do you usually get to sleep with the mistress of the house? Was I supposed to be thrown in as part of the deal?'

'I don't know what you mean.' He took a step towards her, but she backed away behind the low wooden counter he had built along one side of the room.

'No,' she agreed, 'I don't suppose you do. I'm talking about sexual liberties.'

'Hey, I don't take liberties. You wanted it.' He suddenly moved around to the other side of the counter and reached out his hand, grabbing the hem of her skirt and pulling her towards him.

'Let me go,' she said firmly, disentangling herself and moving away. The last thing she wanted to do was provoke him into leaving the apartment, but at the same time it was important to establish the new boundary lines between them. 'You've been employed to do a job of work, and it doesn't involve giving the kind of service you're used to providing. Just leave out that side of it from now on, and we'll get along fine.'

Ray stared down at his boots, as if he had been caught betraying a trust. 'You just made a mistake,' he said finally. 'I really need you. But if that's the way you want it, you got it.' He returned to work without another word.

After that she tried to spend as little time in the apartment as possible. Chance meetings with Ray merely invoked injured looks and uncomfortable silences. She left him money to purchase the materials he needed, and passed long evenings working late at the office. At the beginning of November she took a two-week vacation to visit her parents in Florida.

When she returned she found the apartment finished and a set of neatly labelled keys on the new kitchen counter, along with a final handwritten bill for labour. There was no sign of the builder. He had left her no personal message of any kind. She wrote a cheque for the bill and forwarded it to an address in Queens. Then, as a peacemaking gesture, she invited Alison over to inspect the property and come up with a few furnishing ideas.

'It's unbelievable,' Alison marvelled as she passed from room to room. 'I'd never have known it was the same apartment.'

Even without furniture the transformation was nothing short of miraculous. Every lintel and surround gleamed with proud detail. Alison sat on a packing crate staring about her as Laurie made coffee in a kitchen of grey slate and black marble surfaces.

'I'm sorry for what happened between us,' said Alison as she stirred her coffee. 'It was all my fault.'

Beyond the windows, a flotilla of tugboats heralded the arrival of a large South American freighter. Laurie came over and stood beside her friend, watching the pale sunlight sparkle against the bows of the ship as it progressed up the river.

'Forget it,' she said. 'It was nobody's fault. I chose to let it happen.' She fell silent for a moment. 'Help me pick out a dining table instead.'

'A dining table?' said Alison, equally eager to change the subject. 'What do you need a dining table for? You don't cook.'

'No, but I eat. And I may learn to cook.'

'I'll believe that when I see it.'

'You know, I'm going to love living here,' Laurie said, sitting down on the broad window ledge. 'It feels right.'

On that frosty autumn evening of dying sunlight, Laurie had no idea that her troubles were just starting.

By the first week of December most of Laurie's new furniture had been installed, and the first bad blizzard of the winter had thundered into the Manhattan streets.

In her Hoboken apartment Laurie sat in her soft blue lounge overlooking the river, curled in her mother's old patchwork blanket watching a rented video movie and eating peanut-butter sandwiches. The film had almost reached the end of its running time when the picture suddenly faded and died. Laurie irritably jabbed at the remote unit, but nothing happened. The screen remained blank. The video machine refused to play or rewind.

'Goddamnit.' She unwrapped the blanket from her body and walked over to the set, but there was nothing she could do to restart the tape or remove it from the machine. A minute later, the film started up by itself. By now, though, Laurie had grown tired of watching television, and prepared for bed.

After she had rinsed her cup and plate, she walked into the gleaming bathroom and ran the shower. Immersing herself in the cone of steaming water, she replayed the events of the day. The publishing house was looking at ways of cutting back on personnel, and after Laurie's recent failure to secure the rights to Dig's hotly sought-after new novel, she knew that it was time to strengthen her position in the company by putting in some extra hours.

She was just considering the best way of doing this when the shower jets slowed to a trickle, then ceased altogether. The sound of roaring water fell away to a single echoing drip as she started to shiver and reached over the frosted cubicle door for a towel.

But instead of cotton brushing her hand, something cold and slippery seized it. Yelping with fear she pulled free and jumped back against the tiled wall. She could feel her heart pounding as she slowly pushed open the glass door. The towel lay neatly folded across the heated rail, just where she had left it.

'I tell you, that's the last time I watch a horror movie by myself,' she told Alison over the telephone at work the next day. 'I could have sworn there was something there.'

'Don't tell me.' There was a pause as Alison lit her customary cigarette. 'I can't even watch the eleven o'clock news without getting goosebumps.'

'You mean the mugging reports?'

'No, George Bush. Too scary. Speaking of which, did you see the news last night?'

'No, I went straight to bed and slept with the lights on. Why?'

'I guess if you're nervous I shouldn't tell you. It's in all the papers this morning.'

'I don't have time to read the papers. Tell me.'

Christopher Fowler   93

'Okay. Hold on.' Laurie smiled, knowing that Alison was making herself comfortable on the other end of the line. 'You remember all that trouble at Rockaway Beach last July when those AIDS-infected syringes washed up on the sand?'

'Didn't they find a pair of legs as well?'

'That's right, and a bunch of dead laboratory rats and a human stomach lining. Well, it's started again. Only this time they don't think it's medical waste.'

'What do you mean?'

'Some woman just got washed up on the shore at Rockaway last night, or rather parts of her. She'd been taken to pieces with a bone saw.'

'Allie, I haven't had my lunch yet. Why are you telling me this? You know I live alone, you know how I get!'

'Sorry.' Alison did not sound very sorry at all. 'I thought you'd be interested. Maybe there's a book in it.'

'No thanks. We already did a children's guide called *Things to Look for on America's Coastline*.'

'I'd buy you a drink after work . . .'

'But you know I'm working late. And I am. I'll have to take a raincheck. The weekend, maybe.'

'Okay.'

Laurie worked until nine, then went home and reheated some lasagne. As she ate it she studied the freezing silver river which glowed dimly beyond her window. The apartment was so warm that the snowflakes melted the second they touched the pane. She undressed in the bedroom and emerged in a loosely tied kimono before heading for the television and turning it on. The screen showed a policeman being interviewed by a CNN reporter on a bleak, snow-swept beach. Behind him on the sand a pair of fat white female legs protruded from one end of a tethered tarpaulin.

'Fears are growing that another consignment of laboratory waste is being washed up on New York's beaches,' said the announcer. 'Last summer's outbreak saw the closure of many beaches and plunging attendance figures at nearly all of the major resorts. But with the thermometer staying at around the zero mark, that's one problem New York may avoid. This is . . .' The picture suddenly dwindled to a point of light.

'Damn it to hell!' Laurie searched for the remote unit, but it was nowhere to be found. 'This is ridiculous . . .' She pulled out the sofa cushions and stacked them on the floor, running her hand around the back of the seat. After a fruitless search she rocked back on her heels, perplexed. 'It has to be here somewhere,' she said to herself. 'Things don't just vanish.'

Finally, she gave up looking and went to bed.

That was the first time she heard the rat.

At least, it sounded like a rat. Its movements were small and sharp, and could only be heard if she kept very still and held her breath. There, behind the familiar sounds of the old building, beneath the creaking of the floorboards and the clicking of the cooling waterpipes, was another noise, like nails tickering across wood. Laurie sat up and reached for the bedside lamp switch. She clicked it on, half expecting to see a rabid laboratory rat crouching on the counterpane ready to pounce, but there was nothing unfamiliar to be found in the room. The sound continued, so faintly now that she began to wonder if it only existed in her imagination. Laurie did not sleep well that night.

'There's nothing wrong with the set.'

To prove his point, the TV repairmen switched it on and off several times in rapid succession. 'Or the video. It has to be your supply source.'

'What do you mean?' Laurie gave the television a dubious look.

'The electrical system. You've just moved in?'

'What has that got to do with it?' she asked, sharpness in her voice.

'These buildings have old wiring. Half the time it's dangerous and you don't even know it.'

'I've just had new wiring installed.'

'There could be a fault in that, something overloading. Are you running any other appliances while the TV is on? The iron, maybe.'

'I don't do the ironing while I watch TV,' she said coldly. 'I'm from New York, not Ohio.'

'Well, I think it's your circuitry,' said the repairman, closing his toolkit and heading for the door. 'Get your electrician back in to take a look.'

The next evening, an hour before Peter and Fran came by the apartment with Chinese food, the bedroom lights started to misbehave. Laurie was just changing into her jeans when the room was plunged into darkness. Swearing to herself, she checked the bulb and the fuses but found nothing wrong. Ten minutes later, the lights worked again. It was a very puzzled Laurie who opened the door to her old friends that night.

'So, how are you enjoying the place?' Peter asked through a mouthful of noodles. 'It really looks great.'

'There are one or two teething problems.'

'What kind of problems?'

'Oh, lights, plumbing.' She tried to make it sound casual. 'And I think there's a rat.'

'You're being melodramatic,' said Fran, passing a cardboard

box filled with bean sprouts across the table. 'Every building has mice and roaches.'

'I guess so. This sounds bigger. I hear it almost every night.'

'You want me to take a look?' Peter offered, but he didn't seem too enthusiastic about the idea.

'No, it'll sort itself out. It's OK.' She picked at the bean sprouts, wishing she was as confident as she sounded.

The next morning Laurie was seated at the kitchen counter dropping pieces of grapefruit into the blender when the Channel Eleven local news report began. Her mind was half on the preparation of breakfast, half on the day's planned meetings as the image on the screen changed. Lettering stripped across a beach scene: ROCKAWAY BEACH VICTIM NAMED.

'Police today identified the body of the murdered woman found on Rockaway Beach as Mrs Irene Bloom, a forty-two-year-old CPA who went missing from her Upper West Side apartment last Thursday . . .'

At first Laurie failed to register the name. It wasn't until she looked up at the picture that her blood ran cold. The grapefruit knife slipped in her fingers, gashing the back of her hand. Blood welled in the wound and dripped heavily on to the marble counter as she continued to stare at the network's photograph of Mrs Irene Bloom.

She was standing proudly in an apartment that appeared to be an exact duplicate of Laurie's own.

'It was the woman I spoke to, the women he recommended I call to check his credentials. And her apartment is exactly the same as mine! He decorated it in an identical style, don't you see what this means?'

'This is stupid, Laurie, you know that? It's just a coincidence. You want to go to the police? You want to walk in there and say, "Excuse me, officer, but I shared the same interior decorator as the murdered woman"?'

'You know damned well that we shared more than just the decoration.'

Alison sighed. She hadn't minded changing her route to work so that she could meet a near-hysterical Laurie in the coffee shop on East Fiftieth, but she was bothered by the sight of a good friend seemingly falling to pieces.

'Every painter has a style,' she said, trying to sound as calm and rational as possible. 'The apartments he designs are bound to be similar to some extent. You're working too hard, you know that? You should get out more.'

'Maybe you're right.' Laurie seemed to back down suddenly. 'My imagination's been a little overactive of late.'

'If you're so worried, I'll set your mind at rest. After all, it was me who put you in touch with this guy in the first place. I'll call him. Do you have his number?'

'I thought you had it. You gave it to me.'

'That was just a temporary line. He was moving to somewhere in Queens.'

Laurie thought for a moment. 'That's right,' she said, remembering. 'I posted his cheque on.' She began to rummage in her handbag. 'I think I threw the piece of paper away.'

'It doesn't matter. We know his name. I'll find out where he lives and give him a call. And you've got to promise me that you'll start taking things a little easier.' Alison held out her hand and they shook. Laurie's fingers were freezing.

'Do we have a deal?'

'A deal.'

* * *

Exactly two weeks before Christmas Laurie's ex-boyfriend turned up at her office. He had been meaning to see her for a while now, he said, just to bury the hatchet. Coincidentally, he had just broken up with his girlfriend Carol. Laurie was surprised but hardly flattered. Still, in the spirit of Christmas she went for a drink with him and actually managed to have a good time. At the end of the evening he tried to kiss her and she pulled gently but firmly away. She did, however, give him her new home telephone number, which was certainly more than she meant to do. Jerry was a louse, but a charming one, and she figured that he deserved something for at least possessing one good quality.

The following Saturday there was another strange occurrence in the apartment. Laurie had arrived home from work and was playing back her messages – one from Jerry suggesting dinner – when there was a thud and a bang in the room next door. Clicking off the answering machine, she moved back against the wall and listened. For a minute or so there was silence. Then a weight shifted and a floorboard creaked, not from the apartment above or the one below but right next door, the weight falling against the wall with a sudden heart-stopping thump. Laurie moved across the lounge to her work-desk and picked up the Indian letter opener of sharpened brass which lay on the desktop blotter. Slowly she crept towards the archway into the dining room. Poising herself on the threshold, preparing to attack, she suddenly felt foolish. Here she was, a grown woman, acting like a child of six just because she'd heard a few unexplained bumps and thuds. With an uneasy laugh she began to lower the knife. The apartment lights extinguished themselves.

The darkness was complete and solid, like a black wall. She had always hated the dark, ever since she'd been a small child. As she ran across the lounge to the front door her shin caught the edge of the coffee table and she fell sprawling, her knee tearing open on its sharp steel edge. When she reached the doorway to the hall she found Jerry standing there with his finger still resting on the apartment buzzer.

Seconds later, the lights came back on.

The last thing she had intended to do was cry on his shoulder. Perhaps it was a culmination of the month's events that caused her to behave in such an uncharacteristic manner, but she hung on to Jerry and told him all her fears – about her job, her private life, and even the inexplicable problems of her apartment.

When she had finished he smiled and poured her a brandy before taking her to bed and tucking her in. He sat with her for three hours and didn't try to lay a finger on her. It was a side of him she had never seen before.

That night, for the first time in what felt like an age, she slept soundly.

The next night was a Friday, and Laurie returned late from a meeting to find that she had been burgled.

'That's the whole point,' she told the officer. 'I'm not even sure if there's anything missing.' She was standing in the lounge amid the wreckage of the shattered glass coffee table and the stuffing of the slashed sofa. The young policeman picked his way from room to room with a distant, indecipherable look on his face.

'Forgive me for saying so, Ma'am,' he said, 'but this is kind of a regular problem at the moment, and we don't have too much of a chance of catching anybody. A lot of folks resent the yuppies moving in and forcing up the local property prices.'

'I understand what you're saying,' said Laurie angrily, 'but I've as much right to protection as the next person and I don't think it's your job to make value judgements.'

'Listen, I'm just trying to tell you how it is around here.' Now armed with a legitimate excuse to lose interest in the crime, the police officer moved away towards the door. 'Just make a list of the missing items and bring it down to the station, Ma'am, and we'll do what we can. Also, give me the names of anyone you know who might have done this.'

Halfway to the door, Laurie halted. 'What makes you think I know anyone who would do something like this?' she asked.

'Well, there's no sign of a break-in. Either you forgot to lock the door or whoever it was had a key.'

'Nobody has a key to this apartment except me.'

'Then you left the place unlocked. If it's not one, it has to be the other.'

'Terrific. You've been a great help.'

After slamming the front door, she returned to the ruins of the sofa, sat down and cried.

She found nothing missing. Her jewellery box was unopened, and some dollar bills lay on her dressing-room table untouched. The damage was less serious than it had at first seemed. Even so, the coffee table and the expensive designer sofa would have to be replaced.

Peter and Fran came by to help Laurie tidy the place up, and suggested that she install a burglar alarm. At least, they said, it would prevent the same thing from happening again. After the last dustpan of broken glass had been emptied into the bin they opened a bottle of red wine and toasted the coming new year.

'You have to get an entryphone to this place, you know that?'

'Jerry, what are you doing here?' Laurie stood in the doorway in her bathrobe, unprepared for visitors. To be honest though, she was pleased to see him. 'You'll have to be quick, I'm getting ready to go out to dinner. But while you're here, you can do something for me.' She moved aside to let him enter.

As he walked into the lounge he pulled a champagne bottle from his jacket. 'To warm the new apartment,' he explained. 'Better late than never. What do you need me to do?'

Laurie led him by the hand down the hallway and through to the strange crystal-and-mirror bathroom that Ray Bellano had designed for her. Taking the champagne bottle from him and standing it down on the washbasin, she positioned Jerry in the centre of the room and held her finger to her lips.

'Listen,' she whispered, 'and then tell me what you hear.'

Jerry cocked his head on one side in an exaggerated gesture of attentiveness. He listened for a while, then shook his head. 'Zip,' he said finally. 'Nothing at all. What was I supposed to hear?'

'I don't know. There's this weird sound I keep hearing at night. Maybe I really *am* imagining it.' She shook her head, then picked up the bottle and headed into the kitchen.

'What do you mean?' asked Jerry, following her through. 'What are you imagining?'

'Oh, I don't know, rats, mice, you name it. Something. You need a haircut.' She reached up and touched the back of his neck.

'This is the Frankie Avalon look. I happen to like it.' Jerry patted his hair back in place. 'So, have you had a fumigator in?'

'No, it doesn't seem that serious.' Laurie found two glasses and opened the champagne. 'It comes and goes.'

'Forgive me saying so, but it looks like it's keeping you awake at night.'

She poured, then touched Jerry's glass with hers. 'You know how I always used to worry about little things? I'm just doing it again, that's all.'

'You want me to stay with you tonight?' His smile became a sly grin.

'I know it's Christmas,' she said with a chuckle, 'but I'm not quite that full of goodwill yet.'

An hour and a half later, though, she was.

It was the first time she had had sex with anyone since the departure of the master builder, and for a while it was a very different experience to get used to. Jerry was a courteous, considerate, conservative lover. He took into account a woman's needs. He took things slowly. He massaged her body gently. In fact, she had completely forgotten how boring he was in bed.

He lay heavily on top of her, his hands kneading her breasts. His clothes were folded neatly on a nearby chair. The bedroom lights were all turned off. He was moaning softly in what he considered to be a sexy manner. Laurie felt her left leg falling asleep as he shifted his weight, pulling the sheets out again.

Suddenly the room began reverberating with a series of deafening rhythmic bangs. Jerry leapt from the bed with a cry as if he had been electrocuted. As the hammering continued he ran to the wall and slapped on the lights. Immediately, the noise stopped – as swiftly as it had begun. Laurie cautiously removed the pillow she had pulled over her ears to block out the sound.

'That's a hell of a plumbing problem you've got there,' he said as soon as his heartbeat had returned to normal. 'Jesus, does that happen often?'

'Quite often,' replied Laurie.

'Where was it coming from?'

'The apartment,' she said, still shaking. 'It just comes from the apartment.'

'Laurie, you *have* to meet up with me tonight for a Christmas drink. I've a present for you.' On the other end of the telephone, Alison already sounded a little merry. In the background Laurie could hear an office party in full swing. She looked from the receiver to the stack of paperwork on her desk and sighed.

'Allie, I'm flying down to spend Christmas with my folks tomorrow night and I have all this work to catch up on . . .'

'Meet you in one hour's time at fourteen, Christopher. If I'm there first I'll have Michael get us a table. Be there or I'll tell everyone that you rekindled an old flame last night.'

'How did you know that?' asked Laurie in amazement. 'Word sure gets around fast.'

'You forget that Jerry still works in my department.'

'Yeah, but I didn't expect him go to around telling everyone.'

'Not everyone, just me. Oh, about Ray Bellano . . .'

'You managed to get hold of him?'

'No, I didn't. Nobody seems to have seen him alive since you had him, you maneater. Listen, do you still have the blue-prints he made up of your apartment?'

'I've got them right here in my desk drawer.'

'Good, bring them with you to the restaurant. I have a little surprise for you.'

The line went dead.

An hour later in the restaurant at 14 Christopher Street, Laurie and Alison exchanged gifts and drank a toast to each other. Then, at her friend's request, Laurie unfolded the plans to her apartment and laid them flat on the tablecloth.

'Remember the woman who was washed up on the beach? After she died, they put her apartment up for sale,' explained Alison, fishing about in her handbag as she spoke. 'I applied to the realtors and they sent me a copy of the floor layout.' She found the piece of paper she was looking for and studied it carefully. 'I thought it might be interesting to see if your suspicions – whatever the hell they're supposed to be – are well-founded.'

Laurie leaned forward and perused the two sets of plans. She was disappointed to find, however, that in blueprint form they bore little resemblance to each other.

'Kind of a letdown, huh?' said Alison, draining her glass. 'I can't say I understand what you were expecting to find.'

'I'm not sure I know any more,' replied Laurie as she reached for the wine bottle. 'Let's just forget about it. Be happy I was wrong.'

On the 28 December Laurie returned from her parents' condominium in Florida and climbed the stairs to her apartment. As she opened the front door she could see the red light on her answering machine ticking on and off. She put down her bags in the hallway, then went into the bathroom and turned on the central heating. While she waited for the flat to warm up, she played back her messages.

'Laurie, call me the minute you get in. Something awful has happened. It's Allie.'

Laurie raised the receiver and speed-dialled the number on the handset.

'Thank God. I didn't want you turning on the TV and hearing about it on some news show.'

'Here about what?' asked Laurie. 'What are you talking about?'

'It's Jerry. I don't know how to say this any other way. He's been murdered.'

The room dipped before Laurie's eyes. 'No, that's not possible.'

'Laurie, listen to me. Don't watch the news, OK?'

'When did this happen?' She reached out for the arm of the chair and slowly sat down.

'Yesterday. He was found in his apartment in a very bad way. I really don't want you to hear about it. Stay there, I'm on my way over.'

Alison came and stayed at her friend's apartment for the next two days. The police called by a number of times, but only made the situation worse by describing the murder in greater detail. Jerry had been at home sitting in front of the TV when he was attacked by someone wielding a hammer, or a similarly heavy blunt instrument. By the time his attacker had finished, there hadn't been a whole lot left of Jerry to take downstairs. The door to his apartment had been torn from its hinges. There had been no witnesses to the crime, and the police had no direct leads. Was there anything at all she could tell them that would shed some light on his death? Laurie tried to think of something tangible, some concrete piece of evidence that would link the half-formed suspicions in her mind. In the end, though, she settled for promising to call the detective at the station if she remembered any further details of their final meeting.

'You sure you don't want me to stay with you again tonight?' asked Alison for the third time. 'Absolutely sure?'

'Go, go, for God's sake, I'll speak to you tomorrow morning.' Laurie pushed her friend to the front door and opened it for her.

'All right, but you know where I am if you need me. I'll call you before I leave and we can go to the cemetery together.'

Jerry's funeral, delayed by the need for a post mortem, had finally been scheduled for eleven o'clock the following morning. Laurie was grateful for her friend's concern, but was relieved to be left alone for a while. Beyond the windows the river lay in darkness, ebbing sluggishly in the freezing night air.

She went to the kitchen and made herself a cup of herbal tea, then sat in the lounge with a paperback novel. She felt more enervated than she had at any time since moving into the apartment. As she scanned the page and tried to concentrate on the complexities of the plot, her fingers explored the knife-rips in the fabric of the sofa. Because of the Christmas rush, the new covers she had ordered had yet to arrive. The jagged striations across the material which she now absently touched seemed to recall the fine red scratches which had once adorned her back like tribal markings. On a nearby table the telephone rang, making her start. She reached across and answered it.

At first she thought there was nobody on the other end of the line. Then a strange tapping sound began, like someone running a stick back and forth across the bars of a wooden cage. Behind this, she could hear a man steadily breathing, the air in his throat being forced out in a series of sexual spasms.

She dropped the receiver back into the telephone cradle with a gasp of disgust. Now was not the time for someone to be playing practical jokes. She wondered if perhaps she should ring the police and report the call, then decided against it. She had had enough questions from them in the last two days. The only way to outwit cranks was to get an unlisted number. She sat back on the damaged sofa and tugged her robe more tightly over her breasts. Slowly but surely the apartment felt as if it were becoming her prison, and the containment of all the unnamed things she most dreaded.

Alison entered the claustrophobic chaos of her Soho flat and headed for the kitchen. Something had been bothering her on the journey back from Hoboken. She pulled out the drawers beneath the cluttered kitchen counter and began to search among the balls of twine and special-offer coupons. Finally she located what she was looking for – the blueprints Laurie had accidentally left behind in the restaurant just before Christmas.

Unfolding the plans, she held one end down with a cookie jar and began to study the geometric diagrams inch by inch. Then she took a piece of tracing paper and began to draw.

Laurie reknotted the robe-cord around her waist and headed into the bathroom. Turning on the basic tap, she splashed cold water over her face in the vain hope that it would make her feel less exhausted. She was debating whether to run a bath when the telephone began to ring once more in the lounge. She hesitated, her hand resting on the handle of the door. Her parents sometimes liked to call her at this late hour. She walked across the darkened lounge and picked up the handset.

This time the sound was clearer, a steady clicking, wood on wood, expanding and contracting. And beneath it was the rasping, quickening breath of a man fast approaching orgasm. She slammed the receiver down hard and cleared the line, her heart thudding in her chest. She was about to pick it up and dial the police when it rang again. Gingerly, she raised the earpiece and slowly moved it closer.

This time the voice was a familiar one. It was Alison, probably calling to say that she had arrived home safely.

'Laurie, thank God! Now listen carefully. You must do as I say.'

Laurie frowned. The voice at the other end of the line sounded taut and strange. 'Allie, what's—'

'Shut up and listen! You have to leave the building, right now. Just grab your bag and walk to the front door.'

'Are you nuts? It must be minus five degrees out there.'

'Please,' pleaded the voice, 'do this for me. Just get up and go.'

'Why?' asked Laurie, puzzled. 'Just tell me why.'

'Your apartment, I checked the plans.'

'So?'

'I kept thinking something was wrong. The way the place looked didn't seem to match the way it was on the blueprint.' Alison sounded out of breath. Had she been running? 'Ray Bellano, he built it according to the plans that he presented to you, but he built it the other way around.'

'What do you mean?'

'If you flip the drawing over, you get a different-shaped apartment. I tried it just now with a piece of tracing paper. There's a second wall running all the way around the place. An inner skin.'

'I don't understand,' said Laurie, shaking her head as if to clear away her gathering fears. 'What are you saying?'

'I'm saying that he's in there with you.'

Horrified, Laurie looked up from one wall to the other. Away in the background, the clicking wooden sound had started up again. This time it was not being transmitted over the telephone, but was coming from somewhere within the apartment.

'Laurie, are you there? You see what this means? He's been there with you all the time. He must be watching you right now.'

The receiver slid from her hands. She knew that Alison was telling her the truth. Everything made sense. The builder had been controlling her every movement from the start, forcing her to reveal her nakedness in the sudden glare of the bedroom lights, slowly baring her body beneath the drying taps of the shower, sending her from room to room, feeding on her growing anxiety.

She rose and moved into the centre of the lounge, searching the walls, listening for the smallest sound. Now other details began to fall into place. She remembered forsaking her blanket and crossing naked to the TV as she tried to fix the picture, a hand touching hers as she emerged from the shower stall, the sense of someone standing over her bed watching her as she slept, the jealous rage which hammered in the bedroom walls because Jerry had made love to her. The burglary had been nothing more than a display of anger at her leaving. How many cracks and crevices, peepholes and passageways could he have built into the apartment?

As the creaking wooden noise became more urgent, she recognised its origin. He was breaking through the slats of the wall in the lounge. No more sneaking from secret openings, the master builder was about to make his grand entrance.

She ran for the kitchen and the knife rack above the sink as he appeared behind her in a showering explosion of plaster and wooden staves. For a second she caught sight of him striding across the room through a spray of dust, and the madness that glittered behind his blood-streaked eyes spurred her on.

'Stay away from me!' she screamed, grabbing a bread knife from the rack and holding it with both hands in front of her stomach. Ahead in the hallway, he paused. His erect, bloodied penis swayed from side to side as he began to move forward once more. She backed against the counter, desperately trying to think above the noise of her racing heart. Turning, she peered ahead through the doorway of the kitchen into the hall, but now there was nothing to be seen. It was as if he had suddenly disappeared.

The apartment had fallen silent. Laurie took a step forward, then another, carefully shifting her weight as lightly as possible. She began to think clearly again. The first priority was to get out of the flat. Her neighbour below worked nights, so she would have to go into the street for help. And to do that she would need clothes. The bedroom was at her back. Her jacket and car keys lay on the bed. She listened once more. There was still nothing to be heard from the lounge or the hall. Out on the river, the sound of a barge-horn was muffled by falling snow. Slowly she lowered the bread knife, then turned and walked into the bedroom. Into his awaiting arms. The power of her scream was matched by the thrust of the knife as she pushed it deep into the master builder's chest.

'You'll feel better if you drink this down in one.' The young officer holding out the brandy to her was the same one who had called after the burglary. 'Do you have someone you can stay with tonight?'

'I guess so, yes.' Laurie accepted the drink and sipped at it. Although the blanket was pulled high around her shoulders she was unable to stop herself shivering. The doctor had told her it was shock, not cold. The officer watched dispassionately as they removed the builder's body from the room. The handle of the bread knife thrust out above the edge of the sheet, firmly wedged between his ribs, just below the heart.

'He designed the apartment, huh?' The officer looked about, approvingly. 'He did a nice job. Got a real good finish on these units.' He ran his hand along the edge of a shelf, then looked back at the blood-spattered body as it went through the door. 'Guess he took too much pride in his work.'

'Ray Bellano started rebuilding the place right after I broke off with him,' said Laurie, unfolding her napkin and dropping it into her lap. 'I was hardly ever there, so I never noticed what he was up to. He was able to come and go as he pleased, and I was none the wiser. The police say he'd tried the same thing before on a smaller scale, when he rebuilt Irene Bloom's apartment.'

'That poor woman,' said Alison, burrowing her fork into a stuffed mushroom. 'She obviously wasn't quick enough for him. You're lucky you didn't get washed up on the beach as well. These are delicious.'

'All that time spent between the walls, watching.' Laurie reached across to Alison's plate and stole a mushroom. 'The police wouldn't let me see inside. They said he had – things – in there.' She shuddered. 'No more fixer-uppers for me. My next apartment is going to be completely ready to move into.'

'Just think,' said Alison through a mouthful of food, 'if you hadn't slept with him in the first place, none of this would ever have happened.'

Laurie narrowed her eyes at her companion as she continued eating.

'He knew that you'd never have sex with him again,' said Alison, refusing to let the subject drop. 'He must have gotten so frustrated.'

'That's the worst part of it,' said Laurie, slowly lowering her fork to the table. 'I have a horrible feeling he never did.'

They finished the rest of the meal in silence.

The *Trafalgar* Lockdown

They say that in the reaches of space, far more easily than on Earth, one can become fixated upon a person or procedure. In the freezing aridity of a planet's orbit, obsession can bloom until all sense of private perspective withers and dies. How do we think if our world no longer exists? As yet, no one fully understands the psychological problems wrought by venturing out into the universe. How could they? To understand the monstrous agoraphobia of the void is to imply the conquest of inner space. And even now, with all the scientific advances in the world, no one can explain the darkness of the human heart.

My first sight of the ship is the one I will always remember; a vast curving gun-metal grey wall filling my sight from the square launch-hatch window, condensed-air hissing from a hundred pipe outlets, engineering crew buzzing up and down the fascia on tiny pressure-platforms. I'd seen footage of her sister ship, HMS *Imperial*, but it was hard to gauge the size of the *Trafalgar*, to point and say, that's where the navigator works, or these are the storage holds. It was difficult to absorb what I saw. This was no sleek voyager to the stars, unfolding like a silver spider as it reached a new atmosphere. Instead it reminded me of an engraving I had seen of a Victorian prison hulk docked at Portsmouth. Yet it was so beautiful to behold that my eyes started watering.

I wanted to draw what was in my vision, but my Macpad was strapped into my back-pack and we were to board immediately, so I joined the crew shuffling through customs toward the embarkation point and waited for ages in a smelly grey plastic tube, just as I had the week before, taking a shuttle flight to Brussels, Belgium, the other side of the galaxy; boarding procedures were much the same, one was just a few hundred miles away, the other millions. I wasn't sure exactly how many miles, but that is because I'm an artist. I don't think with the logical side of my brain. I can't tell you the cubic capacity of the *Trafalgar*, its speed capability or technical specifications, but I could paint it for you, and I think the *mélange* of pigments would be just as truthful and a lot easier to understand than strings of figures.

To speak with honesty, I was still surprised that the shipping line had agreed to allow me on board. I'd been told it was against regulations to permit non-government employees on export ships. Although I was a civilian, I had been hired on a freelance basis by the contractor, provided I agreed to sign the standard working-condition approval forms. Before the ship's Commander confirmed my passenger status I was required to pass fitness and safety tests. I was also given instruction in basic crew emergency procedures and made to take a short examination, but these were formalities, because in the unlikely event of a real emergency I wouldn't be allowed to touch a thing on board. They were far too worried about their expensive equipment to allow a twenty-three-year-old civilian operate it. They couldn't have checked my psyche-evaluation thoroughly, because there were a couple of problematic incidents in my personal history that should have prevented me from being allowed to undertake the journey. But they passed me and I didn't question their decision. I just couldn't believe my luck. I had longed to do this all my life. Indeed, it felt as though everything that had gone before had been leading to this moment of departure.

The HMS *Trafalgar* would be gone for thirty-two years and four months, that's sixteen years out, four months there, sixteen years back. The amount of earthtime that would elapse was a little over four years. For a one-in-a-million chance like this, I could handle the loss of four years from my life, although I doubted that Dex would wait for me. Oh, he promised to be there when I returned, but I heard the half-hearted tone in his voice and knew he didn't even believe it himself. He did not care enough to marry me, nor I him, and in these conservative times no other relationship was possible between us.

The *Trafalgar* was about to undertake interstellar travel, a route map to the stars that would draw us beyond Pluto, past the Kuiper Belt of cometary debris, beyond the Terminal Shock Boundary where the solar wind slows down and through the Heliopause where it stops altogether, at the outer edge of the Solar System. Through the birthplace of comets, the Oort Cloud, and on to the nearest star, Proxima Centauri, 4.2 million light years from Earth. Then the real journey would begin.

Unlike its sister ship the *Imperial*, the *Trafalgar* had an observation deck on the bridge (organosilica-synthetics had improved in the production gap) from where I could work. The original plan had been to leave from one of the big docks on Mars and save a little time, but the ship returned to Earth Harbour for a software refit, and I heard about it at just the right moment. They don't advertise these posts, believe me, they get bombarded by the colleges all the time, but I had some connections, and I'd painted for Symax before. Just corporate stuff, but they knew my name, and liked my work.

I was expected to provide around seventy paintings and at least a hundred subsidiary drawings. The full list of subjects and angles had been sent to me a few days earlier. It was pretty daunting, and I don't think the *Trafalgar*'s quartermaster was thrilled by the amount of art material I requested, but I could imagine how embarrassing it would be to run out of an essential colour on the wrong side of the galaxy.

I entered the ship with the rest of the crew, sixteen of us in all, twelve men and four women in matching blue suits. While the luggage was being stowed I was shown to a communal area rather like a hotel lobby. The others all had chores to attend to, so I was left alone sipping coffee on a grey plastic bench while everyone else hustled about looking purposeful. It was frustrating to be the only non-technical part of an operation like the launch of the *Trafalgar*; I felt useless and inessential to the journey. But Symax was a highly image-conscious company that, like so many other corporations today, was run by relentlessly wholesome American Christians who greatly valued their perceived contributions to the arts, so I knew that my work would assume corporate importance once I returned to Earth. The crew were nice enough in a busy, disinterested way; after all, I figured we would have plenty of time to get to know each other when we docked beside the *Imperial*.

Not too much time, though. The itinerary allowed us to spend just one week together before entering hypersleep. At the other end of the trip I was due to come out ten days before we reached the *Imperial*, because I had to capture the views on the approach to the sister ship. The rest of the crew were due out a week before me, the Captain earlier and the Commodore earlier still, in order to check that the ship's laserdrive systems were fully operational or something. It was worked out with the hermetic tidiness of a journey that had been made a hundred times before, although this particular trip had only been made once, and that by the *Imperial*.

My cabin was small but cleverly organised to provide me with the optimum living conditions currently available in space flight. There were no handles or buttons to get caught up on, just a lot of pressure-sensitive panels that opened to reveal tiny drawers. Soothing dark wood-textures, too; I'd been expecting a lot of tough white plastic. A full wardrobe of clothes, including boots, was packed into an area just 250 centimetres high. I was still sitting on the bed emptying out my hand luggage when the call went up for immediate departure, so I made my way to the deck and sat with the others, lightly strapped in for my own protection, although the ship countered the force of take-off with its own internal gravitation.

I got talking to a couple of the crew, a handsome Danish-Asian named Dalloway, who was one of the navigation officers, and Kierkemeister, the Spanish engineer who would be responsible for refitting the *Imperial*. They were both old hands at this sort of thing (even though they looked to be about twenty-five years of age), and Dalloway volunteered a little more information than I needed to know about the problems of take-off and landing.

I'm not the world's most technical person, but I was surprised to hear that the latest ships had revived the old concept of manual-override docking, meaning essentially that a mere human being could bring in a ship of this size by him- (or her-)

self in the event of a computer malfunction. I knew computer glitches had become much more serious with the advent of the plasma-chip, but was surprised to hear about anything so important still being controlled by something as squishy and fallible as a human being. Laser engines allow vast ships to be docked into their berths within the width of a fingernail. Instead of being reassured by this, the thought alarmed me.

The take-off was almost dull; except for a sickly feeling in the pit of my stomach there was no sensation that we had even started moving. After we unstrapped and started walking about, I could detect no real change in the ship's gravity, but later I started noticing how objects seemed to stick slightly too hard when I put them down or picked them up, and how my natural momentum kept me moving a little longer than I wanted. It wasn't a problem, but I was warned that it made bruising easier. There was no ship's doctor as such – in the event of an accident advice would be provided from Earth Harbour – but Sanjariit, one of the female officers, doubled as a sort of injury-instructor.

I wanted to meet Commodore Forrester, the man in overall charge of the ship, or at least some of the senior crew members, but only managed to glimpse their silhouettes hunched over consoles on the bridge. There was some talk about Forrester losing his wife on a trip a few years back. Apparently she had contracted a form of encephalitis from a badly sterilised hypersleep pod, and to this day he blamed himself. Many people who flew to the stars had personal, often painful reasons for doing so. Like restless sailors, they never settled well back on Earth.

Donnizetti, the Captain, was always shut away in the communications bay or the cargo holds, and everyone else was working to schedule. This left me walking the grey corridors, searching in vain for something interesting to draw. I'm not a technical artist; computer programs can reproduce dimensions far more accurately than I. The changing light was the thing that interested me, but to draw that I needed windows.

The first time I looked out of one, I was surprised to see how near the searing blue seas of the still-visible Earth appeared to be, until Dalloway explained that the windows (of which there were only three in the whole ship) were manufactured from a dense plastic that greatly magnified the view. This, I knew, would be both a help and a hindrance in my job, for the plastic also distorted, creating prismatic auras around bright objects, and I realised that I would have to compensate for the distension in my drawings.

Because of the staggered shifts we never ate all at the same time, which seemed rather anti-social, but I had read that the social structure of spaceflights was deliberately designed to prevent pair-bonding, because that led to sexual intercourse and jealousies and fights, so it was better to keep the crew members at a distance from one another. I was told that a certain amount of buddying-up was inevitable, though – the theory being that otherwise the sheer vastness of the world beyond the windows induced depression fits on long flights. So I buddied-up with Dalloway, who had a great smile and barn-door shoulders and seemed to like me.

My main disappointment was that I only met the Commodore once, and then for about three minutes. I had been taken to the bridge, which remained in almost total darkness, in order that the outside view from the main-deck window would be bright enough to clearly discern star clusters. Obviously, nobody navigated by sight, but I got the feeling that the great view of space was used to give the Captain and officers some kind of mental gyroscope, a sense of being the right way up in the universe, and therefore the ability to sense when something was wrong. I imagined that it was like being aboard a Victorian fishing vessel at night, a tiny haven of life and light in an ocean of hostile blackness. Apparently, in space as at sea, a good navigator can discern even slight changes in speed and approach-angle from the shifting patterns of the stars. Dalloway tried to point out one such shift when we made a course correction, but I saw and felt nothing different.

Forrester barely bothered to turn from his console to say hello to me, and I got the feeling that his stiffly pleasant greeting was something he had learned, rather like speaking in technical commands. As he was seated in a high-backed chair facing away from me, I was unable to really tell much about him, but he seemed nice enough in a distant way, younger looking than his fifty years, slim, with cropped black hair and a tiny diamond-shaped beard. The other informed me that he was a good man, with deeply held religious convictions, rigid about the flight rules but fair, and his end-of-trip crew reports were apparently admired by everyone because they were usually complimentary enough to push career-ratings up a notch.

During that first week out, I became painfully aware of how little I knew about space exploration. One thing the rest of the crew shared was a kind of religious fervour about their jobs. They were intensely proud of what they did, and to be honest discussed the subject to the exclusion of pretty much everything else. Few had attachments at home, and the ones in formally bound relationships had been placed in buddy situations, with the partner working as ground crew (both partners aren't allowed to fly at the same time). Like old-time fishermen they were profligate with their pay packets when docked, and probably behaved just as badly until the time came around to find another flight. Dalloway had spent the last few years shipping lead potassium and sodium zinc – the ingredients for gypsum – from Europa, Jupiter's second moon, which turned out to be a very lucrative job since the cost of manufacturing concrete had become so high on Earth.

The *Trafalgar* and the *Imperial* had been designed as cargo ships, and therefore lacked the niceties of passenger space travel. The air-conditioning was over-efficient, keeping everyone at a rather chill seventeen degrees, but this helped to counteract the drowsiness incurred by operating in a time-free environment. As far as I could tell, the top part of the ship – that is, the part immediately below the navigation deck – consisted of confusing concentric walkways leading to a vast sealed area which was the cargo bay. Like the cargo bays on regular aircraft, it was unheated, but also airless.

At the end of the first week I had finished making plans for the sketches, but it was harder to map out the paintings; these would require a more spontaneous approach, and would depend upon my reactions to what I saw. My brief was to capture the wonder of the ships and the stars, the complex relationships of light and size from the intense viewpoint of an outsider, a first-timer in space.

But before that: hypersleep. I was pretty scared by the idea of being placed in a flat tank filled with viscous liquid and being told to breath normally, but Sanjariit made me practice with a small face-bowl full of the stuff, and after a few minutes I was less wary of the idea, although the first time I drew the grey jelly down into my throat I panicked and nearly choked, and afterwards, noisily blowing it out of my nasal cavities was not a pleasant experience. Sanjariit told me it was either this or undergo ageing at the normal rate, so I figured it was worth the discomfort. She showed me how to set the revival time from inside the glass. Then I called my mother to say goodbye, and swiftly broke the connection before she could start crying.

Dalloway led me to the life-suspension chamber, and so to 'bed'. I stripped naked and neatly folded my clothes at the foot of the tube. I was the first one into my tank, but even as the opalescent gunk flowed over my vision and into my system I could hear other people preparing for their big sleep. I tried to imagine Dalloway snuggling down beside me for the next fifteen years and eight months. It was a relaxing thought to lose consciousness to. I had expected the sensation to be womb-like, but it was less comforting than that. The state felt much deeper than a good night's sleep. It was slightly suffocating, like being too far down in the sea and becoming aware of the immense weight of water above you, pressing down. Then nothing more than a vague uneasiness. Our bright, silent ship slipped on through the void, its crew lost in that vast inner space between death and life that we call sleep, our hopes and dreams as fleet as falling stars, as dark as worlds beyond our knowing.

And I awoke.

Surfacing too fast into bright cold light, my tank draining noisily, the glass lid of my coffin sliding up to reveal a reluctantly woken princess, harshly jettisoned back into the real world.

As my eyes focused and the last scraps of dreams fled from my mind, I imagined I saw someone leaving the sleep-bay. The place was empty, the other suspension pods vacated too, drained and as dry as if they had never been used. I was indeed the last to be revived, and there was no one here to check my health status. There was a rumpled mylar sleeping bag beside my tube. I remember thinking it was odd, but those first few moments were strange, muzzy and disorienting.

My muscles refused to obey my commands. I longed to return to sleep. My bare feet slipped away as I was climbing out and I fell on to my backside. I slithered about, trying to stand, and finally managed to slip and slide to the washroom, an aluminium pod that cleansed by blasting my body with steam. I donned the first clean staff uniform I could find and went in search of the rest of the crew. According to a readout in one of the corridors, the elapsed flight-time was eleven years and four months, but if that was correct, something had gone seriously awry.

I couldn't find anyone. The *Trafalgar* appeared to be running itself. Its brilliant deserted walkways and corridors were undisturbed by human activity. I found my way to my cabin, so that I would have a point of reference from which to orientate myself, then set off for the bridge. Perhaps, I thought as I walked, the Commodore had called the crew to some kind of emergency meeting, but in that case who had unsealed me from my sleep, and why hadn't they waited to check that I was in good health?

My head was still full of questions as I stepped onto the bridge and found Forrester seated alone before the great window. He was dressed in formal military uniform, a navy-blue suit with slim bands of gold at the sleeves, his appearance striking unfortunate resonances with that of Jules Verne's ill-fated Captain Nemo, except that he was eating a bowl of Chinese food.

'Ah, you're awake,' he said distractedly, and beckoned me to join him. 'Take a seat, will you? You need to eat something. Here.' He popped out a second bowl and slid it across. He looked terrible, much older than I had remembered. Wrinkled patches of dry skin had formed at the sides of his head, and there were deep bags beneath his eyes, as if some

Uncut

awful weight was pressing on his conscience and had kept him awake for days. His grey eyes looked far past me to the depthless galaxies beyond the window. His hair was grey, too. I was sure it had been black. He seemed to suddenly recall his manners, and poured beakers of mineral water from the console. We sat eating in silence for a few minutes before he could bring himself to speak.

'Sadita Kobe, that's right, isn't it?'

'Everyone calls me Sadie.' I gave a little smile.

'Sadie, these things – they occur in space, there's nothing anyone can do, and no one who can help,' he began awkwardly, his eyes avoiding mine. 'I mean to say, there are lines of communication but you must understand that communication is only that, it can't help us physically.' He paused to gather his thoughts, setting down his fork. 'The *Trafalgar* has been travelling for eleven years, and for most of that time it has been malfunctioning. The software refit didn't take. It's a problem that occasionally occurs on these older ships. Although never on one of mine before.'

'What's happened?' I asked.

'According to the logs, not long after we entered hyper-sleep our mainframe computer crashed at source, taking sections of our various back-up systems with it. Our preset on-board navigation course was wiped out. The life-support systems folded. Live-time communications with Earth Harbour were lost. I haven't been able to determine why or how this happened, and I don't suppose that I will without expert help.'

'I thought the *Trafalgar* had three separate back-up programmes. How could they simultaneously fail?'

'It can only be because the installation software was faulty in some way. The offworld manufacture of counterfeit components has become as sophisticated as anything we can use to detect them. The fact is that this calamity has happened and we are alone out here.'

I must have stared at him stupidly, because his tone grew colder. 'Do you understand? The others are all dead. Our entire programme has flatlined. Just you and I are left alive on board the *Trafalgar*, and that occurrence appears to have been determined by luck. When the mainframe crashed, only a random selection of function-circuits were able to remain open. Obviously, I have aborted our original mission in order to plot our return to Earth Harbour.'

'My God . . .'

'There's more bad news, I'm afraid. I don't know how long the journey back will last because I am unable to take any accurate readings. I can't access anything below these decks. There's no life-support available. There are no longer any hypersleep facilities. We're in what is known as a signoff situation.'

I was familiar with the term. Government organisations used it when the cost of repairing was greater than its worth. If a project went into signoff the debt was offset against potential profits. Annual margins were adjusted and the workforce was accordingly downsized.

'Isn't there anything you can do?'

'This isn't a veteran automobile, Sadie, I can't climb underneath it and tinker about with a few tools. There are no on-board navigational or biological support systems that are within the capabilities of mere humans beings.'

'There must be something we could . . .' I let the sentence trail lamely. Perhaps there was something he could do, but I was an artist, I knew nothing about spaceflight beyond the little that Dalloway and the others had told me during our first week out. Poor Dalloway.

I remembered that the tubes were empty, and asked Forrester what he had done with the bodies of his crew. He seemed unhappy about providing me with an explanation, but when pressed explained that he was legally required to incinerate the dead and jettison their sterilised ashes, in order to avoid any risk of contamination to the remaining crew members left on board. I tried not to imagine the two of us stuck aboard a ship that had become a floating mausoleum, drifting through space for all eternity.

'Will we get back?' I asked anxiously, starting to feel claustrophobic. 'What about oxygen?'

He dismissed my fears and took up his fork once more. I wondered how he could sit there eating. 'Oh, don't worry about things like that. There would be enough air left on this vessel even if we stopped manufacturing it. My main concern is to re-establish contact with Earth Harbour. They'll know that something is wrong by now, but there's nothing much I can do from this end. I have to wait for someone back there to find a way of cutting around our dead components and contacting us. That's all either of us can do, Sadie, wait.'

I forced myself to continue breathing normally. 'Tell me what I can do.'

'I suppose you can paint. It's what you came out here for.'

'It won't be the view they were expecting,' I warned forlornly.

'Perhaps not, but I think it's a good idea. You should start work at once. It'll help keep your mind off things.'

And that's what I did. I knew that if I started to think about the awfulness of our situation, I would go mad. I am not easily frightened, but I have a strong imagination; a quality of great artistic benefit, but a liability in a life-threatening environment. I thought of life back on earth, and how Dex would be thirty-seven years old. I was not close to my mother, but for all I knew she might now be dead. I felt ashamed of my selfishness in undertaking the journey, annoyed by the wastage of eleven years, and scared of what the future might hold. The universe was littered with the corpses of travellers. Who would notice one more?

In the days that followed, we fell into an awkward routine of working apart and dining together in the great empty vessel. Forrester left the communications system on all the time in case Earth Harbour found some way of reaching us. Much to my discomfort, the Commodore insisted on only lighting those parts of the ship that were in use, in order to save energy. After dinner, I allowed him to walk me back to my cabin. Sometimes the elevators stalled between decks. I hated the long shadowy corridors, the faint echo of my boots in empty blackness. Sometimes I stopped and listened, and watched the distant darkness in the tunnels, half expecting something to emerge from the gloom. Sometimes the longer passageways creaked and moaned like the timbers of a storm-tossed ship.

When I started thinking too hard, that's when it grew dangerous. I would begin to breath too fast, and the oxygen mix would grow too rich to absorb. I would feel panicky and light-headed. I spent more and more time beside the window, looking out into infinite darkness, anything to stop thinking of this steel coffin. Forrester gave me some sedatives, and I was able to sleep for a few hours at a time, but thoughts of our dead crew were never far from my conscious mind. It was about this time that I noticed something odd.

It seemed to me that the Commodore was watching me. I would look up from my Macpad and catch his surreptitious gaze from the corner of my eye. He would instantly become aware of a change in my mood, and busy himself. I wondered if he was evaluating my mental state, speculating on my reliability in an emergency. Then I began to wonder if he was being drawn to me sexually, seeing me in a different light. After all, it was just the two of us marooned up here. I hoped that this was not the case. I had no intention of reciprocating any feelings he might be developing towards me.

Still, I sensed that he was holding something back. He seemed to be suffering under the weight of some terrible knowledge, so constantly at war with his own emotions that he barely heard me when I spoke. And yet he appeared to hold me in esteem – awe, even. Often he would escort me to my quarters – my door had stopped sealing properly, ever since the system had crashed – and I had the feeling that he waited outside until I was asleep, as though protecting me from some unseen danger.

Every situation, no matter how desperate, brings about its own behaviour pattern. Whether we realise it or not, we humans crave order. Our days soon took on a regular form. I am not a person much given over to hysteria; I'd experienced my emotional-rollercoaster period at a much earlier age. Apart from the odd panic attack I simply got on with the paintings, in an attempt to fulfil at least a part of my commission. As I was now unable to paint the *Imperial*, I contented myself with mapping sections of our own ship that could be seen from the windows, delineating the twisting silver spirals of the galaxies. I painted the colours of everlasting night, the pigments of cold dry death, and as I did so it felt as if the universe shrank, until it was bound up inside the shadows of my heart.

It was during one of these painting sessions that I made an odd discovery. From my angled view at the window I could see a grey section of the ship's stern, and, twisted far above it, the yellowish curd of a great star-belt. In my pencil rough a faintly pulsing line of crimson lights shone somewhere towards the rear of the *Trafalgar*. But as I looked at the scene afresh, where the lights had shone there was now only darkness. Red, the colour of danger. It was as if a warning sign had been extinguished.

The Commodore had finished his watch and was asleep in his quarters when I made my way back to the stern of the ship. It was hard to locate the exact spot from within the windowless corridors. I had expected to find myself brought to one of the storage cells, but instead the hall opened out into the unlit life-suspension chamber. I don't know what it was that I expected to find. I knew that the glass coffins of our suspension pods had been dried and emptied. But as I reached the far side of the bay I saw the column of faint crimson lights blinking in the distance once more, and walked towards them.

As I came nearer, I saw that the diodes were indicators on a section of the hypersleep life-suspension system. I found a wall light and pushed on it.

Sanjariit's tube was stacked with the others on its side, and as I approached, I realised that his body was still suspended in the liquid, but now the liquid had become cloudy and spoiled. Beyond, I could see Donnizetti's corpse in a similar situation, clumps of olive mould clotted against the inside of his glass. Horrified, I shifted from one pod to the next. When I reached Kierkemeister's tube, I saw what was causing the lights to blink on and off. The engineer lay in front of them, periodically blotting them from view. He was still alive and twisting in the tube, even though he was floating in his own excrement. The blood vessels had burst in his eyes, and for a moment he caught me in his vision. He appeared to be in terrible pain, but there was nothing I could do for him. I had no technical knowledge, no way of breaking into the sealed tubes. Besides, I felt sure that the shock of doing so would finish him off.

A growing sense of vertigo tried to rob me of my balance as I ran back to my cabin. The *Trafalgar* had become a labrynthine steel cemetery, a repository of redundant systems and defunct circuitry unsuitable for human habitation. I pulled my cabin door shut and crawled up on to the bed. All I knew for certain was that Forrester had lied to me, and that I would have to broach the subject with him. After an hour of nervous indecision, I rode up to the bridge and found the Commodore seated in his usual position. I told him that I had seen the bodies of the crew lying in their polluted pods. He barely took his eyes from the console as he replied. I knew then that he would tell me some lie to shut me up. Sure enough, he glibly explained that although the official manual required the corpses of suspension-failures to be removed, burned and ejected, he hadn't felt right about denying their relatives the opportunity to conduct Earth burials for their loved ones.

'They're not all dead,' I countered, carefully keeping my distance from him.

'Oh, they're dead all right, it's just that I can't turn off the pods' chemical support processes. Their corpses may appear to be moving, but it's just the intravenous drugs still channelling through them. There's nothing I can do about that.'

'Then why keep them on board?'

'I told you.'

'Suppose they contaminate the ship? You should have told me the truth.'

'Obviously I didn't want to upset you. Now you're upset.'

'You're damned right.'

'I think perhaps you should take a tranquilliser, Sadie, try to get some sleep.' His speech was slightly slurred, as if he had been drinking.

'What about you? How long have you been on shift?'

'Oh, I'll stay up here for another hour.'

I tried another tack. 'Still no news from Earth Harbour.'

'Nothing.'

'How long do you think it will take them to get in touch?'

'I don't know. There's no precedent for this situation.' He remained at the console, staring back as I left, waiting for me to leave. There was something odd behind his eyes, something that frightened me so badly I couldn't bear to think about what was going on in his mind. My life lay in this man's hands, and I could not trust or understand him enough to reassure myself in any way. Despairing, I slowly wandered back to my cabin, but when I reached it I decided to go to the deck beyond, to Forrester's quarters. I needed to get some kind of handle on the situation. I had to be sure that he was telling the truth.

Forrester's door stood at the end of a half-lit corridor and was shut, as I knew it would be. But I also knew that the doors were no longer sealing properly. I came to a halt and listened, but could hear only the soft thrumming of the oxygen generator in the ceiling. I gently pressed my shoulder against the door – they pushed in a centimetre before sliding back – and released it.

The entrance to Forrester's cabin stood open before me. It was dark inside. I slapped my hand against the power panel, and the lights flicked on.

The suite was much larger than mine and very untidy, but I could see nothing unusual about it from where I stood. I ventured further in. Beyond the bed was a cream plastic

Uncut

workstation holding a Macpad and several hardcopy maps and communiqués. I flicked through the sheets, but learned nothing from them. The Macpad was in Sleep mode, so I was able to activate it without re-entering codes. It was formatted as a ship's log, and I scrolled back through the pages. It appeared that Forrester had been using it as much as a personal diary as an official document. At the end of each shift there was an entry. First a technical enclosure detailed the ship's course, its condition and its problems. Then Forrester had added his own thoughts, mostly questions concerning the possibility of overriding various automatic procedures, and sad speculations on the lives of his crew members.

A thought troubled me; if I had been drawn from hypersleep after eleven years and four months, when had the Commodore been woken? I skipped back through the Macpad, reading the dates of the entries, but they did not appear to be broken. Back and back they went, further and further into the years, each as detailed as the one before, until I realised the truth.

Forrester had not gone into hypersleep. He had remained awake through the lonely endless night while I slumbered on, chemically protected from the ravages of real time. No wonder he looked so much older. He had aged naturally. I stared at the pages before me and tried to understand what had made him do it. Confused by this sudden knowledge, I shut down the pad and left his cabin. On my way back along the corridor I passed the ship's chapel. The octagonal room was less a place of worship than of meditation, and housed one of the ship's three windows in its ceiling, so that the congregation might contemplate the vastness of the universe and the relative unimportance of their own fears.

I had seated myself against a midnight blue wall when I sensed a presence in the doorway. I did not need to turn.

'You've been to my cabin.'

'Yes.'

'My thoughts weigh heavily upon me, Sadie,' he said softly. 'I know you want some answers. You have every right to them.'

'You lied to me,' I said simply. 'You never went into hypersleep.'

'I could not help myself.' He came in and wearily slumped against a bench. Even from here I could smell the alcohol on his breath. I could see how heavily the years had marked him. 'It was I who allowed you on this flight, Sadie. I chose you from all the others. You would have been rejected, you know. I managed to get you on board.'

I had wondered about that; a couple of minor misdemeanours in my late teens, but drug offences never come off your records. The fleet would not have overlooked them.

'The software fault occurred when the rest of the crew had already entered hypersleep. I thought about trying to repair the system damage, then something – I don't know – your sleeping face . . .' He turned away, ashamed at the thought. 'You're so like her, it's uncanny. I watched you sleeping safely in your pod. The way you lay with your arms folded across your pale breasts, the way you twitched your fingers as you dreamed. I remembered how she had died in hers. I couldn't bring her back, and I couldn't let anything happen to you. I wanted to protect you, but to do that I had to keep watch over you. There wasn't time to do anything else. I shut down the others and cut Earth communication so that I could concentrate on you, and you alone.'

'You watched me for *eleven years*?'

Uncut

'I hardly ever left your side.'

Like some eighteenth-century mariner locking down the slave holds of his vessel to prevent insurrection, he had condemned the rest of his crew to death by suffocation. The cabin swam before my eyes. Eleven years!

'You were so beautiful in the pod, so peaceful. A character from a fairytale. Your eyelids barely moved. I longed to know what you dreamed about. I rested my hands on the curving glass, fascinated, my face lying inches from yours. I began to think you would never wake.'

'But it was you who freed me.'

'No. The time is set within the glass. The chamber's manual override no longer worked. I had to be there when your eyes opened, to make sure that you lived.'

I wanted to run from the chapel, but where could I go? Suppose I managed to evade him, even though he meant me no harm what would I do? I had no idea how long it would take for us to reach Earth Harbour again, and from the sound of it neither did he.

'I wanted to tell you how I felt, Sadie, to explain what I had done,' he replied, 'but once I saw that the draining process had started I lost my nerve. I became concerned about how you would react, and went back up to the bridge. I felt sure you would be angry once you discovered the truth. You have every right to be.'

He gave a great sigh, as if trying to clear the terrible pressure of the last few years.

'What do you expect me to do now?' I asked, hardly daring to hear his answer.

'I don't know.' He seemed genuinely puzzled. 'I am a man possessed by love. These years have been very . . . *difficult* for me. I need your help, Sadie. Please.' He held out his hand, but

I could not take it. I could no longer be the dumb sleeping girl in the tube, the mute object of his fantasies. Any action I decided upon now would be contrary to his wishes, and I knew him to be dangerous.

'How you must have studied this view while you've been painting it,' he said, moving to the window. 'So calm and silent. It exists beyond our empty meanings of life and death.'

'How far do you think we are from Earth Harbour?' I tried to sound calm.

'Oh, Sadie. You don't have to worry about life back there any more.'

I knew then that he had not altered the *Trafalgar*'s course, that we were still spiralling out beyond our own galaxy, far away from life and any hope of rescue.

'Had you always planned to stay awake through the voyage?' I asked.

'Not until I saw you in the flesh.' Forrester turned from the window to face me. 'Not even then. The more I watched you sleeping, the longer I delayed my own hibernation. Now I'd just be happy to be with you like this, forever.'

'But that's not what I want, not in a million years. Not if you were the last man in the world, which I suppose you are.' Fighting tears of panic, I rose and ran from the chamber, with no idea of where I could go or what I could do.

'Sadie, come back! We have to talk!'

His cries were muffled by the matt plastic walls. As I blundered on, a door hissed shut ahead of me and another opened. I was switched in my track like a rat in a maze. All of the doors could be operated from a distance by an infra-red device I had seen the officers use. I didn't have one, and had no idea of its range. Forrester knew every tunnel, passage and shaft in the ship, and could make me run straight back towards him if he so desired. He could starve me out, trap me wherever he liked. I wished I had paid more attention when Dalloway was showing me the floor plans. Hopelessly lost, I ran on until I was fighting to draw breath. Finally I came up against the third of the great windows in the darkened crew recreation area. Outside the starfield moved at an infinitesimal pace.

And the ship sailed on. How, why and where, I did not know. All thought of passage to the *Imperial* was gone. Our stately wake through the eternal seas of night was beyond my control. *Why*, I wondered, *when there is so much to explore outside, do we end up becoming the prisoners of everything that is within us? How can we consider outer space when we can't even control inner space?* I was dimly aware that the ship could be docked manually, but had not the first idea how to go about doing so. Besides, such a manoeuvre presupposed that the Commodore would stand idly by while I did so, and that I had something to dock on to.

Of course, I knew at once that the situation was hopeless. As I walked back through the ship I found that only two directions were open to me, one which led up to the navigation deck where Forrester was doubtless seated in his usual position, and the other generously leading back to my cabin. He could control my every movement within the creaking corridors of the vessel.

Eventually, I did as I was bidden. I sat beside him on deck. I ate with him in what passed for our evenings. He seemed to have no sexual interest in me. To him, I represented something more than any mere chemical reaction. During the increasing amount of time we spent together he rarely spoke, and preferred me to remain just as silent. My presence seemed to ease some great terror of loneliness inside him, a sense that is perhaps in all of us, but attenuated by time spent too alone. And while the Commodore drew solace, I felt that an hour spent like this was an hour lost for ever.

I knew he would not hurt me, but he would not let me live. I could not be myself, but only exist as some dim saintly memory of the woman he had lost. I had become an icon, as remote and necessary as a distant star. He had no intention of ever returning to Earth Harbour, and would sail on into unchartered territories with me forever by his side.

Or so he thought.

Oh – perhaps you expect me to tell you there was a fight, resourceful woman against deluded male, that I overcame him and piloted the ship back to safety. Let's be realistic about this. I am small, light, slim, unused to the concept of aggression. But there was one thing I could do, one method I had within my means to defeat him. It was something women have learned to use against males across the centuries, a form of survival born of a passive and private strength. I turned and walked out into the corridor, pausing briefly to regain my sense of direction, then picked up my pace until I found myself breaking into a run. The same thought must have occurred to the Commodore, for ahead of me I heard the elevator descending. But then the motor died, and the lift stalled before reaching its destination. I ran on to the hypersleep chamber, never daring to look back.

There was no time to remove all my clothes. The glass revolved and sealed above my head before the pod filled up. I forced myself to breath normally as I tried to remember how to set the code for my revival time. I could hear Forrester's boots slamming urgently along the passageway, but he was too late. The glittering grey liquid was speckled with stinging ice granules. It folded itself over my face just as he burst in, and all he could do was run to the tube and cry out helplessly as I was taken back into the void.

I set my new internal life for half a century. I had no way of knowing if the system would allow me to survive for such a length of time, beyond the fact that it let me key in the numerals. I knew that Forrester would stay awake, a sentinel beside the glass, watching and waiting for my return, until the last vestiges of his dying strength deserted him. I knew that I had won. I thought of slaves in the hold of their ship, cruelly battened below decks by their commander. But this time the slave had chosen to lock the door from her side, and would not emerge until she was ready to do so.

The *Trafalgar* crested the oceans of infinite night, without a destination, home or harbour, its plans destroyed, its communications dead, its crew gone, its captain mad, its sole surviving passenger drifting as slowly as space itself, and I remained safely locked in the embrace of my own dark dreams.

Perfect Casting

It was the season of sulphur. The autumn air already held a sharp smell of fireworks. Just beyond the edge of Regent's Park, the keepers were raking a bonfire. Peter Tipping noticed spirals of sparks above a sore amber glow of dead leaves just before he turned into the north end of Baker Street. Night had fallen before five. For the next few months darkness would achromatise the days. London was a private city in winter. People remained hidden inside, leaving the buildings to come alive in damp air.

The curving cream stone of the apartment block drew close, and then he was standing below the entrance. Climbing the steps and reluctantly withdrawing his hand from the warmth of his overcoat pocket, he pressed the brass stud and bent close to the intercom, waiting for the familiar sound of Jonathan's voice.

'You're late, Peter.' A hurt tone filtered through. The buzzer sounded, and he stepped into a marble hall. Beyond that, rich crimson carpet and a trellis lift. Chalfont Court was not at home to the twentieth century. There was still a porter's lodge beside the main entrance, still a mahogany box affixed to the wall for the placement of calling cards. The building lodged liverish retired colonels, ancient widows with tiny hyper-active dogs, a couple of discreet escorts agencies and a few old show-business types.

Jonathan belonged to the last group. His apartment on the fifth floor had been his combined office and home for the past thirty years, during which time business and leisure had lived in easy symbiosis. It would have been impossible to imagine any other arrangement, as the elderly theatrical agent was attuned to receiving lengthy telephone calls near the midnight hour. At this time he would calm his nervous charges, soothe their fears of thespian inadequacy, listen to their analytical appraisals of the night's performance, always reassuring, calming and cajoling.

He wouldn't be doing that for Peter tonight. Peter had let him down again.

'So, you finally made it.' Jonathan pursed his lips and stepped back in the doorway, a balloon-shaped figure balancing on tiny feet, allowing Peter to enter. The passage was lined with posters for shows misbegotten and forgotten, the disco Ibsen, the reggae Strindberg, a musical version of *Bleak House* called *Jarndyce!* starring Noele Gordon, fading signature from faded stars. Jonathan's fat right fist contained a tumbler filled with gin and irregular chunks of ice, and there were telephones trilling in the distance. Peter was always comforted by the changeless disarray of the flat. This was a place where actors were cushioned and cosseted, heard out and then fed with alcohol. Jonathan puffed past, rings glittering in the dim hall, ready to make Peter a drink even though—

'Even though I'm terribly, *terribly* angry with you.' He entered the kitchen, chipped off an ice chunk and dropped it into a tumbler, pausing to push his spectacles back up the bridge of his nose. Jonathan was constantly in a sweat. It leaked from beneath the auburn wig that fooled no one and trickled beneath his bulging eyes so that his clients were misdirected into believing that news of their backstage woes had moved him to tears. 'One should always be grateful of an audition, Peter, *bitterly grateful*, and you do yourself no favours by acting otherwise.'

Peter had thought the job beneath him, but he hadn't had a decent audition in nearly three months. Playing a jolly dad in a commercial for frozen lasagne wouldn't have been the zenith of his performing career, but it would at least have brought in steady residuals.

'The director was a complete arsehole, Jon.' He accepted the drink and followed the agent through to his desk. There was parkland below the windows of the semicircular lounge, but even during the day it was barely visible through winter mist and traffic fumes. 'I was kept waiting for over an hour, and then asked questions about my motivation by some ad-speaking agency slimeball,' Peter complained. 'I answered him back a little sharply, nothing more, and they told me I wasn't needed any longer.'

Jonathan waved the explanation aside. 'I know, I had them on the phone for half an hour warning me never to send you there again. You're going to be blacklisted by the agency, Peter, the third largest advertising agency in London.' He pushed back-issues of the *Stage* from a leather sofa and sat, daintily crossing his legs at the ankle. 'What have I always said is your biggest stumbling block?'

'Arrogance,' Peter admitted, knowing he was about to receive the usual lecture.

'You've been with me for nearly a year now, and you've hardly worked. You come back with the same story after every audition. You had three – it *is* three, isn't it? – agents before me. You can't go on blaming your representation. It's a matter of learning to handle authority.'

Peter felt the need to explain himself. 'I couldn't see that there was much authority coming from—'

'*Authority* is anyone who employs you, Peter, and you simply can't afford to alienate them. At least you could wait until you've got the job and you've established a working relationship. Christ, even Larry managed to do that.'

'But you're sending me along for rubbishy little parts directed by ignorant children.' He could feel the gin and the heat of the apartment forcing colour into his face. 'Half of these brats are barely out of film school.'

'You want me to change the system for you? I can't help it if the industry is getting younger around you. That's all there is, you either take it or leave it.'

'Perhaps if I had some new shots done . . .' He had been considering an image change for some time. A new haircut, sharper clothes.

'Photographs aren't going to make any difference, Peter. Let's be honest, you don't look like a classic leading male. Your nose is too long, your eyes are too small and your weight fluctuates. You'd make a good villain, but you're never going to have juve leads. You won't take serious theatrical roles—'

'I can't remember long speeches,' Peter admitted. 'Lots of actors get by without classical theatre.'

'You're not prepared to do panto, so what does that leave? There's no British film industry any more and the network franchises are carving each other up, so you should face the fact that if there's an audition – *any* audition – you have to go for it.' Jonathan wiped the sweat from the edge of his wig. 'That's if you want to work. You're too old to have tantrums, and there's always someone else willing to take the part. As

Coward used to sing, "There's another generation knock-knock-knocking at the door."'

Even though he realised that Jonathan was trying to help him, Peter wanted to punch the smug little man squatting opposite with his empty tumbler balanced on his paunch. He knew the agent meant to shock him into better behaviour but he wasn't prepared to waste his career behaving like a sheep, being pushed about by some snotty MTV kid turned commercials director. Hadn't Hitchcock said that actors were cattle? Had nothing changed since then? It was fine for the pretty teenagers flitting in and out of the office on casting calls, busy enjoying their fifteen minutes of fame, happy to do what they were told, but he was an adult with opinions of his own. He looked across at Jonathan, who was waving his hands as if acting out part of some wailing chorus.

'Oh, I don't know what more I can say to you, Peter. I've always had a lot of working people on my books, some of them very successful—'

'If you're referring to the little queen you placed in the Channel 4 presenter's job . . .'

'That's uncharitable and you know it. He got the part because he was young and he looked right. I mean people like Marc Ford.'

Peter know all about Marc Ford. Among actors, it was a famous success story. The young player hadn't worked for almost a year. He was down to his last penny, and his wife was pregnant. He'd been offered a small speaking role as a Nazi storm trooper in a low-budget German film being shot in London. As there was hardly any money left to pay the actors, the producer had offered him points at two and a half per cent, and he had accepted. Three weeks' work, standing in a tank of freezing filthy water, then he'd forgotten all about it. The damned thing had won an Oscar for best foreign film and subsequently played to packed houses throughout the world. Marc had retired, a millionaire. He had been advised to take the part by his agent, Jonathan.

'Actually, something did come in today. Not terribly interesting, but worth a bit of money.' Jonathan was a practical man. Having delivered his standard speech he would not attempt to perform some kind of positive deed that would help his boy. They were all his boys and girls. He hadn't much hope for Peter, though. He'd pegged him as one of the bitter ones, an actor who resented success in others and bore the fatal flaw of being unable to acknowledge his own faults. Actors were supposed to see things more clearly. You couldn't trip blindly through life always blaming the director.

He moved back to his desk and unclipped sheets of fax paper from a chrome letter rack, checking through them. 'I had a call from a company called VideoArts. They make corporate promos, and they're looking for featured extras. The first call is Hampstead Heath on Friday morning, early start, dress in your own clothes.'

That means 6 am, thought Peter. *Have to book a cab there, stand around freezing in the pitch dark waiting for the director to show up.*

Jonathan was watching him, waiting for his reaction. It was a test to see if he would show willing. 'Well, do you want it?'

Time to be a good boy. Reluctantly, he agreed to go along.

'Good, now we're getting somewhere.' Jonathan's smile only affected the lower part of his face. He waved the sheet of paper, ineffectually fanning himself. 'The company produces ten promos for the same client every year, and they like to keep their cast consistent. It's just extra work, but they might take you on permanently, which would mean a regular monthly cheque.'

And a regular percentage for you, thought Peter. Another dead-end job that would advance him nowhere. He'd see how it went, but after this perhaps he wouldn't need an agent at all. He had recently heard of a more interesting proposition, a casting call that hadn't come through his agent and had far greater possibilities than a god-awful boring sales promo.

At the Fulham Road gym the following morning Peter checked out the details with Fanny, who worked in the coffee bar. As far as she knew, the rumour she had heard a few days ago was true. One of the actors using the free-weights room had told her – she couldn't remember who. He'd casually mentioned a feature film that was due to start shooting in less than a week. It was being produced by a Dutch, or perhaps a Belgian company, a thriller set in present-day London, but she hadn't been able to understand the title. Filming would take place in central locations for a minimum of six weeks, and because of casting problems a number of male speaking roles were still to be assigned. She remembered the name of the contact but had no telephone number. It would take a bit of sleuthing to find that out.

Fanny was happy to pass on a professional tip, partly because she still hoped that Peter might find her attractive. She was an actress but had been disabled by a childhood illness, and only took roles that allowed her to appear in her wheelchair. The rest of the time she worked at the gym, running the bar, strengthening the upper half of her body with weights and waiting for a man like Peter to ask her out. She had once thought that working here would make her more independent, but the male patrons arrived with inflated egos that pushed her own flimsy sense of courage back into her wheelchair.

Peter tried not to look too excited about the tip. The gym was full of actors who might overhear and get there first. 'You mean it's being shot in English?' he asked, lowering his voice.

'I suppose so. A lot of these people dub or subtitle according to the territory, don't they?'

'Was this guy up for one of the parts? Did he have a script?'

'God, Peter, I don't know. I've only ever seen him a couple of times before. I imagine they'll give the script out to anyone who auditions.' Fanny reached her hand along the counter, hoping he would absently take it. No such luck. She could tell he was already planning his audition piece. She wrote down the name of the production company for him, and Peter headed for the phone booth. At least the kiss of thanks he blew her seemed genuine enough.

Directory Enquiries failed to find the name listed and suggested that he wasn't looking for a company but a specific building. Had he tried the Yellow Pages? He was surprised to find the address registered to a fruit and vegetable market. The woman who answered the number explained that they were indeed auditioning in rooms above the stores. She had an unplaceable European accent, admitted that the film was soon to start production, and agreed to check out his *Spotlight* photograph. If she was interested, she would bypass his agent and call him at home to discuss his CV before making an appointment.

She rang him at seven o'clock that evening and they talked for a full half-hour. Peter exaggerated a little about his recent work and was officially invited to audition on Friday afternoon. Fighting to contain his excitement, he wrote down the address and agreed to be there. For the first time, he could feel the spotlight shifting towards him through the darkness.

As he entered the southern corner of the park, Peter spotted the other extras. They were standing huddled together in the gloom, like sheep preparing to be attacked. Instantly he wished he hadn't accepted Jonathan's proposal. In a few hours' time he would be auditioning for a real film. He walked over to the nondescript group and stood a little way off. Actors, that is those performers with speaking parts, do not mix easily with extras, whom they consider to be little more than unskilled fans. He knew that they would be forced to speak to each other, though, as there seemed to be no one else around. In the distance bare elms stood on the brow of a hill, thrusting up blackened bones like the spine of some half-buried animal. A sour pink glow edged the sky, the first intimation of dawn.

'Where is everyone?' he asked, breath clouding around him.

'The director's gone with the first AD to sort out payment with the park keeper,' said a small man in a brown raincoat. Shooting on the heath cost two hundred pounds an hour and had to be paid in advance. 'They've already had us rehearing. There's a lot of mud about. I've just ruined a pair of trousers. Make sure you put in a dry-cleaning bill.'

This was typical extra conversation. They were obsessed with dry-cleaning. Too bad he'd lost the frozen lasagne commercial. At least he'd have had some national exposure in that. Corporate videos never really saw the light of day. Perhaps that was a good thing, though. He wouldn't want some embarrassing early performance turning up to hamper a successful film career.

After a few minutes the director's assistant appeared and explained how he wanted them to move. Lack of enthusiasm dulled his instructions, as if he was being forced to describe the least interesting part of the day's filming. He simply wanted them to move this way and that. Peter's questions were cut short. If actors were cattle, the assistant made it clear that extras were plants.

Half an hour later, Peter could no longer feel his feet. The temperature was hovering around zero. He and the other extras had been running back and forth along the ridge of the hill while the camera recorded their movements from a hollow two hundred yards below them. Peter was taller than the rest of the group and deliberately hung back a little so that he would at least stand out. Occasionally a microphone would crackle and the first AD would warn him to keep up with the others. Apart from commands to go again, there was no other way of telling that they were even being filmed

'I hate early starts,' said one of the extras suddenly, as if Peter had shown signs of valuing his opinion. 'I live in Barnet, and the travelling does me in. There aren't many showbiz people where I live. You can't buy the *Stage* in Barnet.'

Then they were off again, running up and running back down. No one had told them why they were running, or where they were supposed to be running to. None of the extras had seen a script. Only the main actors were given copies, and they were waiting inside a warm pavilion at the bottom of the hill. Peter could feel resentment building within him. How could the director see them if they couldn't see him?

'Could we go again, quickly please,' called a disembodied voice, as if their movements were being orchestrated by the trees themselves. Peter broke away from the group as it prepared to run once more and set off down the hill holding his arms high, like a surrendering Indian.

'Wait a minute,' he called, 'I have a question. Why are we doing this over and over? You can't possibly see us from down there.'

A bearded man rose from behind the camera and stood with his hands against his thighs. The rest of the crew impatiently dropped their arms to their sides, siding with the director.

'I'm trying to get you lot silhouetted against the rising sun, Mr Whoever-You-Are. Can you go back up *at once* please.' It wasn't a question.

'I appreciate that,' called Peter, continuing nearer, determined to make his reasoning understood. 'You could bring the camera a lot closer and still have the sun rising in the background. At least that way you'd be able to see us a bit better, give us a bit of identity.'

'I don't want to see you any better.' The director separated himself from his assistants and walked up to meet Peter, ready for a fight. 'You're just a group of generic running people. You don't have identities. You could be anyone. That's the whole point.'

'Well, nobody explained that—'

'Because the sun rises fast and we wanted to get the shot quickly.' He looked up at the hill. 'But that was our last possible take, and now the sun is too high. I think you'd better go, don't you?'

It was humiliating, having to walk away from a group of people who were so obviously angry with him. Upsetting the extras didn't matter, but he hated falling out with the crew in case he found himself working with them again. Clapper loaders, first assistants and sound men freelanced in each other's crews, and turned up all over the place. Sound crews were usually men because of the weight of their microphone booms, which had to be constantly held aloft. Peter liked crews and got on well with them. They were professionals, like him. Extras were nothing, star-struck spear carriers who got paid a tenner a night for standing behind a throne through three acts.

He hoped Jonathan wouldn't hear of this latest fiasco too quickly. The misunderstanding could jeopardise his film audition. It would be easy for someone to put in a call and spoil his chances. All work was supposed to go through the agent. Peter was expected to call at the end of the morning shoot, so he went to the public library at Hampstead and hung around until lunchtime, then ran from a pub callbox. He assured Jonathan that everything had gone well, and the agent's replies were relaxed and pleasant, as though the day's first bottle of gin was already improving his view of the world.

Back out in the street it had begun to rain hard. Shoppers loitered disconsolately beneath awnings, waiting for the downpour to ease. Peter kept a beret in his pocket and pulled it on to keep his hair dry. It would have helped to know something about the role he was going for. He checked the address he had written down and headed for the tube station.

The afternoon was already darkening when he arrived at the Edgware Road, skirting filthy puddles to locate a small turning between the kebab shops and falafel bars. Walking to the far end of the street, he found himself in the remains of a cobbled road, facing an old Victorian warehouse of the kind beloved by film location managers. Heavy steel shutters sealed what had once been entrances for horses and carts. The base of the graffiti-stained building was steeped in rubbish and chunks of rotting vegetable matter, swept from the market that operated inside during the day. Several small windows had been shattered, but all were barred and lined with spikes. For any normal job interview, the building would have sparked feelings of anxiety and revulsion. Peter knew better than to be alarmed. He could see the fierce yellow light shining behind the broad first-floor windows, light that could only be thrown by the 10K lamps of a film set.

As he searched for a door, he marvelled at the extraordinary manner in which film business was conducted. A pretty girl could be picked from the pages of *Spotlight*, her agent called and an appointment made. She could then be sent to an abandoned farm, a lunatic asylum, a den of rapists, and she would happily go along in the hope of landing a film part. It seemed so obviously dangerous he was surprised no one had put a stop to the practice. But that was the way the system had always run. Casting agents were tucked above tube stations. Rehearsal rooms sat behind strip clubs and chip shops. Dressing rooms were converted toilets. But not for the ones at the top. And not, he hoped, for him.

Peter found the notice pinned across a narrow doorway set in the end wall. It read, simply: AUDITIONS 1ST FL. As he climbed to the top of the unlit stairs, he passed a man of his own age coming down. The other actor threw him a cold smile before passing into the street, a sure sign that auditions had started. Pushing open the landing door, he found himself in a vast wood-planked room that ran the entire length of the building. At one end the windows had been whitewashed over, and a simple screen-test area had been constructed. Before it, half a dozen people sat in plastic chairs softly questioning a nervous-looking young man. Peter approached and was waved to a bench against the wall. After a few minutes the actor ahead of him was dismissed, and the team made notes, consulting with each other. Then he was beckoned to the vacated seat, like a patient customer about to receive a haircut.

One of the men rose, shook Peter's hand and introduced himself as Mr Ostendorf. Behind him stood a collapsible plywood table with a single sheet of paper on it. He consulted the typed list. 'You must be Mr Tipping.' His voice bore a trace of an accent.

'That's right.' Peter beamed a smile at the assembled group and shifted in his chair. It was hard to tell which one was the director. Ostendorf ticked his name on the sheet before re-seating himself.

'Allow me to introduce everyone. Miss Deitch I think spoke to you on the telephone.' He gestured along the line of chairs, starting first with an attractive young woman who turned out to be the producer's assistant, then pointing to the director (why did all directors have little beards?), the cinematographer, the writer and an arrestingly beautiful woman of middle years, the costume designer. 'I myself,' Ostendorf explained, tapping his chest, 'am merely the producer.' Everyone laughed politely. 'In my own country I have much experience in casting, but here it is more difficult, and you must be patient with me. So –' He gestured about himself with a friendly shrug. 'We are casting now only one role, and we shall perhaps tell you a little of this character and his story. Then we have you read a page from the script, yes?'

'Fine,' agreed Peter, trying to see how many other names there were on the page Ostendorf had consulted. Christ, it looked like they had seen fifteen people already. All eyes turned to the director. He was an elderly, tanned figure in an immaculate Italian suit and reminded Peter of photographs he had seen featuring Bertolucci's cinematographer, Vittorio

Storaro. Could it even be him? But no, the old man introduced himself as Joachim Luserke and had a strong, almost
comic German accent. As he spoke, he paused to draw on a
heavy, wet cigar that appeared to have burned itself out.

'We are a Netherlands company,' he began slowly, 'releasing feature films through Columbia Tri-Star in Europe. This
film is a modern-day thriller entitled – in your language –
Hours Of The –' he looked around for help, unable to trans-
late. '*Jackals*,' said the writer, an exhausted-looking man in
his late twenties.

'There is already a film called *Day Of The Jackal*,' Peter
interrupted, then stopped himself from saying more. Better to
take Jonathan's advice and get the job first before offering his
opinions.

'This was long ago, yes?' Luserke waved the problem aside
with his cigar. 'It does not concern us. People go to the cinema
for only seven years of their lives, that is the average, and the
film you mention is more than seven years old I think.' Peter
was impressed. He was not used to having someone listen to
what he had to say.

'I explain the plot to you now because not all of the script
is translated to our satisfaction. It concerns a wealthy businessman whose son, Jack, is kidnapped one night while working
late in his office. He searches for the young man – here, there
– but he does not find him.'

The others were watching the elderly director's gestures
with amusement. They clearly enjoyed seeing him act out the
story. It was probably the sixteenth time he had done so this
afternoon. 'Then he discovers the truth. Jack had been taken
by –' He checked with the others for the approved designa-
tion of the phrase, 'social terrorists, who plan to keep him
imprisoned as an example to the complacent business world.

They will use his capture as a propaganda weapon that will bring them great power. The police – pooh! They do not believe our hero. He alone must come to the rescue. He finds out where Jack is being held, but it is too late. One of the terrorists argues with the young man about his privileged position in life, secured for him by his father, and kills him in a fit of fury before he can be rescued. Now they will come after our hero's wife, and he must convince the police of the conspiracy—'

'Wait, wait.' Ostendorf raised his hand. 'I think this part is not necessary to tell. Wait until we have the new translation.'

'When could I see a fully translated version of the script?' asked Peter. The project sounded interesting, the plot uncompromising. This was the kind of subject matter European film makers handled so well. It was probably a metaphor for the human condition, very profound.

'We will not give you the complete script unless you win the part, but you may read the pages which feature your role.'

'Which part is on offer?' he asked. Was it too much to hope for the lead?

'I hope you won't be offended when I tell you it is the part of the evil terrorist,' laughed Ostendorf.

'Not at all.' Peter smiled back. Jonathan had thought him perfect for a meaty, villainous role.

He was handed half a dozen pages on which the character of Dr Emil was scored through with a yellow highlighter. In order to provide him with some interaction, the producer's assistant read the role of Jack, the hero's captive offspring. The tone of the piece was sombre and oblique, the exchanges awkward, as though English was not the author's first language. After the read-through, Peter raised his hand. 'There's a problem with the English translation,' he pointed out. 'It's very stilted. I could paraphrase my lines and get a better reading out of it.'

'I think for now it would be better if you stayed with the words you have,' replied Luserke firmly.

Peter could take a hint. Tidying the pages, he sat back and waited for a response. The group talked quietly among themselves. Heads were nodding. Only the art director seemed to be in dissent. Finally Ostendorf rose and turned to Peter with an outstretched hand. 'We believe we have found our evil doctor,' he said, smiling warmly. 'You are happy?'

Peter thrust his hands in his pockets and beamed his thanks back at the group. 'I am very happy.'

'Good. Now we take some test pictures of you to show our backers.'

'What do you mean, they're shooting before signing your contract?' asked Fanny. 'I've never heard of such a thing. Your agent certainly wouldn't allow it.'

'My agent is never going to find out about it.' Peter reached across the counter and emptied a container of apple juice into his cup. The gym was empty and about to close. Rain pattered against the skylight far above them. 'The guy playing Jack is a big-deal star in the Netherlands and they only have him for four days. It's not a large part but it's the key to the film. I'm going to be playing my lines with a stand-in. Obviously I have to do it before the set is struck, so they'll film my performance at the same time.'

'Then why not put the two of you together in shot?'

'For Jack's scene with me he's tied to a chair with a bag on his head. He doesn't need to be there.'

'Just make sure you get the contract signed as soon as possible.' Fanny was growing bored with all this talk of Peter's success. He never asked her how she was doing, why she still spent her evenings serving sandwiches to walking lumps of muscle tissue when she could be pursuing her dream, running a course for disabled actors. She had known all along that she would never be much of a stage success, but she was sure she could teach. She was prepared to settle for something more satisfying than pouring coffee. What she needed now was advice.

'But you'd advise me to do it even though the contract's not through, wouldn't you? I mean, they seem like pretty trustworthy people. It's a big company. They're not going to run off without paying me.' He was looking at her intently, waiting for an opinion. She threw up her hands, knowing that he would only hear what suited him. So many actors were like that. 'Sure, take the job. It's what you want.'

'I knew I could rely on you to steer me to stardom.' Peter reached down and kissed her on the forehead. 'I'd better go. Big day tomorrow.' He swung his gym bag onto his shoulder and headed for the door.

She could have killed him. It was the forehead kiss that made her most angry, as if he didn't see her as a woman, or the possessor of any kind of sexual identity. Grunting furiously, she wheeled her way back behind the counter and began turning out the lights. Peter was a typical bloody actor, completely closed to the real needs and purposes of other people. She hadn't seen it in him before, or perhaps she'd hoped that he would be the one to break the mould, but he was the same as all the rest. She didn't mind them lying, but it was boring when they lied to themselves. No wonder his girlfriends never stayed around for long. She certainly wouldn't be there for him after tonight. Far too much acting, she decided grimly.

* * *

Rain blanketed the city, sheathing the rooftops in a grey shower curtain of mist. It flooded the gutters, coursed over pavements, breached the drains and ruined Peter's chances of making a decent impression with his new shoes. Filming was about to commence in another old warehouse. This particularly rundown specimen was tucked behind the tube station in Tufnell Park, hidden by a row of shops that were either covered in For Sale signs or already derelict and seemed to be spouting water from a thousand broken pipes.

Peter looked for the telltale glare of the spotlights, but found none. Studio lighting was always turned off between takes because of the intense heat it generated. Besides, the set was supposed to be low lit, so he doubted that anything could be seen from the road. He found the producers waiting on the second floor with a small crew (below British union requirements, certainly) and a simple set of rubble and straw, in the centre of which was a single wooden chair. Bound to it with ropes around the torso and legs was a rather unrealistic dummy, intended to represent the young hostage. Luserke came over and greeted Peter warmly.

'I hope the late hour does not upset you, Mr Tipping,' he said apologetically, 'but we have been having some trouble with the lights.'

'Nothing serious, I hope?' Peter looked over at the single cable trailing behind the set. There didn't seem to be enough lighting here to go wrong. But then, the scene they were about to film was an intense one, and every element had to be exactly right.

'You will be pleased to know that our "Jack" is so far very good,' the director continued, anxious to please. 'He finished his part of the scene today. I would have liked him to stay here for your lines, but he is a big star in his country because of a television show, how you say *sitcom*, and he will not sit with the bag like so.' He indicated the linen sack gracing the head of the mannequin, whose left leg looked as if it was about to detach itself completely. Wherever the money was being spent on this production, thought Peter, it certainly wasn't going into the props.

'The dummy doesn't look very convincing,' he complained. 'Couldn't you make the scene more realistic by getting someone to take its place while we film?'

'I think we will not need to do so. Watch please.' Luserke gestured to one of the crew and the set lights came on, throwing a dingy blue haze across the chair and its occupant. With the figure half buried in indigo shadow, its imperfections were lost to the darkness. 'I am more concerned with your close-ups tonight, and your speech, which we will do in one take. I think we will not need to feature our Jack in clear focus. If you would like to take your mark on the set—'

'I haven't been made up yet.'

'Made up.' The phrase seemed new to him. Luserke looked over to his producer, who said something in German. 'Now I see. This was not made clear to you before I think. No make-up for this scene. The light, the blue light, will be on your face.' Peter looked back at the low glow of the set and hoped it would be bright enough for his facial expressions to register. This was to be an emotionally draining moment. He didn't want his performance to be lost in the gloom, like it had been with the extras on the hill.

He made his way past the shattered-looking writer, who was sitting with his head in his hands, nodded to Ostendorf, who was whispering into his mobile phone, and found the gaffer-taped cross on the floor of the set. Ostendorf had told him that he needed to learn only two pages of dialogue for this first night's shoot, which involved the end of his scene with the hostage and the moment of fury in which he kills him. The producer felt that, as he would be addressing a plastic dummy rather than a live actor, it would help to start with the least interactive part of the sequence.

Peter studied the lolling, strapped-up figure and rolled the handle of the carving knife between his fingers. Although to his eyes the set appeared absurdly unrealistic, he knew that through the camera lens it would take on a strange reality, so that even the luminous turquoise lighting would somehow be appropriate. The lengthy scene was divided into sections, the last part involving ranted monologue from Peter, which culminated in him stepping forward and thrusting the knife into the mannequin's chest.

By the fourth rehearsed take of his 'fury' speech, the crew were egging him on and applauding. Encouraged by Luserke, who sat forward on a stool beside the camera studying Peter's every movement with glittering eyes, he grabbed the chair back with one hand and with a despairing scream thrust the knife deep into the gut of the dummy, splintering the plastic shell to bury his fist deep within the kapok and foam interior. The director wanted his inner rage to surface, to slam against the floor and walls until it exploded into unstoppable violence.

During the final rehearsal Peter caught himself thinking, *This is what it's really about, to be in the centre and in control, to reach inside and draw emotion from the heart, to feel the sheer naked power of performance.* He had reached this point by his own efforts, not through some agent looking to cream off a percentage. This was just the start, a glimpse of the future making itself clear to him, a fabled city appearing through a calming sea. *Enjoy the moment,* he told himself. *Make it last.*

They took a short break and the film magazine was loaded for the first take. Peter returned to his mark and stared across as the battered dummy strapped to its chair, chunks of torn rubber clinging to its cream plastic chest.

'Peter, could you come here a moment please?' Luserke called him over to query an inflection at the end of the monologue, tapping the speech with a nicotine-stained finger.

'I can handle it that way if you like,' he conceded, 'but it's a long speech, and by the time I get to the end my voice has risen so high it's hard to control.' Peter promised to try his best, but he knew that he'd do it his way. The matter was out of his control. He could only give his talent full rein and shape the power as it grew within him.

'Your mark, please. Quiet everybody.' The crew quickly returned to their places.

Peter reached his spot and looked up. Rain still blurred across the skylight. The knife handle was warm in his hands. The lights dimmed even lower than in the rehearsals, and the room fell silent, so that the only sounds came from the rain above and the breath catching in his chest. He could see nothing beyond the shadow of the dummy and the straw-lined edge of the set.

Slowly, carefully, he began the speech.

The anger flowed from him as he accused the captive young man of having all the things he could never have, of squandering his inherited power, of wasting a life that paid lip service to truth and decency while perpetuating an immoral, divisive society. He felt the bile rise within him, felt real hatred for this golden boy who knew nothing of the real world, who had never tasted the hard lives of working men and women, and forward he ran with the knife at his waist, thrusting it out into the bound ribcage of his captive in an explosion of bare rage.

The first spray of warm liquid jetted into his face, blinding him as the next boiled hotly over his fist, which still clutched the knife. He tried to pull his hand free from the dummy's chest but it was trapped, caught between the flesh and bone of the hostage's ribcage. There were no lights at all now, only the scuffling of feet and the slamming of a distant door. As he fell to his knees he knew he had cut into a real, living body with the foot-long blade and that even now the roped-up figure was sinking fast within the coils of death, leather-soled shoes drumming madly on the floorboards until the chair toppled onto its side and the form bound to it lay still and silent, but for the steady decanting of its blood.

The crawl across the room in darkness seemed to last a lifetime. When he finally found a light switch he was frightened to turn it on. Two bare bulbs served to illuminate his blindness. He looked down at his shirt, his hands, his trousers, at the gouts of blood, as if someone had emptied the stuff over him in a bucket. The camera, if that was what it had been, had gone. There was nothing left in the room except the 'set', a pile of bricks and straw, a pair of gel-covered standard lamps set on the floor in either corner, a wooden chair and the cooling corpse of a young man, bound at the hands and feet, and taped at the mouth.

It took him a moment to realise that the room wasn't quite empty. Something else was over everything. His fingerprints – on the body, the chair back, the floor, the walls, the knife.

And even as his confusion lifted to be replaced with mounting fury, he wanted to know not why but how. How had they come to choose him, of all people? Because even now he could not see the blindness in himself.

And then what hurt most of all, what really cut into his heart and burrowed into the little soul he had, to lie there stinging and burning in a wormcast of purest agony, was the disappearance of the audience who had witnessed his greatest performance, and the knowledge that his moment of triumph had not been captured.

It was a pain he had only just begun to nurse when the police broke in the door.

In Persia

And once again I am in Persia.

As always, the first sight that greets my tired eyes is the brilliant white colonnade of the harbour building twisting away in mad perspective, overrun with fleshy green cacti. The sapphire waters cast shimmering planes of light across the marble courtyard of the squares beyond. The jetty ends in smooth semicircles of warm stone, where young women sit in the blossom-crusted shade with open books in their laps.

As we tie up and begin to disembark, several of these girls rise and set aside their volumes. Gathering their robes below their bare pale breasts, they stand and shield their eyes from the sun as they watch us bobbing at the edge of the harbour wall. They turn excitedly to one another and reach for the rush baskets they had earlier settled at their feet. Delving into these containers, they fill their hands with rose petals and hurl them at us, pink clouds spiralling in the breeze which carries them to the sea edge, where they descend upon the jetty steps like falls of fragrant snow.

But of course, no one here has ever seen snow. If I could only have brought some from my travels, what a sensation it would cause! For here in Persia there are no seasonal changes, and nothing happens to disturb the pleasant, peaceful cycle of our lives. The sun-drenched sea laps against the white walls of the inlet, blossom-laden trees rustle faintly on the verdant hillside, swallows chase a path across an azure sky, and everyone is quite content.

It is good to be home.

The cabin-boys help me with the brass-handled baskets we have filled with the booty from far-off lands. As we set them on the dock, I see a distant robed figure shake herself from her dozing trance and leave the coolness of her *exedra*, raising her arms in heartfelt welcome. The splendour of the scene overwhelms me, and I almost lose my balance as I seek to hold the moment in my mind. Everything is blue and white and yellow, the open saffron robes of the young women, the domes of the sea palace shining in pale alabaster, and in the distance the rich green hills still veiled by rainbow mists that will slowly dissipate as the trees unfold to the warmth of the day.

How I love this land! My travels are arduous and rarely pleasant. On every trip a smaller crew returns. I survive these brute excursions in the knowledge that at the end of each journey I will return to my true homeland, to the country I love so dearly. It is still early in the morning, and the air is filled with the freshness of a new day. As I fill my lungs I can taste the seasalt on my tongue. My nostrils detect the sharp smell of newly scythed grass, the sweet tang of cut nectarines.

The girls arrive in trains of rose petals, kissing us in welcome, their smooth skin warming our sea-chilled cheeks. Laughing, the bo'sun opens his bag and passes out gifts of scented almonds and painted beads, wrapped in multi-coloured parchment and tied with silk ribbons. He does this at the end of every trip, and the girls lead him on in an elaborate teasing charade that everyone knows and understands.

The happy crowd parts as my beloved approaches, her head shyly lowered, her dark hair garlanded with blue poppies and braided with gold at her exposed white bosom. As she raises her eyes to mine she smiles, and the world grows brighter still. We embrace, her arms linking behind my neck, and her lips touch mine as the warm breeze settles her robe around my thighs in silken folds.

We walk home towards the dazzling gold-roofed temples of the Handmaidens of the Sea Priestess, and I feel as if I shall never leave Persia again. High above us parrots are calling to each other, shocking vermilion flashes passing in high-looping rituals. I know their cries, and stop to watch, thrilled by the familiarity of their ascent. Their lovecalls counterpoint the distant chopping of the sea at the wall. Here everything has a familiar feel, the hand of my beloved pressed in mine, our steady rhythmic walk, the neatly cropped cyprus trees that line the pathway leading to our house, the Ionian blue of the mosaics that swathe the walls of the orchard.

Here in Persia, I am safe.

'You must tell me all about your trip,' she says softly, pushing back the gate that leads into the sunfilled courtyard of our home. 'I am so happy to see you safely returned once more. Did you encounter cut-throats, trolls, brigands, sea monsters?'

I laugh as I seat myself between the stone satyrs half buried in the ivy behind the white marble *labarium*. 'No, my dear, I encountered men, mere mortals only, but bad ones all the same.' My smile fades with the memory, and I turn my tanned arms over, revealing the tight red scars so newly healed.

'Tell me about these creatures,' she demands. 'Are they not like us?'

'Not at all. They are natural aggressors, broad men with

red hair and red faces who would do us harm without a single prick of conscience. Anger is their natural state, righteousness and hatred their weapons. They are Christians, men who wish us to be like them, and who become dangerous when we refuse to exchange our gods for theirs.'

'What is their country like?'

'Cold, and brown, and wet, and harsh. Many thousands of them live there, many more than us.'

She passes me a pomegranate and I dig my finger into the tough yellow hide, breaking the skin to reach the bitter scarlet globes within.

'Did these men attempt to capture you?' she asks, alarmed. 'Whatever did you do to save yourselves from such barbarians? Did you take their leader's life?'

'We fought,' I say, suddenly weary as my muscles loosen in the soothing heat. The sun is a wheel of flame, bleaching away my darkest memories. 'We fought and freed ourselves, and other captives too.'

'So there was no bloodshed,' she asks carefully, watching as I pick apart the globules, the crimson juice running between my fingers.

'I did not say that,' I reply. 'We lost several members of the crew, good men and true.'

'But you are here, safely returned home. I wish you would never leave Persia again. If only you would promise me to stay this time.'

'Yes,' I say, embracing her as tears break from my eyes, 'this time I will stay here with you for ever.' As I bury my head in the honeyed perspiration of her breasts, I pluck open her robe, run my tongue across her sweet salt stomach, and know that nothing can ever separate us again.

* * *

By the angle of the sun in the copper sky it is far past noon when I awake. The shade has shifted beyond the sputtering green fountain on the far side of the courtyard, and my beloved is seated within the villa. Her silhouette is set within the window as she sews, slowly drawing the golden thread through the frame, her needle casting a spear of sun as it arcs above the cloth.

For weeks I have been without warmth, and now the suddenly renewed heat has awoken a restlessness within me. I stand and take an earthenware pitcher to the fountain, fill it to the brim and slowly allow the delicious cool liquid to trickle across my burning brow, my arms and chest.

'Are you hungry yet?' My beloved stands at the window batting at herself with an ostrich-feather fan, watching as I rearrange my robes. 'I am planning a special meal in honour of your homecoming. Pheasant and partridge, marinated in nectar and roasted in roses.'

'In that case, I should take a walk to strengthen my appetite,' I say, and set off in the direction of the High Priestess's watergardens.

Here, passing between featherbeds of white and purple bougainvillaea, I see the familiar faces of friends and neighbours, all of whom pause to smile and wave, offering their pleasure at my safe return.

'Returned again, Franciscus!' calls a round-faced man on a mule. 'We had given you up for good this time!'

Before I can reply, my attention is distracted by the laughter of two young women who stand at the steps of the *tepidarium*. They are waving silken kerchiefs in my direction. 'We missed you, Franciscus!' they cry in perfect unison, for they are twins and share a common mind. 'You shall not leave again so easily!'

I pass my father's grey-haired servant at the garden entrance. He gives a toothless smile and doffs his woven sun-bonnet in respect. 'So glad to see you have returned, young master,' he says gratefully. 'May the gods always protect you.'

How could I not have returned to such a glad arcadia, where life maintains its pure and simple stride, passing each day in peace and harmony? Here amidst the fantastic buildings of the Royal Court, where children laugh and play below the flower-twined columns that surround the High Priestess's palace, where everyone is always happy, never sad . . .

The watergardens are filled with flowers of every scent and variety. Pure stream-water from the hills is lifted and sprayed from a hundred fountains of varying sizes, filling the air with vaporous rainbows. Carp and angelfish flick and turn in the crystal pools below them.

At the farthest end of the parade is another sunlit square, larger than all the rest. This one is filled with tall bronze statues of our gods. Some are over thirty feet in height, and stand guarding the entrance to a sacred valley. I love walking between them, feeling their benign, imperious gaze upon my head as they reach out their arms to protect us, who worship and tend to them.

I step between the stripes of shadow, the fingers of a giant hand, and gaze up at these noble likenesses of our gods, filled with awe.

I would like to walk further, but know that if I do so I would be late for the evening meal which my beloved has painstakingly prepared for me. And so I turn, and retrace my steps to the villa.

By the time I return home the sun is setting in the hills, filling the distant woodlands with hesperidian fire. Lamps are burning in copper bowls within the garden, filling the air with a richly wooded scent. Off towards the harbour someone is singing, accompanied by *auloi* and *tympani*, a melodious sound that lightly drifts above the walls.

The cooked meats are quite magnificently prepared, as befits a homecoming meal. My beloved wears a revealing robe of peach chiffon, and golden bands of entwined snakes on either arm, gifts I have brought her from my travels. It is only after we have eaten that she says what I know she has been wanting to speak of since I returned from my walk.

'You were gone so long I had begun to worry.' She tears a mint-leaf from the fruit bowl and touches it to her lips. 'How far did you walk?' Her question is deceptively casual. I know that beneath the lightness of her tone there is genuine concern.

'As far as the Valley of the Gods,' I reply. 'Just to the entrance, you understand.'

'Darling.' She reaches across the table to touch the tips of my brown fingers with her pale hands. 'You have only just returned home, and you have made a promise to me.'

'I know,' I reply, chastened by my irresponsible behaviour. 'Sometimes I have to see.' Although I have to admit that usually the urge to do so does not seize me for many months following my return.

'This time, Franciscus, you must try to stay away.'

I agree, and the rest of the evening passes as it should do, in perfect harmony.

And so the pattern of life is restored. One day I visit the Royal Court, and I and my fellow shipmates gain an audience with the Handmaidens of the High Priestess herself. Another day I fish, and work in the courtyard, building a crib for the child we soon hope to have. And always I write, filling my journal with pages of inky scribble. My beloved cannot read, and so I am teaching her. Little by little we progress, question and answer, filling the days.

But my curiosity returns, and like a buried fire slowly builds.

On the day my beloved announces that she is with child, we celebrate by driving up into the hills. I tie a canopy of orange silk across the mulecart and load it with picnic provisions, although we will find all the fruit and fresh water we need in the woods. As the cart trundles higher and higher across the ascending pastures, bluebirds swoop about us like falling pieces of sky. Here the flowers grow in even greater profusion, tangled nests of poppies and anenomes hosting banquets for explosions of blood-red butterflies.

We seat ourselves in a grassy nook far above the distant water, where we can watch a flotilla of triremes setting off across the ocean like ponderous migrating seabirds.

The mulecart's canopy billows like a ship's sail, responding to the call.

'Do you think you will always be content here?' asks my beloved. She is facing away from me, looking out to sea. She tucks a strand of ebony hair behind her ear. I cannot see the expression on her face.

'I believe so,' I reply as honestly as I can. 'This is my home. And soon we will have a child to consider.'

'Then why did you leave before? Your interests are scholarly, and yet you set sail with rough men for places I can only guess at, far-off lands, dark and terrible . . .'

'Only one land, and that against my will, as well you know.'

'If only you never had to leave my side again. Everything you could possibly want is here for the asking.'

'Sometimes we discover things we do not want to know.'

'Then why discover them at all?'

'Because it is in our nature to do so. We are human and naturally inquisitive, and cannot help ourselves.' I reach over through lush talons of grass and still her questions with my parting lips.

Just two days later, I find myself back at the entrance to the Valley of the Gods.

The morning is crisp and still. The sun has only just begun to rise. I stand between the marble bases of the towering statues, which appear a hazy blue in the half-light of dawn. At home my beloved lies curled in slumber on a golden bed of swan-down. Unable to sleep, I have come here to visit the statue of the High Priestess. Few others ever do so, although it is not expressly forbidden. Nothing is forbidden here in Persia, so long as it is for the good. Here there is no crime, no jealousy, no hatred, no bitterness. Instead there is enchantment and endless joy, day upon day of peace and safety.

It is not forbidden to visit the statue of the High Priestess – but it is considered unwise to read the words she has had inscribed across the marble fascia at her feet. For so profound is her wisdom that it affects mere mortals like heady liquor on an empty belly.

As I approach the soaring figure I look up, becoming lost in the beneficence of her calm gaze. She stands with her head held high, her blind green eyes staring out across the harbour far below. Her feet are placed together, her arms outstretched. In the open palm of her right hand is a proffered laurel-sprig. On the back of her left hand stands a dove. Hers is the voice of wisdom, rationality and goodness. She is the representation of all I hold dear, the embodiment of all I value in my life, the shining symbol of Persia itself.

So why may I not hear her message?

My eyes travel down from the verdured bronze folds of her gown to her sandalled toes. In the trees behind me, the first of the morning songbirds begins to trill.

Below I see it, the carved legend that has been inscribed across her base. My eyes alight eagerly upon each word, as with pounding heart and trembling breath I read: *What Have You Done With The Fucking Gun?*

At first I cannot comprehend. Is this some form of foreign language? A cryptogrammic reference, perhaps? I stand there frowning, attempting to decipher the puzzling message. Then a familiar roaring fills my ears and the pale dawn splinters into searing, soaring shards of light. My safe surroundings rush away from me and Persia vanishes, sucked into the darkness as I hear the anguished cry of my beloved replaced with the bark of my interrogator, pacing a room of corrugated tin.

'I said what have you done with the fucking gun?'

He hawks and spits on the hard clay floor, stepping back to allow the other American, the mad one, closer access. I smell the stink of their sweat, and my own fear. The wire tying my wrists together cuts white-hot bands of pain through my mind, and for a moment it is impossible to concentrate. My mouth is filled with blood and I find it difficult to speak. Earlier they loosened my teeth with a hammer.

'We know there was a gun, you little Iranian bastard,' says the mad one. 'Your pal wouldn't tell us where it was so we blew his fucking head off.' I can see him from the corner of my remaining eye. He lies on the excrement-smeared floor like a flyblown sack. There is nothing solid left above the bridge of his nose. Insects are swarming in the glossy viscera which protrude from his gaping stomach.

'If you don't talk, you're gonna wind up like your little

fuck-buddy here,' said the first one, leaning close. He waits for a reasonable period while I try to compose an answer, but I am still confused. Was there a gun? There had been rumours among the other students, but if there was a weapon I did not see it.

'This is a waste of fucking time, man,' cries the mad one, suddenly lunging forward. 'He ain't even in the room with us. Let me stick a knife in him.'

'Wait, he's trying to say something.' The first American raises his hand. He listens carefully. I bring burning air from my windpipe. I shape my lips. He leans closer as I try to say it again.

'*Persia?* What the fuck is that?'

'It's what they used to call this place,' said his partner, lowering the knife. He thrusts his head at me and grins. 'It don't exist no more, you dumb fuck,' he shouts, brandishing the blade again. 'It ain't nothing but a state of mind.'

He punches the knife into my shoulder with the heel of his hand, popping flesh. Blood sprays out like punctures in a hosepipe as he bumps the blade over my chest, jamming the tip against my ribs. The pain redoubles its assault and consciousness begins to slide away once more. The stench of shit and sweat is overpowered by the bitter fragrance of freshly opened lemons. The imprisoning agony of the abductor's knife is replaced with the freedom of the harbour winds. The men retreat. The tin walls fade. The sunlight beckons.

. . . And once again I am in Persia.

Black Day at Bad Rock

I have this irrational desire to kill Mick Jagger.

I've never told anyone about this until now. To explain why, I have to relate a story. Most of it is true, but one part isn't. Just for protection, you understand. You can figure it out for yourself.

At every school there's always one kid everyone hates and shuns. I was that kid.

Obviously I hadn't intended to be. It just worked out that way. It didn't help that I was stick-thin and wore glasses with sellotaped arms and hung out in the library when I should have been caving in heads on the rugby pitch. Pens leaked in my shirt pockets. I was born unfashionable, from Oxford toe-caps to short-back-and-sides. I still owned a clean cap. I was a classic hopeless case. Worst of all, I knew it.

The sporty set had a low tolerance level for kids like us. A boy called Bates in the year below me announced that rugby was for thickos and got hit in the face with a cricket bat. It knocked his nosebone right back into his skull.

This school was a posh school near posh Blackheath, the only posh bit of shit-ugly South London. I lived miles away, in chip-paper-strewn Abbey Wood, gateway to teen delinquency. The neighbourhood kids were neurotic, doped-up, walking scar tissue, groomed for early failure. Hanging out with them wasn't an available option. My mother, a study in thwarted gentility, faded, thrifty, lower-middle-class, never expected much from life and certainly didn't get it, but she expected more of me. My dad was the Invisible Man. He left all the major decisions to his wife, preferring to devote the whole of his adult life to revarnishing the doorframes, a job he had still not finished when I last went home. I got to the posh school because I got good exam marks. Most of the other kids were paid for by their parents.

School was a train journey to a different planet. Blackheath was full of dark antique shops and damp tea-rooms, and called itself a village. Ideally, the shopkeepers would have built a moat around the place to keep out the trash.

The timeframe may slide a little here, but I think this happened at some point in the very early seventies, when the 'village' was still full of crimson-painted boutiques selling lime-green miniskirts and military tunics. Trends weren't so nakedly motivated by marketing then. They seemed to evolve in a happy coincidence of mood and style. *Bonnie And Clyde* had been playing on and of at the local fleapit since 1968, and much to the horror of our elders everyone at school imitated the doomed gangsters as closely as possible. Me and Brian 'Third Degree' Burns, the kid I sat next to for eight years without running out of things to talk about, went up West and stole two guns from Bermans & Nathans theatrical costumiers with a forged letter purporting to be from the Dramatics master. The guns were fake, but were cast in metal and came in real leather holsters, like Steve McQueen's in *Bullitt*, which was good enough for us.

The music around this time was mostly terrible. Of course, now everyone thinks it's great. But it wasn't. Marc Bolan wanking on about fairies and stardust, Groundhogs and Iron Butterfly sounding like somebody masturbating in a roomful of dustbin lids, Jethro Tull hopping about on one leg playing a flute for Christ's sake. About the only bands I could bear to listen to were Mott The Hoople and – the great white god Jimmy Page – Led Zeppelin. 'Whole Lotta Love' received some major suburban bedroom turntable time. It was an antidote to the local disco, where everyone sat at the corners of the room nodding their heads and grooving along with little spastic gestures of their hands. The girls wore floor-length crushed maroon velvet dresses and had long kinked hair, pre-Raphaelite virgins on cider and joints. The generally accepted idea of a good time was getting very, very stoned while carefully listening to the screaming bit from Pink Floyd's 'Careful With That Axe, Eugene'. The sixties had finished swinging and the seventies hadn't started doing anything. My formative years. If my parents had only waited a while before having kids I could have been a punk.

I did have a few friends, but they were all like me i.e. shunned and/or regularly duffed up. The other kids had a collective noun to describe us. Weeds. We were the school Weeds. Do you have *any idea* how humiliating that was?

We mostly spent our spare time dodging our classmates, revising Latin, sneaking into double-billed X movies like *Dracula, Prince of Darkness* and *Plague Of The Zombies*, and reading Ian Fleming novels. Everyone was talking about Bond having his balls tortured in *Casino Royale* I think it was, and Jane Fonda's see-through clothes in *Barbarella*. Also, there was this Swedish movie called *Seventeen* which had female pubic hair in, but some of us thought this was going too far. Nobody in my class ever got to speak to an actual live girl because it was an all-boys school where strapping chaps played lots of healthy contact sports in shorts. (I found out much later that those contact sports involving our revered head boy and the gym master extended to the shower room after games. Years later I heard they were running an antique shop together. A fucking *antique* shop. I'm not making this part up.)

Homework was four hours a night minimum, caps were to be worn in the 'village' on penalty of death and the boys from the nearby comprehensive, whose parents voted Labour and were therefore common, used to nightly pick fights with us at the bus stop. The one time we had a chance to meet girls was when our sister school teamed up for the annual joint operatic production, and obviously only dogs and germs signed up for six weeks of vocal strangulation in the company of *Die Verkaufte Braut*.

For the weaker members of the pack it's always a strange, cocooned existence on the sidelines of the action. We enviously watched the other kids as they honed their social skills, getting their hands into drunk girls' shirts while they danced to 'Ride A White Swan'. We weren't like them. We were still making Aurora model kits of mummies and werewolves. None of us were rebels. The school had a good name. The head and his teachers, tall and stiff and imperious in their black gowns, stalking the corridors like adrenalised vampires, were grudgingly respected because they kept their distance and occasionally maimed their pupils. We'd seen the movie *If*, in which Malcolm McDowell machine-gunned his teachers, and it just wasn't us.

We spent our time discussing *The Avengers*, *Monty Python* and the lyrics to the songs in *Easy Rider*.

One day, all this changed.

Mike Branch, the relief art teacher, arrived.

He was about thirty years younger than any other member of staff, and came for the summer. Of course, everyone instantly liked him. He was handsome and funny and mad-looking. He let you smoke in the kiln room. His hair was over his collar. And *he wore jeans*. To schoolboys who were expected to wear regulation underpants, this was nothing short of frankly amazing. He asked us to call him Mike, and explained that as long as he was around, classes would be very different from what we were used to.

The first time I saw him, he was lounging with his brown suede boots on the desktop and reaching a long arm up to the blackboard to wipe the masters of the Florentine renaissance away with his sleeve.

'I want you to forget the heavy stuff for a while,' he casually explained. 'We'll be concentrating on the Dadaist movement.' Then he wrote 'Rebellion in Art' across the board in red and threw the heavy chalk block clean through a closed window. There was a crack of shattering glass and we all came to attention, filled with borderline homoerotic admiration.

'Don't misunderstand me,' said Branch, sliding his legs from the desk and rising. 'We'll be working hard. But we'll be taking a new approach.' And with that he revealed the school record player – a big old wooden thing, never known to have been removed from the office of the headmaster – plugged it in, and began to acquaint us with his personal taste in rock.

Suddenly Art became the hot class to take.

Branch's periods were unpredictable and (something unheard of in our school) actually interesting. We created Anti-Meat art and Self-Destruct art and Death-To-The-Ruling-Class art. The other teachers tolerated our displays because technically speaking they weren't very good, which made them less of a threat. Besides, as pupils we were Showing An Interest, thus achieving a prime educational directive. The fact that we would have donated our kidneys for vivisection if Mike had asked us hadn't passed unnoticed, either. The other teachers realised they could learn something from watching the art class.

One day, Branch placed a single on the turntable and played it. I was fist deep in a gore-sprayed papier-maché duck when 'Paint It Black' by the Rolling Stones came on. I'd never really liked the song. It already sounded dated when it was first released. Too dirge-like. It reminded me of 'House Of The Rising Sun'. But Mike had a special reason for playing it.

'For the climax of our season of Anti-Art,' he said, strolling between my paint-spattered classmates, 'you are going to Paint It Black.'

'What do you mean?' I asked. He turned to look at me. He had these deep-set blue eyes that settled on you like searchlights, looking for truth.

'A day of artistic anarchy. The idea is to take all of the work you produce this summer and paint it matt black. Then you're going to glue it all together, along with anything else that looks suitable, stick the record player in the centre, and stand it in the middle of the quadrangle.'

It seemed a bit stupid, but nobody argued.

'What if someone tells us to take it down, sir?' asked the pudding-basin-haircutted Paul Doggart, fellow-Weed, a boy who was born to say *sir* a lot in his life.

'You don't take it down. You don't obey anyone's orders

until the stroke of noon. Then I'll appear and we'll play "Paint It Black" from the centre of the sculpture. The art will last for the duration of the song, and then we'll destroy it.'

'But won't we get into trouble, sir?' pressed Doggart.

'No, because I'll forewarn the other masters. They'll be turned on to expect some unspecified action of guerrilla art.' (Yes, embarrassing as it may seem, people really spoke like this in the early seventies.)

So, preparations were made, the date was set for the last day of term (third Tuesday in June) and we painted everything we could lay our hands on and added it to the pile. Clocks. Chairs. Tyres. Lampshades. Toys. Clothes. Tailor's dummies. Car exhausts. A washing machine. And all the time, the damned song played and played until it wore out and had to be replaced with a new copy.

Mike Branch strolled around the artroom, shifting from table to table, stopping to watch as Ashley Turpin, a fat kid with almost *geological* facial acne, attempted to get black paint to stick to a brass candelabra. The master nodded his head thoughtfully, running his thumb beneath his chin as he considered the sheer anarchy of his loyal pupil's work. Finally, with lowered eyebrows and a crooked smile, he turned his attention to the boy. 'Extremely groovy, Turpin,' he said. Turpin, who had previously shown no promise in any area of scholastic endeavour beyond O Level Body Odour, was pitifully grateful.

Identified to other classes by our laminated badges (black, circular, blank – oh, the *nihilism*), we suddenly found ourselves behaving like some kind of creative elite. Me and the other despised and shunned creeps had finally found our cause. For the first time ever we were part of a team, and the fact that the Sport Kings all hated us worked in favour of our anarchistic behaviour.

We began to be *bad*. I mean bad as in modern bad, good bad. By the week before end of term, we were discovering the non-artistic application of 'Paint It Black'. Minor league anarchy. Having pizzas with disgusting toppings delivered to masters COD. Gluing their wipers to their car windscreens. Brian 'Third Degree' Burns upped the stakes by removing the wheels from the French teacher's moped, painting them black and adding them to the sculpture.

Then someone found a masters' home address list. Crank calls to the wives, made from the caretaker's phone by the dining hall. Then obscene calls. Anyone who whined that it was wrong was ditched from the group and returned to the status of a Weed. His badge was ceremoniously taken back. To wimp out on the rebellion was to fail as a human being. The Sport Kings stopped thundering up and down the pitch to cast jealous sidelong glances at the Black Brigade. (Funny thing, we had only had one kid in our year who was actually black, Jackson Rabot, and he wasn't interested in anarchy at all. He wanted to be a conservative MP.)

Of course, the shit soon started coming down on us. Efforts were made to find the culprits. There were extra detentions, cancelled privileges. But end-of-term pranks were expected, and so far we weren't far beyond that.

On Monday, the day before term ended, the day before *B Day*, we stepped up the action and went too far. (You saw this coming, didn't you?) It's blindingly obvious now that some of the group didn't appreciate the subtleties of Mike Branch's orchestrated artistic protest, but had just joined for the party attitude. One of these B-stream holdbacks threw some kind of concentrated acid over the geography master's car. It stank and made an amazing mess, melting clean through to the chassis. Incredible.

News of the attack spread around class like wildfire. Paul Doggart blanched beneath his pudding-basin haircut and threatened to leave the group, but didn't because there was nowhere else to go, and even Brian 'Third Degree' Burns was impressed. Nobody dared own up. We were given until noon the next day to produce a culprit, or the whole brigade would be kept back while everyone else left for the summer. But by now there was an *all or nothing* atmosphere in the group, and we stayed solid. When the head took his record player back, someone brought in their own hi-fi system. The damned song played on.

There was never much studying done on the last day of term. Leisure activities were tolerated. We were allowed to bring in – wait for it – *board games*. I shit you not. And we could wear casual clothes, so everyone made an effort to look hip. Recently I found an old photograph of us Weeds together, taken on that final morning. You'd think we'd been dressed by blind people. Poor old Doggart.

Mike had arranged a double art period for his brigade of rebels. All of the black-painted stuff was arranged in chunks around the room. The record was playing as high as the volume would allow, the sound completely distorted. The artroom was christened The Rock Shop. (I know it's embarrassing now but at the time you'd narrow your eyes and go 'Hey, if anyone wants me I'm at The Rock for a Study Period.' Highly cool.) It was in a separate annexe of its own, and inside it seventeen maladjusted kids were free to do whatever they liked.

The party really started when Bates Junior brought in his mother's hidden supply of mixed spirits (the woman must have been an incredible lush, there was about six litres of the stuff). There were joints, courtesy of Simon Knight's brother, who was possibly the most corrupt customs officer in Britain, and there was acid, although I didn't have any. Everyone went into the kiln room to smoke (force of habit) and soon you could get high just by opening the door, walking in and breathing.

Everyone knew that the gym teacher was a queer because he brought this skinny hairless dog to school. A Mexican thing, big eyes, ugly little teeth. He never watched us in the showers or anything (the teacher, not the dog), because he was too scared of losing his job, but he had this stupid mutt. *Had* being the key word, because Brian 'Third Degree' Burns came up with the great rebellious artistic act of luring it into the kiln room with a piece of bacon. The old art master had always warned us that the inside of the kiln, on full power, was hotter than the surface of Mars, so we decided to test it. A scientific experiment, like sending Laika the Alsatian into orbit with no hope of getting him back. The idea was to dip the dog in slip clay and bake it, then paint it black and add it to the sculpture.

The kiln was squat and wide, with these thick stone walls, so you couldn't hear the dog whining once the door was shut. After about an hour we unsealed it and found that the only thing left was a small patch of blackened sticks. Doggart started moaning about cruelty to animals, so we covered one side of his body with glue and pressed him against the art-room wall until his skin stuck.

Then we began to assemble the sculpture. Forming a chain, we passed the sections out into the school quadrangle, a pathetic damp square of grass surrounded by rain-stained concrete walkways. As the sculpture rose above the height of a man, an interested crowd gathered. The gym teacher asked us if we had the authority to do what we were doing and we said yes, so he went away. I figured he hadn't found out about his dog yet.

At a quarter to twelve the sculpture was fifteen feet high and we still had a load of stuff to add. Table legs, television sets and doll's arms poked out from the twisted black heap. The record player was wired up, but we were going to be late for our noon deadline, mainly because we were all so ripped that we were repeating each other's tasks. The assistant headmaster, a sickly wraith-like creature who looked as if he hadn't slept since Buddy Holly died, asked Simon Knight if he'd been drinking and Simon said no, which was true, although he had dropped acid. Behind his calm, reasonable, innocent exterior he was tripping off his face. Back then the teachers didn't really know what to look for.

The big moment arrived and we were still building the sculpture. Most of the school had turned out to watch. Everyone knew that something special was about to happen. The event had been whispered about for weeks. There were all kinds of rumours flying around – most of them far more imaginative than what was actually planned. Even the Sport Kings were here. Then the headmaster appeared to see what all the fuss was about. He stood in front of the crowd with his bony arms folded behind his back like the Duke of Edinburgh, a look of thin tolerance on his face, tapering towards displeasure.

This was our brief flicker of fame. All eyes were on us. We were the kings. The *bollocks du chien*. The members of the brigade stood back while Brian climbed into the sculpture and started the record player. The opening guitar riff heralded Mick Jagger's voice, a voice which always sounded as if he was leaning obscenely into the mike mouthing distilled insolence. We looked around for Mike. Our Mike, the leader of the Black. No sign. Then we noticed the headmaster.

His displeasure had changed to – well, not pleasure but something sourly approximating it.

'If you're looking for Mr Branch,' he said in a clear Scottish Presbyterian voice that ran across the square, 'you will not find him here. He left the school last night with no intention whatsoever of returning today.' He pronounced the 'H' in whatsoever.

The headmaster triumphantly turned on his heel and led the other teachers back to the common room. And the record stuck. It stuck on the word *black*. The repeated syllable taunted, and the derision began. The Sport Kings just drifted away, snorting to each other, too bored to even beat us up. Suddenly we were Weeds again. It was as if the natural order had been restored, as if everyone had been returned to their correct status, with us back at the bottom, and the holidays could now begin.

'No intention whatsoever.' It was the *whatsoever* that hurt, as if he'd been ready to bottle out all along. The last of the Sport Kings were hanging back by the bike sheds watching us, evidently planning to crack a few Weed heads after all. We didn't care about them. We were too choked to even talk.

Brian ripped the plug from the record player, snatched off the record and returned to the artroom close to tears. He tipped over a table and threw a chair across the room, then so did a couple of the others, and suddenly we were smashing everything in sight. I guess none of us had expected to be betrayed at such an early point in our lives. Perhaps if we could have had sex right then, nothing more would have happened. But we hardly knew any girls, so we had to make do with violence.

Paul Doggart was still stuck to the wall. We'd forgotten all about him. He started making a fuss about wanting to leave, but he couldn't get out of his clothes. His blazer and trousers were cemented fast to the white-painted concrete. So was his fat left cheek. His bellyaching went against the general flow of energy so we spray-painted him black with the leftovers in the cans, hoping it would shut him up. Of course this had the reverse effect, so someone (to this day I don't know who) finally obliged by putting a foot against the wall and tearing him free.

Doggart came away, but not quietly and not in one piece. His cheek left a grisly triangle of flesh stuck to the wall. The last time I saw him that day he was stumbling between the tables clutching his face, crying in hoarse angry sobs. By the time we had finished in the artroom, paint was dripping from the walls and there was broken glass everywhere. We knew someone must have heard the noise by now and didn't dare open the door, so we went out through the windows.

Our adrenaline was really pumping. Using the knives from the artroom we slit every tyre in the car park as we left. I cut the fingers of my right hand to the bone at the second joint because I was gripping my knife so hard.

That night most of us met up and went to see *Woodstock*, but by this time all those Country Joe And The Fish peace songs could only leave us cold. A bridge had been crossed. An unspoken bond had been forged between us.

It's funny how moments can change lives.

Doggart nearly died. The black paint infected his wound and formed some kind of poisonous chain reaction, so that the damage to his face became a whole lot worse. He had a load of skin grafts over the next seven years. And his mind got all fucked up. Nothing he ever said again made much sense. I think his old mum tried to sue someone, but was forced through ill-health and lack of funds to give up the case.

I visited him in hospital once.

I remember walking along a wax-tiled corridor, shoes squeaking, pushing open the door at the end. He was lying in a darkened room, unfriendly eyes staring accusingly from a mess of taut shiny skin. As I made to leave, his right hand grabbed my wrist. I think he was trying to thank me for coming to visit him. I gave him a Get Well Soon card from the members of the B-Brigade. A fold of plain paper, blank shiny blackness. So hip.

The entire brigade was expelled, but the school took no further action. They had too many paying parents to risk getting a bad name. As I said, it was a posh school. Most of the Old Boys were masons. Money changed hands; word never got out. With the time I had spare I attended art college. Cue tears from mother.

Years later, someone heard what had happened to Mike Branch. It turned out that he never was an art teacher, relief or otherwise. He'd played in a band once, opening for the Stones. That was his sole claim to fame. He'd walked into our school with credentials that no one had bothered to check. Then, the day before our big event he'd simply walked away again, gone to the North to do something else. Somebody told me he's in property sales now. That sounds about right.

Still, I wonder if he had the remotest notion of the effect he had on us. He changed the lives of seventeen boys. Thinking about it now, I find it incredible that we trusted someone who regularly wore a turtleneck sweater and gold medallion beneath a brown patch-suede jacket, but there you go. I owned a mauve two-tone shirt with a huge rounded collar that fastened with velcro, a fashion crime I compounded with the addition of yellow hipster bellbottoms.

Personally, I blame Mick Jagger.

Chang-Siu and the Blade of Grass

Long, long ago in China, at the time of the Sung dynasty, a poor farmer named Chang-Siu lived with his daughter in the bleak hinterland of the Hopeh Plain near the city of Ch'in-huang-tao. Their home was as barren and austere as the dark mountains at their backs, but Chang-Siu was content in the knowledge that he would one day be buried beside his ancestors, most of whom had expired after lifetimes spent breaking the hard dry soil by day, and shielding themselves from the bitter winds which crossed the plain at night.

Chang-Siu's frail wife had died giving birth to their only child, and the farmer had been left to raise his daughter, whose name was Ti-Pu, alone. Ti-Pu's beauty was as flawless as polished chalk, and Chang-Siu's love for her had the strength of the sky. Nothing grew on the desolate land that surrounded their house, not even a blade of grass, so each morning, while the misty sun was still low beyond the plain, Chang-Siu would take his daughter to the sluggish river at the base of the mountains where they would gather rushes. After this, they would return home to place them in racks for drying, and Chang-Siu would empty the old racks so that his daughter could begin to weave the hardening stalks into mattering. From this simple trade they were able to buy the few necessities they required to silence their bellies and keep them warm.

Half a day's walk from Chang-Siu's modest house, a village sat sheltered in shadow at the base of the mountains. Although small, it was situated at the edge of a much-used trading route, and it was here that the couple were able to sell their wares. On the few warm days of late summer, when the sun cut free from the towering horizon and shadows withdrew from the village like a retreating grey tide, Chang-Siu would sit in the square and play checkers with the merchants, while his daughter remained seated obediently beside him, and the old hound that lived in the square slept with its tail gently twitching. On these days their life together gained a pleasurable respite from eternal toil, and Chang-Siu felt the fleeting luxury of leisure.

As the years passed, Ti-Pu's beauty grew until it exceeded her mother's, and as Chang-Siu escorted her through the town he saw heads turn and men whisper as she passed. The old rush-farmer knew that their hard life on the plain would soon rob his daughter of this delicate beauty, and because they spent almost every waking moment of their day together, he turned his admiration of her golden days into a fear, and then an obsession. He knew that unless a good marriage could be made for her they would die without advancement, as poor as they had been upon their arrival in the world, with nothing to show for their lives of labour.

There lived in the next village a handsome young merchant named Wang-Lin. At an early age he had inherited a fortune from his father, who had once been a painter to the Emperor Chao Hsu himself at the Imperial Palace. Wang-Lin's father had fallen from grace after painting a picture that was wrongly interpreted, and had expired in comfort and regret at the house of his son. The young merchant was barely older than Ti-Pu, and although he had no need to work he did so in order to contribute to the fortunes of his village.

To strengthen his family following its depletion by the sudden inertia of his father, Wang-Lin was rumoured to be searching for a wife. It became Chang-Siu's deepest wish to see his daughter married to the merchant. All who had met him spoke of the boy as kind and noble, the perfect partner for a girl as beautiful as Ti-Pu. Soon, the residents of both villages had linked the couple's names in anticipated harmony. The arrangement of their meeting and their subsequent marriage were regarded by all as an occurrence as inevitable as the rising sun.

For his part, Chang-Siu let it to be known that he would allow his daughter to meet with Wang-Lin, to discuss the details of the impending nuptials. Ti-Pu's dowry would be her beauty, a gift more precious and fleeting than summer rain. Accordingly, Wang-Lin replied that he would consider it a great honour to receive a visit from Chang-Siu and his daughter.

Just before dawn on the day they were to travel to Wang-Lin's village, Chang-Siu was seized with a terrible foreboding, and leapt from his rush bed with a fearful cry. As soon as he saw that his fears were founded, fingers of ice began to close over him, and in an instant he sensed that his dreams for the future would never be fulfilled. Ti-Pu, who always faced the day with clear eyes and a hopeful heart, was crying. Between her sobs she explained that despite his desirability as a husband she had no wish to marry Wang-Lin, for she loved another, a scholar who lived in their own village, and that worse still he was penniless.

'How could this be?' demanded Chang-Siu, for in all their years together his daughter had never been left alone in public. Ti-Pu explained that she had fallen in love with the scholar, whose name was Liu-Yen, in the square while her father played checkers.

'But surely this means you have never even spoken,' Chang-Siu gasped, unable to believe his ears. Ti-Pu explained that they had no need for words, and that all was understood between them. Chang-Siu considered his afternoons in the village square and recalled the scholar, who was as thin and pale as he was poor.

'It is out of the question for you to marry this man,' he cried, quite enraged. 'Does it mean nothing to you that we have slaved and sweated to survive on this land, where not even a single blade of grass will grow? Why should you seek to destroy our family's only chance to change our lives for the better? I am your father, and it is right that I decide whom you should marry. I will not countenance the idea of your betrothal to a pauper. I forbid you to ever look upon this man again. Furthermore, today we will journey to the house of Wang-Lin to formalise the forthcoming nuptial ceremony.'

At this, Ti-Pu cried anew, and her misery was deepened by a dark cloud passing above the house, which Ti-Pu took to be an omen of death.

Chang-Siu sought to console his daughter, and tried to explain that his actions were compelled by his concern for her happiness, but Ti-Pu was deaf to his entreaties, and ran from the room in tears.

As the day passed, she refused to go with her father to see Wang-Lin, insisting instead that her suitor be informed of the situation. When he saw the pain in his daughter's amber eyes, Chang-Siu set off alone, and with every step he took towards Wang-Lin's house, he watched his dreams slip away. Wang-Lin was disheartened when he heard that Ti-Pu loved another, but Chang-Siu was sure that there was still time for his daughter to admit her folly and return to the marriage he so desired for her. Love was more powerful than Chang-Siu's anger, and although he forbade the girl from ever seeing her lover again he took her back into his heart, hoping that she would quickly see the error of her ways.

Several nights later, there arose a terrible thunderstorm. Lightning cracked the sky in two and filled the great plain with fire, and the rushes beside the river clattered like the bones of the returning dead. Hail hammered over the little house so that it sounded as if a flight of stallions was riding across the roof. Inside, Ti-Pu's misery broke like a dam, flooding into anger. Bitterly she begged her father to allow her a single visit to the man with whom she had fallen in love, but Chang-Siu furiously refused. His rage against his daughter followed the course of the storm, finally blowing itself out when Ti-Pu threw open the door of the little house and fled into the rain.

Chang-Siu's weeks of loneliness were preceded by the knowledge that he had lost his only child. The storm abated and the bare plain dried, but Ti-Pu did not reappear. The rain channels which had been carved into the hard earth slowly dried and filled, and the pale sun climbed to the sky once more, and Chang-Siu no longer dared to leave the house for fear of missing his daughter's return.

* * *

Finally, when he was forced to venture into the village for supplies, he heard the women gossiping outside the teahouse. In truth he wished to overhear, for he had no other way of discovering the whereabouts of his child. In this way he ascertained that Ti-Pu had become the wife of the scholar Liu-Yen, and that they lived in a tiny hut beside a rocky outcrop at the foot of the mountains, in the place where her new husband had been born. The one thing that marred Ti-Pu's happiness was the loss of her father's devotion. It was only her fear of his wrath, said one of the women, that kept her from calling on him. Sadder by far, said another, was the news that the heartbroken young merchant, Wang-Lin, had arranged to marry another for the favour of financial convenience, and not the grace of love.

That night the old farmer raged around his threadbare home, greatly vexed. Eventually exhausted by his rage, he tried to sleep, but the cold air which invaded his bones seemed the coldest air that had ever been, and the darkness which filled the room was darker than the blackest night that had ever fallen on the plain.

The next day, Chang-Siu arose with a stubborn ache in his heart, and bitterly returned to the routine of his daily business, resolved that he would never set eyes on his daughter again.

For six days and nights Chang-Siu saw no one. He made war upon his work, using it to combat the enemy of his memory. His gnarled hands had not the dexterity of his daughter's, so that the mats he wove were imperfect and unfinished. On the seventh day he returned to the village, but managed to sell little more than a third of his wares, and those out of pity for his loss. The merchant, a man whom Chang-Siu had known for most of his life, seemed uncomfortable talking to him, and was relieved to conclude business so that the old farmer would finally leave his store.

Chang-Siu returned home, to his work, to his empty house, and to his rancour, which ate into his chest like a deep-rooted poison, and clouded his every waking thought. At the end of the week he returned to the village, but now the merchant said he could not take even a few mats, for he had found a more reliable supplier.

Disconsolate, Chang-Siu sat in the square and searched for challenges. He tried playing checkers, but his friends all drifted away from him shaking their heads, refusing to be drawn into a game. Everywhere he went it was the same. Those who would once have cheerfully passed the day with him now lowered their eyes and searched the ground, anxious to be gone. Even the ancient hound in the square slunk guiltily from his presence, preferring the company of flies.

Chang-Siu knew he had done nothing wrong, and could not understand the behaviour of the villagers. Was it not the lot of man to better his station, and marry his daughter to the best advantage of his family? One old friend, an elderly merchant full of travelling tales, now pointedly refused to sit with him. Another refused to eat with him. Chang-Siu sensed that something terrible had occurred, but could find no one to tell him what had passed. And so, as his melancholy deepened, his life took on a pattern quite empty and devoid of meaning. His house, uncared for by any human hand, accepted the embrace of nature. What little savings he had accrued in a lifetime of toil were soon exhausted in the purchase of provisions. Each trip to the village was filled with dread as children darted from his sight, and even the birds refused to alight on the ground where he walked.

One morning, Chang-Siu arose with the familiar ache filling his chest and stinging in his joints, and resolved to visit a physician, a kindly old man who lived on a windswept hilltop. The physician held his hands across the farmer's heart, then stared long and hard into the pupils of his eyes. Finally, he told him that he had discovered the root of the problem. He asked the farmer how long he had been suffering from aches and pains. Chang-Siu explained that his health had begun to fail after the terrible fight with his daughter that had resulted in her departure from the family home, and that the moon had passed three times since.

'Well, that's it,' said the physician, nodding sagely. 'I'm afraid I have some bad news for you. You are dead. Your demise most likely occurred on the night that your daughter became lost to you. Your ill-humour overpowered your heart. You have been dead since that time, but neither you nor your friends can see your death, only sense it. The light of life has been extinguished from your eyes, but your angry spirit is unwilling to leave your body.'

'What will become of me?' asked Chang-Siu, appalled.

'Unless you find a way to make your spirit leave soon, your body will start to corrupt even though it continues to perform its normal duties,' said the physician, 'and although the chill winds still sweep our village, summer is coming.'

Devastated by this news, the old farmer returned home and sat alone in his hovel. He looked out on the bare plain where nothing grew, remembering the death of his lovely wife, and the departure of his beautiful daughter. It was as if the land itself had taken a hand in robbing his family of life and happiness. Chang-Siu grieved for the end of his line. Dead! How vastly the grim truth of his mortality differed from his imagined demise! Instead of exhaling on silken cushions, to perish in such dismal penitude! Finally, his self-pity was usurped by the search for a solution to his problem. At first light the following morning, he began the journey to his daughter's house.

As Chang-Siu reached the end of the rocky promontory above his daughter's home, he looked down and saw that the tiny shack had been painted vermilion, and was surrounded by small plants that bristled with blossoming pink buds. As he watched, Ti-Pu appeared at the door, and he saw that her waist was thickening with child. When she saw him she ran to his arms, and it was as if they had never been apart.

They walked together beside the house and spoke softly of the past. Chang-Siu decided not to mention that he had died, for he did not wish to alarm her. Ti-Pu told him how Liu-Yen had gained a position teaching, and although their income was modest it would be enough to support their child. Chang-Siu fought his natural indignation, but still he found his daughter's choice hard to understand. For it seemed to him that even if he worked as hard as the old rush-farmer had done all his life, Liu-Yen would still have nothing to leave his wife and child.

'It wasn't as if I attempted to wed you to an ogre,' he said. 'Wang-Lin was a fine catch, but you refused to even meet him. Our family owns nothing, not even a single blade of grass. How could you think of marrying this man?'

Instead of being hurt by his words Ti-Pu smiled, and took her father by the hand. At the back of the house she knelt in the small green garden, then arose with her fist closed. 'This is where my child will play,' she said, slowly unfolding her fingers. 'It is more than we have ever had. Look at our riches now.'

In her palm lay a single blade of grass.

At the end of two days, Chang-Siu took his leave of Ti-Pu and her husband. As he walked back along the rocky path of the promontory, he felt the warmth of the setting sun slowly fill his limbs, soothing away the soreness in his joints and the ache from his heart. His body fell softly, fading away in the gentle spring breeze. Last of all to disappear into the earth was his closed right hand, and the slender emerald treasure it concealed.

Thirteen Places of Interest in Kentish Town

These places of interest in Kentish Town may be enjoyed in a single pleasant stroll through the area. You should allow a time of approximately two hours. Unlike most walks, which only take in buildings of local historical interest, this walk is designed to give a flavour of daily life in the neighbourhood.

If you would prefer to take a shorter route, may we suggest commencing from Camden Parkway Cinema, walking up to the base of Parliament Hill near the Gospel Oak Lido, then down to Burghley Road in time for tea. This shorter journey should take no more than forty minutes, or less if you are walking briskly with a companion. If you are walking at dusk, be careful crossing the base of Parliament Hill, as the ground is often muddy and it is easy to slip over.

1. *Bentinck's Grocery Store, Angler's Lane*

This unassuming one-storey house once stood on the bank of a tributary of the River Fleet. When the river was enclosed and connected to the Grand Union Canal at Camden, it became part of North London's new sewer system and a roadway was constructed above it. At that time the building was converted into a vegetable store, and has remained so to this day.

The store stocks a wide variety of traditional market produce, mostly grown in Kent, although some non-seasonal items are imported from the Canary Islands and certain fashionable fruits are shipped in from the West Indies. At Christmas Bentinck's extends its range to include nuts, dried fruit, floral wreaths and table centrepieces. The store is used mainly by housewives living in the immediate streets to the south and west of Angler's Lane.

A typical visitor to the store would have been Mrs Kathleen Atherton. Every week for thirty years she purchased the family's fruit and vegetables here. A native of Kentish Town and the last surviving member of one of the area's oldest families, the strong-willed Mrs Atherton was always careful to balance her family's dietary needs with the availability of fresh farm-produce. She continued to patronise the shop after growing infirmities limited her mobility, and refused all offers of help from staff, preferring to select produce personally. A lifelong Conservative, she found it difficult to express emotion, and preferred to take action, however inappropriate.

Since the opening of two hypermarkets in the vicinity, custom has declined at Bentinck's Grocery Store. The little shop could not compete with low prices brought about by the bulk-purchasing power of the superstores, and is now closing its shutters for the last time.

2. *Kentish Town Baths, Prince of Wales Road*

This elegant Edwardian building with art-nouveau flourishes started life as the St Pancras Baths and Wash-houses. It was provided with four swimming pools, one hundred and twenty-nine slipper-baths and a public laundry which is still in use to this day. Like many housewives in the neighbourhood, Mrs Atherton preferred to pay someone to do her laundry twice a week, and disliked the idea of owning her own washing machine.

On the first floor of the Baths, a state-of-the-art gymnasium now caters for the area's young professionals, and its apparatus provides much-needed physical stimulation for local men and women of all ages.

In charge of the exercise class is Ms Pauline Metcalf. Thirty-two-year-old Pauline hails from Derby, and moved to London with her young son Neville, on whom she doted, to escape unhappy memories of a difficult divorce. Twice winner of the National Physical Prowess Certificate, Pauline took step-classes and aerobics every day except Sunday, enjoyed swimming, and liked to keep herself in shape.

In November 1986 she gave up her classes following a painful personal tragedy, and moved back to Derby in February of the following year. Like many young women, Ms Metcalf grew lonely on cold winter nights, and sought solace in the arms of married men.

3. *Number 236, Kentish Town Road*

Formerly the headquarters of E. H. Olive & Company, Tailors and Outfitters, who inhabited the building from just after the turn of the century, this property is now occupied by Abba Electronics, which sells reconditioned televisions, radios and all manner of electrical household equipment, available on easy terms of payment.

It is odd to think that in 1903 an overcoat purchased in E. H. Olive & Co. cost just eight shillings and eleven pence, which in today's decimal currency is just under forty-five pence and would not buy a lightbulb in Abba Electronics.

The stables at the rear of the shops on Kentish Town Road were constructed to house the horses from nearby Highgate Racetrack, and after the Second World War were converted into warehouses for use by the high street's various stores, including Abba Electronics.

The former manager of the establishment, Mr William Atherton, worked here and at two other branches located in Camden Town and Belsize Park until 1987, when he was forced into sudden retirement on the grounds of ill-health. Mr Atherton would describe himself as a good but essentially weak man.

4. *Bus shelter, Fortress Road*

This small, unprepossessing concrete shelter was built in 1946 when the new bus routes to Highgate via Archway came into use, and has been twice featured in the national news.

In March 1953 a coach full of nuns visiting the Richard Stanhope Catholic School in Prince of Wales Road mounted the kerb and ploughed into a party of agnostics waiting at the bus stop, killing two and injuring seven. Father O'Hanlon, the driver of the bus, was subsequently found to be drunk, and was jailed for four years.

Then, on 11 November 1986, the shelter was photographed and described as the site where a young schoolboy, Neville Metcalf, aged nine, was last seen alive. Witnesses recalled spotting him on one of the red plastic seats, dangling his legs and studying a comic in the late-afternoon drizzle while he waited for a bus to take him in the direction of Camden Town.

Neville Metcalf was a shy, quiet pupil at Richard Stanhope who had learning difficulties, and was usually supervised on outings because of his willingness to be led by strangers. He was, however, a member of the school cinema club, and enjoyed swimming and football. He was an Arsenal supporter and an avid fan of the James Bond series, and would see each 007 film several times.

Despite an extensive police search lasting for several months, little Neville's whereabouts were never ascertained, and his disappearance remains one of the area's most enduring mysteries. Shortly after the disappearance his distraught mother made an emotional appeal on national television, but the resulting leads all proved to be dead-ends.

5. Number 24, Burghley Road

This is an Edwardian terraced house of a type typically found to the north of Kentish Town's main thoroughfare. The high-ceilinged, well-proportioned rooms of these houses were created for well-off middle-class families at a time when Kentish Town was still considered to be a leafy suburb of London, long before it gained its present 'inner city' reputation. The house, within walking distance of Parliament Hill Fields, was for many years the home of Mr and Mrs William Atherton, typical residents of Kentish Town.

Uncut

The airy, pleasant rooms of the houses were intended for families who could afford several children, but shortly after the couple's marriage Mrs Atherton discovered that she would never be able to bear a child, and the upstairs rooms she had planned as a nursery and live-in nurse's quarters remained empty for many years.

In early November 1986, Mrs Atherton suffered a nervous attack and disappeared overnight, returning the next day only to lock herself inside her back bedroom. She refused to come out for two days, and then only agreed to do so after her husband had left the house. She subsequently converted to the Catholic religion, and redecorated the upper floor of the house for her own habitation, leaving it only to cook her husband's meals and to care for him after his retirement.

Mr Atherton died nine years later in 1995, after a tragically prolonged illness, at which time the house was sold and divided into four flats.

6. Number 5, Cathcart Street

This modest home, typical of the area, was rented by Pauline Metcalf, who lived there with her son Neville for a number of years. The street takes its name from one of the generals of the Crimean War, which was fought just before these houses were built. Many of the surrounding area's street names recall battles from that glorious folly in the Valley Of Death. The residential properties were originally constructed to provide homes for immigrant Irish workers, who were employed by the council in 1860 to build the railways extending from the north of the city, and many of these houses are still occupied by their descendants.

Today the original cobbled street remains much as it appeared in the previous century. The Crimea public house, which stood on the corner of Cathcart Street and Alma Street, once acted as a secret rendezvous-point for public-school spies Burgess and Maclean, and was a focus for much of the street's social life. It has recently been converted into apartments for young professionals.

Ms Metcalf's house, rented from council, typically suffered from condensation and occasional flooding, being situated close to the underground river beneath Angler's Lane, but, like the other dwellings in this overlooked area, offered a small oasis of calm in an inner-city neighbourhood. Ms Metcalf eventually vacated her home following the tragic loss of her son.

7. *The Vulture's Perch, corner of Islip Road and Kentish Town Road*

This popular public house, while not as famous as its nearby neighbour The Assembly Rooms, which still boasts one of the finest collections of Victorian etched glass in England, began life as the Oxford Vaults. Many fine brewery products are available on tap, including London Bitter and Kronenberg lager. Its Saturday-night discos, a throwback to seventies entertainment, are extremely popular and attract a mixed local crowd of all ages.

A typical customer would have been Pauline Metcalf, who often came here after she finished conducting exercise classes at the Kentish Town Baths. Ms Metcalf started attending the Saturday-night discos in October 1984, and continued to enjoy drinking and dancing there for the next two years.

Just before Christmas of that year, Mr William Atherton also began frequenting the pub on Saturday nights while Mrs Atherton visited relatives in Belsize Park. He subsequently took up weight-training at the gymnasium in Kentish Town Baths in order to lose the stomach he had gained through drinking.

8. *Holmes Road Police Station, Holmes Road*

If you stand outside this fine late-Victorian building, built in 1895, you will see the old arch of the stables to your right, and a sympathetically constructed modern extension to your left. Many Victorian police stations still retain their original architectural features and compete in the maintenance of their summer flowerbeds, and Holmes Road is no exception. In the basement of the building are four overnight holding-cells, still with original Victorian fittings, and at the back of the ground floor is the interview room where Pauline Metcalf was first questioned about the disappearance of her only child, Neville, in November 1986.

After a highly emotional series of interviews, Ms Metcalf was released pending her availability for further questioning. She was particularly upset that a two-month sentence for shop-lifting seven years earlier appeared to be prejudicing the course of the investigation, and later sued the police, winning her case.

During the course of her penultimate interview, she admitted that she had been involved with a married man for over two years. Although officially she refused to name him, it is believed that Ms Metcalf later revealed her lover's identity to the officer in charge, and that the gentleman was subsequently brought in for questioning.

The unnamed man explained that he had been drinking in The Vulture's Perch, Kentish Town Road, on the evening of Neville Metcalf's disappearance, and his alibi was confirmed by the bar staff and several customers. Visibly distraught, he was released without charge. Shortly after this time, Mr Atherton's health began to deteriorate, and he was forced to retire.

9. The Old Post Office, Leighton Road

This attractive red-brick postal sorting-office, which finally shut its doors to the public in 1994, was built during the reign of King Edward VII, and the initials E.R. (Edwardus Rex) may still be seen on the building and the adjacent railings. In the decades of its public service it saw the style of its staff change from smartly uniformed, courteous post officials to louts in trainers. A letter could be collected from this building if, for some reason, it proved impossible for the postmen to deliver it.

Taken at random, a typical letter might have been the one posted to Mr Atherton on 9 November 1986. The recent heavy rainfall has rusted the spring of the letter box at Abba Electronics, a popular high-street shop, and the postman was unable to deliver the mail that morning.

Responding to a Royal Mail form she found in the breast pocket of her husband's shirt as she took it to the laundry, Mrs Atherton was able to go to the post office that evening and collect the letter, which bore a handwritten return address in Cathcart Street, Kentish Town.

10. *Parliament Hill Fields, Upper Kentish Town*

There is much confusion as to where exact boundary lines fall between Parliament Hill, Kentish Town and Gospel Oak, but it is a fact that the rolling green hills bordering all three areas are enjoyed by residents from every part of the borough. At the foot of the main hill are numerous tennis courts, a bowling green and refreshment rooms incorporating a special play area for children. The nearby heath is particularly popular with gentlemen who prefer to take their constitutional at around two in the morning.

The grass at the base of the fields was wet on the evening of 11 November 1986, and shone a livid green even in the sickly winter light. A lost item, such as a boy's red-and-white Arsenal scarf, would have stood out quite clearly, even at a distance.

Later that night, the year's fiercest storm broke out above the town, blackening the sky over Parliament Hill, where several oak and beech trees were rent asunder by lightning, and the downpour soaked the ground so thoroughly that all footprints were washed back into the soil.

11. *Gospel Oak Lido*

This charming open-air swimming pool was constructed in 1934 in an art-deco style, complete with curve-fronted cafeteria and sapphire-blue moulded fountains, and has played host to thousands of local children and parents who have braved the chill waters of its Olympic-sized pool. In June 1996 Camden Council completed an extensive refurbishment programme on the lido, improving its sixty-year-old facilities for a new generation of bathers.

During the excavation to the west of the car park, below Parliament Hill Fields, a gruesome discovery was made when the body of a small child was dug from the upturned earth by a passing dog. The skeleton lay in builders' rubble, which had been used as landfill for the shallow ditches that had lined this quiet corner during the previous decade.

Unfortunately, lime from builders' bags had soaked through to the skeleton, damaging it so badly that identification was rendered impossible. In an area as rich and diverse in population as this, great personal tragedies are certain to unfold, and we might only ever glimpse small parts of these interesting human stories.

12. *Odeon Cinema, Camden Parkway*

This popular venue was constructed in the nineteen thirties and featured an elegant interior design typical of cinemas built in central London before the war. During the box-office slump of the seventies the auditorium was divided into two screens, and the foyer featured a stylish bar where nightly live entertainment could be enjoyed by patrons between film performances. No more than five hundred yards away, another cinema, the Camden Plaza, showed continental and art films. In the late eighties both cinemas were closed down, although the public protest that accompanied the closure of the Camden Parkway eventually resulted in it reopening as a bland modern multiplex reeking of overpriced stale popcorn.

A typical bill-of-fare on a random date, say an early-evening performance on 11 November 1986, would have featured the most recent James Bond film *A View to a Kill* in its main auditorium, and a typical audience at this time would have included local schoolboys, and housewives from Kentish Town filling in the angry, empty hours before their husbands' return from work.

13. *Raglan Road Day-care Centre, Raglan Road*

This day-care centre run by Camden Social Services is a second home to local elderly ladies, many of them widowed, alone and bewildered, who attend during weekdays and enjoy a chance to socialise with others of their own age. On Tuesdays there is a singalong with Mrs Birch, a local schoolteacher, at the piano, and a wide variety of other pursuits are available for the enjoyment of those attending.

There is a limited number of permanent residents who through bereavement and ill-fortune have found themselves destitute and alone in their twilight years.

One such resident is Mrs Kathleen Atherton, who came to the centre in late 1995, and stayed on until her hospitalisation and subsequent death three years later. This colourful character outlived her husband after nursing him through the course of a crippling wasting disease, for which doctors could find no cure, or indeed cause.

Mrs Atherton was a familiar sight, who touched the hearts of everyone passing the centre on their way to and from Bentinck's Grocery Store in Angler's Lane. On most summer days she could be seen seated at the open window, framed by the dingy net curtains, draped in an old Arsenal football scarf, and she would tell anyone who cared to listen to her fanciful stories of infidelity, rage and retribution.

Last Call for Passenger Paul

Passport. Tickets. Washbag. Walkman. Cassettes. Batteries . . . no, no batteries. Paul pushed everything back into his flight bag and headed for the airport stationery shop, threading his way between hordes of holidaymakers and pyramids of suitcases. He'd need at least four Duracells for the trip. The ones in his Walkman were dead. He entered the stationery shop, passing racks of brightly-coloured trashy paperbacks, teatowels decorated with scenes of Buckingham Palace and St Paul's Cathedral, headsquares and cuddly toys. Outside, the public address system boomed loud and indistinct. Paul pulled a pack of batteries from the stand and paid for them with the last of his English money.

It was early August, and Heathrow airport was a scene of total chaos. Frazzled check-in clerks dealt patiently with mislaid tickets and last-minute arrivals, while passengers complained about missed connections and missing baggage. Queues extended across every concourse. Moslems unrolled prayermats in the corners and children chased each other around video machines and parents lay stretched out asleep on benches and in chairs, oblivious to the announcements detailing further delays and more cancellations.

Paul hitched his flight bag further onto his shoulder and aimed himself at the upstairs restaurant, past a congregation of confused nuns and a group of fifty elderly American tourists, each one neatly nametagged, all standing in the middle of the floor waiting to be told what to do next.

The restaurant was no quieter. There were no seats to be found, and tiny Pakistani ladies dragged vast green plastic sacks from table to table, attempting to keep pace with mounting stacks of dirty crockery. Paul stood his bag down in a corner and fitted the batteries into his personal stereo. At twenty-eight, he was pretty much an old hand at dealing with crowded airports. His job as a CBS record executive saw to that, regularly requiring him to board the transatlantic flights for Chicago, Los Angeles and New York. This trip, however, was purely for pleasure. The last six months had been hellishly hectic, culminating two nights ago in a spectacular launch party from which Paul was still feeling the effects. Now he was preparing to board the next flight to Larnaca, Cyprus for two weeks of well-earned R&R.

Adjusting the volume on his Walkman, Paul walked through passport control and into the passenger lounge to await the arrival of his flight. On the column ahead of him the screens announced the first call for Cyprus. Paul decided to wait until the actual departure time was closer before heading for the gate. He sat back in the chair and closed his eyes for a moment, letting the music surround him completely. After working with rock bands every day of the week, he found his own tastes straying to Beethoven and Mozart in his leisure hours.

The voice on the PA system announcing the final call for flight 203 to Larnaca brought him back from Mozart's *Marriage of Figaro* with a start. Paul swung his bag back up on his shoulder, ran a hand through his cropped blond hair and made his way to the gate.

The flight was full, mostly with holidaymakers of the worst kind, it seemed. He leaned on the counter while the check-in girl stamped a boarding pass and handed it to him. Just as he thanked her and moved off, she called him back.

'Sorry, sir,' she smiled. 'You'll be needing this.' She pressed a small blue sticker onto his ticket and returned it. Paul looked at the sticker, which had a tiny figure printed on it. The ink had blurred, but it appeared to be a man riding on the back of another – St Christopher, perhaps? Either it was a new computer symbol, or the airline had turned religious.

He hung back until the last passenger had moved out into the corridor before handing in his boarding pass. As he made his way onto the Tristar, he fingered the control button of his Walkman nervously. Actual flying did not bother him – taking off and landing did.

As soon as he had located his seat, he secured the belt in his lap, refastened his earphones and lay back. He planned to stay that way until they were in the air. There was an elderly man of presumably Turkish origin in the seat next to him, happily emptying the contents of a holdall into both his seat pocket and Paul's, oblivious to the revving engines outside. Paul shut his eyes and kept them that way until they were safety off the ground.

The first thing Paul saw from the window when he finally opened his eyes was Windsor Castle, far below and briefly glimpsed through racing clouds. He turned from the scuffed plastic porthole and looked around. The palms of his hands were slick with sweat. As the cabin levelled out and the seat-belt sign was turned off, he released the back of his chair, kicked off his trackshoes and began to relax. Two weeks away from the office with nothing to do except lie in the sun – it seemed too good to be true. He had been careful to tell no one where he could be reached. He knew only too well how likely it was that he would be called back to deal with a crisis otherwise.

A stewardess arrived with the drinks trolley, and Paul requested a gin and tonic, watching while the girl – tall and tanned, with strong white teeth – continued smiling as she filled the glass. The elderly Turk in the seat next to him had presumably become bored with rummaging around in the seat pockets and was already comatose, remaining so until woken for his meal. Paul ate and drank with a hearty appetite. After idly thumbing through the flight magazine as he sipped his brandy, he turned to stare out at the motionless azure sky and his eyelids began to fall. By the time the stewardess quietly slipped his meal tray away and folded his seat flap up, he was lost in a deep and dreamless sleep.

The first thing Paul became aware of upon awakening was the heat, even before he felt the hand shaking him. The steward's face swam before his eyes.

'Sir, wake up, sir, time to get off. All the other passengers have disembarked.'

Paul blinked and rubbed his eyes, then pulled the earphones from his head. The air in the cabin was stiflingly hot. He sat up and stared about at the empty seats surrounding him. Up ahead, two stewardesses stood by the galley entrance talking as the last of the passengers threaded their way through the exit door.

'Boy, I was out cold,' Paul said to the steward, smiling. His mouth felt hot and dry, the after-effect of drinking in an air-conditioned atmosphere. The heat surprised him. Already he could feel sweat forming between his shoulder blades.

'Don't forget your hand luggage, sir,' said the steward, moving off.

Paul pulled his bag from beneath the seat and stood up. The cabin was empty now except for the crew. He checked his seat to make sure that he had not left anything behind, then stooped and peered out of the window. A large white concrete terminal, arched with the architecture of a harem, stood at the end of the blurred, dusty airstrip. Somehow, Paul had expected Cyprus to be prettier at first sight than this. He made his way down the aisle to the exit door, where a smiling stewardess waited to bid him farewell.

'We look forward to seeing you again soon, sir,' she said. 'Have a pleasant stay in Amman.'

He had almost passed through the doorway before he realised what the stewardess had said, and turned back to her, puzzled.

'Where?' he asked.

'Amman, sir,' said the stewardess, her smile fading as she realised something was wrong.

'This isn't Cyprus?'

'No, sir. We left Cyprus over an hour and a half ago.'

'Oh my God, I was supposed to get off there,' said Paul. 'Why didn't someone wake me?'

'I'll get the cabin director, sir, if you'll hold on for a moment.'

A tall, square-jawed man in a crisply cut blazer came over. 'What seems to be the problem?' he asked, in a deep, relaxed voice.

'I've gone past my stop,' said Paul, aware that he sounded like someone addressing a bus conductor. Just then, the stewardess who had served Paul his meal came over.

'I didn't wake this gentleman up because I thought Amman was his final destination,' she told the cabin director.

'Did you look at his boarding card?'

'Yes, it was in the seat pocket in front of him.'

'That wasn't mine,' explained Paul, producing his own. 'It must have belonged to the guy sitting next to me.'

'We were on the ground for over an hour,' said the cabin director, turning to the embarrassed-looking stewardess. 'Didn't you think to check?'

'I'm sorry, a lot of people were staying on. I had my hands full.'

'I'm afraid you'll have to sort this out in the terminal,' said the cabin director apologetically. 'It shouldn't take long to get you back to Cyprus. In fact, I think there's a flight later on this afternoon.' Paul sighed and hitched up his flight bag. He couldn't believe how dumb he could be, falling asleep like that. Outside, the temperature was astounding. Before he could reach the terminal building, his face was popping with beads of sweat, and the strap of his bag was leaving a wet bar of heat across his right shoulder blade. The vast white strip of concrete over which he walked glared up at him. Where the hell was Amman? He had a vague recollection that it was somewhere in Jordan. Was it safe here? Jesus, what a way to start a vacation!

Inside the terminal it was fresh and cool. He explained what had happened to the woman on the desk, who happened to be English and therefore quite amused by the situation, much to Paul's annoyance.

'Oh, it happens all the time, sir,' she said after checking his ticket and examining the small blue sticker. 'We often have people disembarking too early, grandads getting off at Singapore when they're supposed to stay on until Australia. It's just like the buses. We're always leaving passengers in strange places because the flights are full. And where their *luggage* turns up is nobody's business.'

Paul failed to see the amusement in this. 'Well, when can I get back to Cyprus?' he asked, already suspecting that he knew the answer. The concourse behind him was disturbingly free of passengers.

'That's the trouble, sir. Our direct flight to Larnaca has been cancelled today because of an aircraft fault.' Her smile was extremely apologetic.

'Does that mean I just have to hang around this airport until it gets fixed?' asked Paul with mounting irritation.

'Well, let's see.' The counter clerk consulted her timetable. She looked like a holiday courier, heavily tanned, with auburn hair swept back in a ponytail. 'What we could do is transfer you to an airline which does have a flight going out this afternoon. How about that?'

'Fine, fine,' agreed Paul. 'I just want to get there before nightfall.'

The clerk dutifully transferred his ticket to a local airline, and arranged for his luggage to be forwarded.

So it was that, two hours later, Paul found himself boarding an Alia flight filled with Jordanian businessmen.

At the entrance to the aircraft, the stewardess checked his ticket and directed him to a business-class seat. Obviously he had been upgraded in order to recompense in part for the inconvenience of having to switch airlines. Paul felt uncomfortable in these unfamiliar surroundings. As the plane reached its cruising altitude he found it impossible to concentrate on the pages of his paperback, and instead donned the earphones of his Walkman to relax with a soothing symphony. When he became aware of a voice speaking in a foreign tongue above the sound of the music, he turned down the volume on the Walkman to listen. Unfortunately, the announcement was not repeated in English, so he summoned a stewardess.

'What was that last message?' he asked.

'Owing to a problem at Larnaca airport we are having to put down in Adana,' said the stewardess. And then, in a lower tone, she confided, 'I think they are bringing the hostages in to Larnaca. No other planes can come in or out for several hours.'

'Thank you, but where the hell is Adana?'

'It's in Turkey, near the coast.'

'Great, just great.' Paul was beginning to wonder if he would ever reach his destination. The papers had been full of news about the hostages for the last few days. They had been expected to be released at any moment, but they could not have picked a worse time, he thought uncharitably.

Adana turned out to have an even hotter and dustier air-strip than Amman. Its terminal building was old and filthy and crowded with the most extraordinary people. Despite reassurances from the Alia stewardess that his luggage would be forwarded, Paul doubted that it would even find its way out of the airport, since it was quite obvious that no one here spoke any English.

Once inside, he fought his way over to the nearest flight desk and attempted to make himself understood to the clerk. By now he was hot, tired and angry, his sour shirt sticking to his back. The clerk, in hopeless fractured English, attempted to placate him. Eventually Paul went to sit with the others from his flight on a long wooden bench by one of the gates.

The terminal was packed. There were old men in shawls asleep on the floor, and tired women clutching huge bundles of clothing, and at one point a mange-ridden mongrel hobbled over to where Paul sat and peed against his flight bag.

After he had rinsed off some of the sweat and changed into a crumpled but fresh T-shirt in the washroom, he returned to his seat to find his fellow passengers swarming through two gates onto a pair of newly arrived planes.

The mad scramble for seats was alarming. Paul tried to gain the attention of one of the passing passengers, a woman he had seen on his previous flight. He waved his ticket before her in a desperate effort to attract her assistance. She was obviously torn between helping him and rushing onto the flight herself.

'Larnaca?' he shouted above the babble of the tannoy. 'Larnaca airport is open again, yes?'

The woman stared at his ticket, with the little blue sticker fixed to its corner, and suddenly seemed to comprehend. 'Yes!' she cried. 'You want Larnaca, next gate, hurry now!'

'Thank you! Thank you very much!' Paul grabbed her arm gratefully, but the woman pulled away in alarm. Quickly he made his way over to the second of the gates and held his ticket before the man at the door. Around them swarmed girls with wicker baskets, ancient men with their belongings bundled into sacks, and children of every size and description. There seemed to be nobody issuing boarding passes. The man at the door glanced at the ticket, then nodded and waved Paul through and onto the aircraft.

He hadn't had a chance to look at the outside of the plane, but inside the cabin seemed narrow and cramped. Paul found himself without a seat allocation, and after failing to reach either of the stewardesses, seated himself next to a fat Turkish woman bouncing a child on her knee. There seemed to be a 'first come, first served' policy regarding the seating arrangements.

Eventually the cabin doors were closed, the stewardesses managed to find everyone a seat, and the plane jiggled along the runway in the direction of the afternoon sun. If Paul had been nervous about taking off before, this time he was petrified. The overhead lockers creaked and juddered as the aircraft revealed its stress points in the airstreams of the sky. Children began crying and old men wandered from their seats, attempting to light their pipes until the stewardesses insisted on extinguishing them.

Paul slumped back in the uncomfortable seat and plugged into his Walkman once more in an effort to shut out the surrounding noise of the children playing in the aisles. He wanted to ask someone how long the flight would take, but was loath to become involved in a linguistic wrestling match with any of his fellow travellers. He was seated in an aisle seat this time, in an area which may or may not have been designated as a smoking zone for all the notice anyone was taking around him. As he tried to let the music blot out all other sounds, he imagined the problem of relocating his luggage, and was glad that he had not packed anything of value.

Beyond the cabin window afternoon was slowly turning into evening, and the sky was filled with heliocentric hues. The edges of the scudding clouds were flashed with red and purple as, far below, the sea glittered with dying light. There was nothing to do now but wait.

The aircraft was approaching the runway below at an alarming angle. On both sides of the cabin people were craning out of their windows to see the airport terminal. When Paul managed to locate it, his stomach dropped. This could not be Larnaca. Against the dusty orange walls of the low concrete building ahead lounged two armed policemen. In the distance stood a truck, filled with what looked like goats, and further afield the lights of a small town twinkled against low velvet hills. As the plane taxied to a standstill, he read the cracked sign along the wall of the airstrip.

Ajdabiquh.

They had landed in North Africa. There could be no other explanation. This time Paul contained his rage until he was inside the terminal building, threw his bag onto the counter of the first official he could locate and demanded to know what was going on. The official, a young customs clerk, spoke no English, and after five minutes of shrugging and face-pulling went to fetch his superior. He returned with a broad, heavy-set African wearing flamboyant gold insignia.

'Do you speak English?'

'Certainly, sir. Now what seems to be the trouble?'

'I've just arrived on this flight . . .' Paul indicated the candy-striped aircraft standing on the runway outside, 'and I was told that our destination was Larnaca.'

'Well, whoever told you that was wrong, sir,' said the senior official in a simple, placating tone. He looked at the sweating young man with interest.

'Is there any way that I can get back to Larnaca tonight?' asked Paul. He wiped his forehead with an unsteady hand, refusing to let his paranoia rise to the surface.

'I don't know about that, sir. We have no scheduled flights going there from here . . .'

'Here being where?'

'This is Libya, sir.'

'So how am I going to get back?' he demanded, panic

creeping into his voice. Outside, darkness had fallen, and the runway lights had come on.

'Can I see your ticket for a moment, sir?' The senior official reached out a broad pink palm. *Why not?* thought Paul. *Everybody else has*, and handed it to him.

The two men behind the counter examined Paul's ticket closely. The young clerk pointed to the corner of the ticket and said something to his superior, who slowly nodded his head in agreement.

'I think we may be able to help you,' he said as he returned the ticket. Paul found himself following the two men through the sand-blown terminal towards one of the far exit doors. He had to virtually run to keep pace with them as they chattered on in their native tongue, completely ignoring him. Paul's sole consolation, he told himself, was that he was seeing places he would never otherwise see. And, he mentally added, they were places he'd never bother trying to see again.

The outside of the terminal building was lit with grey tin lights which swung crazily in the warm night breeze. Here, on a low bench along a wall, were four other travellers, one of whom appeared to be of European extraction. The senior official pointed to a smartly suited pilot who was crossing the tarmac from a small passenger plane.

'He is a charter pilot. He will take you to your correct destination,' said the senior official. 'These other people have been misrouted as well. You should be in Larnaca before midnight. I am sorry you have had such a bad journey.'

'Me too, but thanks for your help, at least,' said Paul. 'I thought I was never going to find anyone who spoke English. Are you sure this pilot knows where he's going?'

'Don't worry, he knows. This sort of thing happens all the

time. Enjoy your trip.' He turned to explain what he had just said to the junior clerk, who let out a snort of laughter.

The pilot walked along pass the bench to Paul, took his ticket from his hand, checked the destination and returned it. The officials re-entered the terminal, leaving Paul and the other four passengers alone outside. The pilot beckoned them forward, and they crossed the tarmac to the steps of the plane. Paul manoeuvred himself so that he was walking by the middle-aged white man he had seen on the bench, and took the opportunity of introducing himself. The man turned out to be a French businessman named Bernard. He spoke a fractured form of English, and was able to explain to Paul as they climbed the aircraft steps that he too had been re-directed, and had boarded his flight in Paris at nine thirty that morning.

Paul was relieved to find a kindred spirit, and decided to sit next to him for the flight. Inside the aircraft, which Paul reckoned would have seated about thirty people, there was no stewardess to be seen. He pushed his flight bag under the seat and sat down by the Frenchman. Within moments, the co-pilot closed the cabin door, the engines revved, and the plane shot up into the night sky, circling the airport once before heading south.

'This cannot be right,' said Bernard. 'We are heading in the wrong direction. We should be going north.' He peered from the window into the blackness beyond.

'You mean Cyprus is to the north?' asked Paul, sensing that something strange was going on. Behind them, the three other passengers were peering from the windows.

'Cyprus?' said Bernard. 'You mean Athens.'

'What?' Paul's eyes widened. He could not believe his ears. 'We're not going to Larnaca?'

'Not to my knowledge. I am supposed to be in Athens. I thought this was where we were heading, but we are going south. Look.' He drew out his travel folder and opened it to reveal a small map of central Europe and Africa.

'Here, the airport we just left faces north, but we took off to the south. We are heading down into Chad.'

'This can't be happening,' said Paul shakily. 'Let me see your ticket.' Bernard pulled out his ticket and handed it across. There in the corner was the same square blue sticker that was affixed to Paul's.

'Do you know what this means?' he asked, pointing to the sticker.

'No, I have no idea.'

Paul examined it closely under his seat light. It definitely showed two men, one of whom appeared to be seated on the other's shoulders. He passed the ticket back and stared helplessly out of the window as the aircraft buzzed on through the cloudless night.

Paul looked at his watch. It read a quarter to twelve. The plane had just come to a stop. Beyond the runway lights, nothing could be seen. The other passengers were looking from one window to another, confused. One of them, a young black girl, was crying. Paul walked back to her seat and took the ticket from her hand. It too had a blue sticker on it.

'What the hell is going on here?' he shouted as the main cabin door suddenly opened from the outside with a dull bang. Grabbing his flight bag from beneath the seat, Paul strode to the front of the plane and trotted down the floodlit steps. The ground beneath his trackshoes was not tarmac, but earth. Beyond the perimeter lights marking the airstrip, there was nothing. Passing in front of the aircraft, Paul spotted a squat, dimly lit building ahead, the only one on an unbroken desert horizon.

'Come on!' he turned and called to the others, but nobody appeared in the cabin doorway. Why were they so reluctant to leave the plane?

As Paul headed towards what he presumed was the terminal building, the cool desert air ruffled his hair and calmed him slightly. He heaved the flight bag back onto his shoulder, and paused to toss the dead batteries from his Walkman into the long grass, which rustled drily several feet from the runway.

A hundred yards from the terminal, he realised with mounting horror that it had been completely burned out. Bats flitted around the cracked bones of rafters which could be seen against open sky through its huge windows. And yet there were moving lights inside. Paul redoubled his pace.

He reached the entry door, which was ajar, and looked back at the plane. One of the remaining passengers was standing in the cabin doorway, hesitating before descending the steps. Turning back to the terminal door, he reached forward and pulled it open.

The building was just a concrete shell. Several fires burned on the remains of the tiled floor. Groups of men stood clustered around the fires, drinking and laughing. They were dressed in brown ragged cloaks, as if part of a tribe of desert nomads. Against the far wall, just beyond the largest fire of all, the flickering light revealed a sight that made Paul reel.

On a long wooden pole attached to the wall, several bodies hung by their feet. They were naked, and each one had been slit from waist to chin. Beneath their heads the ground was caked with dry brown blood. Paul stumbled back against the door, which banged against the wall and startled the men before him to attention.

Uncut

There were cries of delight around the gutted room, and several of the men rushed forward to seize Paul's arms. Two of them pulled his flight bag away and tore it open, as the others propelled him across the floor towards the far wall. It was then that Paul noticed that the brown cloaks worn by the tribe members were made of human skin.

One of the tribe, a large, grinning man with gold teeth, revealed a long, hooked knife in his waistband. As Paul shouted, the men holding him ripped the shirt from his back and threw him to the floor.

Before him, painted on the wall ahead, was a huge blue square, a grand version of the sticker attached to his plane ticket. It depicted a man not carrying another on his shoulders but someone donning the complete skin of another human being. The man with the gold teeth advanced towards Paul with the glittering culling knife in his hand.

'Why?' screamed Paul. 'Why me?'

Gold-Teeth leaned forward until Paul's sweat-sheened face was right beneath him.

'Your airline owes us for our land,' he hissed, then turned and called to the elders of the tribe. 'See! Nice blond boy, soft white skin make very special coat!' Gold-Teeth smiled spectacularly and nodded to the men surrounding Paul. They fell on him as the elders started the bidding.

They never did figure out what the Walkman was for.

The Unreliable History of Plaster City

When Otis Dagg decided to swat blackflies from the wall of his motel room he shouldn't have used the butt of a loaded twelve-bore shotgun, because the damned thing went off and some of the pellets perforated the plasterboard room divider, rupturing the left eardrum of the woman next door. Her name was Betty Segal, and she'd been resting her head against the wall watching a game show, trying to think of a six-letter country beginning with *M* and waiting to see who'd won two weeks of amoebic dysentery in Mexico, when suddenly she found herself smothered in specks of blood, and buzzing in the ears like a nest of pissed-off hornets had been tipped over her head.

It took Betty a while to figure out what had happened, but when she finally did she went even crazier, physically attacking poor confused Otis, who was still casting puzzled glances from the end of his gun to the ragged hole in the wall when she burst screaming into his room like a Valkyrie in a nylon housecoat. She managed to bite him on the face a couple of times before one of the porters pulled her off, and later successfully sued his ass in a brief but embarrassingly ugly court case.

Naturally, Otis didn't have too much to lose – he wouldn't have been staying in a joint called the Forty Winks Motor Lodge if he had – but he skipped town at the first available opportunity just to get away from the Neanderthal brothers of the woman he had rendered deaf, both of whom looked like members of the World Wrestling Foundation and had threatened to tear his arms off if he failed to meet his payments. Since Otis Dagg didn't hang around long enough to cough up any compensation money, the court took away the only piece of property he owned, a small clapboard building with a collapsed front porch that stood at a crossroads in the industrial end of a small town called Plaster City, 217 miles from Los Angeles, and they granted the deeds to Betty Segal.

Betty had spent all her adult life in a trailer park and the prospect of living in something that didn't have wheels appealed to her, so she moved in. She passed her time happily there, leaning out of the slanting porch window to watch the trucks roar by, and eventually compounded this pleasure by finding a man uglier, deafer and richer than herself to marry. Tony Marco sponsored the local basketball team and made his money in the furniture trade, so when he rebuilt the old Dagg property he turned it into the only furniture store in the area that had a full-sized basketball court in the car park. The parents of the players attending Plaster City Junior High could often be seen leaving after a game with armoires and dining chairs loaded into their station wagons, and pretty soon the old store sold anything you could name, provided there was a demand for the item and it could be turned around for a profit.

And so it was that, twenty-two years later, after a spectacular vein-ripping heart attack had slam-dunked Tony

Marco out of life's final quarter, his widow took to her room above the store and left the daily running of her business in the hands of an experienced manager who had recently relocated from San Diego.

The manger was a tall, stooped man with narrow eyes and an uncomfortably furtive attitude that made his customers think he was in the Witness Protection Programme. His name was Taylor Hollings.

By this time the property sported a large red and yellow plastic sign reading VALURAMA, which sounded more like a Hindu god than a discount furniture store, and until 1987 it functioned as the Plaster City equivalent of a shopping mall. Extensions had been added to the front and back in violation of every known zoning law, which was okay because the councillors all shopped at Taylor's store and knew that if they complained about what he was doing with the property he'd accidentally cease to stock their favourite monthly magazines. Business was good and life went on, most of it bypassing Plaster City completely and barely bothering to call in at any other town before hitting the West Coast.

Taylor met a widow called Barbara Stokely, who was driving through in a beat-up Oldsmobile Cutlass one summer and made the mistake of stopping for gas and directions. Something in the store window caught her eye, Taylor probably, and she married him and pretty soon had three kids, Big Joey, David, and, with a sigh of relief, Julie. Shortly after this her biological clock threw a cog and she became tranquilliser-dependent. But in the meantime there were golden years, while her three children grew up in and around the old store.

To an impressionable youngster the place was a spidery Xanadu, filled with corridors that led nowhere and storerooms full of forgotten end-of-line items, stuff that didn't sell and hadn't been returned. Behind the stacked boudoir chairs and plastic-covered vanity bureaux were all manner of hidden delights: X-ray goggles, Aurora model kits and packets of dried sea monkeys, BB guns and useless boxes of magnets, Hallowe'en masks, back issues of *Aquaman* and *Famous Monsters Of Filmland*, and giant weather balloons that no one knew how to inflate. The building even provided its own scary monster in the form of old Mrs Marco, still deaf, still crazy and still living in the room at the top of the house. Barbara fed her and changed the bed, and the children took turns to visit her in the evenings, but the room smelled of piss and lavender and she never did anything except complain about the weather and how terrible the TV shows were and what a lousy hand life had dealt her, so going upstairs to see her became something of a reverse lottery.

David Hollings used the make-believe possibilities of the furniture store more than anyone else in the family. Although he hero worshipped his older brother, Big Joey was practical and unimaginative and spent his spare time helping their father with deliveries, and Julie was an asthmatic china doll who wasn't allowed to play near dust, which ruled out all of the downstairs storerooms.

It was a lucky thing David enjoyed staging complex battles in the labyrinthine depository, as Plaster City had little else to offer a hyperactive child. It wasn't a proper country town with a summer creek you could jump into from a rope and winter hills designed for tobogganing. The only river ran past a factory that made rubber grommets for faucets, and nothing with a central nervous system could survive in it for long. There was a large, perpetually arid park, mainly used by Mexican families for barbeques, and a lookout point that didn't look out over anything and should have been renamed

Drop Point, considering the amount of dope that changed hands out there. This was where most of the town's kids went to lose their virginity, and on Sunday mornings the grass around the car park was slick with knotted condoms.

More than anything Plaster City was like a suburb, but there was no nearby metropolis to which it could attach itself. For many years the nearest place with a population of over five thousand was Bakersfield, and that was a damned long way off. Every August, choking grey dust blew in from the distant fields, and the furniture store became Flies-R-Us. Every January, shiny new snowploughs came out to clear the streets, only to return to their garages when the powder failed to settle. Still, there was always religion to keep idle souls occupied. Plaster City was a Baptist town with a vengeance. It seemed like there were more churches than any other kind of building and twice as many preachers as believers. Everyone could offer an explanation for the extreme zeal of the religious community, but no two explanations were the same. Some said the area had once been designated a holy ground, but if there was any evidence of this, it had long since been covered over.

At some point in the early eighties the main street became notably more prosperous as the chain stores moved in and VALURAMA became as anachronistic as a tram token, a twilight zone of a store, in which you half expected to find old geezers playing checkers on a cracker barrel, now stranded between a pair of mammoth glass and chrome retail outlets staffed by relocated New Yorkers.

Those were the bad years, when the old customers died and moved away, and business dried up like a high-season river bed. Taylor lost weight and developed a peptic ulcer. Barbara cried all the time. The store seemed to shrink in the shadow of its competition, and the children, now teenagers, grew claustrophobic and trapped and angry with each other.

Two days after his eighteenth birthday, David left home, but he didn't leave town. Los Angeles was just too big a jump and there was nothing much else on either side of the freeway to interest him so he stayed on, renting an apartment with an old schoolfriend over near the freight yard on the other side of town. He told himself that he hated the idea of not being near his brother, and Julie needed him to help her out with homework. But he also knew the truth, which was that he felt safe here, in a place he understood, in a town that underpinned his life.

By this time, Plaster City was in danger of turning into a real one. It was nearly ready to be designated one of the new edge cities, racially integrated and classless, vaguely liberal, slowly replacing its farm hands with computer punchers. Property developers built a kind of yuppie Olympic village called Greymeadow at the edge of town, and then came a mall that had Tower Records and Sharper Image and Radio Shack and an ice rink and soon the main street began to look just like everywhere else. David was nineteen years old and working in his father's store when his life arrived at its purpose and conclusion.

The most famous thing about Plaster City is that Ethel Merman once made a phonecall from there when her car broke down. She probably couldn't get out of town fast enough. Back in the sixties there was nothing to see but a main street composed of the usual mix, dry-cleaner's, food store, garage, diner, and rows of neat ranch-style houses with carports, yapping hounds and lawn sprinklers. On the road out of town a crazy old guy called Elmer Boricswyn had spent his retirement years building the House Of Mud, a grotesque clay outhouse studded with thousands of crimped bottle tops that he charged people two bucks each to photograph. According to Elmer, whose conversational English was exactly like that of Mr Rogers, it was the only one of its kind in the entire state. When you saw it, you had to ask yourself if you were entirely surprised.

The nearest thing Plaster City had to a nightclub was the Hot Spot, a joint appropriately situated down by the coach station in an area that boasted a lone Catholic mission run by Mexican nuns, an old wino called Stick who lived in an abandoned dumpster and spent his days outside the truck depot telling people he could talk to the devil, a couple of seventies time-warp topless bars, one of which was actually, honest to God, called the Boom-Boom Room, and a single adult book store populated by perspiring kids with poorly forged IDs.

The neon sign outside the Hot Spot showed the profile of a woman poised with a phallic cigarette holder, and the name of the place uncurled as if she'd just blown it out in a puff of smoke – real sophisticated stuff. David had been there a couple of times with his roommate. Brett wasn't a very social guy. He spent most of his time watching uncut horror videos and hardly ever went out, except to go to the Safeway for beer and to hide when his creepy mother came by to leave him some money and see if he was okay. David had never been invited into his room, which was fine because he probably had a dead body in there or something. Brett was kind of involved in a romantic relationship. He dated a tiny blond girl with a squeaky voice who lived outside Phoenix on the Gila Bend Indian Reservation, where she was studying anthropology, and as the Colorado Desert stood between her and Plaster City they didn't get to see a whole lot of each other.

Thinking about it later that night, David was careful to recall every detail of that freezing Saturday in late October. It was a couple of weeks before the bad weather settled in, and he and Brett had been drinking in a fake Western bar called the Twisted Wheel over on Third and University (typically there was no university on University, just like there was no plaster industry and it wasn't a city). The Just Say No To Alcohol campaign hadn't made its mark in town – everyone was still slamming the stuff back as though the end of the world had been scheduled for a midweek appearance. The two young men recognised everyone's faces in the Twisted Wheel and, worse still, were recognised in turn, so they decided to head over to the Hot Spot, where there might just be someone from out of town on the dance floor.

Brett was a year older and a foot taller than David, with the burnished complexion you get from using too much spot cleanser and the kind of thin sandy hair that leaves you semi-bald by the age of twenty-five. He could always be spotted across a crowded bar because his wardrobe consisted of fluorescent tour shirts advertising bands he had never heard of, let alone seen. He worked for a company that made portable office partitions, so if you rented floor space and didn't want to sit looking at the guy next to you, you'd call up Brett and someone would come and construct these chipboard dividers to cut you off. The company motto was something like 'Integrated Wall Systems For A Divided Environment', but only David could see the sad side of it.

It began with a tingling in the pit of his stomach, the kind of feeling you get when you realise you're about to have a terrible fight with someone. Brett had gone ahead, and he was left walking alone towards the club, a low brick building blocking off the end of the road. It had been built away from residential properties so that they could keep the music cranked up until 2 am without getting complaints. The night winds were wild, thumping at the ground in smudges of dust, and the neon flickered through the trees, tall beaten pines with top branches that thrashed in the turbulent darkness and sounded like TV static. For a moment it seemed that someone was following him. David stopped and turned around, half expecting to find something dark and heavy descending from the sky, but there was nothing to be seen. The highway was deserted for miles. It was a clear night, and a chain of cross-street lights wound all the way across town, swinging green bulbs that made it look as if the earth was moving.

Every Saturday the club found an excuse to have some kind of theme party, and tonight's was billed as 'erotica', presumably because the DJ remembered that Madonna had once chosen the title for an album. In the car park, among the chopped hogs and tinted-glass RVs, there were plenty of new Datsuns and Mazdas, a sure sign that the Greymeadow yups had ventured over for the evening. The building's entrance corridor was designed like a space-shuttle ramp, a reminder of the club's previous incarnation as a Trekkie hangout called the Final Frontier Disco. David caught up with Brett and they paid ten bucks apiece, for which they were each given an indelible-ink hand stamp and a drink ticket.

They never had much to say to each other. Like a lot of the people in town, Brett wore an expression of perpetual dissatisfaction, because he was pissed off with his job, his folks and his life but didn't seem capable of changing anything. Although he was technically an executive he wasn't a business graduate and was aware that he had no real skills or qualifications. He'd once considered moving away, until he realised that the money he'd make in San Francisco or Los

Angeles wouldn't leave him enough for an apartment, so why swap a solid, predictable existence for a set of unknowns? Plaster City had become enough of an urban area to stop them from feeling like hayseeds. There was a mall and a multiplex; it wasn't like they were homeboys or anything and yet – there were those who left. Guys you went to school with who couldn't wait to get out, girls whose idea of heaven was Plaster City in their rear-view mirror. Sometimes David envied them, in the summer when the store was empty and the streets were hot and still, and there was only enough air to breathe if you stirred it yourself. Other times he was happy in the knowledge that his life was unlikely to hold many surprises, either good or bad ones.

David could see his roommate on the other side of the dance floor with a girl called Kathy who sold condos on the Greymeadow estate. She dressed like an anchorperson, pastel suits and big bold earrings, and drank spritzers with a bunch of man-hungry women in property sales, and he was surprised to see the two of them talking.

The main dance area was illuminated by a large rotating silver light bank, another remnant of the building's former Star Trek theme, and crimson velveteen banquettes were arranged in horseshoes all the way around the room. At one time the place must have been a movie house because there was still a stage area separated by heavy black drapes, from which the heady aroma of dope billowed constantly.

The guys David and his brother had gone to school with still came here at the weekend because this was the closest they could find to any place fashionable or disreputable. Just lately, some of the girls from Greymeadow had been spotted slumming, mainly because the promised Greymeadow Leisure Center never got built and there was nowhere else for them to go at night. There were also the ageing Lotharios, overtanned men in silk shirts and cream suits, Wayne Newton lookalikes who shot each other finger .45s and drank bourbon like it was tap water. The music wanted to be West Coast fresh but was a little too far from LA to stay current, so the DJs opted for a loud nondescript techno drone with a bass beat you could feel pulsing in your belt buckle.

David checked his watch and made it nearly midnight. On the suspended screens above him were endless MTV clips and Nike ads. The place was full but uninteresting, as if everyone wanted a good time but couldn't be bothered to help create it. Brett came over and stood nearby, something he usually did when he'd run out of drink money.

'What's the deal with Kathy?' asked David. 'I didn't know you guys even knew each other.'

'It's nothing.' Brett dismissed the idea and held his friend's beer up between two fingers to see how long he would have to wait before David offered to buy him one. 'All she ever talks about is real estate, like she's had a character bypass or something.'

'Maybe she's offering you a piece of her property.'

'Hey, I'm not proud,' Brett admitted with a shrug. 'I'd take her up on the offer. It's your turn to go to the bar.'

'It's always my turn.' David pulled a squashed ten from his pocket and stuck it in Brett's hand. 'You go.'

The music had become a series of modulated thuds offering no hint of a tune. David walked towards the dance floor and studied the stage beyond. The black velvet drapes were slowly undulating back and forth. It looked like the wall was gently tipping, as though they were all on board a ship. A sharp tingling ran across the ends of his fingers, and tiny, painfully bright lights speckled the edges of his vision, causing the room to shift. In the middle of so much movement he felt more than mere alarm. He was suddenly disturbed that he was alone. No one else seemed to notice him. Perhaps they could no longer see him. It was as if for a moment he had slipped into an entirely new realm of existence. Then, as quickly as it had appeared, the tingling and the lights receded. The music, the cigarette smoke and the fake painted-marble walls of the Hop Spot closed in around him once more.

When Brett returned with the beers David asked, 'Did you feel anything just now?' and Brett just screwed up his face.

'What, you mean like an earth tremor or something?' After all, the town was near a couple of dormant fault lines.

'No, it was more . . . I don't know. Something shifted.' David shook his head and squinted around, hoping to see some remaining effect.

'You sure you didn't smoke a joint before you came out?' To Brett, getting stoned could explain most of life's confusions.

'You know that stuff makes me sick. This was – different. Skip it.'

He stayed watching the dancers for a while, but the evening's experience had unsettled him, and he soon decided to leave. Brett was nowhere to be seen, so he walked back to his car alone. He rounded the mud-splashed hood of the old blue Chrysler, and his heart thudded hard in his chest as a figure lolled forward from the shadows.

'Jesus, Stick, you nearly gave me a fuckin' heart attack. Ain't you in the wrong end of town?'

The old tramp thought for a moment, then remembered. 'I just heard the news. You best get back to your daddy's store, boy, an' be quick about it.' Stick heard voices all the time. They were always telling him to warn people about the devil's return to earth, or some damned thing. Stick was mostly harmless. People liked him and often left food packages by his dumpster.

David checked his pockets for the car keys, making conversation. 'Why, what's happening this time?'

'Bad things comin', the worse you ever saw. Worse since – since – hell, I can't remember when.' That wasn't surprising. Stick couldn't remember anything, not even where he lived.

'You've been drinking, haven't you, Stick? My pa leave you out a little drop of whisky tonight?'

The old man threw his hands wide and nearly fell backwards into the rustling hedgerow. 'No, I swear! It's the people from inside the ground, coming to take back the town. Didn't you feel 'em arriving a few minutes ago? I sure as hell did.'

David stopped halfway into his car and stared back at Stick, who was trying to look as serious as a man could be wearing a floor-length raincoat and a back-to-front truck cap.

'I felt something, yeah. You're trying to tell me that was a train coming in?'

'Jeez, you think these people travel by train? They don't catch no trains, and they don't *drive* here neither! They just – just –' he gestured drunkenly at the night sky, 'open up th' air and step through. That's what you felt. The air tearing open to let 'em in.'

'I thought you just said they lived in the ground.'

'They do – that is, that's where we nailed 'em. Jest ask your daddy if you don' believe me!'

This had gone far enough. David climbed into the car and tried to close the door, but the old man moved with surprising agility, catching him by the wrist. 'You get back to your store, boy, an' you look after your family. They're gonna try and take down Plaster City tonight, you just watch an' see!'

He'd seen Stick drunk plenty of times before, but the wino's urgency was beginning to rattle him. 'Why would anyone want to take over Plaster City?' he asked, pulling the car door shut. 'There's nothing here worth having.'

'I didn't say take it over, I said take it down – down into the ground. Plaster City's time just ran out. Tonight we're all gonna burn in hell!'

The engine turned over first time. David gently edged the Chrysler forward around Stick, who was twisting his head into the wind, listening. David knew he had to ask as he passed.

'Why, Stick? If that's gonna happen, why this town? There's plenty of other crummy places this side of the state line that no one would ever miss.'

'Talk to your old man 'bout what they're doing here – he knows the reason good enough. And so does that old deaf bitch your ma takes care of.' As David pulled away into the road, Stick stumbled after him. 'Ask Taylor about the spike! But you'd better do it quick 'cause I hear 'em coming, right around the next hill!'

David cruised up through the speed limit as he hit the empty highway. Behind him the stars were blotted out by the encroaching black outline of the hillside. He could feel it now, the change in air density, the faint humming that didn't come from the telephone wires. Something had been displaced. A coldness spread across his chest, filling him with panic. Something terrible really was coming; he could feel it inside himself – and outside the car.

The crosswinds were whipping his radio antenna so much he couldn't get a fix on any station, not even WX-GOD, the twenty-four-hour evangelical hotline run by the indefatigable Reverend Lowe, who tub-thumped the coming battle with

Satan night and day, interspersing his sermons with depressing country and western songs no one had ever heard of. David hit the Plastic City turnoff at forty plus, wheels barely locking on the dirt-covered shoulder. Sloping away in the distance, the town looked as if everyone in it had died or simply vanished. Only the swinging green lights gave any suggestion of life.

He reached the crossroads where the fitful buzzing of the VALURAMA sign had drawn him home, the only light in a row of glass and concrete boxes, and wondered what he was going to tell his parents once he had managed to wake them. He hadn't brought his keys to the store, and the front bell hadn't worked for years.

The problem of entry was solved when he saw the flashlight skittering through the ground-floor windows. Either his father was still up or the place was being burgled. He pulled into the customer car park and turned off the engine, vaulting the door and running lightly past the faded backboard of the basketball court. As his trainers touched the ground the soles grew warm, as if the earth itself was changing. Beside a low hedge he saw a body sprawled face down on the concrete. The fawn pants and navy-blue shirt identified him as one of the sheriff's men. A black pool of blood several feet long blossomed from his crushed head. Fighting his fear, David ran on. The porch steps groaned as he climbed them, but the sound was lost in the rising wind. Taylor was moving around inside the store, but he hadn't turned on the overhead panel lights. David pushed against the front door, and it swung open to his touch. As he entered, the smell of fresh wood and packing cardboard brought back a thousand childhood memories. His father was standing at the rear of the room, by the entrance of the depository, his torch beam slowly traversing the floor.

'Dad?' he called softly. 'What the hell is going on? There's somebody dead outside.'

'David? That you?' The beam came up into his face, forcing him to shield his eyes. 'You shouldn't be here, son.' He knew. David could hear it in his voice. He knew what was going to happen to the town. 'Close that door quick and come over here.'

David obeyed the command and joined his father. Taylor looked wearier than he had ever seen him before. He swung the torch beam back and forth as if looking for something but not knowing where to begin.

'What's going to happen to us?' David studied his father's face. Taylor was anxious to talk to someone, even if he would have preferred it not to be his son.

'That kind of depends how much you believe, David.' He flicked his hand nervously across his forehead. 'But you can feel the bad energy, can't you?'

'Sure, it's coming from outside, like it's in the air or under the ground or something. You feel it?'

'Yeah, and I guess a lot of other folks do too, but they're staying indoors, too frightened to come out into the street. I got through to the sheriff's department, told them they're a man down. Last call I managed before the lines went dead.'

'I came past there a few minutes ago. The place is dark.'

'Listen, you can see for yourself something terrible is goin' on, David. They're gonna take Plaster City back, unless we can stop them.'

'Who? No one can take a whole town anywhere.'

'Listen to me.' Taylor pulled him over the step of the depository. 'I would never involve you in anything dangerous, you know that. But I need your help.'

'Just tell me what to do and I'll do it.'

Taylor pointed back at the stairs to the first floor. 'Go on up and look after the women. The wind is frightenin' them. Keep 'em away from the windows.'

'I want to be down here with you. What are you doing?'

'I don't suppose you'd believe me if I told you. Now go on upstairs.'

David wasn't happy about it, but obeyed his father. Deaf old Betty Marco had been brought down to the lounge that overlooked the main street. Julie was sitting motionless with her feet pulled up under her, watching TV from behind a stack of cushions. His mother came from the kitchen and threw her arms around him.

'David, I've been so worried. The lines are down. I couldn't get through to you or your brother.'

There was no point in telling her what had already happened. He prayed she wouldn't see the shattered body lying at the rear of the house. 'I haven't heard from Joey,' he admitted. 'Everyone else okay?'

'Julie's acting strangely. She hasn't said a word for the past hour. Nobody knows what's happening. Taylor won't tell me anything. I looked out of the window a few minutes ago and you know what I saw? Rats! Thousands of them, like a brown carpet, running across the highway. Do you suppose there's an electrical storm coming? Aren't animals able to sense these things first?'

Behind them, the television signal fuzzed and flared, the picture alternately glowing and dying.

'I don't know, Ma. Dad says Mrs Marco can explain all this.'

His mother was fretfully twisting a dishcloth around her hand. He had never seen her looking so frightened. 'What could he mean?' she asked, confused. 'She talks all the time but she never makes any sense, hasn't done for years.'

'Let me try.' David walked across the room and knelt before the old woman. She had been staring out of the window, listening to the rising wind just as Stick had done, but as she turned he sensed a sharp intelligence behind the cold blue eyes that watched him. Slowly, she reached down a thin, freckled hand and slipped it into her bed jacket, twisting a dial, raising the volume of her hearing aid. Her deafness varied according to what she was prepared to hear.

'You know what happened, don't you, Mrs Marco?' Either she had told his father, or it was something Taylor already knew about.

'Nobody ever listens to me,' Betty Marco began, clearly relishing the notion of being in demand. 'Nobody ever wants to hear what I have to say.'

'I do, Mrs Marco, I want to hear. Tell me.'

Her hand snaked out and seized his shoulder, pulling him closer. 'Then you better listen good,' she said. 'I'll tell you what I told your pa long ago, see if you believe me any more than he did then. It was back in the nineteen twenties. A government brush clearance scheme uncovered a settlement out here at the crossroads. Wasn't much left of it, just a few old bits and pieces, rags and bones and burned rocks. Archaeological value, they said. The town was tiny then, barely more than a few shacks. The local people examined the site and decided that the settlers were bad. They'd been without religion – or perhaps they'd chosen to follow some older religion of their own. Early settlers was free to choose back then. It wasn't all damned Baptists, like now. Anyway, there was artifacts, unholy symbols, and weapons, like the stuff you'd use for animal sacrifice. I don't know what else. But the settlers had claimed the area for themselves.'

'What happened to them?'

'I have no idea – I guess nobody will ever know. Maybe they drove out, maybe they just died off. All that was left was these signs that they'd once occupied the site for a while. Perhaps they moved on, further west.'

'I don't understand, what has this to—'

'Just mark what I'm saying.' She raised her head for a moment and listened. Outside the wind was growing again, hammering the window frames. From behind her fortress of cushions, Julie released a squeak of terror.

'The townspeople was all God-fearing Baptists, so they covered up the site and acted like it had never been there. They couldn't have pagan worshippers laying claim to their town, this was where they was going to raise their kids an' build their churches, so they plastered over the remains of the settlement, then later they concreted it into the highway.'

'What happened to the artifacts?'

'Maybe they found their way to museums, who knows? Problem was, the Baptists couldn't reconsecrate the site. They didn't know how to go about doing such a thing, so they came up with a special service of their own. They held a big prayer meetin', and then they hammered a spike into the freshly covered ground, right in the centre of the settlers' camp. It was a foot-long iron spike like the ones the railroads drove into the land to break new territory. On its flat head they engraved the whole of the Lord's Prayer, and they surrounded it with holy symbols. I guess everyone forgot about the site after that. The thing was barely noticeable, and as it weren't near any big roads, no one had reason to go by it. Wasn't until the fifties, just before the highway department was due to lay the new interstate, someone came and stole it, dug the blasted thing right out of the ground. Just think, all that time it'd been in the soil, holding back trouble and protecting the town. It was dug up by Otis Dagg's no-good father who thought it might be worth somethin'. He tore it out of the site and damned us all.' She pointed up at the ceiling, illuminating cracked plaster as pale as bone. 'I been up there all this time. I watched from my window and seen the changes in this place as it went from good to wicked, and I knew about the spike 'cause Otis inherited it when his pa died. I tried to tell people that the town started goin' bad the day the spike was pulled, but nobody believed me. They just carried on buildin' their fancy homes.'

'That's crazy,' David whispered, but even as he spoke he acknowledged the truth.

'I know it's true,' the old lady was saying, 'because the spike is right here, down in the storeroom, where it's been for the past forty years.'

Now he remembered seeing the spike as a kid, even recalled turning it over in his hands. It lay somewhere in the back of the store, among the hundreds of boxes of toys and tools, just another childhood plaything.

'But why tonight?' he asked. 'Why would they return after all this time?'

'They been waiting to gather their strength, until they was strong enough to take the whole town back in one go.'

'And you believe all this?'

She narrowed her ice-blue eyes at him. 'Don't you?'

David took the stairs two at a time, reaching the depository just as a cry from outside brought his father running to the windows. He could see his roommate's Camaro parked outside, at a sharp angle to the road. Then he caught sight of Brett himself, spinning and shoving at something formless as his coat was pulled up about him and the wind plucked at his legs. He was trying to reach the front of the store but was being pushed back, shoved and grabbed at until he screamed and lashed at the swirling darkness in the air. There were slashes of blood across his face and chest. As David ran towards the door, passing the scene from window to window, he saw the boy outside lifted from the ground, pulled and stretched and finally ripped in half by figures barely visible in the raging turbulence.

'We have to find the spike and put it back in place,' he shouted to his father.

Together they tore the cluttered old depository apart. On the floor above them, David's mother forced a chair against the door that led down to the store and fearfully waited with her daughter and the old woman.

The task ahead of them seemed hopeless. There was no way of knowing where the spike could be. They heaved aside spider-filled cases of linen and crockery, gate-leg tables and tea chests smothered with termite eggs, decades of untouched bric-à-brac. David wanted to call his brother, but with the telephone lines dead there was no way of contacting him. He forced himself to think, to try and remember those rainy afternoons passed in the back of the store, playing complex solitary games of make believe – cowboys and spacemen, firemen and sheriffs, werewolves and vamp—

Dracula.

He had always used the spike for Dracula. It looked just like a stake, and it had religious stuff all over the head. Christ, he hadn't thought about the horror games for years and now here were the memories as vivid as the fantasy had once been, waiting to be dusted off and relived. He set off through the maze of furniture, sure of himself.

'Give me a hand with this.' Thousands of issues of

National Geographic, standing in stacks and glued together with mildew. They weighed a ton. Behind them were dozens of hat stands, clumped together like a winter forest. And at the foot of these was a box, a big old tea chest filled with black curtains – vampire cloaks – that had stood in for a coffin until he had grown too tall to fit it any more. The spike still lay there, wrapped in rotting folds of fabric. Although the years had tarnished it, the Lord's Prayer was still completely legible. Perhaps that was why these pioneer spirits or whatever the hell they were hadn't returned earlier to take the town. The spike had been removed from the site, but it was still here at the crossroads, still protecting, even if it only retained a fraction of its power after being uprooted. He lifted it in his right hand, slowly rotating its octagonal stem, and could feel the angry winds suddenly changing direction around the house, as though the ancient settlers could sense that this most hated of religious artifacts had been rediscovered.

'We have to return this to the settlement fast,' said Taylor, shining his torch down into the crate. 'I don't like the sound the timbers are making.'

'It's all highway out there now,' said David. 'How are we gonna find the right spot?'

'We've got the co-ordinates,' his father replied. 'They blacktopped the crossroads over the exact centre of the site. We just have to follow the centre lines.'

In the front of the store they found a pair of heavy steel sledgehammers. Taylor waited for a moment, thinking, then ran back into the depository. He returned with a handful of cheap Mexican-gold crucifixes and threw some to David, who slipped them over his head.

'I don't know if this'll make much of a difference, but it

might keep them away long enough to reach the site. I mean, if the Lord's prayer has such a strong effect.'

The crossroads were a good hundred-and-fifty-yard sprint from the store. Between the porch and their goal, David could make out several hunched black figures picking at the remains of his butchered roommate.

'The longer we leave it, the worse it's gonna get,' said Taylor, pulling open the front door. Instantly, the air was filled with the shrill squealing of the dead. Father and son ran out into the storm, the wind almost lifting them from their feet. They had barely descended the steps and reached the forecourt before the dark creatures fell about them in a fast-closing ring. Instantly, David could see that they had no chance of reaching their destination before being brought down. The things were scuttling towards them on blackened spindles, their fleshless arms pumping back and forth as they flexed and clasped their fingers. They moved at great speed, like clustering insects. David skidded to a halt as he realised the path ahead was already blocked. Taylor was behind him, preparing to swing the mallet as the first of the settlers approached.

Just as the ring seemed about to collapse on top of them, a shaft of bright light fell across the ground and the circle suddenly widened amidst much hissing and crying. David looked back at the house, where Mrs Marco and his mother had turned on the lights of the main store, the first floor and the attic. Thank God his mother had followed his lead and had finally listened to the old woman; the illuminated rooms formed a perfect cross. Seizing their chance, David and his father ran upwards along the lengthy path of light to the top of the crucifix, then on into renewed darkness and the hard tarmac of the highway.

David knew they had only a matter of seconds to spare. Out of the protecting light, they were prey once more to the rallying creatures. His trainers pounded along the central markers leading to the crossroads. Taylor arrived moments after, wheezing badly. He fell on his knees at the spot, barely able to catch his breath.

'Give me the spike.' Taylor held out his hand. 'I'm stronger than you.'

Together they set the tip of the iron rod at the exact point where the road lines crossed. David steadied it as Taylor raised his mallet for the first blow. Behind his father, one of the creatures was already dropping down to attack. He threw his own mallet at the figure with all the strength he could muster. The steel head smashed through its skull as if the bone was just a shell, like the head of a burned match. Taylor slammed his hammer down on the spike, sinking it two inches into the tarmac. The noise around them became insane, a ranging storm of death.

David gripped the spike as his father swung again. The blow connected, thrusting it deeper into the blacktop. Taylor had raised the shaft for a third time when the creatures reached out their melanistic arms and grabbed him, wrenching his head back until the neck broke with a sound that could be heard above the maelstrom. David screamed into the gale, starting towards his fallen father, but the malformed spirits dragged the body back and fell upon it in a frenzy. Grabbing the fallen mallet, David swung at the spike again and again, hammering it deep into the crossroads until the head was flush with the surrounding tarmac surface.

Sweating, he fell back onto the highway and dropped the sledgehammer. The banshee shrieks that had accompanied the first of the blows had died away now. The worst was over.

He raised his face to the night sky and felt the wind in his hair as it began to lessen.

And rise again.

Puzzled, he looked back at the highway. His father's body lay eviscerated and ignored as the pagan spirits now advanced on him in a ragged line, stalking forward like shore crabs avoiding the surf. He crawled back to the glistening stud set in the highway and examined it as the air pulsed in a wild roar, and the rocks themselves were unanchored from the surrounding hillside.

In his determination to slam the spike back in place, he had completely flattened its head with the mallet, obliterating the protective prayer. Instead of revealing a statement of faith, the smooth, shiny surface of the spike blankly reflected an idolatrous moon.

In the moments that followed, David's short life shifted before his eyes, the events of the night recurring as if they had taken place an age ago. He cried now, unleashing his anger in a wail of sorrow not for himself but for his family and the terrified, helpless inhabitants of a town about to be reclaimed by an apostate enemy in the eternal war of the gods.

WELCOME TO PLASTER CITY says the twisted tin sign, but there's no town to be seen any more, just dusty brush and broken concrete, summer scorpions and flies. Stray from the highway, though, and you'll catch a glimpse of something that once existed, the bleached awning of a corner store, a shattered backboard from a basketball court, a piece of kerbstone, now the rubble of history. Who knows what terrors the inhabitants of Plaster City endured that night? None who saw the tragedy remain alive to tell.

These days the nearest town is Greymeadow, smart and

fashionable, growing fast, sporting a finally completed leisure centre, one of the finest golf courses in the country, and churches – you never saw so many churches. Although Greymeadow is becoming increasingly popular with god-fearing young families, they would do well to examine the ruined site five miles down the road and learn from the mistakes of their old neighbours.

They should find a way to plug the fissure and seal off the pagan terrors of the past. Because Greymeadow will soon be crossing city limits, to where an unforgiving hunger waits. And the acolytes of a disrespectful god will once again appear in Plaster City.

Jouissance de la Mort

It was a cool unmisted morning in the rich green fields beyond Rennes. Swallows filled the trees above the Château Saint Vincent as M. Jean-Luc Condorcet set off through the loamy pasture towards his herd. He preferred being in the open air; the château's atmosphere was damp and unhealthy. For decades the building had been shunned by those villagers old enough to remember the Condorcet family's dissolute flirtations with Satanism. M. Jean-Luc was the last surviving member and preferred the bucolic delights of animal husbandry to the arcane interests of his forebears.

The farmer paused and listened; a distant aircraft. An unusual sound in this area. No commercial flights passed overhead. Several cows looked up as the engine noise grew. He searched the sky and glimpsed the tiny silver plane, a customised private Lear jet, banking above a crest of white cloud. The aircraft had been chartered to bear a dance band from Carcasonne to its first public appearance in Nice. Thanks to a leaking fuel lead and a drummer who insisted on smoking in the toilet, they never reached their destination. The plane exploded in midair.

After the bang there was a shocked silence. Everything was

still. A black ball of smoke and debris hung motionless in the sky. Then M. Condorcet was hit on the head by a falling cocktail cabinet with chromium legs and gold glass doors. One of his cows was knocked unconscious by a trombone. A bottle of Remy Martin demolished the henhouse, and two chickens were impaled by drumsticks.

M. Condorcet was in such a terrible mess that they had to cremate him. His staff consulted an ancient family manual, then inscribed four lines from a poem, the first of which was '*Les mouches bourdonnaient sur ce ventre putride*', on the side of the brass urn containing his ashes. Unsure what to do next, they parcel-posted him to the surviving member of his family, an English aunt living alone in a flat in Bayswater.

Elizabeth Fritton had been dismissed by the education board after losing a child on the Northern Line, and the incident had destroyed her life. She and another teacher had set out with a crocodile of pupils heading for an exhibition of molluscs at London Zoo but had disembarked the train to find themselves one short. Extensive searches were made in the tunnels, but no explanation for the disappearance was ever uncovered, and Miss Fritton assumed that the boy must have drawn the attention of a molester, who had stolen the lad away when her back was turned. The police found a French essay book inscribed with the lad's name on the tracks at Camden Town tube station and returned it to the school, whereupon it fell into Miss Fritton's possession. On the last page was part of a poem that began '*Les mouches bourdonnaient sur ce ventre putride*'.

Miss Fritton had not seen her nephew for some years and received nothing in his will, the château being sold to cover debts. What little monies remained from the sale of the property fell to the staff in descending order of loyalty.

When the urn arrived she set it upon the mantelpiece in her sitting room, where it gathered dust for several months and became stuck to the paintwork. Miss Fritton had few acquaintances and fewer visitors. The only woman she permitted within her fringed baroque apartment was an impoverished family friend named Maria Brown, who was Antiguan by birth and longed to return there. Kindly Maria convinced the whey-faced ex-schoolmistress that she should get out more and cajoled her into visiting the seaside one August Bank Holiday.

The morning of their departure, Miss Fritton tried to move the urn but found it stuck fast. Finally she was forced to use a chisel to release it from the paint.

Bedecked in postcards and candyfloss, Miss Fritton strode the seafront and found herself having fun for the first time in years. She even suggested that the two of them should relive a childhood memory and ride the switchback. Unfortunately, the switchback operator had temporarily left the attraction in the hands of his dimwitted French nephew, who noticed an unused car on the side rail and pressed it back into service.

The car's base was faulty, having lost a number of screws in the recent poor weather. In the middle of the first big drop, with the car travelling at forty-five miles per hour, Miss Fritton went through the floor, losing both her feet to the scything sleepers. Due to the centrifugal force of the ride there was scarcely a drop of blood that had not been forced from her by the time the electricity could be turned off.

Maria Brown was deeply traumatised by the accident, but her misery was partially mitigated by the fact that Miss Fritton had left her a considerable amount of money, on the condition that she would take care of the apartment and its contents. Maria Brown dutifully did as she was bid, then booked her passage back to the West Indies. She returned to a wooden house in St John's, Antigua, with almond trees, a pink and green verandah, a VCR and a cellular phone system imported from Montserrat. Feeling guilty but faced with no other choice, she left the urn and the rest of Miss Fritton's belongings in the care of her cousin Bill in Notting Hill.

'Calypso' Bill was considered a bit of a ne'er-do-well and lived up to his reputation by promptly selling off the old lady's furniture. He couldn't get anything for the urn and still had it under his arm wrapped in newspaper when he accidently incurred the wrath of an obeah man in a local pub called the Albatross.

The furious obeah man accused Calypso Bill of trying to steal his woman, which may have been true, and with a mystic pass of the hand 'turned his eyes'. Bill, who believed in the witchcraft of the old country, was instantly blinded, his eyes turning over in their sockets, and stumbled out into the street to be knocked down by a truck delivering skimmed yoghurt from Northern France. On the dashboard of the truck was a copy of Baudelaire's *Les fleurs du mal*.

In the confusion following the accident, the urn was knocked from the bar and burst open, its contents clouding out onto the folded jacket of a young man named Simon Turner. Turner was a frustrated insurance clerk who had long considered leaving his job to live a life unfettered by convention. He wanted to be an artist but lacked the necessary bravery to break free. That afternoon, though, he dusted off his jacket and returned to the insurance office with a determined look in his eye.

He demanded an interview with his superior, resigned on the spot, received a cheque for his back pay and walked from the building a liberated man.

Within a month the change in Simon's appearance and personality was remarkable. He rented a tiny studio apartment in Shepherd's Bush, filled it with art equipment, dyed his hair into a red and yellow striped mohawk, put a silver pin through his nostril and strolled through the market in purple tartan bondage trousers. He was not a very talented artist, but at least he felt like one.

Simon's former colleagues would never have recognised him – and in fact they didn't when they staggered out of a local wine bar called Vive La France late one night and saw him standing on Shepherd's Bush Green studying the configurations of the stars. Irrationally annoyed by someone who clearly dismissed notions of conformity by refusing to wear a regulation grey suit and black nylon socks, they drunkenly kicked him to death.

Simon's jacket, still heavily impregnated with the urn's contents despite a visit to the dry-cleaner's, was given to Oxfam and bought by a girl called Amanda, who worked for a Bloomsbury publishing house. She embroidered an ornate collar around the jacket, tutting at the greasy grey dust that emerged from the unpicked material, and wore it to a smart French restaurant that was hosting the launch of the publishing house's most successful author.

Being a lowly assistant, Amanda's job was to stack the author's new book – a poetic romance set in nineteenth-century Paris – in attractive piles that would draw the attention of reviewers and photographers. The room was filled with literary celebrities, magazine writers, minor television personalities and tabloid journalists, in that order, and Amanda, taking time off from her stacking duties, enriched her vocabulary by chatting amiably with the first group.

Returning to her book display to straighten a wayward

pile, Amanda was shot in the face by an assassin's bullet that had been intended for Salman Rushdie. She died instantly, and Mr Rushdie was safely hustled from the rear of the building into a waiting car. It seems callous but necessary to mention that Amanda's jacket was ruined. As her broken body was removed from the restaurant, the embroidered collar became detached and landed under a table, where it was later discovered and pocketed by one of the cleaning staff.

The cleaner, a young French girl named Gabrielle, was visiting London with her mother and had taken a temporary job to earn a little extra cash. She sewed the dusty collar onto a white work blouse but, failing to find pleasure in the effect it produced, folded the garment away into a valise that her mother was sending back to France. Two weeks later, the package containing the bag was delivered to their gloomy apartment in Paris and taken in by Alice, a friend who was staying there.

Alice had been dating a jazz musician who was killed in an air crash on the way to his first professional performance. One night, a heroin addict named Charles broke into the apartment and ransacked it, looking for money. Alice, returning late from a poetry reading, surprised the thief in the act and was clubbed to death with the nearest weapon to hand, a ceramic chamber pot. The addict grabbed a gilt mantel clock, a jewellery box and Gabrielle's package, and fled down the fire-escape.

Charles bought his fix by fencing the contents of the jewellery box, then boarded a train and alighted at Rennes, where his former girlfriend worked, cleaning house for a young farmer who was purportedly the master of the Château Saint Vincent. However, when he reached the château he found the building locked up, the windows barred and bolted.

Although the property had been sold, the new owner had become seriously ill and was, as yet, unable to take possession.

Charles sat down on the overgrown steps of the building to think through his next move. He could not return to Paris, for he was too well known to the police, and they would now be searching for a murderer. He studied the crusted needle marks on his arms and knew that he would soon be needing another fix, another chance to keep himself suspended between pleasure and death. What was there left for him to barter now? In the back of his brain, a strange fragment of poetry surfaced; something to do with flies humming over the guts of a corpse. *Les mouches* . . . The words were buzzing in his head like the insects themselves.

He still had the package containing the valise and opened it once again to see if there was anything at all that he could sell. But there was not. Angrily, Charles tossed the case onto an iron drainage grate at the foot of the steps and searched his waistcoat for a joint. He found a squashed brown stub and jammed it in the corner of his mouth. Then he scratched a match against the heel of his cowboy boot.

He would not have done so had he known that several months before, his former girlfriend, being the last of the château's departing staff, had failed to turn off the kitchen gas taps, and the pipes beneath the house were now filled to capacity with highly flammable vapour.

The force of the match igniting the combustible mists leaking from the drain upon which the valise stood blew Charles into the air like a mad rag doll. He landed on his head in an ornamental garden seventy feet away. The explosion shattered a stained-glass window in the small chapel, which stood to one side of the main building, and blew the contents of the case through it, so that Gabrielle's white shirt with the embroidered collar fluttered down upon the chapel altar with a silken sigh, to drape itself neatly over the upturned brass crucifix, which stood there patiently awaiting the arrival of the damned surplice.

The satanic history of the Condorcet family is well documented. Of less common knowledge is the fact that, in exchange for their success in the black arts, the Condorcets were not permitted to leave the Château Saint Vincent. It was written that if they did so, catastrophe would befall all who impeded their restitution and that even in death they would be forced to return and remain, whole or in part, on the ungodly site. The prophecy was now fulfilled.

Night After Night of the Living Dead

The best thing about the dead is you can't get pregnant from sitting on a chair they've just been sitting on like you can with live people. When live people warm up the seat (especially the toilet seat – that's where AIDS really comes from) and you sit on it after them and it's still warm, the heat activates the hormones in your body and fertilises the egg, and nine months later you have a baby. But the dead don't leave warm seats because their body temperature is about the same as winter tap water.

The worst thing about the dead is they don't sleep, so if you go downstairs for a glass of water in the middle of the night you're liable to find my grandpa sitting at the kitchen table staring off into the dark, and frankly this gives me the creeps. We have the Night Of The Living Dead to thank for all this. The most interesting thing about that occasion (apart from the fact that it happened in the middle of the afternoon) is that such a cataclysmic event didn't seem to bother many people at the time. Personally speaking I find that weird because I was only eleven when it happened and it fucked me up considerably, I can tell you.

You probably know all about it – I mean you'd have to have been living in a monastery on the Orkney Islands for the last three years to avoid knowing – but I'll tell you anyway, because a) it will give like a personal perspective on the whole thing and b) I'm doing this as my mid-term English essay.

For a start, it was nothing like the movie, which was made many years before. If you saw that particular classic (I wasn't supposed to watch it, but a kid in our street lent me the cassette – he'd relabelled it with a *Winne the Pooh* sticker), you'll remember how the dead came out of the ground and stumped about in waist-high mist with their arms stretched out like sleepwalkers. This was not exactly accurate. Think about it; when they bury someone the coffin is sealed and put in a hole that's packed with earth and tamped down, so we're talking about several hundred pounds of wet dirt to push up, assuming that you can get the lid of the box open in the first place – which you wouldn't be able to do because there's not enough depth in most coffins to give your arms the necessary leverage. The simple fact is, nobody came out of the ground. When the dead came back to life it was only the ones in the morgues and hospitals that reawoke, and if any others were lying around above ground for any reason, they would have risen too.

They didn't walk with their arms raised either; their hands hung limply at their sides and they didn't really move about much, although they did fall over a lot. But the main difference from the film is that they didn't kill people and try to eat their brains. If you think it through logically, how could they? They were dead, and that means brain dead, and wanting to eat someone else's brain suggests conscious thought, which they don't have. Eating a brain isn't going to restore your own. That's like saying if you eat part of a cow you'll grow four stomachs. Also, if you wanted to eat someone's brains you'd have to get their head open, which I shouldn't think is as easy as it looks on the screen. It's like the vampire thing in movies. You know, the biting part, where Dracula makes two holes in someone's neck and sucks the blood out. Excuse me, but did someone just cancel the laws of physics or something? When you open a tin of condensed milk you have to make a hole on either side of the can to allow the milk to escape. So a vampire would have to make sure that his mouth only went over one of the holes, otherwise, he wouldn't be able to suck any blood out – unless he could *really* suck hard, in which case the person he was sucking would sort of dent inwards like a punctured football.

So. No coming out of the ground, no eating brains. That's the trouble with the living dead, they're nothing like their movie counterparts. In fact, they're really boring. These days some of them can do rudimentary root-memory things like read the *Sun* or hum songs from *Cats*, but you can't train them any more than you can train really stupid insects or our biology teacher's dog. You can point up in the air and they'll follow your finger but then they'll stay like that for hours, like chickens expecting rain. And it's because they're dead, end of story. I mean, dead is it, *finito*; after you're dead, you don't understand the punch lines to jokes or remember to set the video, it's all over, baby.

What was really weird, though, was the reaction of the adults. They didn't think about the basic absurdity of the situation. They didn't wonder how the whole thing could be physically possible. They weren't interested in the mechanics of the dead returning to life. They just completely freaked, screaming the place down every time they saw one, and stopped us from going near them or even looking. You'd expect this from my mother, who has a nuclear meltdown when I so much as bring a dead sparrow into the house, but not from Ted, our revolting old next-door neighbour who lost an eye in the war and talks about stringing up darkies to our West Indian milkman.

I don't specifically remember much about the night it happened except that it was a Wednesday, it was raining hard and I was late home from school. I'd been caught unravelling the elastic inside of a golf ball during social studies and had been made to stay behind for detention. I remember walking home and seeing one of the dead shuffling ahead, a man of about fifty. My first sighting. It was a weird experience, as though I'd been waiting all of my admittedly short life to see something like this, and now that I had it made sense of everything else.

The figure before me was drifting more than walking, his feet barely rising from the ground. As far as I could see in the fading light, he was dressed in normal street clothes, although they were dirty and one jacket sleeve was torn, as though he'd been in a fight. His head was lowered a little but he was staring forward and seemed to know where he was going. As I drew abreast of him I caught an overpowering stench of chemicals, formaldehyde I supposed, as though he had just heaved himself up from the mortuary slab. His face was grey and speckled, the texture of my Dad's IBM slipcase, but his eyes were the real giveaway. They had this fixed dry look, like doll's eyes, I guess because there was no fluid to lubricate them, and they were stuck in one position. They looked like a pair of jammed roll-on deodorant balls. I kept pace with him as I passed, and it was then that I realised I wasn't really scared.

When someone is dangerous they give off warning signals,

and if you're receptive to the signals you back away. But this guy was just dead and there weren't any signals good or bad, and I instinctively knew that the worst thing that could happen was he could fall over and land on top of me. The street was pretty empty, and the few people who passed us didn't seem to see anything wrong. I guess in the rain-hazed dimness there was nothing unusual to see beyond the fact that the old man didn't have a raincoat on and was getting pretty soaked. Finally I arrived at my turning, and the dead bloke just shuffled onwards into the gloom. I watched him go for a while, then headed home.

I missed the early evening TV news but asked my mother if there had been anything about the dead coming back to life and she made a face and said of course not. I remembered noticing that her eyes were puffy and red, as if she'd been crying about something and was trying not to let me see. Later, on the portable in my room, the footage appeared. There, right in front of me, live on some crappy Sky channel, the anchorwoman was awkwardly reading a report that several cadavers from a hospital morgue in Leeds had been found walking along the corridors of the building. She said that similar phenomena were being reported all over the world, although I don't think she believed a word of it. Then some ecosystems guy who looked like he'd just got out of bed kept patting down his hair and saying it was all to do with the ozone layer, and I thought *As if*. I mean, you don't have to be a rocket scientist to figure out that there's no link between the depletion of the ozone layer and the reanimation of dead tissue. That's like saying Nintendo games give you rabies or something. Get a grip.

I retuned the TV to CNN because they repeat the same stories over and over when they're not quoting Iowa wheat prices, and there it was, actual footage of ZOMBIES lumbering along roads and bumping into walls and generally looking thick. I rang my friend Joey 'Boner' Mahoney to tell him to turn on the TV but his dog stepmother answered and told me it was too late to talk to him.

The next day I attempted to discuss what was happening with my friends at school, but no one was that interested except Simon Waters. Unfortunately Simon believes that crop circles are made by Venusians, not by a couple of sad guys with a piece of rope and a plank, and is desperate to believe in any scenario that's more interesting than his own miserable existence, which consists of getting lousy marks at school and going home to a father who is having an affair with a foot specialist. That was when I began my Deadwatch, which is a notebook marked out so that I can record each dead sighting as it happens.

With each passing day there were more and more sightings as the walking dead took to the streets. Soon I was recording as many as ten or fifteen on a single Saturday morning (the women are particularly fond of milling around the trolley collection point outside Sainsbury's), and I stopped bothering with the book because there were too many to keep up with. To begin with, most of these ambulatory cadavers were in pretty good condition. I mean their jaws and ears weren't hanging off or anything, but once in a while you'd see one in a really bad state. There was a guy on the bus in a hospital gown, and the stitches down the front of his chest had burst open so that his intestines were hanging out and rolling from side to side as the bus turned corners. There was no blood and his guts were blue-grey, like piles of old school sausages. That was pretty gross. But in the early days most of the corpses seemed to stay in one piece.

You see, it wasn't just a Night Of The Living Dead, as we had thought at first. It was Night After Night. The effects of whatever had revived them were sticking around, so the authorities had to come up with some kind of legislation to cope with the problem. They simply arranged for bodies to be buried at a new standard depth and for mortuary doors to be kept locked. There was talk of freezing and vacuum packing for a while, but I guess it seemed too disrespectful, bowing out like a pork chop. Still, an awful lot of Deadies seemed to be walking around, more every day, so either someone was letting them out (which I'd seen a Right-To-Life group doing on the news) or they were finding ways to escape prior to burial.

The government couldn't settle on a reason for what was happening, and still haven't come up with a satisfactory cause to this day. They set up an independent enquiry to investigate what was going on, i.e., cut open some corpses and had a poke around, but found nothing conclusive. The corpses were just inert organisms that wouldn't lie still. They had no heartbeats and coagulated blood and hardened veins and leathery skin and dry staring eyes. At first the scientists thought it was radiation in the atmosphere, then Rogue Viral DNA, but I knew they really didn't have a clue when everyone started to blame the French.

Anyway, none of this really touched my family or our lives. We continued to see the dead sitting in bus shelters looking neither happy nor sad (looking like they were waiting for a bus really). We saw them in gents' outfitters staring vaguely at the shelves. We saw them standing shell-shocked outside cinemas and pizza parlours (they weren't allowed near food but they seemed to enjoy being in queues). We saw them watching football through the windows of TV rental stores, their foreheads pressed against the glass. We saw them sunbathing in park deckchairs with newspapers over their faces, and the only way you could tell they were dead was because it was raining.

I guess this was about a month after the actual NOTLD, and now that everyone could see the dead weren't going to hurt anybody, all kinds of trouble started. For one thing, no matter how harmless they were, the dead tended to creep people out. It was only natural; the way they looked and smelled was depressing to say the least. The police wanted special powers to round them up because they were always falling onto railway lines and wandering into busy traffic, but all kinds of groups began protesting, arguing that because the dead were walking around they still had souls and therefore had human rights.

Then doctors began worrying that the bodies would decompose and put everyone at risk from germs, but the corpses didn't really rot. Because the newly dead leaked so much they slowly got drier and more leathery, and this was helped by the fact that it was winter and a lot of them had taken to sitting in libraries where the central heating caused an arid atmosphere.

They got damaged and tatty from constantly bumping into things, and some of them lost fingers and clumps of hair, which made them even creepier looking. (Oddly enough, they managed to keep a natural sense of propriety. If one of them tore his trousers he would tug the hole around so that people on the tube wouldn't have to sit facing his willy.) While television shows and newspaper articles preached respect for the dead, teenage gangs began going out and tampering with the bodies, cutting bits off or dressing them in inappropriate clothes to make them look silly. My friend Joey once saw an old man in the high street wearing a glitter wig and a ballet tutu. Sometimes if you were out with a bunch of friends and saw one shuffling along ahead of you, you'd run up and pull his trousers down, then all run away laughing. Also, some unscrupulous entrepreneurs hung advertising on them, but most people disapproved of this.

The dead weren't supposed to travel on the tubes because they never bought tickets, but one or two always managed to get through the barriers, only to spend the entire day trying to open the drawers on the platform's chocolate machines. They never made much noise. I think their vocal chords sort of dried out over time, but God, the older ones started to look awful. The problem was, even if they fell into the river and floated about for a few days being run over by motorboats, they would eventually drift to the shore, only to climb out and begin aimlessly walking around again. Hospital crews collected the most disgusting ones and took them away somewhere.

Around this time I remember seeing an old woman fall off a Routemaster bus and get dragged around the block on her face. I followed her just to see what would happen if her coat strap managed to disentangle itself from the pole. When the poor old love finally hauled herself to her feet (nobody was willing to help her – the dead are kind of ignored now, like the homeless) the remaining part of her face fell off like torched wallpaper, leaving her with tarmac-scraped bone and an expression of annoyed surprise. It was not a pleasant sight.

A few weeks after this, one wet Saturday afternoon, my grandpa died. He had lived in the house with us for years even though my mother had never liked him, and at first nobody even realised that he had died. He just stayed in his armchair all day staring at the television, but I knew something was wrong because he would normally start shouting at the screen when the wrestling came on and today he didn't.

He did make himself a cup of tea, but he left the teabag in the mug, drank it scalding and immediately peed it back out onto the floor. My father wouldn't let my mother call the hospital and they had a huge row, after which it was decided that Grandpa could stay for a while so long as he didn't get in anyone's way. My mother refused to change his clothes, but Dad argued that they wouldn't need changing very often as he no longer had operative sweat glands. Still, it was difficult to break the old geezer of his tea-making habit. I guess when you've been making ten cups of Brooke Bond a day for sixty years you don't need motor neurons.

Grandpa wasn't allowed out by himself because he had a tendency not to come back and we would have to go looking for him. Once I was allowed to go on a grandpa hunt with my dad and we had to search the park just as it was starting to get dark. There were dozens of them – Deadies – sitting motionless beneath the rustling plane trees. They were seated in deckchairs around the bandstand with their hands in their laps, quietly waiting for the music to start. Two of them were sitting on the enclosure railings with their arms around each other like lovers, except that the railing spikes had gone through their thighs. It was a strange sight. I stopped going to the park after that.

A few days later I took Grandpa to the cinema. I guess it was an odd thing to do, but I was supposed to be looking after him and there was a film I really wanted to see, one of those slasher films with music that creeps up on you, and I managed to pass Grandpa off as alive, although the usherette looked at us suspiciously. Halfway through the film, just when the heroine had gone to the cellar to look for her cat even though she knew there was a homicidal maniac loose, I turned to find the old man staring at me with wide, flat eyes.

He wasn't breathing of course, and his mouth hung open to reveal a thick dry tongue that looked as if it had been carved out of Spam. What bothered me most was the way he repeated one of his living mannerisms, tilting his head slightly to look at me, so that for a moment I couldn't tell if he was really dead. It was just the illusion of life, of course, but an unsettling one.

A few weeks after that, Grandpa took it upon himself to revive another root memory and peel some potatoes. He remembered the peeler but unfortunately forgot to use it in conjunction with a vegetable and succeeded in removing most of the skin from his fingers before I came home from school and found him staring at a set of bony protrusions that looked like badly sharpened pencils. The very next day he sat down on the stove while the burners were lit and branded his trousers. My mother threatened to leave us if my father didn't arrange to him to be put somewhere, so the following morning found me standing on the doorstep waving goodbye to Grandpa as he stared sightlessly back and stumbled off across the flowerbeds, led away by a disinterested hospital porter smoking a joint.

A short while after his departure, I was walking home from late detention and took a short cut past the backs of the terraced houses a few streets away from where we lived. Ahead, only half visible in the grey fading light, a dead man was standing with his head titled to the sky, studying something. As I drew closer he sat down with a thud, as if his legs had suddenly given way, and I realised that it was Grandpa. He'd come back. It looked as if something had been eating him, rats perhaps. There were little bite marks all over his face and neck, and one of his arms had hardly any skin at all, only shredded brown muscle. Then I realised where we were, and what he'd been looking at.

He'd slipped out of care and returned to the house he had shared with Grandma when they were just married. I knew he'd been standing there watching for the sight of her passing by the windows. But she had died long ago. An idea occurred to me – that I could take Grandpa to the cemetery where she had been buried and that they could somehow be reunited. Perhaps I could explain to the caretaker, and he would allow her body to be disinterred. But I wasn't sure where the cemetery was, and every time I tried to lead Grandpa away he started pulling back. Finally I had to leave him there, standing before the glowing kitchen windows of his youth, staring up through a half-remembered past.

I never saw him again. I rarely leave my bedroom. I don't go to school any more. There are just too many dead people about, and it bothers me. They blunder into the garden at night and follow you to the shops and fall down the steps of public lavatories and float past you on the ferry, and it's undignified. My mother seems to understand how I feel and lets me have most of my meals in my room. She's become overfriendly with the cocktail cabinet these days, anyway. The extraordinary thing is, the living dead don't seem to count any more. It doesn't matter that the stench of corruption is all around us. We've grown used to the smell. The government continues to chair pointless debates and issue toothless white papers. The general public has ceased to care or even notice. The fabric of society is gently rotting through, even if the dead aren't. So I'm formulating a plan, because someone has to do something. Somebody has to care. Somebody has to take affirmative action before it's too late.

Kevin Grady, Upper 4B

* * *

'It makes you wonder what he thinks about,' whispered Mrs Grady, pulling the tablecloth in by the corners and removing it. 'He'll sit like that for hours on end, just staring down into the street, watching the people come and go.'

'You should be thankful,' said her neighbour, helping her clear away the cups and saucers. 'My Joey's a holy terror these days, out every night mixing with heaven knows what kid of riffraff.'

She looked across at the chalk-faced child seated before the window, and a cloud of doubt momentarily formed in her mind. It was unnatural for a teenaged boy to sit so still. When you spoke to him he stared back in accusing silence. And the terrible way he looked at you, with murder in those deep-set eyes. 'Joey tells me he's doing his homework,' she continued, 'but I know damned well he's running with that gang of his. I have no control over him, and his father's absolutely no help at all. But your Kevin . . .' She furrowed her brow and uneasily turned aside as the boy glanced at her in suspicion. No wonder Kevin's mother was bashing the Bristol Cream these days, with her son wandering about the house dressed in black, narrowing his eyes at every passing adult. He'd probably grow up to be a serial killer.

'Kevin's a good boy,' said his mother firmly. 'He's terribly bright. And sensitive. He and his grandad were very close. He's been a lot quieter since the old man died. Wouldn't even come with us to the funeral. I hope it doesn't have any lasting effect on him.'

'I shouldn't think so,' the neighbour whispered back. 'Children are resilient. He's very quiet, though. He should go outside more and get some fresh air. Mix with the others. Swim. Play football.' She threw the torpid child a look of desperation. 'Anything.'

Mrs Grady unfolded her arms from her ample chest and looked about for the sherry bottle. 'I wish he would, but he prefers to stay in his room watching horror films all the time.' She poured overgenerous measures into a pair of amber glasses. 'It gives him such an overactive imagination. I think Kevin sees the world differently to most children. He has some very odd ideas. I'm sure it's just a phase, but right now, well . . .' She turned to her friend and brought her face closer, confiding. 'It's . . . the way he looks at us sometimes. Almost as if he wishes we were dead.'

Jumbo Portions

' ''Ere, this chicken don't half taste funny.'

Sharon squinted through mascara-caked lashes at the thing on the end of her fork. It was orange and lumpy and battered, and it was dripping grease on to Sharon's copy of *Girl About Town*.

'I told you we should have had a bloody tandoori.' Tracy looked up from her crossword puzzle and waggled the suppurating chicken chunk between her thumb and forefinger. 'No wonder you never see a bloody cat in the West End.'

'There was a big queue at McDonald's. I don't like to wait. Anyway, their chips are crap. Is your chicken funny?'

'It depends on what you mean by funny,' said Tracy. 'If you mean "Am I amused by it?" the answer is no. If you mean "Does it taste like a long-dead mackerel?" I'd be forced to answer yes.' Tracy propped her half-gnawed chicken leg against her typewriter and wiped her hands on a Supermoist Lemon Towelette. She and Sharon spent their days typing out invoices for discount furniture in the dingy little room which overlooked Oxford Street. The work was slow, repetitive and undemanding. But then so were Sharon and Tracy, although their hearts were in the right place and we should think none the worse of them for merely being ordinary.

Their lunchtimes were usually spent in the office with a meal in a polystyrene box purchased from one of the many takeaway food outlets in the area. The pattern varied on Fridays, when instead of eating, they went with the downstairs mailboys to a nearby wine bar and got drunk.

'Of course, you *know* about takeaway chicken, don't you?' asked Sharon as she continued to stare in fascination at the object on the end of her fork.

'What do you mean?' Tracy's Birmingham accent was as spikily pronounced as Sharon's heavy cockney.

'Well, they're all battery grown, you know, like in them little wire cages, millions of 'em. And they never see the light, so they never grow feathers. And there's no room to move, so they lose the power of their legs. They just sit there, all white and hairless, screaming at each other. And they're trained to eat from these chutes that pump fishmeal into them until they're full to bursting. That's why it tastes fishy.'

'Oh, bloody fab.' Tracy emptied the oily remains of her fried chicken carton into the wastepaper basket with a grimace.

'Only this tastes . . .' Sharon groped for the word. 'Funny.'

'Why don't you take it back and complain?' Tracy wiped her hands on her seat and proceeded to tear open a Toffee Crisp.

'I think I will. In fact, I think I'll go right now.' Sharon shook the dripping lump free from the end of her fork and let it fall back into the box, which was leaking grease on to her desk. Carefully wrapping the carton in a plastic carrier bag, she rose from her chair. 'They're supposed to give you sporks with the food, anyway.'

'You what?'

'You know, sporks, them white plastic spoons with jagged points on the end. That's what they're called.'

'Oh.' Tracy returned her attention to a magazine article on unreliable smear tests. 'If you're goin' past the sandwich shop, bring us back a sardine and tomato.'

Sharon pushed open the door of the fried chicken take-away outlet and dumped her carrier bag on the counter. The little Indian at the back of the store lowered his chip basket into a tank of boiling fat and waddled up to the service bay.

'Yes pliz?'

'Your chicken tastes funny.'

'What you mean?' The little Indian wiped a lock of lank hair from his eyes and peered into the plastic bag as Sharon withdrew a half-eaten piece of breast.

'You taste it.' She proffered the piece.

The Indian made a face. 'Ugh,' he said. 'No thank you. Is horrible.'

'Don't give me Is Horrible, you expect other people to eat it.' Sharon dropped the breast back into the box with a look of disgust.

'Is not my fault I don' eat chicken. Nobody else complain.'

'That's 'cause they're probably not alive afterwards.' She shook the carrier bag. 'I want my money back.'

'You wait here.' The Indian waddled off and disappeared behind several plastic sacks full of defrosting chips. A few moments later he returned with a sweaty young man in a vest that revealed the navel of his beer-swelled stomach.

'Wassamatter with the chicken?' he asked belligerently. Perspiration, if such a delicate term could be used, dripped from his pale, chubby face.

'She say it taste funny.'

'Funny?' The podgy young man thrust his hand into Sharon's carrier bag and withdrew a chicken leg. He took a large bite, chewed for a few moments, and with the delicacy of a veteran wine taster spat the lump of chewed meat into the palm of his hand.

'The batter's off.' He turned to the Indian, who in turn looked at Sharon with embarrassment.

'You 'aven't been using the batter in the bowl above the frozen yoghurts?' The Indian nodded nervously. The fat young man rolled his eyes heavenward. 'No wonder. I could have told you that was off. You should have chucked it out before the weekend.'

'Well, it's unhygienic,' sniffed Sharon as she unstuck her hands from the glistening counter. 'That meat could be curdled. You should stick a warning on the side of the box – "Danger: Might Be Off".'

'Look, you can 'ave a refund if you're gonna be funny.'

'It ain't me that's funny, it's your chicken, mate.'

The Indian dropped three pound coins and four grease-slippery ten-pence pieces into Sharon's outstretched palm. Tossing her spray-glazed curls at the duo, Sharon clumped out of the takeaway and off along Charing Cross Road to find a Tandoori.

The young man stared after the closing door and tutted. 'These people come in here expecting the earth.' He turned to the Indian, who was gingerly removing Sharon's abandoned plastic bag from the counter. 'It's all very well for them, all they got to do is eat the stuff, they don't have to sell it. They don't understand the problems you get with poultry.'

'Thass right,' said the Indian. 'Me, I like a nice piece of fish.'

'Well then, have a piece of chicken.' The fat young man laughed. Then his face grew serious. 'She had a nice bum on her, though,' he said.

* * *

'How's your Tone these days?' asked Tracy as she stood at the photocopying machine collecting the printed advertisements for Dralon Boudoir Stools which were popping out of one end. 'Is he still out of work?'

'No,' said Sharon, 'he's got a job on a van, deliverin'.'

'Nice,' said Tracy. 'Deliverin' what?'

'I dunno.'

'Oh.' Tracy collected her copies and carefully squared their corners. 'Still, nice though. Workin' an' that. I wish my Damon could find a bloody job.'

'How long's he been out of work now?' Sharon folded a piece of gum between her glossy crimson lips and began snapping it into shape.

'Six bloody months.'

'You should tell him. It's no good being trained up in wicker repair if there isn't the call for it.'

'Yeah I know, but – well, you've met him – there's his problem to consider.'

'What problem?'

'He can't apply himself.' Tracy stuck a ruler up her skirt and scratched the top of her tights. 'This heat's giving me a terrible rash.'

'Can't apply himself? What, you mean he's stupid?'

'Basically, yeah. I'm gonna have to put something on this.' Together they clumped away from the photocopying machine. 'Let's get some lunch in.'

'Good idea,' agreed Sharon. 'All I 'ad for breakfast was Fruit Crunch.'

'What's that, health cereal?'

'I suppose so. It turned the milk red.'

Sharon dashed through the rain along Oxford Street, heading

for the nearest hamburger bar. When she arrived outside she was surprised to see plastic cladding draping the front of the building and a CLOSED FOR RENOVATION sign slung across the entrance. The rain was spoiling her spiky blond coiffure, and would be bound to start leaking into her boots in a minute. Darting between the taxis, she found herself at the bottom of Tottenham Court Road, where shoppers hurried between broken paving slabs and flooded drains. Here in a no-man's-land of stereo component stores populated by listless Tunisian salesmen, there was only one takeaway within sprinting distance.

The little Indian recognised Sharon the moment he laid eyes on her. She stood at the counter shaking the rain from her hair like a spaniel, the only customer.

'Today we have good chicken, miss. You want try?'

'It had better be good or I'll bring it back.'

The Indian tonged hot battered chicken into a carton, added a variety of sachets and passed it to her. Sharon tucked the box under her arm and headed back out into the rain. The fat young man stuck his head out from behind the rotisserie.

'Her again? Glutton for punishment. I bet she brings it back. She'll find something wrong, you'll see. I know the type. Complain about finding hairs in their soup. Real moaners.'

'She won't bring it back,' said the Indian. 'Bring it back up, perhaps. I don't know how you people can eat such rubbish. Kebabs. Fish and chips. Fried chicken . . .'

'Tandoori takeaways,' added the fat young man. 'Your lot's got quite a bit to answer for as well.'

The Indian gave him a cool look and returned to his fat fryer.

'Now, this isn't so bad,' said Tracy with her mouth full of chicken. She sucked a huge gulp of Diet Coke and carried on chewing. Her ancient desk was littered with magazines, spilled correcting fluid and polystyrene coffee cups with cigarette ends floating in them. There was little work to do today. 'It's sort of' – she sought to articulate an impressionistic response – 'you know . . . less fishy.'

'Yeah, more, er . . .' Sharon stared at the gnarled lump of battered meat with a single bleached bone protruding from the end of it. 'More burgery.'

'Yeah, there is an aftertaste of burger, isn't there? Quite nice, actually.' Tracy peered into her chicken box as if half expecting something to leap out of it. 'I wonder why it tastes like that?'

Sharon tore the skin from a chicken leg and held it up to the light, examining it as she pondered the problem. 'It's probably just from storage.'

'What do you mean?'

'Well, the chickens, after they've been slaughtered – 'cause they're killed in vast numbers at a time 'cause it's easy killing them, the chickens being very weak and unable to walk and nude from not growin' any feathers – well, after they're chopped up into the appropriate parts like breast an' wing, they get stored in huge fridges, then they get moved to smaller fridges which probably have hamburgers on some of their shelves, an' the hamburgers drip meat juices on to the chicken, probably.' Sharon sucked the chicken skin into her mouth, smearing her lipstick as she did so. 'It's all just meat, nothing to worry about.'

'So what happens to the heads an' feet an' stuff?' asked Tracy with a sickly look on her face. 'You never see deep-fried chicken feet.'

'There's no call for them – in white countries,' Sharon replied darkly. 'They get ground up an' made into other chicken-flavoured products. Like when packet soup says "chicken extract" on the side. It's the ground-up bits no one else wants to have anything to do with. Beaks and things.'

'You're putting me right off,' said Tracy, blanching beneath her make-up. 'I think I'll stick to sausage sandwiches in future.'

'You're no better off there. Cow lips and eyeballs, all squashed up in skins, that's sausages for you.'

While Tracy visited the toilet, Sharon turned back to her deep-fried thigh and read an article on cervical cancer in *Wow* magazine.

'Hang on, it's slipping.' Tony shouldered the fruit machine upright and together they lowered it from the ramp of the truck. Standing it down on the pavement with a thud, he leaned on the Formica top and wiped his brow. 'How many more we got today, Steve? I'm knackered.'

Steve consulted his notebook. 'Just one more. We should be through by six.'

'We'd better be. I'm meeting my Sharon outside Tottenham Court Road tube station at six.' Tony smoothed down his flat-top and hitched up his white socks. There was no mirror available but he presumed he still looked terrific.

'That'll be handy for you,' said Steve. 'We're delivering just around the corner from there, to a Mr Patel.'

Tony checked that the rolled sleeves of his tight white T-shirt were still in place and prepared to shoulder the machine once more. He looked good when he was lifting things. His muscles bulged.

'Okay, let's get this one inside.'

After installing the machine, bolting it to the floor of the Chinese takeaway and leaving the bemused manager with a set of instruction booklets showing him how to operate the Mississippi Gambler 2000 Electronic Blackjack game, Steve and Tony climbed back into the van.

Tony checked his appearance in the rear-view mirror and quickly slid a comb over his immaculately styled square hair. He squeezed a spot on his neck, then straightened the golden Taurus horoscope symbol Sharon had given him to wear as an earring.

'Where you off to tonight?' asked Steve as he started the engine.

'We're goin' up that new cocktail bar in Camden, opposite the market. We went there last week but we didn't stay long 'cause someone got knifed. Then we'll go for a kebab at the Chinese place next door.'

'I've been there,' said Steve. 'They do really good curries. Real bum-burners.'

'Yeah, there's nothing like a good curry, is there? Mind that old dear.'

Steve shot the van over a zebra crossing and narrowly missed an elderly lady who was struggling with the wheels of her shopping basket.

'You gonna marry Sharon, then?'

'Nah. She wants to but I can't at the moment.'

'Why not?'

Tony studied his reflection in the window. 'I've got a kid. From this girl I used to be at school with. Sharon doesn't know. I keep meanin' to tell her. Watch out for that bloke on the bike.'

'Well, you'd better pop her a postcard. It's quite important, something like that.' Steve swung the van past a cyclist, who was forced to pull into the kerb.

'I was gonna tell her before. The trouble is, I'm still seein' the mother.'

'You randy sod,' laughed Steve. 'Go it, my son.' The van turned into the one-way system at Tottenham Court Road, scattering pedestrians in every direction.

'Talking of food,' said Tony, 'you ever had frogs' legs? They're great. They taste like chicken.'

'I'm never sure about French stuff. I mean, they eat horses, don't they? An' that's barbaric, to my mind.' Steve cut into the next traffic lane and considerably surprised the driver of an invalid carriage.

'Me, I like all them exotic things,' said Tony. 'Snails, they're like whelks.' He thought for a moment. 'Whelks in garlic.'

'I couldn't eat snails,' admitted Steve. 'I mean, you see 'em in the garden leaving slimy trails, don't you? An' when they're cooked, they look like something you'd find up a horse's nose.' He pulled a face and beat a Ford Marina to a parking space outside the fried chicken takeaway which Sharon had patronised only yesterday.

'How can you have it here when you ain't got no power point to connect it up with?' Steve stood up and wiped his dusty hands on the knees of his jeans. The little Indian shrugged.

'You will have to speak to Mr Duncan. I will get him for you.'

'Thank you, Mr Patel.' Steve turned to Tony. 'We ain't gonna get this machine fixed up tonight. They haven't got a proper junction box for it.'

Tony looked over at the dormant fruit machine and scratched his head. 'I could put in a bit of overtime late tomorrow an' sort it out,' he offered. Just then, the Indian reappeared with the fat young man in the grease-stained shirt.

'I'm Duncan, the manager,' he said. 'Is there a problem?'

Steve explained the hold-up, and offered Tony's services the following evening. Duncan blew his nose on a paper serviette and agreed that tomorrow would be fine.

'Anyway,' said Steve, 'it's all fixed up and ready to go. Tony here will patch in your electrics. What time do you close?'

'At eleven pm,' said Mr Patel, 'but you can come earlier. We're not very busy, early evening.'

'That's no good,' said Tony. 'I've got to turn off your electrics, and that means turning off your fryer. I'll get here just before you shut.'

'We'll be off, then,' said Steve. 'You got a chicken leg for us to be going on with?'

'There's a baby here that's been born with its head on backwards,' said Tracy, setting her hamburger down on a folded copy of the *Sun* and reading the headline. She carefully dabbed bun crumbs from her lipstick. 'The doctors are blaming it on faulty spermicide. What does your hamburger taste like?'

Sharon considered the question for a moment. 'I dunno,' she conceded. 'You can't describe it really.'

'You know what mine tastes like?'

'What?'

'Well, if you tore up an empty cereal packet, like into tiny, tiny pieces, and then mashed it up with Bisto for about two hours, then let it set . . .'

'Yes?'

'Well, that's what it tastes like.'

'That's 'cause cows, when they're slaughtered, these great hammers—'

'Don't bloody start that again,' said Tracy. 'Why's your Tone workin' late?'

'He's puttin' in a bit of overtime,' said Sharon. 'At one of the places where he's deliverin'.'

'You don't think he's seein' someone else, do you?' asked Tracy.

'No,' said Sharon. 'He's not that bright. Can I have your ketchup sachet?'

The last customer had just left the fried chicken takeaway when Tony arrived. The night was warm, and the greasy heat in the store was almost unbearable. It clung heavily to his clothing as he unpacked equipment from his toolbox. Behind the counter, Mr Patel was cleaning down the shelves of the rotisserie. Further out at the back, Duncan was resealing sacks of frozen chips. The fruit machine sat dark in the corner. Mr Patel paused in his labours and poured himself a cup of instant tomato soup. He slurped it thickly, leaving a fluorescent red circle around his mouth. Tony sorted out his tools and carried them across to the fruit machine.

'So,' he said genially, talking to the wall as he worked, 'how long you been here, then?'

'Two years,' answered Mr Patel as he finished his soup and prepared to wash the floor in the back of the shop. 'It was doner kebab place but Greek boys got closed down by the health peoples.'

'Why was that?'

'They had a really disgustin' problem with the toilet drainage system,' called Duncan. 'Blowback. You don' wanna hear about it.'

'Blowback?' Tony grimaced and went about his work.

Presently, he looked up from the tangled mass of cable on the floor and called to Mr Patel.

'Excuse me, do you happen to know where this lead goes?'

'Sorry.' Mr Patel shrugged and continued mopping the tiles.

'What appliances have you got wired up there? How many wall sockets? Hang on, I'll come back and have a look.'

Tony raised the red Formica counter flap and let himself through to the back of the store, where Duncan was wringing a grey cloth into a bucket of filthy water.

'Mind you don't slip on the floor.'

Tony traced the cable he was looking for, and sat back on his haunches to strip it.

'This wiring's a real old mess,' he pointed out. 'I wouldn't let anyone from the council see it if I were you. Here, I've been meaning to ask you something. What do you do with all the chicken that don't get sold? Do you take it home, like?'

'Urgh, indeed we do not,' said Mr Patel earnestly. 'Chicken cooked in this manner is no good for you.'

'Funny that,' said Tony, 'you not liking chicken and workin' here.'

'It's because he works here that he became a vegetarian,' chided Duncan. 'Ain't that right, Patsy?'

'I do not like you calling me that,' said the little Indian as he angrily tossed the remaining soapy water in his bucket across the tiles.

'Me,' began Tony, 'I love a good curry, but that's . . .'

He never finished the sentence, because as he spoke he moved forward towards the exposed box of electrical circuitry, slipped on the tidal wash of soapy water from Mr Patel's bucket and fell face first into the junction box.

There was a loud bang, and a spectacular array of sparks fizzed in a halo around Tony's electrified head. His body jerked erect as the blast of electrical current from the mains supply tore through him, then he was suddenly thrown backward with his arms flailing, like a scarecrow in a hurricane. He hit the edge of the deep fat fryer with his pelvis and fought for a moment to retain his balance, both hands flying first to his blackened face, then clawing the air as he somersaulted backwards over the rim and into the fryer with an oily splash.

Duncan and Mr Patel looked on in horror, their jaws dropped and their eyes bulging at the scene taking place before them. The fryer was built to hold three pans of chips. It was far too small to contain a human being. Unfortunately, however, Tony had fallen head first, and as he fell had raised his knees so that he had entered the fat in a crouched position. Consequently, when the boiling waves subsided, all that could be seen of Tony were the soles of his trackshoes.

For a moment the only sounds in the little takeaway were the crackle of electricity and the gentle bubbling of boiling fat as it popped and plopped around Tony's cooking body. Finally, Duncan spoke.

'Why didn't you turn the bloody fryer off?'

Mr Patel suddenly became aware of the extreme likelihood that Duncan would try to pin the blame on him. He began to sweat profusely.

'I was not expecting anyone to fall into it,' he said lamely. 'Anyway, you are the manager, and you are not supposed to let anyone else back here for reasons of hygiene. It says so in the company manual.'

Successfully countered, Duncan stood with his arms at his sides thoughtfully staring into the fryer while the device was turned off.

'Do you think he's dead?' asked Mr Patel timidly.

Duncan exploded into life. 'Dead? Of course he's bloody dead!'

'How can we get him out of there?'

'We'll have to wait until the fat cools down.'

Already, a delicious smell of cooking meat was filling the room. Duncan peered into the fryer once more. 'Oh Christ, he's starting to crust up.'

Mr Patel wrung his hands fearfully. 'Whatever will we do?' he asked the ceiling.

'They'll take away our licence if they find out, that's for sure.'

'But we cannot just leave him in there cooking!'

'What time do the dustmen come by?' asked Duncan, shaking Mr Patel by the shoulders.

'A little after midnight, I think. It varies. Sometimes they do not appear until seven in the morning.'

'Let's pray this isn't one of those times,' said the sweating young man. 'What we'll do – when you've finished jumping up and down panicking – is first of all turn the fryer back on . . .'

'What? This is craziness!' the little Indian screamed.

'Listen to me,' said Duncan. 'We'll cook the corpse until it's unrecognisable. Then we'll drain off the fat, remove the body and put it into one of those heavy-duty hundred-weight bags that the chips come in. We'll leave it with the other rubbish out on the pavement. If anyone opens it and looks inside, all they'll see is a jumble of burned meat and batter.'

'And this will work?' asked Mr Patel.

'For both our sakes,' said Duncan, as he switched the fryer back on it, 'it had better bloody work.'

After the fat had been boiling for more than an hour, the air in the takeaway store was filled with the powerful aroma of overcooked meat. If he had not known exactly what was cooking, Mr Patel might have found the smell quite delicious. Instead, he could scarcely keep from regurgitating his lunchtime samosas. Duncan appeared from around the corner dragging a heavy plastic sack.

'Smells good, don't it?' he said, lifting his porcine nose in the air and sniffing. 'Almost seems a pity to waste it. 'Ere.' He nudged the distinctly queasy-looking Mr Patel. 'I bet we could make a fair bit of dosh if we changed the name of the store to Sweeney Todd's.'

Mr Patel gave him a look of utter incomprehension.

When the fryer had been turned off and drained, Duncan beckoned Mr Patel to come and take a look. Reluctantly, he came over and squinted into the grease-coated stainless steel basin. Inside, standing on his head and his kneecaps, was an unrecognisable Tony. If he had not been dead when he tumbled in, he would certainly have been battered to death by now.

'You get around one side of him,' said Duncan. 'Put your ovengloves on. I'll get around the other side and we'll lift him out together and stand him on the floor.'

'I cannot do this,' moaned Mr Patel. 'We are committing a sin.'

'Yeah, well.' Duncan tried to console his partner. 'It's a good job you ain't a Catholic. This wouldn't sound too good in the confessional.'

Mr Patel gave a pained look and donned his floral ovengloves. Then he gingerly lowered his hands over the side of the fryer. Together they lifted the body out inch by inch. They had almost got it clear of the basin when there was a cracking noise, and it broke in half. Although Duncan swore angrily, this desiccation of the body made its removal much easier, as all the fluids had been dried out and the corpse could now be broken into several pieces, mixed with the day's batter scrapings and tipped into a number of different bags. Mr Patel agreed to help, but kept his eyes screwed up tight throughout the operation, especially when Duncan cracked off Tony's deep-fried fingers and dropped them into a separate bag.

'You got all the loose pieces of batter up your end, Patsy?'

'I think so, yes.'

'Good, then give me a hand with these sacks and we'll get 'em out before the dustcart comes by.'

After the sacks were secured and placed outside the two men returned to the back of the store and wiped up the puddles of grease which had formed all over the floor. As Mr Patel was mopping up the last pool, Duncan came by with the air freshener.

'Mmmm, lavender, that's better,' he said, spraying everywhere. 'You'd better put that cheesecake back in the cold cabinet or it'll go off.'

Once they had finished clearing up, Duncan and Mr Patel turned off the shop lights and sat outside in Duncan's car until they had seen the dustcart load and crush the sacks containing the hapless Tony to a pulp. Then, after promising to open the store as usual in the morning, they went home to their beds. For Mr Patel, at least, it was a sleepless night.

Sharon and Tracy sat at their usual places in the dingy office with their lunch spread out before them. Sharon was processing a requisition form for Buffalo Suede Reclining Chairs, and Tracy was waiting for her nails to dry before starting into her box of fried chicken. She held up two cans of fizzy drink.

'Which one d'you want, Shar? Orange?' She pointed from one to the other. 'Or yellow?'

'What's the yellow?' asked Sharon as she opened her carton and removed the napkins, sachets and spork.

Tracy examined the printing on the can. ' "Tropical Fruit

Mix",' it says. Could be anything. "Produce Of More Than One Country. Made From Concentrate. Contains Saccharin."'

'Causes cancer in laboratory rats, does saccharin,' said Sharon as she pulled out a chicken leg and bit into it.

'Well, we're not laboratory rats, are we?' said Tracy.

'Oh, give me the orange.'

'Did you see your Tone last night?' asked Tracy, passing over the soft-drink can.

'No. He was supposed to come round but he never showed up. Men.'

'Is he normally reliable, then?'

'Not really, no.'

'No, well they're not, are they?'

Silence fell in the office while Tracy opened her chicken box and started on a wing. She looked over at Sharon.

'Blimey, you polished off that leg in record time.'

'I was hungry,' she said through a mouthful of meat. 'Friday tomorrow. You gonna come up the wine bar?'

'Yeah, but I don't much like that house wine they have. It comes out of purple plastic barrels. It doesn't seem to have travelled well.'

'I should think it's travelled very well if it's in plastic barrels. It's probably been all over the place.'

'That's a point.'

Silence fell once more. Sharon set down her denuded chicken bone and delved into her box for another piece. Tracy drank her Tropical Fruit Mix and studied the portion of cheesecake sitting on her desk. She leaned forward and sniffed it.

'I *thought* that's where it was coming from,' she said. 'This cheesecake smells of lavender.'

'Probably a new flavour.' Sharon chewed on slowly. 'Now this chicken really *does* taste funny.'

'Oh Shar, you always say that. You're too bloody fussy, that's your problem.'

'No, it really does.' She carefully examined the piece in her hand. 'And anyway, what piece of chicken makes this shape?' She held it up to Tracy to have a look. The battered piece was small and semi-circular, and rather flat.

'I dunno,' said Tracy, puzzled. 'It's shaped like someone's ear.'

'Chickens don't have ears.' Sharon peered at it more closely. Set in the bottom of the fried portion, something glittered. She carefully picked away at the batter.

Underneath, pinned through the meat, was a small golden Taurus horoscope symbol.

Sharon's subsequent scream was so loud that shoppers in Oxford Street stopped dead when they heard it, and even Mr Patel, in the middle of serving a customer, looked up and wondered.

The Laundry Imp

'That wasn't the way I heard it,' said Charlene, folding her arms across her heavy chest. 'Whoever told you that was lying.' Her wonderbra sailed past the window twice, then vanished from sight.

'You know how these stories get exaggerated.' Lauren readjusted the crotch of her jeans and stared back at her rotating knickers, hypnotised. 'I mean, it's obviously not true or anything. It couldn't be. Someone would have heard the screams, or seen the blood leaking out.'

'Well, it was late at hight. There wasn't anyone around to save her.'

The two girls sat back on their grey plastic bendichairs and watched as the huge grey steel washing machines thudded and hummed and shook.

A freezing wind moaned fitfully under the glass entrance door, to be dissipated in the tropical steam heat of the laundromat.

'This place gives me the creeps,' Charlene complained. 'The lights are too bright and the air smells funny.'

'That's from the soap. My sister Beverly got a panty rash from the powder they put in the dispensers. She accused her boyfriend of sleeping around, and by the time she'd found out the real cause of the problem he'd admitted he was seeing someone else, so . . .' She allowed the thought to vaporise and replaced it. 'So she died, then, this girl?'

'I'm not sure whether she did or not. But if she did, it wasn't in the way you'd think. I didn't know her personally, but then you never do, do you? It's always a friend of a friend. Hard to ever know what's really true.'

This much is true.

It was a bitter, desolate winter night. Vernie wouldn't have bothered venturing out to the laundromat, but earlier that day she had spilled a strawberry milkshake down the front of her dress and the stain had stayed even after she had hand washed it. Gary always left his dirty washing in a white plastic bag beneath the sink, so she added the dress to it and set off, knowing that he would never get around to taking his turn with the laundry.

The Albion Laundrette was set in a parade of semi-derelict shops in a high street that nobody used any more. Respectable townsfolk headed for the vast shopping mall at the edge of town, a spotless climate-controlled dome filled with clowns and children and the scent of hot bread. There they could buy Belgian chocolates and novelty greetings cards. Here there was just a sauna, a restaurant of vaguely Arabic origin, a mini-cab company, a takeaway kebab counter, a porno book store, a closed-down electrical repair shop and a smeary-windowed room filled with fat Greek men playing cards.

On this night the laundrette was the only illuminated store-front in the parade. It stood behind a blizzard of litter, a large rectangular room lit by buzzing fluorescent strip lights. It contained twelve large washing machines, two heavy loaders and six tumble dryers. There were black and white rubberised tiles on the floor, twelve grey plastic chairs, two powder dispensers and a folding bench on which sat a pile of soft, dog-eared women's magazines. A cubbyhole at the rear was reserved for the manageress, who came by at nine in the morning, noon and eleven o'clock at night to lock up.

Vernie pulled the fake-fur collar of the cheap coat around her throat and set the plastic bag at her feet. At first she thought the place was closed, but the door was just stuck. Inside, the sticky warm air smelled of exaggerated cleanliness. The room was empty, but one of the huge front-loading tumble dryers was on. Presumably someone would be returning soon for their laundry. It wasn't a good idea to leave your clothes unattended in this neighbourhood; they were likely to disappear.

Vernie selected a machine and dumped her bag on the top. This was the most depressing place she could imagine spending the evening in. Especially when she knew that her friends were having fun somewhere else. But she couldn't go with them to the club tonight because she had no money, and because Darryl was going to be there with his new girlfriend, the one he'd been seeing while he was going out with her. Instead she was left in the flat with Gary and his boyfriend, feeling like a gooseberry while they sat on the sofa feeding each other scoops of chocolate-chocolate chip Häagen-Dazs.

As she carelessly loaded the machine she nearly started crying. She could not understand why life had to be so unfair. Everywhere she looked other people had jobs and lovers and something to look forward to. Nobody ever asked how she was. They were all too wrapped up in their own lives. She slammed the lid of the machine and dropped in the correct change. Pipes hissed somewhere in the wall as the drum began to fill.

Why should it be me who ends up spending the evening alone in the laundromat, she wondered, *wasting another page in the book of life, dropping another stitch in the tapestry of existence?* It didn't help that she was too damned smart for most of the guys around here. They wanted someone pretty by their side, someone to hold their beer while they took their pool shot, someone who didn't spoil it all by talking too much.

She folded the empty bag neatly and place it on the table, then checked through the rumpled magazines, but nothing excited her interest. The room was slightly cooler now, and she realised that the tumble dryer had stopped. The metal ticked and tapped as it contracted. The owner of the clothes hadn't returned to collect them. What if he was attractive and single, as lonely and alone as her? Love could flourish in the most mundane places. Hadn't her mother always told her that?

She checked the dusty clock above the machines. Her laundry was still on its first cycle. The room was growing cold. She tugged the hem of her old brown sweater over the waistband of her jeans. What if the owner of the clothes in the dryer *was* cute? She'd dressed in her sloppiest outfit. Perhaps he'd think she was being fashionable in a grungy waif kind of way. What if it wasn't a man? There was one way of finding out. She could remove the clothes from the dryer and fold them for him. It would give them a conversation opener when he finally returned.

'*How kind of you! You shouldn't have gone to so much trouble!*'

'*Oh, it was no trouble. It gave me something to do.*'

'*I don't understand what a pretty girl like you is doing in here.*'

'*Well, one needs a rest from partying occasionally.*'

'*I know what you mean. Why don't I give you a hand with your laundry, then we can go and get a cup of coffee?*'

'*That would be lovely. I don't know your—*'

The crash of something falling heavily against the glass doors snapped her from her reverie. A grey-bearded drunk had fallen against the step and was trying to get up without releasing his grip on the litre bottle of cider he carried.

'Fuckin' hell's teeth!' he shouted, rolling uselessly onto his side and thumping the reverberating door. Vernie backed away to the dryers, making sure that he couldn't catch sight of her. She counted to twenty beneath her breath and looked in through the dimpled window at the dried clothes, tying to ascertain the sex of their wearer. When she looked back up, the drunk had moved on and the street outside was once more empty.

She pulled open the dryer door and emptied the warm clothes into one of the red plastic baskets stacked below. The wash definitely belonged to a man. Faded jeans, denim work shirts and underpants, quite sexy ones. She pulled the full basket aside and began sorting the socks into pairs. It felt strange, touching the warm clothes of a total stranger, as if she was breaking some private taboo.

Something rattled in the dryer behind her. Or rather it made a scrabbling noise, as if a lizard was clinging to the roof of the perforated steel drum. She immediately thought that a rat had somehow jumped through the open door, for the warmth perhaps, but it scarcely seemed possible. The interior of the dryer was still scorching hot. She approached the drum and pulled back the door. Perhaps he had lost a cufflink or a bracelet in there and it had become entangled in the holes of the curving steel roof. Enveloped in the searing dry heat, she put in her right hand, extended her fingers and felt about.

Nothing.

She moved her arm further into the drum. Something rattled again, skittering towards her bare skin and clamping down on it. She screamed, jolting upright, cracking her head hard on the top rim of the machine. For a moment her vision clouded and she lost her balance, falling back against the plastic chairs. She briefly sensed something peering out at her from the drum, something dark and spiky with glittering back eyes. Then it was gone.

The air seemed warm and hazy, filled with choking motes of dust. Perhaps the blow to her head had left her with a concussion. Vernie glanced at her arm fearfully, expecting to find a bite wound, but there was nothing, not even a scratch. Her head throbbed, though. She looked at the gaping dryer drum, then across at the glass entrance door with the wind moaning beneath it. Perhaps she had imagined the whole thing. Somebody had been horribly murdered in one of these desolate places recently, a friend had told her all about it. Alarmed, she sat on a corner of the folding table and allowed her breathing to return to normal. And as she sat listening to the flopping and sopping of her laundry in the far washer, she remembered the story that Mrs Delphine had once told her, when she was just a tiny little girl.

Mrs Delphine was from Venezuela but had spent most of her life in Trinidad. She was a heavy, downcast woman who grudgingly visited Vernie's mother once a week to 'help out' as she called it; a matter of pride prevented her from thinking of herself as a cleaning lady. Every Wednesday afternoon after school, Vernie would sit and watch Mrs Delphine as she ironed and folded the household sheets, and would listen as she grumbled about the English weather before fondly recalling her life in an unimaginable tropical paradise.

One day Mrs Delphine held up a corner of a cotton vest in her plump right hand and tutted. 'Dear oh dearie me,' she said sadly.

'What's the matter?' asked Vernie, struggling to see. The centre of the vest was torn to shreds, as if it had been repeatedly slashed with a razor.

'Somebody's brought in the Laundry Imp,' she replied, bundling up the vest and taking it to the bin.

'What do you mean?' asked Vernie. 'What's the Laundry Imp?'

'I shouldn't be telling you, it will only give you nightmares.'

But Vernie could see that it wouldn't take much for the woman to speak. Her mother wouldn't be back for a while yet, and Mrs Delphine loved to recount scraps of lore from her homeland, particularly if they were of an unsavoury, doom-laden nature.

'See, the Laundry Imp is the fiercest little creature you can get in your house. It has a nastier mind than a mongoose and sharper teeth than a weasel, because it's born of lazy dirt.'

She upturned the laundry basket and began looking cautiously through the remainder of the unwashed clothes.

'At first it's very small, see, so small that you can hardly see it, like a shiny black flea. It grows in the clothes that folks have worn too long and worked too little in.' She looked off through the windows of the laundry room, at some middle-distant point of the garden. 'It feeds from the secretions of the rich and the idle, and it moves from one pile of dirty laundry to another to keep from being cleaned. As it moves through the clothes sucking in all the stains and the smells, the imp grows until it is the size of two knotted hands' – she entwined her strong brown fingers in demonstration – 'and it looks like a cross between a lizard and a monkey, with shiny black scales like pointed toenails, and a soft, bare underbelly, and tiny needle teeth, and beady little eyes and long sharp claws. It moves very fast and jerks its head like a bird because it's watching all the time.' She approached the unnerved girl, who had gingerly raised her feet from the floor. 'And because it has grown in the lazy waste of warm, slow bodies, it is very, very poisonous.'

'But what does it want?' Vernie asked, sitting back on the table and surreptitiously checking underneath it.

'It's searching for the scent of the poor,' Mrs Delphine murmured beneath her breath. 'It's a mean-spirited creature of supernatural origins, born from a curse once placed upon a cruelly idle man.'

'Tell me.'

'I'll be getting in trouble . . .'

'Please!'

'Very well.' She moved the iron to one side of her workbench and sat for a minute.

'In Venezuela there was once a nobleman named Count Arturo Lombardini who was very rich but also very mean and lazy. He was searching for a wife, but no woman would stay with him because he never washed, and although his clothes were imported from France with finely embroidered *dentils* and epaulettes and silken panels, the count wore them until they fell from his back because he was too mean to wear them out by washing them. He proudly boasted that he had not washed is hair in sixteen years but he went to great pains to pomade and arrange the sleek black tangle so that a row of greasy curls ringed his forehead. Such a look he felt no woman could resist.

302   Uncut

'Every morning a gypsy girl passed beneath Count Lombardini's bedroom window, hawking warm bread from her basket. The nobleman was in love from his first sight of her and had his servants fetch her to him. But when she was ushered into his chambers (a suite of rooms he rarely left), the terrible smell of his body overpowered her and she fled from his residence, dropping her basket of fresh bread.

'The next day, the count instructed his men to lie in wait for the gypsy girl, and they kidnapped her as she passed the palace doors. In a fever of anticipation, Lombardini sprayed himself with eucalyptus water, but this only produced a more emetic effect on little Sapphire, for that was the girl's name. Her parents had perished at sea long before, and she had been raised by an aged uncle who had taught her that daily acts of cleanliness were something even the poorest could perform to bring themselves closer to God.

'Incensed by the girl's obvious repulsion, the count bound her hands with rope and tied a silken bandana across her mouth. Then, with the help of a corrupt family priest, he arranged a simple wedding ceremony, so that even though it was against her will she would be betrothed to him, and he would be legally entitled to enjoy his conjugal rights.' Vernie did not need to know the meaning of that word in order to appreciate the unpleasantness it conveyed.

'That hot night he bore her to the stifling bridal chamber, and she was horrified to see that when he tried to undress himself the shirt he was wearing was so matted with sweat he could barely remove it from the stickety flesh of his back.' At this point, Mrs Delphine exercised rare restraint in her decision to gloss over the more grotesque details of the wedding night.

'Thankfully,' she added, 'no moon rose in the sky to

illuminate the scene, but after the unspeakable terrors of those endless darkened hours the gypsy girl became crazed with grief for her lost decency and decided to take her own life.

'At daybreak, while the count was still asleep, Sapphire ran to the filigreed bedroom balcony and leapt from it, only to be trampled by the count's own thoroughbred horses, which the ostlers were riding below in the street. But before she finally expired, she cried out to the heavens and placed a strange curse upon the count.

'Lombardini was sorry to lose his new wife but thought only of himself in the matter. Raising his sweat-stiff wedding shirt from the bed, he donned it once more and considered how he might secure another bride. The next evening, when he tried to remove the shirt before retiring, he found something growing in the silk – a tiny black imp that hopped from the chemise onto his back before he could stop it. The little mite burrowed into the skin between his shoulder blades, just at the point no man can ever reach to scratch. And it got plumper and heavier with every passing hour.

'Lombardini soon found that he could not sit back in a chair, or lie in a bed, for fear of squashing the imp. You see, every time it was squeezed it screamed and chattered and dug its claws deep into his flesh, almost until it could touch his spine. It crushed his nerves and twisted his muscles and burned his skin, but no one else could see the imp, so they simply thought the nobleman mad. He remained in his private chambers even more than before. All his meals were brought to him and were left outside the door. He cut the backs from his chairs so that he could sit after a fashion, and hacked a large hole in the headboard of his bed so that he could doze without disturbing the imp, but nothing would dislodge the hellish creature, which screamed and hissed as it grew wise to Lombardini's ways and chattered all night to prevent him from sleeping.

'Soon the count was a shadow of his old self, a wasted, yellowing skeleton with dark-rimmed eyes set in a gaunt, haunted face. His hair fell out in slimy clumps and he developed a stoop from the constant cramping of his back. He stalked the rooms at night, whimpering and whining for the pain to end, but was granted no relief. Often the servants stood at the door listening to his half-mad moanings.

'One night he drew a poker from the blazing fire in which it had lain and repeatedly slapped the glowing orange shaft across his back, searing his flesh, trying to dislodge the imp. But it was too quick for him and uprooted itself, scuttling around to his chest, where it tightened its grip more than ever before.

'When the servants finally broke down the doors and found the count with his codfish eyes turned over in their sockets, they saw that his spine had been scratched and frayed until it had severed, as if a hundred cats had reached inside and clawed away in a crimson frenzy.

'But the imp lived on in the nobleman's old clothes. It bred through the palace, multiplying in the rumpled sheets and the piles of rancid laundry left by other idlers, spoiled relatives of the count who lived lives of waste. Then the imps headed out into the streets for tastier, riper fare.'

'So the gypsy girl's curse backfired,' said Vernie. 'She had her revenge, but the imps went on to hurt poor people, and she herself had been poor.'

'Curses always find a way of backfiring,' said Mrs Delphine, returning to her work with a sigh. 'These days the wealthy wash and perfume themselves, and the imps spring from unhygienic clothes to spend their lives searching for the acrid scent of poverty. They move from one warm place to another, and when an imp finds the clothes of a working man, or a working woman, it draws its strength and burrows in, building its nest, slashing a bed for itself. And if it is disturbed it will burrow through a person, scratching and scrabbling through an ear or through the mouth or through the belly-button, until it comes out of the other side . . .' She spat on her iron and slapped it onto a shirt. 'So many wicked, dirty things around us, and not even being a good Catholic can save you.'

Two days later, Mrs Delphine was dismissed for filling the child's head with frightening stories. 'What could she have been thinking of,' Vernie's mother asked her husband that night, 'telling the girl such nightmarish things? Isn't the world filled with horrors enough without imagining more?' She felt that Mrs Delphine was insulting the household by implying that her husband, of whom she clearly disapproved, had brought in the Laundry Imp.

But for Mrs Delphine such creatures were real, just as they were for Vernie, who had seen the damaged vest and had spent the rest of her childhood screaming unless she was given clean clothes to wear.

Vernie raised her right leg and gave the dryer door a hard kick with the heel of her shoe. It slammed shut, but she had kicked too hard for the magnetic lock to catch, and it bounced back open. A sharp squeal reverberated within the drum, then there was silence.

Vernie had taken a step-class earlier in the same shirt she was wearing now. She had meant to add it to the wash before leaving the flat but had forgotten. What if the imp could smell her and even now was searching for a way to cleave itself to her sharply scented skin?

She realised with a start that her own laundry had completed its cycle and now required emptying. Even if the imp proved to be more substantial than a product of her childhood imagination, she was determined not to be bullied into leaving the laundrette without her washing. Closing the door more carefully this time, she dug out some coins and switched the dryer on. Surely the heat, magnified by the emptiness of the rotating drum, would prove too much for the creature? She walked to the front of the room and stared at the lid of her own silent machine. Gingerly, she raised the metal flap and lowered her arm inside, scooping out the warm, damp clothes.

There was a noise behind the washer, the sound of tiny scaled feet running along a pipe. It was using the water system behind the machines to cross the laundrette. She slammed the lid down hard and backed away. Suppose it could get into any of the tubs in this fashion? She looked at the clothes she had extracted so far, carefully unfolding a T-shirt and holding it up. To her horror she found herself holding a mirror to her childhood terrors. The shirt was tattered beyond repair, scored with a hundred tiny slashes.

The clatter of the lid made her raise her eyes, and she found herself staring at the Laundry Imp itself.

It was the size of a small cat but stood on curving hind legs. Its thin ebony claws formed sharp little hooks. It was worrying one between its teeth now, an eerily human gesture, watching her with quick, furtive movements. Its lips were pulled back about its tiny black snout, so that it seemed to be grinning at her.

The glass front door twanged open and closed behind her.

She couldn't bring herself to move. She was sure that if her concentration broke for just a second, the imp would set itself upon her.

'Are you okay?' The question took her by surprise and she jumped, involuntarily turning. The owner of the other wash load was everything she had hoped for, but now the thought of a romantic liaison was the farthest thing from her mind.

'Uh, yes, I'm – fine.' She turned back, but the imp had vanished from its place on top of the washing machine. She glanced to the floor. Perhaps it had dropped back behind the appliances.

'I think they may have mice in here,' said the man, watching her. 'I heard something moving about earlier.'

'Yes – I heard it, too.'

'Hey, thanks for taking my stuff out. Christ, it's hot in here, like the jungle or something.' He walked to his basket of clothes and slipped his leather jacket from his shoulders, dropping it onto the folding bench. His white T-shirt was sweat stained at the armpits. As he began shovelling his laundry into a large blue plastic bag, he looked back at her, concerned. 'Are you sure you're all right?'

'I thought I saw – something – but –' Forcing herself into action, she grabbed a handful of clothes and imitated him, shoving them wet into her bag. *Don't think about what's there*, she told herself, *don't try to rationalise.*

'Shouldn't you dry those first?'

'No, I just need to get outside for some fresh air.' She realised that she was speaking more sharply than she had intended and wanted to explain to the nice young man, who seemed so concerned, but as she looked back she saw the dryer doors all opening in unison, and not one but five of the Laundry Imps appeared, drawn by the acrid tang of his sweat. More were disentangling themselves from the overhead pipes like unfolding tarantulas. And then they were dropping through the grey air, and before she could cry out they were landing on his surprised face, leaping to his shoulders where they swarmed about, nuzzling their teeth into his shirt, burrowing beneath his arms, biting chunks of shocking red flesh from his neck. No longer content to simply live as parasites, the newly urban creatures had adopted the aggressive nature of the city streets and were seeking out prey – but not her, not her.

As they buried themselves in his body, churning aside gobs of fat and splinters of bone, her rescuer fell to his knees with a wet crack, and Vernie began to shake uncontrollably. Then, forcing her frozen muscles into action, she fell towards the door and tore it wide open.

The icy gale that hit her almost drove her back. She had left her jacket at the far end of the room. She would have to leave without it. Looking over her shoulder, she saw that the feral creatures were protecting themselves from the blast of freezing air by ducking behind the collapsed corpse of the young man.

Finally finding the voice to scream, she left the laundromat and ran – and ran and ran – on through the deserted, alien streets.

'What happened to her?' asked Lauren as she eyed her undulating lingerie with new suspicion.

'That's the awful thing,' said Charlene, digging the gum from her mouth and fixing it to the underside of her seat with a practised gesture. 'Guess what I heard she finally died of?'

'What?'

'Pneumonia.' She stretched the second syllable so that it sounded even more deathly. 'When she got home, she took off all her clothes and started examining them for black specks, the seed lice of the Laundry Imps. She ripped all of her clothes to shreds looking for their eggs. Went through her entire wardrobe, tearing everything up and burning it in the garden. She couldn't bear to keep any clothes on her skin after that.'

'I don't get it,' said Lauren slowly. 'Why not?'

'Don't you see? The imps didn't kill her because she knew about them. They sensed that they could use her as a breeding ground. They probably laid their eggs in her dirty laundry while she was at the soap dispenser, right here in this laundrette. She wouldn't allow them the chance to grow on her, so she stopped wearing clothes and kept all the windows open, and it was a very cold winter. The poor thing literally froze to death.'

Charlene's machine stopped suddenly. She folded her magazine shut and rose. She looked around. They were the last remaining customers of the evening. Out in the dark night, the wind was rising. Something clattered sharply against the glass of her machine.

'Wait a minute,' said Lauren. 'I thought you said you didn't know if this girl lived or died.'

'Well,' said Charlene, reaching for the dryer door, 'nothing's ever certain, is it? My grandad has wartime stories that would make your hair perm itself. You hear about these things, stuff that's been going on since before you were born, and you're still never quite sure. Before you can really believe, you have to take a look for yourself.'

Her fingers grasped the aluminium handle and she jerked the broad porthole open.

The Most Boring Woman in the World

I can't imagine why you'd want to interview me, I'm the most boring woman in the world.

I'm nobody. Nothing interesting ever happens in my life. I live in a house like thousands of others, in a banjo crescent called Wellington Close in a suburban part of South London, in a semidetached with three bedrooms and a garden filled with neatly pruned roses that have no scent and a lawn covered with broken plastic children's toys. I have a Labrador called Blackie, two children, Jason and Emma, and a husband called Derek. I keep my clothesline filled and my upstairs curtains closed (to protect the carpets from the sun – blue fades easily) and my days are all the same.

Derek works for a company that supplies most of Southern England with nonflammable sofa kapok. I met him when I was a secretary at Mono Foods, where he was senior floor manager. One afternoon he came by my desk and asked me out to the pub. I'll always remember it because he drank eight pints of lager to my three Babychams and I'd never met anyone with that much money before. Six weeks later he proposed. We were married the following June and spent two weeks on the Costa where I picked up a painful crimson rash on the beach and had to be hospitalised in a clinic for skin disorders.

Before that? Well, nothing much to report. I was a happy child. People always say that, don't they? My older brother, to whom I was devoted, died in a motorbike accident when a dog ran out in front of him, and at the funeral they muddled his cremation with someone else's, an old lady's, so that we got the wrong urns and her family was very upset. Also, the dog was put down. Things like that were always happening in our family. On Christmas Eve 1969, my father got completely drunk, fell down the coal-hole chute and landed in the cellar, and nobody found him until Boxing Day. His right leg didn't knit properly so he had to walk with a stick. One day the stick got stuck in a drainage grating, and he had a heart attack trying to pull it out. My mother passed on a few weeks later. They say one often follows the other, don't they? I lost a cousin around the same time, when a gas tap jammed in a Portuguese holiday villa.

No such calamities ever occur now. Now my days are all the same.

When I was young I was a pretty girl, with straight white teeth and hair that framed my face like curls of country butter, but I didn't know I was pretty until I was thirteen, when John Percy from three doors down tried to rape me in exchange for a Chad Valley Give-A-Show projector. I told my mother and she went over to the Percy house. They moved away soon after. They had to. John came around and hit me when I opened the front door to him. He broke my nose, and I wasn't so pretty after that.

When I was sixteen I wanted to go to art college, I wanted to be an artist, but my father said there was no call for it and I would be better off in an office. So I went to work for Mono Foods, met Derek, got married. I didn't have to or anything, it just felt like the right thing to do. He seemed interested in me, and nobody else was, so I said yes. My father joked about it being a relief to get me off his hands, but he wasn't really joking.

For a while we moved in with Derek's mother, but that didn't work out because she hated me for taking away her son and stood over me in the kitchen while I cooked, saying things like, 'That isn't how he likes his eggs,' until I felt like strangling her. Then I fell pregnant and we moved here. We put her in a very nice old folks' home, but the first night she was there she wrote and told me I was cursed for stealing her boy, that she was going to die and that it would be on my conscience for ever.

The awful thing was that she had a stroke that night and died, and I had to go into therapy. Derek took his mother's side, and while he didn't actually call me a murderer to my face, I knew that was what he was thinking.

Since then I always joke that I'm not addicted to Valium. I just like the taste.

My days are all the same.

Here's my routine:

The white plastic radio alarm goes off at seven fifteen. The DJ makes jokes about the day's newspaper headlines as I rise and slip into the powder-blue dressing gown covered in little pink flowers. I'll have been awake since five, lying on my back listening to the ticking of the pipes as the boiler thermostat comes on. Derek sleeps through the alarm. I wake him and he totters off to the bathroom moaning about his workload and complaining about people at the office I've never heard of because I'm just a silly housewife who can't retain any information that isn't about the price of fucking washing powder.

I drag the children out of their beds and pack them off to wash and dress, make them breakfast (cereal and toast in the summer, porridge in the winter), check that they're presentable and send them to school. Derek usually finds something to bitch about, like I've ironed his shirt with the creases going in the wrong direction or there's a button missing from his braces, and tuts and fuffs until I sort out the problem. Then he takes the Vauxhall, leaves me the Renault and the house falls silent. And I sit down with a cigarette, and a nice glass of Scotch and a Valium.

They don't know I smoke. I have to wash the ashtrays and open the windows before the kids get back.

During the day all sorts of exciting things happen. Last Tuesday the knob came off the tumble dryer, on Thursday next door's cat nearly got run over, and on Friday I found out that my husband was having an affair. Her name is Georgina. She works in his department. His pet name for her is 'my little Gee Gee', and she explains all of the awkward, stilted phone calls that take place here in the evenings. If you're going to have an affair it's a good idea to remember to empty the pockets of your trousers before you give them to me for dry-cleaning, that's all I can say.

I don't get on with the neighbours. The stuck-up bitch next door won't talk to me because I once got a little soused in the middle of the day and fell into her fishpond. Sometimes I sit in the car and rev the engine just to blow smoke over her washing.

Jason and Emma come home and lie on the floor on their stomachs in that curiously impossible position children use for watching television. They remain glued to cartoons, space serials and Save The Fucking Zebra updates, all presented by some perky fresh-faced teenager I'd secretly like to ride naked.

I cook. I make sausage, egg and beans with chips, and fish-fingers with chips, and beefburgers with chips, and chop, chips and peas. Everything comes with chips at number 11 Wellington Close. I'm the only one who doesn't like chips. I'd like to cook *langoustine* swimming in garlic, *loup grillé* with capers and shallots. But you can't get *langoustine* around here, just *doigts de poisson avec frites*.

I don't eat with the others. After the smell of frying has permeated my clothes I'm no longer hungry. I have a brandy. I keep a bottle at the back of the sink. Sometimes Derek comes into the kitchen to refill the saltcellar and finds me on all fours with my head somewhere near the U-bend, and I tell him that the waste disposal is playing up again.

Then I clear away the dinner things while Derek provides more news about the people he works with and who, for me, only exist as a series of names with personality quirks attached. The Byzantine intrigue of the sofa kapok world is such that if Lucrezia Borgia applied for a job she'd barely make a secretarial position.

I don't wash up very well. By now the kids are yelling and I'm getting jumpy. Anything I drop goes in the bin. Nobody notices. Nobody notices anything. My days are all the same. I listen to the pounding in my head and watch as the lounge fills up with blood. You can't see the telly when there's blood in the way.

At the weekend I go shopping. Sometimes I go shopping in my mind, but I don't come back with anything. Oh, how we love to shop! B&Q, M&S, Safeway, Tesco, Homebase, Knicker-box, Body Shop, we just wander around lost in amazement at the sheer choice and ready availability of luxury products at the end of the twentieth century. If the excitement was running any higher it would be leaking from our arseholes. Derek doesn't come with us, of course; he stays behind at the house to creep around making furtive phone calls from the bedroom. He says he's 'doing the accounts', presumably a coded phrase that means 'telephoning the trollop'.

On Sunday mornings we rise later than usual and I prepare a cooked breakfast before Derek heaves his flabby body from the chair and chooses between the pastimes of straightening up the garden and hoovering his floozie's hairpins from the car. Do they still have hairpins? I can't remember the last time I saw one. There are so many things you don't see any more. Those little pieces of green string with metal rods at either end that used to hold bits of paper together. Animal-shaped Peak Freen biscuits. Jubblies, sherbet dabs and Jamboree Bags. You never see any of them any more. Instead I see the white plastic radio alarm clock and the powder-blue dressing gown and the hairs on Derek's indifferently turned back.

The first time I took speed I got all the housework done in under an hour. It was great. But I felt so tired afterwards that I couldn't cook, and Derek had to go and buy us all fish and chips. Speed helped me to organise the household. Thanks to the speed, which I got in the form of prescription diet pills, I not only started collecting money-off coupons, I catalogued them all in little boxes according to date, value and type of offer. I just never got around to using any of them.

I have never hit my children. Not even when I caught Jason smoking in the toilet and he was abusive. It would have been hypocritical of me. Is punching hitting? Sometimes I don't remember things very well. I have lapses. Little bits of housewife downtime. Sometimes the children tell me I did something when I'm sure I didn't. The dog won't come near me any more, and I think it's something to do with one of those vanished moments. I think I fed Blackie something bad.

When we argue, which is quite often these days, Derek always tells me that I never learn. I try to learn, but it's hard to get motivated when you're alone all day and you know exactly what's going to happen from the minute the white plastic radio alarm goes off until the time you set it again at night. I don't like the nights. It's when I feel most alone. We go to bed, read magazines and sleep, but we don't speak. I lie there listening. Derek's furry back is turned away from me, the children are unconscious, the streets outside are black and silent. It's like being dead, or being buried alive, or some damned thing.

Wait, here's something new I learned. Cocaine, Valium and Lamb's Navy Rum don't mix at all well. I got the cocaine from a man at the shopping centre because I'd just had a huge fight with Derek and it seemed like a good angry response to his wheedling, wide-eyed denials. I'd already drunk half the bottle of rum to get my nerve up, and the Valium was a matter of habit. I opened the little paper packet of coke and chopped it finely on the breadboard with my M&S card, then snorted it up through a Ronald McDonald straw. The kids were in the lounge watching adults get green slime tipped over their heads on TV, and I was off my face in the kitchen. I threw a careless glance at the lasagna filling the oven with dense grey smoke and thought, hey, it's takeaways again tonight, kids!, chucked the burning lasagna in the dog's bowl and crawled under the sink for another hit of rum. Derek was at the office 'attending an extracurricular staff meeting', which roughly translated as 'bunging the bimbo one in the photocopying room', and I no longer gave a toss about the world or anything in it.

I love my children because they're my flesh and blood. But I don't really like them. Jason, without intending to, has learned to be sly and grasping and is already watching his father for tips at gaining a better foothold on the easy life. Emma is, well, *bovine* is too unkind a word. Slow to catch on, shall we say. She stares slackly with eyes like chips of glass and only becomes animated before certain TV programmes. These children are from me, but not of me. Each day they become a little more like Martians, shifting away from my embrace with each incomprehensible new habit learned in the school playground. And as their language grows more alien, as the cults and rituals they design to be misconstrued by adults grow more elaborate, I lose them a little more each day, meal time by meal time. Every mother knows that her children eventually leave. I just hadn't expected the process to start so fucking early.

Derek works on winning the kids over to his side, of course. He can only allow himself to be seen as a hero. He teams up with them against me. Fathers often do that. Nice habit.

The house is quiet now. But then, it always was quiet. Our fights were conducted in a series of controlled explosions that wouldn't wake the children, muted insults escaping like hisses of steam.

It was important to Derek that we also presented a unified, peaceful front to the neighbours. It didn't take them long to cotton on, of course. The bin bags filled with bottles were a giveaway. Well, Mr and Mrs Rodney Boreham-Stiff next door can go and fuck themselves as far as I'm concerned. They're dead from the wallet up, like everyone else around here; you want to talk about politics or art, they want to ask you how you get your windows so clean. Everyone's a Stepford Wife. We have television to thank for explaining to us the importance of germ-free, pine-fresh tiles in our lives.

I'll admit it now. At some point, I lost the plot. I could no longer remember my set routine. Housewifely duties became unfathomable to me. When the alarm went off I would rise and stand at the bedroom window, looking down into the deserted dawn streets, wondering what on earth I was supposed to be doing. How to function as a mother and a wife. Was it get up, wash the kids and iron the breakfast, or make dinner, fry the dog and kill the husband? I asked the children, but they didn't know. Just got frightened and ran to Daddy. Big brave Daddy.

When Derek came home early one day and told me he was leaving for good, heading off into the sunset with his little Gee Gee, I was heating oil in a copper-bottomed omelette pan. Bad timing, big mistake. The pan left a series of concentric rings on the side of his face, and the oil badly burned his neck. The second time I hit him it dented the back of his head with a crunch, like putting a spoon through a soft-boiled egg. He dropped to his knees in complete surprise and pitched onto his back. I wanted to make sure he was dead, so I cut open a cushion and stuffed his mouth with kapok. I expected my civic-minded neighbours to call the police any minute, complaining of hearing 'raised voices', as if such indications of human life should never be given, and I began to panic. I imagined being led away through a crowd of gawping, tutting onlookers to a waiting car. But before agreeing to go with the police, I would tidy up the kitchen and tearfully say goodbye to the children. And I thought to myself, if only one of you could have met me halfway, just to show that you cared, I wouldn't have had to murder someone. But I had, and he was lying on the kitchen floor, a halo of coagulating blood expanding on the diamond tiles, and I had to do something about it.

So I put him in a bin bag.

Well, not one, about three, but it wasn't at all difficult. I did it without thinking, as though it was the most natural thing in the world to do. Derek wasn't a large man, and I was used to manhandling sacks of rubbish, and before the kids were back from school I had him trussed up by the back door ready for collection. I squeegeed up the blood, rinsed the mop and replaced it, then showered and changed and came back downstairs just as Jason walked in, asking what was for dinner.

That night after the kids were in bed I entered the garage from the house, put the bin bags in the Renault and drove over to the edge of the estate, where there was a gravel pit that the council were landfilling so they could build yet another Tesco nobody needed but would soon be hypnotised into using. I dragged the bag across the back of the car park and gave it a good shove down into the pit, then kicked a load of rubbish on top of it. Then I went home and watched *The Late Show*.

I didn't plan any of this, you understand. I simply acted without thinking about it. The police would turn up and arrest me and that would be that.

But they didn't. The next morning, Derek's office called to find out where he was, and I told them I had no idea. The kids asked in a half-hearted way, and I told them the same thing.

I didn't go to the police and report him missing, because if they came calling I knew I could say he'd run off with his mistress. Instead I opened a fresh bottle of rum, got pissed watching *Pebble Mill*, and got away with murder.

When I was a little girl, I believed that you got what you deserved. If you were very good, you were rewarded with a lovely house, a husband and children. If you were dis- obedient, you would never meet anyone and die a bitter, loveless death. Now I know that it's the other way around; you get what you don't deserve. And I didn't deserve this frozen life where my days are all the same.

Oh, but they *are*. You think they should be different since I murdered my husband? And you wonder why I chose to confess to you?

Well, because I only just made the murder part up.

I didn't really kill Derek, even though I had the opportunity. He's still alive. We did have a row about his fancy woman, but he promised to put an end to the relationship. He hasn't, of course. And I missed my chance to conk him on the head.

But it's always there in the back of my mind, the knowledge that one day I might just go berserk with the Black & Decker. Hack his dick off, saw the dog in half, drink rat poison and set fire to the house while the children are in bed. Sometimes I get up in the middle of the night and watch them all sleeping, and I wonder if they realise how much danger they're in. I stand above Derek as he snores lightly, his head buried deep in the pillow, and I want to pour lighted petrol into his mouth.

Each day they bring themselves closer to a reckoning with me. And they have no idea, because our days are all the same. Soon there'll be screams in the night, power knives, lamps being overturned, doors slamming, flames and madness.

Or perhaps there won't.

I have to go, my husband will be home from work soon and the dinner isn't on. I don't know why you wanted to interview me, anyway. I'm just like everyone else around here – more so. I'm the most boring woman in the world.

At the moment.

Dale and Wayne Go Shopping

'There's nothing else for it,' she said, raising her hands in apology. 'We have to go to the store.'

'Christ, Dale, isn't there another way?' asked Wayne. He walked to the refrigerator, yanked open the door and peered inside. At the back of the bare shelves he found an almost empty jar of peanut butter and two curled slices of packet ham, so dark and stale that they looked like jerky. In the ice-box there was half a pint of mildewing pistachio flavoured ice-cream and a bottle of amyl nitrate. 'I mean, it ain't as if we're gonna be holding any dinner parties in the next few days. We can get by on takeouts.'

'Wayne, my guts can't handle any more pizza.'

'Then we'll get burgers.'

'I don't know what they put in them these days. Last time we ate at BurgerShack I nearly died, remember?' She pulled a bothersome strand of blond hair from her face and tied it back. The heat in the apartment was dishevelling them both. 'Besides, I have a recipe I want to try out. Let's just do it without thinking about it, then it'll be over quicker.'

'I guess you're right,' Wayne conceded as he selected a long-bladed knife from the kitchen rack and slid it under the belt of his jeans. 'I just wish the sun was a little higher. We could always try somewhere different this time.'

'We know the layout of the Pricefair, Wayne. And it's real near for us. We'll be safer there. See what else we need, honey.' Her blue eyes studied his for a moment before flicking away. As her husband checked the kitchen cupboards, Dale chose a short wooden-handled knife with a broad blade and tucked it point down in her side pocket. Then they left the stifling apartment and walked around the back of the block to the van.

It was little more than a three-minute drive to the vast supermarket at the corner of Grove and 23rd. They parked as near to the building's main entrance as they could. As usual, the lot was almost empty.

'Jeezus, it's gonna be dark soon. I don't like this,' said Wayne, searching around. 'Leave the van unlocked, just in case we have to make a run for it.'

They walked across the lot in perfect step, low-slung sunlight yanking their shadows tall across the cracked tarmac. Brightly coloured special offer posters filled the gold-reflecting windows of the store. No details of the interior could be seen from outside.

'Oh Christ, this is it.' Wayne dug his hand into his pocket and touched his silver dollar. 'Make me lucky today.' He looked over at Dale. 'Make us both lucky. Now you touch it.'

Dale touched the dollar.

'Ready?'

'Ready as I'll ever be.'

They stood at the threshold of the supermarket, drawing

one last deep breath before breaking the electronic beam which shot the glass doors wide before them.

'Okay, where's the list?' called Wayne as Dale ran for a trolley.

'In my hand.' She raised a fist so he could see. 'Eggs,' she shouted back. 'We need eggs. Go quickly. I'll meet you there.'

Above them, Henry Mancini's 'Theme From A Summer Place' played on the Muzak system. Wayne dashed into the first section, the steel-tipped heels of his cowboy boots skidding on the tiled floor. He knew where the eggs were, end of the shelf on aisle one, but in front of him was the first sign of trouble. An elderly woman in a heavy woollen coat, burning pretty fiercely. She must have been on fire for some time, because her charred body had collapsed in on itself, and the floor was blackened all around her. Wayne moved cautiously past the crackling pyre. The woman looked like an immolated buddha. Her wire basket had fallen to one side, unfortunately devoid of produce. She'd barely had time to pick up a carton.

That was the problem with the eggs. Sometimes they were booby-trapped with this napalm-like stuff that stuck to your skin and stayed alight for hours.

He reached up and grabbed the box beside the one she had removed, figuring it was unlikely that two cartons next to each other would both be tampered with. Cautiously he raised the lid and checked inside. One dozen fresh farm eggs. A good start.

'Make sure you get Free Range,' called Dale, sliding into view at the tip of the second aisle. 'It's easier on the hens.'

'A whole lot easier on them than us,' muttered Wayne, deciding not to take the risk of switching the cartons. Ahead, Dale's trolley slewed to one side and slammed into a rack of tinned fruit. A can of cling peaches fell to the ground with a bang, followed by a second. Wayne and his wife dropped to the floor with their hands over their ears. but nothing happened.

Dale climbed to her feet and hefted one of the cans into the trolley. 'A nice little bonus,' she said, grinning at him. 'Let's get on.' They had no way of knowing what the noise might have attracted while they were hanging around. She consulted the items on the list. 'Butter and cheese.'

'Oh, not the cold cabinet,' complained Wayne. They both remembered seeing a man torn limb from limb in the yoghurt section last month. They carefully wheeled the trolley past a pair of black-shirted punks who were randomly stabbing at the back and neck of a cowering man, and arrived at the cold cabinet. The Muzak had now changed to 'Lara's Theme' from *Dr Zhivago*.

'This is so unhygienic,' complained Dale, pointing at the various packaged cheeses. 'You'd think they'd clean it out every night.' A black pool of blood lay scabbing over between packets of Edam and Cheddar. Blood spattered most of the products on the shelves. The reason for the mess quickly became obvious. A man with no head lay half out of the cabinet, the ragged stump of his neck glutinously leaking onto the frozen pastries. Some kind of razorblade device had swung down on him when he'd reached in for a pound of margarine. Trying not to look at the twisted form beside her, Dale pointed out the brand of butter she needed as Wayne darted his hands in and scooped it up.

'And grab that cheese,' she said, waving her hand at a block of Emmenthal. 'Don't take the front one. There's some kind of wire hanging out of it.' The front cheeses were indeed wired up, probably to the mains electricity supply. One touch would burn the skin clean off your bones. Wayne leaned gingerly forward and checked at the back of the shelf, but it was overrun with hairless baby rats, plump pink forms that wriggled away, scattering to the touch. 'Could you make do with a piece of Stilton?' he asked.

'Actually, that would be nicer for what I had in mind,' said Dale. 'Is it safe?'

'Nothing is safe any more,' he replied, grimacing as he flicked the tiny blind rodents aside to reach a chunk of shrink-wrapped Stilton. 'What's next?'

'Bleach.'

'Oh, *great*.' He tossed the cheese into the trolley. It was becoming hard to steer because the front wheels had been standing in blood, and were now rolling crooked crimson tracks across the cream plastic floortiles. Above them, the tannoy system was playing the theme from *Born Free*.

The Household Items aisle was notoriously dangerous even by Pricefair standards. A group of drugged-out kids were standing in front of the shelves, popping the tops from economy-sized bottles of bleach and chugging them down. It was a manhood thing, a kind of dare. Lots of kids were dong it now. One child of no more than eight or nine had fallen to the floor and was convulsing as the acidic liquid seared its way through his internal organs.

Two of the taller children moved menacingly towards them brandishing opened bleach bottles. Wayne could see that their lips were badly burned. One of them swung his bottle, spraying bleach at Dale. She ducked behind the end of the aisle as the liquid splashed around her. With a shout, Wayne withdrew his knife and ran at one of the larger children, a girl, slashing a cheek, then an arm. As she screamed and fell back he grabbed a large plastic bottle from the shelf and threw it to his wife. Dale caught it in a seasoned swing as if accepting a Bronco pass. Then Wayne was running, sliding out of the aisle, safe in the knowledge that he could not be followed because the bleachers would never risk surrendering their home turf.

The centre of the store was quiet enough. Here the spoor of violence had grown stale. They passed a half-rotted corpse folded up in a lawn lounger in the Garden Furniture section, black body fluids leaking through the multicoloured fabric. The scene had an ugly peace about it. At least there were no signs of recent disturbance. In Jams & Jellies, sticky gossamer nets of brown crawly things pulsed with life on the shelves between the pots. An old Jim Reeves song was now tinkling from the ceiling speakers. Something with a lot of legs ran past Dale and vanished under Special Offer Soups, brushing the backs of her legs as it went.

'For God's sake let's get out of here,' said Wayne, pulling the cart to a halt. 'We got everything we need.'

'We don't, Wayne. I still have to get some other stuff.' She tapped the paper with her index finger. Wayne looked over her shoulder at the list.

'You can cross those frozen diet dinners off,' he said, grimacing. 'I saw a man lose his nuts trying to get a Weight Watchers meal outta the cabinet.'

Over on aisle six the air-conditioning ducts set in the ceiling had been blocked up with something alarmingly bulky and human-sized, and the rising temperature caused sweat to sheen their faces. Dale smudged damp hair from her eyes and sighed. 'Okay, we'll just get some dessert. Please, Wayne, it's been so long since we had a nice cake. A black forest gâteau, maybe.'

'Well . . . all right.'

The Cakes & Pastries freezer was suspiciously devoid of life. As they wheeled their errant trolley to the far end of the store they could see someone leaning over into the refrigerated cabinet, pushing and shoving at the cartons within.

'I don't like the look of this,' whispered Wayne. 'Slow down.' As they approached the cabinet, they could see that the figure was convulsing, knees jerking back and forth beyond muscular control, shoes banging and skittering against the wall of the freezer unit.

'Hey, mister, you okay?' called Dale. There was no reply.

Suppressing a shudder of alarm, Wayne looked over into the dessert compartment. One of the gâteau boxes had exploded in a tangle of metal coils. He quickly pushed Dale away. 'You don't wanna see this, honey, believe me.' But he could not resist another look himself. The wires had sprung from the booby-trapped box to pierce its victim's face in a hundred different places, gripping flesh and bone with springs of steel.

'Okay, *that* does it, we're out of here,' shouted Wayne, grabbing his wife by the arm and hauling her and the trolley off in the direction of the checkout.

'Wait,' cried Dale, pulling back. 'We're passing right by Savouries. I want some ketchup, and a pack of those little silver balls you put on cakes.'

As the song on the tannoy changed to The Doors' 'Light My Fire' rearranged for xylophone, they ran past the Savouries section, where a pair of leather-jacketed teenagers were sawing the head from a squatting female shopper with a large kitchen-knife. Wayne noticed that the knife worked pretty well considering it was still in a bubble pack. 'I think you can forget the ketchup,' he said.

A bored-looking girl sat playing with her hair at the express-lane till. Dale and Wayne yanked the runaway trolley to a stop beside her and began throwing their purchases onto the conveyor belt. Dale could tell that the checkout girl was stoned out of her mind by the way her eyes kept involuntarily rolling up into her head until only the whites showed.

'We gotta find a new place to shop,' said Wayne.

'Yeah,' his wife agreed. 'I miss the friendliness of the local corner stores.' The girl at the till managed to run each product over the barcode laser but had most of them the wrong way up, so that half of the prices failed to register. Her hair was matted with overperming, and a thin strand of drool hung suspended between her lips and her sweater. Suddenly she jerkily hoisted the bleach and shouted 'Pricecheck on this item', in a slurred screech before letting the bottle slide from her hand. As Wayne deftly caught it, she coughed and blew a chunk of nose-blood onto the register.

Trying not to look, Dale stood the eggs on the conveyor belt. The checkout girl turned her attention to the carton and stared at it with bulging eyes.

'This yours?' she asked in amazement.

'I figure so,' replied Dale sarcastically, 'seeing as we managed to get it off the shelf.'

Wayne stopped filling the takeout bag. 'What's the problem?' he asked.

'Eleven items,' slurred the girl, pressing a button beneath the till. 'This is the express lane. Ten items only.'

'Then we'll put one ba—' Wayne managed to say before the bullet shattered his skull and his body was punched into a backward somersault, landing him in the end aisle.

As Dale's voice rose in a scream another burst of gunfire came, shattering her arm and shoulder, tearing open her neck in a powerful geyser of blood as she spun around with her hands raised and toppled to the floor.

The Pricefair manager, a ginger-haired boy of twenty-one,

dropped the scorching pistol back into his overall pocket and turned to the checkout girl.

'I told you before, Charlene,' he admonished, 'warn 'em before you start ringin' stuff up. I gotta reset the total each time.'

Above them, the overture from *Mary Poppins* began to play.

Tales of Britannica Castle

I. *Ginansia's Ravishment*

The problem with the spiral staircase to the Northeast Quadrant was the plethora of scorpions, small brass ones, set in spiky pairs on either side of each stone step. Their tails tugged at Ginansia's dress, snagging on the sapphire-sewn hem and snatching her back every few feet. Finally she was forced to run with the silken material gathered up at her knee and run she did because she was late for dinner, and the Great Wound never forgave tardiness when it involved the ruination of sweetmeats.

Although the Princess Ginansia had lived here all her life and knew every room, corridor, staircase, tapestry, window, door and hallway in the castle, she often felt that the building as a whole conspired against her. It was too ornate, as fussy and overdecorated as her mother, filled with dangerous shadows, pools of darkness that concealed sharp little objects that tripped toes, cracked nails and tore skin. In terms of acreage the castle was small, but it was tall. The top five levels had been added by Captain Smackthistle after his legendary victory against the Fire-Tribe Boys of the Infected Mountain. He and his men had returned with all manner of disgusting trophies, parts of bodies which they threaded with gold and silver wire and hung in the heavy blue glass jars that lined the whole of the planetarium.

Ginansia knew no other home but sometimes dreamed of visiting white open spaces, vast halls of light that were free of clutter and gloom, where nothing was more than a few moments old and she could breathe without drawing dust into her lungs, stretching out her arms to embrace the flaring sun.

She tripped on the bottom step and nearly overturned one of the huge cracked Chinese vases that stood on the marble pedestals at the base of the staircase. Catching sight of herself in the vestibule's towering scabrous mirror, she readjusted the dried clematis petals in her hair, carefully tucking them into the auburn folds. She liked clematis flowers because they had no smell; the castle held far too many extraordinary odours to require further olfactory obfuscation by its residents.

Ahead was the narrow, uneven flagstone corridor that led to the Tarnished Hall and the Seven Sepulchres Of Shame, and beyond that the strangely shaped area formerly known as the Heart Of All Sorrow, which was now simply called the Dining Hall. The floor here was always wet and slippery, 'perspiring tears' according to her mother but in reality slick with condensation, because the flues from the kitchen passed across the eastern archway and the fissures in them released steady wisps of steam, wreathing the entire ceiling in swirling mist.

Ginansia was about to open the enormous iron door to the Tarnished Hall when an elegant figure divorced itself from a cobwebbed clutter of crockery and stepped in front of her.

Leperdandy pulled a handkerchief from the top pocket of his purple quilted smoking jacket and flicked it under his quivering narrow nostrils, enveloping them both in an over-powering scent of lavender.

'You're as late as I,' he sniffed. 'Your stepfather went in ten minutes ago. The Great Wound will not be pleased.'

'Have you ever seen him pleased about anything?' she asked, falling into step beside her half-brother.

'Now that you mention it,' said Leperdandy, 'no.'

'I dread tonight.'

'I know you do. You must be strong.'

They passed across the puddled stones of the angular hall, the damp air clinging to their clothes, fattening the fabric with droplets of moisture. The shadowy stone alcoves on either side mercifully concealed the sepulchres, which had given Ginansia such nightmares as a child. In front of her stood the towering armoured suit of St Ethelbar Squeam, one rusted red arm raised high with his spiked mace still gripped in a battered gauntlet, the other perched effeminately on his steel-lace hip. The mummified corpse of the Squeam himself was still inside the armour, and if you raised the protesting visor and peered in you would see that the rumours were indeed true; the ancient knight had somehow turned himself around within the mail so that he was facing back to front – a sign of cowardice before the enemy, some said.

Opening the doors of the Dining Hall tugged a chain that rang a sharp little bell somewhere beneath their feet, a warn-ing to the kitchen staff to be on their toes. The great table, arranged in cruciform and draped in holly-green cloth, was occupied along its far side, and the inhabitants swivelled their eyes disapprovingly to the latecomers.

'Is it too much to ask that we might share a meal together

on the eve of your age-coming?' boomed her stepfather, his sole good eye glaring wetly beneath a bunched, bushy brow as he jutted from the table, an acre of emerald linen splayed at his throat. Globules of venison soup hung in his immense beard. A dripping spoon jutted from his meaty fist. His vast shoulders rose and fell, rose and fell with the wheezing passage of his breath, like an old steam engine labouring with its load. Scarabold the Third of the royal family Bayne, the Great Wound himself, Doer Of Dark Deeds, Rectifier Of Wrongly Wrought Rites, Warrior, stepfather to Ginansia and father to Leperdandy (by a different mother), had watched the severed heads of his enemies bounce down the steps of the Imperial Museum during the Great Siege of '28 with less passion that he now displayed at the tardiness of his offspirng.

'The Italian Courtyard is half flooded,' replied Ginansia glibly. 'I had to go all the way around and through the Under-Chapel.' She had, in fact, spent too long at her toilette to register the crepusculation of the hour. These days she was rarely on time for anything. It was one of the few ways she had left of showing dissatisfaction with her circumstance.

'Your father has something to tell you, dear,' called her mother, ignoring the steaming monarch at her side, 'just as soon as you are settled.'

Mater Moribund Bayne had outdone herself tonight. Her sticklike form, so thin that her ribs could be discerned through the purple bombazine of her gown, was bedecked with ropes of jewellery that glittered and shone and swayed about like the lights of a pier in a gale. She was guyed up with so many cascading loops of amethyst and opal that it was a wonder she managed to hold herself erect.

'Come and sit near me, both of you,' said Dwindoline with a kindly smile. Leperdandy's mother was Scarabold's other wife (it being quite legal in these parts for a king to operate a marital duopoly) and, because she was wed to the Great Wound second, occupied a slightly inferior role in the household to Mater Hari (as they called her behind her back).

Plump and lumpen and draped in various shades of pheasant brown, Dwindoline was pleasing and pleasant and resigned to the sidelines of the royal menagerie. She tended her weakling son and her infuriating half-daughter unobtrusively, trying to provide the maternal concern they deserved and certainly didn't receive from Moribund. As the children (children! Ginansia was hours from her eighteenth year and Leperdandy was soon to leave his teens behind) accepted their places opposite, she looked along the table, nodding to the Decrepend so that he might commence the Blessing, smiling blandly at Asphyxia, who was sulking behind her goblet, and at the bulbous, bibulous visage of the Quaff, who had already drained his.

'O Cruel, Cruel Gods, Please Hear The Lowly Call Of This Great Family,' bellowed the Decrepend, who clearly had little faith in the power of prayer and planned to be heard through the more physical expedient of shouting, 'We Give Most Humble Thanks –'

Most humble, thought Ginansia, *the word has been excised from the castle dictionaries.*

'– For The Sheer Lack Of Harm You Have Bestowed Upon Us In Your Infinite, All-Seeing, Wicked Wisdom –'

Ginansia caught her half-brother's gaze and held it. Their aptitude for passing messages was so finely honed that the merest ocular twitch could signify histories. They had grown up side by side in the tall moss-green castle, had hidden together from their ranting, stamping father, had rescued each other from the freezing grip of the moat's shattered crust, had fought secret battles behind the dust-filled curtains of the Red Theatre in the attic. They were childhood allies now standing on the cusp of adulthood.

The Decrepend droned on, his narcotic tone pitched above the sound of falling rain. Scarabold's thick forefinger impatiently traced the edges of the livid ridged scar that crossed his face, the result of a sword blow that had honourable granted him the title of the Great Wound. He threw the Decrepend a look of hatred. The Blessing had to be given again in full if someone joined the table late. Beyond the windows of the tall, narrow Dining Hall, the sky was black and greeny grey, bruised clouds implicitly inclement. Here in the castle the family was safe and secure. Outside the forces of chance raged on.

So did the doddering Decrepend, who suddenly ended his prayers with a thud, smiting the table with a brittle-boned hand in an attempt to drive home his celestial-bound message.

The soup was now cold and curded, and Moribund snapped her fingers at the servants, who scurried to remove the bowls, Scarabold seized the moment to address his stepdaughter. The clearing of his throat was like someone shovelling coal.

'Ginansia, your arrival at the eighteenth year of your life demands the surrender of your maidenhood, and it is my duty as your father—'

'*Step*father.'

'– to appoint a suitably equipped suitor. In short, it is time for your deforestation.'

'Deflowering,' nudged the mater.

Ginansia stared furiously at her stepfather, whom she grudgingly respected as a warrior but considered an odious beast as a human. Since the death of her real father, his every entrance into her mother's bedchamber had multiplied her loathing tenfold. 'I suppose I have no say in this matter.'

'Certainly not,' thundered Scarabold. 'You have no knowledge of allegiances, alliances and allegations. You could not possibly know who would be most suited politically to this penetrative act. The decision has already been made, the bargain struck. The rupturer of the royal crust will mount you at midnight in the appropriate manner, in accordance with the law of the land. The ceremony will commence at half past eleven. Your mother will attend the preparations, and Dr Emeric Fangle will be on hand to instruct you in matters of hygiene.'

'Dando,' hissed Ginansia beneath her breath, 'you have to set me free from this.'

'We agreed you'd go through with it,' replied her half-brother quietly. 'It's an awful obligation, but it's not as if you have to marry him or anything. You never even have to see him again.'

'I know I said I'd do it but I can't. It's a stupid, revolting law.'

'Oh, for God's sake,' snapped the Quaff suddenly, slopping his claret, 'it's just a matter of keeping your legs open and your eyes shut. The women of the family all undergo the ceremony.'

'The women of *this* family,' replied Ginansia sulkily. Somewhere beyond the walls of the castle was another way of living, where families weren't knotted together like rat kings, biting, baiting and barely breathing in the tightest of tangles. Somewhere were places where the young ran wild, where freedom abounded and life was open to an endless azure sky . . .

'Drifting! Drifting!' screamed Aunt Asphyxia suddenly. 'See, she barely attends to your words, the minx! She needs the member in her fast to take her mind from rumination!'

'Surely you wish to know the identity of your pronger?' asked the Decrepend.

'I wish to know nothing!' cried Ginansia angrily, shoving away from the table and grabbing her half-brother's hand. 'Dando, come with me to my suite.' The boy pushed awkwardly back and joined her, grimacing apologetically to his parents. Dwindoline pouted in sympathy.

'And see she is ready at the appointed hour!' called Moribund, already losing interest as she twisted in her chair to berate the servants for the delay between courses. Behind her, the senior chef bore a huge tureen of bloody meat and knobs of bone, his gore-streaked apron a testament to his bitter, frantic labours. Asphyxia licked her fingers in anticipation.

Ginansia ran. Behind her trailed Leperdandy, the crimson side ribbons on his striped leggings flapping and snapping as he raised his knees in pursuit. 'Gin, please wait, I can't run as fast as you!'

She flew ahead, vanishing around each stone corner with her sapphire gown ruched up around her knees. *She will have to calm herself*, he thought, *or accept sedation before she discovers the identity of her romancer*. Abandoning pursuit, he watched her fleeing figure fold into the misted gloom.

Scarabold was breaking wind in the armoury. His efforts thundered through the filigreed gilt portcullis of the baroque chamber, resonating through the trellis like pummels on a tambourine. A luckless valet named Ratachet shared the room while he attempted to attach a pair of scarlet epaulettes to the fidgeting monarch's ceremonial battledress. The Great Wound raised a cheek of his ample rear and released an alarming fusillade, then fell back against the ambergris velvet cushions on his dressing bench. The valet grimaced and continued thrusting needles into a doublet.

'She has never shown any respect for the traditions of her family,' Scarabold continued. 'And now this unseemly fuss over her Maidenhood Ceremony. She should be pleased to mark her passage into womankind in so firm a fashion.'

'If it please Your Grace,' coughed Ratchet cautiously, 'perhaps the Lady Ginansia has deduced the identity of her suitor and is less than happy to allow him admission.'

Scarabold's face crumpled as completely as if it had been drawn on paper and crushed into a ball. Valets had no opinions, and if they did they should never be allowed to voice them, and even if they *did* voice them should never, ever mention subjects of such indelicacy.

'I mean,' stammered Ratchet, sensing the heat of the royal glower upon his vulnerably thin neck, 'how fiercely she cast her glance aside when introduced to Earl Carapace in the Cathedral of Pons Minor.'

'I do not give a maggot's egg what you think of my choice, you oafish seamster,' he blasted. 'The land is much changed since last they met. Carapace's armies are now the finest warriors in the Dunghills and make better allies than enemies. He has long shown an interest in the youthful glory of the princess.'

The withered valet remembered only too well. During Ginansia's confirmation, on her thirteenth birthday, Carapace had barely been able to tear his gaze from the pale flesh of her bare shoulders. Ratchet gave an involuntary shudder as he recalled the eerie clicking sound the earl made with his throat when considering matters of a carnal nature. Even now he was beetling towards the castle in his iridescent ebony armour to claim the soon-to-be supine body of the princess.

As Scarabold's eruptions, anal and oral, continued un-
abated, Ratchet returned to work, despairing the fate of
females born into nobility. Many years ago he had been
employed by the gracious Lady Dwindoline, and look what
had happened to her, poor thing, forced to become the Great
Wound's second wife because Mater Moribund had failed to
secure him a son. Three girl babies had been ceremonially
drowned before Dwindoline had finally given birth to the
milksop Leperdandy. As the golden needle slithered through
his gnarled fingers, Ratchet considered the night that now lay
ahead for the princess and her suitor. It was well known that
Carapace never travelled without his skittering 'courtiers'.
He prayed that Ginansia would somehow find the strength to
survive her grim ordeal.

The Great Clock Of Fascinus would have been easier to
interpret if it had still sported hands. Unfortunately a slow-
turning central spindle and a racing quarter-second arm were
all that remained of the timepiece's horological abilities.
Ginansia kept it mounted above her bed because the mother-
of-pearl face shifted like a sunlit sea. But now the remembrance
that Fascinus was a phallic god brought fresh qualms.

'I don't understand why you're so reluctant to help me
escape,' she sighed, staring up at the shimmering clock face.

Leperdandy moved the princess's lolling leg and perched
himself on a corner of her purple coverlet. 'I don't want
you to incur Scarabold's wrath. You know how slow he is
to forgive, and a matter such as this bears great importance to
him.'

'What about its importance to me?' she cried.

'I mean that the congress carries political weight.'

'And the intrusion upon my body does not.' She sat up

sharply and narrowed her eyes. 'Do you know the identity of my despoiler?'

'I have my suspicions.' He coughed awkwardly into his fist.

'Dando, you must tell me the truth. Is it someone I abhor?'

Her half-brother's cough turned into a hacking fit.

'Not that awful man who smelled like a pond and was covered in mud, Plum-somebody . . .'

Leperdandy, crimson cheeked, shook his head and spluttered.

'Or the fat little king who paid court to Mother, the one with the leaky eye . . .' She froze with a sudden thought. 'Not Carapace.'

There was a horrible, confirming silence.

'No, Dando, not the Lord Of Beetles . . .'

'He campaigned long and hard for you,' admitted the boy. 'Scarabold won't be moved from his ruling, and if you fail to bide by his decision he'll treat it as a matter of treason . . .'

'Treasoners must be entombed for life. He wouldn't do that—'

'You are not his blood daughter, Ginansia,' warned Leperdandy, who had once visited the grim, stinking dungeons beneath the castle to see for himself the pitiful bone creatures captured as prisoners of war by the king. These weary albinos with flaking skin and wheedling voices had been forgotten by all except Fumblegut, the jailer, who was rumoured to play elaborate sexual games with his charges in return for food and water.

'Then you must find a way to save me,' she cried desperately.

Her half-brother fidgeted with the quilt, running the fronds of a crimson tassel between his bony fingers. 'There is a way, but you'd be on your own beyond the castle walls. I couldn't come with you.'

'I wouldn't ask you to,' she said, her face softening. 'Just take me to the broad night sky, and I will do the rest.'

At eight o'clock, Dwindoline knocked at the bedroom door and asked to sit a while, but her offer was curtly refused. Ginansia hated to offend but feared that sharing the plan of her escape would place those she loved at risk. Besides, she was not entirely sure that her secret would be safe. As she prepared, she found herself bearing no malice towards Scarabold. Her stepfather had no desire to hurt any member of his extended family, but it was necessary for him to place duty before affection.

At a quarter past eleven, Ginansia rose from her dressing table in a high-necked robe of plain green silk that whispered across the flagstone floor, curling about her like a cubicle. She raised the hook of a slim lead-glass case containing three lit candles and left her apartment, locking the bedroom door behind her, not daring to glance back at her lifelong home.

Tonight the corridors of the West Quadrant seemed alien and friendless. Fewer lamps had been lit than usual, and the leaping shadows were of a deeper hue. The entire edifice was sealed in darkness and cold air like a refrigerator, with the servants waging an eternal battle against rising damp and leaking ramparts. Yet there were pockets of warmth within the castle, and the princess knew them as well as the kitchen cat. She measured her tread to the funeral drumbeat that sounded within the Chapel Of Consummation. The sexangular stone room held a comfortable curtained bed and a basin of warm spring water on an iron stand, having been designed for a single purpose. Mater Moribund had – quite illegally – slept there on those nights when her husband had returned victoriously drunk and muck-encrusted from his public skirmishes in the skink towns of the lowlands. As Ginansia approached it now, her heart sank.

The mater was already in attendance, talking softly with Dr Fangle as she watched him wiping his pudgy hands on a strip of linen cloth. Ginansia balked at the chamber entrance. What if Leperdandy had fallen asleep? Consciousness slipped from the sickly youth as easily as an oilskin cloak. She was forever nudging him awake during the Wednesday sermon. What if he failed to keep their finely timed appointment?

'Come, child,' beckoned Moribund, her amethyst wristlets chattering. 'Let Dr Fangle examine you.'

The short, wart-bedecked physician, an unwelcome temporary replacement for Scarabold's dropsical family doctor revealed an arrangement of yellow teeth and strummed his hand across his housecoat before offering it to shake.

Seated in a wooden-stirrupped chair that seemed to have been designed for the sole purpose of internal examination, Ginansia gave an involuntary shudder as his freezing fingers touched the insides of her thighs. She was frightened that her mother, peering over the doctor's shoulder, would spot the heavy woollen travelling clothes hitched up beneath her gown. A sudden sly icicle ran across her exposed aperature. Fangle grinned into her face. '*Intacta,* veritably,' he whispered. 'Most encouraging.' He reluctantly removed his digit and ran it beneath his nostrils like a fine cigar.

'That's enough, Fangle. Your job here is finished.' Moribund pushed him aside as Ginansia hastily dropped her gown.

'But surely the princess must be taught how to avoid conception and infection,' pleaded the doctor, still staring at her veiled cleft with his forefinger extended.

'Carapace is responsible for the former, and there shall be

no need for the latter,' snapped Moribund. 'The earl is also undergoing examination. On your feet, child. You have little time to spare.'

Sweating from her layers of clothes, Ginansia clambered to an upright position. She longed to run screaming into the torch-lit corridor but forced deliberation into her movements so that nothing should seem amiss. In a few minutes she would be on her way to freedom. She took her leave of the ogling physician and fell in behind her mother, who was already retreating from the chamber.

'Of course you're nervous, just as I was long ago,' intoned the mater, swinging her beads. 'Before my coring I presumed all kinds of painful pleasures lay in store. Imagine my disappointment when the great sweating brute dropped upon me like a felled tree and tore at my flowerpot of femininity with a fleshy little twig that discharged its sap and promptly vanished into the shrubbery. No danger of that happening to you, though, as I understand from Carapace's physician that the earl's maleness could steer a tea clipper if raised as a mast.'

Ginansia thought it best not to comment. The fireplace was approaching.

It was common knowledge within the castle that the chimney breasts of all the fireplaces in the Western Quadrant were linked to a central passage lined with ceramic bricks. The original idea had been to light one large fire in the basement boiler and so provide gusts of warm, dry air from fireplaces on every floor, but this plan had been abandoned when the Squeam's mother perished after she fell into the boiler trying to light it. Leperdandy was even now pushing through the elasticated cobwebs of one such passage that ran parallel to the hallway along which Ginansia followed the queen.

Separated by a mere three feet of stone, he strained to catch the sound of their progress but could discern nothing.

'I was sure I'd be able to hear them. Bumscuttle!' He blundered into a whiskery nest of spiders, batted the skittering insects from his vision and wiped the webbing from his eyelids. He could hardly see a thing. How would he be able to time his emergence from the fireplace in order to snatch Ginansia?

On the other side of the wall the princess slowed her pace, gradually dropping behind. She needed to put as much distance as possible between herself and Moribund before reaching the great carved maw of the fireplace.

'Don't dawdle, girl!' The queen looked back. 'Carapace is not a man to be kept waiting.'

'I'm sorry, Mother. My hem is caught.' She stopped and affected making a study of her ankle. Leperdandy, hearing the exchange, drew a great breath, burst from beneath the marble mantelpiece in a cloud of soot and grabbed his stepmother, who screamed and stabbed him through the shoulder with one of the many silver hatpins she kept concealed upon her person to deal with Scarabold.

'You've killed me!' gasped Leperdandy, clutching at the protruding pin, his great white eyes bulging out of his sooted face like night-time sea beacons.

'You stupid, stupid boy,' screamed Moribund, whipping the pin from his stinging flesh and tossing it aside. 'This is no time for your idiotic japes!' And with that she seized Ginansia by the wrist and thrust her into the chamber ahead.

'Dando!' Ginansia flung the cry back plaintively as she was swept inside and the door boomed shut behind her. Horrified by his failure, the boy limped into shadow to nurse his burning shoulder.

Moribund was nowhere to be seen.

Her role as procuress completed, she had slipped beyond one of the six chamber walls, leaving her daughter alone with the earl. Carapace stood between a pair of flickering lanterns, barely discernible in his oiled black armour. The susurration of his breath was punctuated with tiny clicks, like an insect rattling its mandibles. Ginansia felt the chill splinters of the door on her back. There were no windows in the cell. Only a bed, a bowl of water, and a freshly sliced lemon set upon the stand 'to cleanse and heal your wound' as Moribund put it. As her eyes adjusted in the gloom, she registered a shimmering movement behind Carapace, as though the purple counter-pane was attempting to escape the bed. The earl removed his gloves with deliberation, the leather creaking over his knuckles, and began to unbutton his glistening tunic with a series of little cracking sounds.

'Come closer into the light, my little one,' he croaked, his throat lacquered with lust.

Ginansia took a small step forward and studied the figure before her. His uncorseted belly hung above his ebony cod-piece, but his features were more handsome than she had expected. A goatee hung on his bone-white face like a small black shovel. Elaborate silver rings adorned the rims of his ears. Whatever happened, she would not speak to him. How could the older ladies of the castle have allowed themselves to undergo such an abhorrent ritual? It had no purpose, save to satisfy some ancient law laid down by long-dead ancestors.

There was definitely something moving beneath the cover-let on the bed. As Carapace seated himself in order to remove his leggings and boots, the cloth shifted and rippled around him.

'Come, let me touch you. You have nothing to be afraid of. I am a gentle man.' He raised his arms to receive her. Like a clockwork doll Ginansia shifted forward, her legs moving in tiny spasms.

'If I must be penetrated for the sake of my family,' she stated clearly, 'I will receive no overtures of affection from you.'

'Penetration!' he cried. 'Who taught you to think of love in so clinical a fashion?'

Ginansia was incensed. 'This mockery, sir, has nothing to do with love!'

'But I have loved you from the first moment I saw you, on your thirteenth birthday. I would have broken your hymen upon your communion dais.'

'Oh, this is blasphemy!'

He stopped the shocked oval of her mouth with a searing perfumed kiss. One icy hand slipped into her bodice and cupped her breast, the calloused thumb brushing across the thimble top of a nipple. She tried to pull herself free as he tilted the pair of them back onto the bed.

'This is too intimate – I was not warned—'

'Stay your fears,' he whispered. 'The night is young and we are enormous. We have plenty of time to acquaint ourselves.'

'The night! I was told that the ceremony would last but a few minutes!'

His snickering laugh followed her down as he cantilevered her onto the counterpane. Through the eider feathers she could feel things moving, hard-shelled creatures the size of gravy boats shifting this way and that. Reaching out in puzzlement, she seized a corner of the quilt and peeled it back. Hundreds of black beetles filled the mattress, their polished wing-cases flickering over each other. Recoiling in horror, the princess fought away from the pulsing morass of segmented bodies.

'My courtiers are here to further our conjugal ecstasy,' he hissed, dipping his hand into the heavy, chittering insects and allowing them to run across his arm. 'Now we must obey the natural impulse of their bodies.' One of the beetles was upon his neck, its feelers tentatively entering his mouth.

'Repugnant barbarian!' she screamed, punching at his chest. Her gown tore in his grasp, and the woollen travelling dress beneath slipped free from its silken shell. She fell back from the bed, her shoesoles popping and crunching on the squirming, living floor. Reaching the far wall, she searched for the handle to the door.

'Listen to Lady High-A-Mighty,' laughed Carapace, sitting back on the bed so that the insects could fill his bared lap. 'As if you could afford to choose a suitor for yourself.'

'I will give myself to whomsoever I please!' she shouted, close to tears, scrabbling for the inset brass ring which refused to turn.

'You might try, but who would have you? Who would want someone from Britannica Castle? The door is locked, so calm yourself.'

She turned to face him, sliding her body along the wall. The hidden exit through which her mother had vanished, that was the only answer now. If she could find the door itself she could locate the catch. All secret passageways within the castle opened similarly.

'What do you mean?' she asked. 'Our family is the finest in the land, generations of warriors brave and fair—'

'Is that what they told you? What does the castle look like from outside?'

She caught her breath. 'They speak of golden spires and colonnades so fine that only—'

'They speak? *They* speak? You have never seen the building from beyond it, and do you know why? Because it is not safe for you to leave this edifice. You would be murdered in the winking of an eye. You are prisoners here, outcasts, lepers, Jews. We have left you to peter out, to breed inwards and die. For us to speak with you is taboo, to touch you is punishable by death. Do you know what I risked to be with you tonight?'

'You're lying!' she cried. 'I will not listen to such lies!'

Carapace leapt from the bed in a shower of beetles and pinched her face so hard she squealed. 'Then learn for yourself. Ask your stepfather about your family name, ask him about the noble family from which you are descended. You will find nothing noble beyond the escutcheon that bears your arms.'

'The Baynes are an ancient family, good and wise, just and kind.' She knew this to be true. It was the foundation of all she believed. But she spoke for another purpose; to hold the earl in conversation was to hold him at bay.

'Arrant nonsense, my dear little Ginansia,' he spat, his phlegm-flecked lips an inch from hers. 'Answer me something else. If none of the serving maids dares to enter or leave the castle, how do you think you survive here? What do you live on? What feeds and fattens you?'

'The livestock beyond the river—'

'– are all dead of lung rot and have been for years. No, my dear, you cannot beg the question quite so easily. But surely it is time for you to discover the truth for yourself. Remove the lids of the kitchen cauldrons and look inside if you dare. Or listen to me.'

And he proceeded to tell her what he knew.

'I will not hear this!' The princess buried her fingers in her ears. Carapace reached for her, but she evaded him.

'Ginansia, please believe that I have no desire to hurt you.'

Warily, anxiously, she lowered her hands. 'Do not lie to me in this matter, my lord, I entreat you. This is the only world I know.'

'I merely seek to open your eyes, lady, and to show you what your family will not – cannot.'

But now the passage entrance was at her back with its catch between her fingers, and she fell thankfully into the tunnel, shoving the wall slab shut and running away through the freezing stone space. Behind, she heard him bellowing her name. 'Open your eyes, Ginansia!' came the fading call.

The only light in the dripping tunnel leaked from the cracks between the bricks. When Carapace could no longer be heard, she slowed her pace and drew breath. Wet, steep steps led down, and the corridor curved. She pulled the woollen dress around her, longing for the comforting arms of Leperdandy, the yielding warmth of her own bed. But before that, she had to ascertain the truth. Rest and peace would come only with knowledge that the Lord Of Beetles had lied.

The far end of the corridor was misted with the spicy scent of cloves, revealing the proximity of the kitchens and providing her with a means of irrefutable proof. To her right, a rectangle of buttery light marked the passage's egress. Locating a wooden catch and depressing it, she carefully opened the panel and stepped through. A wall of moist warm air instantly enveloped her.

The crimson-tiled scullery was deserted at this late hour. The gigantic butcher's block table, around which utensils stood in earthenware pots like bunches of steel flowers, had been scrubbed clean. Pulpers, colanders and dough knives dangled in clumps from S-shaped hooks. Light was thrown from the flickering burners of the huge iron stove that extended along one side of the room. Beneath the dull roar of flames below the pots, the princess could hear logs and coals sifting and shifting in the boiler.

She approached the stove, where four great shining saucepans, each of them several feet deep, simmered on the glowing hob. The handle on the lid of the first was too hot to be clasped, so she plucked up a muslin dishcloth and wound it around her fingers. The ring of flame beneath the metal cauldron illuminated her flushed cheeks as she slowly raised the lid.

At once she smelled a dizzying aroma of marjoram, spackwort, cumin and meat, meat most of all as she waved a path through the steam and peered in.

The bubbling brown liquid revealed nothing but surfacing chunks of carrot and fennel. She found a wooden spoon, two feet long and slotted at the bowl, which she carefully lowered into the boiling gravy. The joint within was heavy and hard to raise without slopping juice everywhere, so she was forced to use both hands to balance the spoon.

It was a head, human and male.

Its hair had been shaved away, and the lenses of the eyes had boiled into bulging orbs as hard and white as peppermints. The grey skin seemed loose and ready to separate from the skull. There were no teeth in the mouth, and the lower lip had come loose from the flayed gums. Ginansia screamed and dropped the boulder of meat and bone back into the fragrant depths of the pot, sending its juices hissing and splashing in waves across the burners.

Carapace's words came humming back into her ears. 'For you feed on human flesh!' he had cried. 'The Bayne family, so proud and so regal, are eaters of corpses, devourers of humanity! Why even the name itself is a corruption, from Sawney Beane and his cannibal horde – these are your fine ancestors! And you dare to call me barbarian!'

Bile had risen in her gullet. 'Lies, all damnable lies!'

'Go to the dungeons and see what your father breeds before you damn me treasonous, see what happens to the war prisoners you take. See how their souls reside in the colons of the royal family Bayne! And consider how you yourself have been nourished on the bones of your enemies!'

With a painful howl she ran from the infernal kitchen, leaving the boiling vats of human flesh behind her.

Dwindoline rocked forward in her chair and ran her fingers lightly over her son's fine hair. The boy had slumped his carcass before her fireplace and had barely moved in an hour. Now the apartment was lit only by sinking embers.

'You can't blame yourself,' she said softly. 'None of us can be protected beyond a certain age, and I'm afraid that your half-sister's time had simply arrived.'

'It seems so unfair,' said Leperdandy. 'Why can't we stay innocent forever? Knowledge can only destroy us.'

'You mustn't believe that, child. There always has to be hope for the future.'

Leperdandy raised his head and glared at her. 'What kind of hope? That one day we will be allowed to walk free beyond these walls?'

'Until Scarabold has found success in his endeavours there can be no freedom for any of us.'

'It might help if he didn't cut the heads from those who failed in his negotiations.' Unsnagging his muscles, he rose slowly to his feet. 'I'll go and await Ginansia's return. No doubt she'll need some comforting after her ordeal. Thanks for the advice, Mother, but it's clear you don't have a solution to our predicament any more than I.'

She sighed. 'The young are impatient.'

'And the old complacent.'

Dwindoline watched her son take leave with anguish fevering her breast. She knew she could not change the path of the family, only suffer in silence as each new generation discovered its dark heart.

For the remaining hours of that night, Britannica Castle was filled with tortured bruits: the bitter screams of the mortified princess, the enraged, insane laughter of the beetle earl, the muffled confusions of the boy Leperdandy – and the comfortable, well-fed farts of a slumbering king.

II. *Leperdandy's Revenge*

'You must eat something,' coaxed Dwindoline, raising the steaming ladle of bone broth to her half-daughter's parched lips. Ginansia coughed and knocked it aside, spattering an Arthurian arras with ruby droplets and shreds of gristle. She dropped back onto the bed, sinking into the dull-gold pillows.

'How can I eat, knowing what I know?' she asked. 'My bile rises. I shall never eat again. The shame of it, to think we are descended from common cannibals!'

Dwindoline knotted her dimpled hands in her lap and sighed. 'So many generations ago,' she whispered, her breath clouding in the chill bedchamber, 'and born of desperate necessity. How could we help but follow their tradition when it was all we ever knew?'

'Decency should have told you to desist. I despise the entire Bayne dynasty.'

'Then you must despise yourself, my dear,' said Dwindoline gently, 'for you were fattened on the braised flesh of traitors, just as we all were.'

Ginansia's opal eyes turned to her. 'Did you never think it was wrong?'

'I thought it the way of the world.' Dwindoline tugged at a stray brown thread poking from her dirndl. 'When we are children, we assume that everyone else is like us. When we discover the truth, we have to adapt.'

'Then I shall adapt as well.' She reached down beside the bed and pulled out a raffia parcel of carrots and radishes that Leperdandy had thoughtfully delivered. 'The family has found its first vegetarian.'

'Your father won't be pleased.'

'My father is dead. Killed in the stupidest of all the stupid wars. My stepfather can be buried alive by the blind grave-diggers of St Minch for all I care.' She bit disconsolately into a carrot. The sound was like snapping wood.

'Scarabold is too angry to countenance your presence at table. He has allowed Carapace to stay on at the castle and is attempting to placate the earl, whose alliance he needs. Your Maidenhood Ceremony may yet take place.'

'Not while this body has a breath left in it.' The girl flummocked onto her side, the bedsprings chiming. The wind moaning through the arrow slits of the East Quadrant turrets sounded like a distant mad organist. Dwindoline felt she should deliver a warning.

'The Great Wound will not wait for your agreement in this matter, Ginansia. As I try to placate him, Mater Moribund goads him on.'

'I can fight my own battles.' Ginansia raised herself on one arm, studying her stepmother with returning affection.

'Don't fret. I'll meet with Scarabold and disarm his argument.'

'That, my doveling, is something warrior kings have failed to do,' said Dwindoline, sadly stroking her hair. In these grim times, she seemed to be forever comforting her disillusioned offspring. Outside, the wind wailed in sympathy.

'I must see for myself,' said Ginansia firmly, 'and you must take me.'

Leperdandy uncrossed his skinny legs and rose from the marble dais, pacing to the window and staring down through the smeary stained-glass at the weatherbeaten hedgerows lining the moat. His face was as pale as lightning. 'I once descended deep into the heart of the prison chambers,' he murmured, 'and it is not a sight for female eyes – not any who value their sanity.'

His ears pricked, and he yanked open his bedroom door before the second knock. Aunt Asphyxia, all velveteen and liverspots, stood with her bony fist still raised.

'Conspiring!' she cried, the word emerging from her frayed vocal cords as a muzzled scream. 'Always tucked away, the two of you, whispering and plotting!'

'How could we be, Aunt Asphyxia, with you lurking around to spy on us?' asked the boy in mock exasperation. 'Ginansia wants to visit the dungeons. Shall we let her?'

'Germs!' screamed the old lady. 'Disease, deformity and diarrhoea! No woman is allowed to take such risks!'

'Did you want something specific?' asked Leperdandy, looming in the doorway to prevent her entry.

'Tell the girl she must asquiesce!' Asphyxia suddenly screwed up her eyes and scratched her mottled nose to prevent a sneeze. It gave her a face like a diseased parsnip.

'She must apologise to Carapace and beg for his carnal attentions!'

'I don't think there's going to be much chance of that, Auntie.' He started to shut the door, but she thrust at him in an angry cloud of mothball musk.

'You have no inkling of the consequences, you useless young fop! We cannot afford to make an enemy of the earl! Loyalties must be forged!'

'Then the Great Wound will have to exercise some diplomacy for once.' With that, he slammed the door shut.

Leperdandy raised a slim finger to his lips, halting his half-sister's laughter. 'She'll be hovering outside for ages yet,' he whispered, 'and she's not as harmless as you might think. From her ears, straight to Britannica's war room.'

'Will you take me down to the prison cells or must I go alone?' his half-sister asked.

'Fumblegut will never admit you, and you should be glad of that. His tastes are more exotic than the excesses of your imagination. Better by far to begin with Scarabold.'

'Do you really think so, Dando?' Her headstrong ideas were usually mitigated by Leperdandy's guidance. 'Then I should go to him now. Reparation without surrender. I will have my wishes observed.' She rose from the bed with a creak.

Leperdandy worried a cuticle and watched as she washed her cheeks in rosewater and donned an evening robe of deepest sapphire. She showed her mother's determination, even if she lacked the authority to access her desires.

'Gin, if Scarabold consents to a confirmation, you will try to be –' he searched for a word that would not annoy her, '*reasonable*, won't you?'

'Reason is as reason does,' she replied, clasping a gold opera necklace over her breastbone. It was a family heirloom, a pendant chain hung with six flawless cabochon-cut rubies, Scarabold's favourite. Leperdandy furrowed his alabaster brow. The princess was unversed in the art of discretion, and her stepfather would not take kindly to accusations. He began to regret suggesting a meeting so clearly fraught with dangers . . .

The Great Wound had wondered how long it would take his errant stepdaughter to come a-creeping back in abject apology and gave a smile of satisfaction to see her humbly seated on the edge of the battered crimson recamier in the reading room. He strode across to the vast granite fireplace and scratched a match into his overloaded briar, filling the chamber with a smell akin to burning sweet wrappers. Ginansia had woven tiny violets in her hair and laced them through her bodice, appearing an image of innocence in the mistaken hope that it would sway scarabold to her argument.

'Gad, you're a headstrong minx and no mistake,' he complained, 'but I'm prepared to bygonify your quarrelsome attitude if you are willing to renounce your vestal status and comingle with the Earl Carapace.' He tamped down his pipe bowl with a fat sepia-tipped thumb, clearly expecting no response.

'That is quite out of the question,' the girl replied hotly. 'I came to speak of another, far more serious matter.'

'What could be more serious than the perpetuation of our line?' The Great Wound hissed and sucked at his pipe, peering at her with his good eye through a cloud of cinders as though discoursing through a raked bonfire. 'If we fail Carapace now he will deny us the alliance that secures our future. Don't you see, you silly girl, how our fate is entwined with his?'

'You hated him once,' answered Ginansia. 'You told me

that the iron rule of the Bayne dynasty held the entire valley in its grip.'

The old king softened as he remembered. 'The world has changed, my petal-pudding, and we are driven to befriend our former enemies. That is why I ask your help and pray that you can understand our predicament.'

Ginansia had no wish to hurt her family; her life knew no one else, for the castle had few visitors. She began to appreciate her role in the destiny of the Baynes – and to understand the bargaining power it afforded her.

'I shall attempt to do as you wish, stepfather – on one condition.'

'Condition?' asked Scarabold suspiciously. 'We don't have conditions.'

'I must visit the dungeon chambers wherein you keep our war prisoners. If you deny me this, I would never surrender myself to the Beetle Earl in a thousand years.'

'But why would you wish to enter such a dreadful place?' demanded her stepfather, genuinely confused.

'To meet the people we eat,' she replied, trembling with indignation. 'I wish to see the men we breed like cattle and slaughter to fill our bellies.'

Within the undergrowth of his vast beard, Scarabold's lips were pursed in anger. Who had informed the child, and to what purpose if not to upset her? Even he could see what damage the knowledge might have on one so lacking in the family ways.

'So you know,' he said simply.

'We are butchers of men and that is all you can say?' cried Ginansia, ending her determination to remain calm. Before Scarabold could formulate an appropriate attitude, the princess burst into a furious fit. She accused her stepfather of

Uncut

treason and murder and much worse besides, of lying and hiding, of cowardice and bestiality. She said many things she had no intention of saying and wrecked any chance of a reconciliation between herself and the king. More harmful still, she ended the diatribe by renouncing her name, something no member of the family had ever dared to do.

Scarabold was apoplectic. In a fiery cloud of briar embers he banished the girl from his limited sight and ordered that she should remain confined to her quarters. Ginansia ran from the room in a flood of tears and ransacked most of the East Quadrant searching for the bonily comforting arms of Leperdandy, but he was nowhere to be found. She returned to her chamber and fell onto the bed, drifting quickly into a bitter, miserable slumber.

An hour later she was awoken by the sound of nails being heavily driven into her bedroom door. She counted forty of them, long iron shards that protruded through the oaken piers of the door arch. She tried the handle but it would not budge even a tenth of an inch.

She was sealed in.

Forced to reply to her bellowed questions, two servants shifted from spandrel to keyhole and admitted that they were carrying out Scarabold's wishes. Her meals would be delivered through the gap beneath the door, and she was to remain incarcerated until she saw the error of her ways - however long that might take.

Spackle and Peut were running through the corridors of the castle's skewed seventh floor playing Dead Man's Sting, a game requiring intimate comprehension of its convoluted rules and an attitude of extreme spite. The twin progeny of Aunt Asphyxia were spoiled brats with barely a single original thought to share between them, and were consequently used by their mother to spy on the rest of the family. Asphyxia was not, in fact, a genuine aunt but an embittered widow inherited by Scarabold after he had made a promise to her dying husband on a gore-soaked battlefield. In the emotional turmoil of the moment, the Great Wound had forgotten that his old friend's wife was pregnant and so had found himself providing for the only family inhabiting the castle that was not directly blood related. He did not approve of the twelve-year-old twins; their sly, underhand meddling offended his warrior sensibilities. He would have approved of them even less now, for they had been sent at their mother's command on a spying mission. Spackle stood at Earl Carapace's door, and Peut stood on his brother's shoulders, peering through an engraved blue crystal transom. The cut and thickness of the glass gave him only the vaguest of refracted views but magnified the voice of the Beetle Lord into reedy sharpness.

'There must be a way to make her see reason,' he was insisting, unaware that she had already glimpsed it after unsealing the kitchen's cooking pots. 'Why, she's no longer a girl but a mature woman, luscious, full, bulging, a fragrantly moist plum, ripe for plucking and peeling.'

'Your trousers, sir.' That was the valet's voice. 'The buttons are undone.'

'Is it any wonder,' sighed the earl, attending to his groin.

'He's smitten with Ginansia,' Spackle whispered downward, always prepared to state the obvious. He resettled his boots on either side of his brother's spine. 'I don't know why he doesn't force himself upon her and have done with it.'

'Not everyone's like you,' hissed Peut, arching his sore back.

'And now that the Neanderthal Scarabold has sealed her up inside her bedchamber, how am I supposed to plight my troth?' There was a rip of silk as Carapace put his elbow through his shirt. The exasperated valet was attempting to dress his master as he paced. 'His loyalty to me is touching, if transparently political. Presumably the Great Wound hopes to curry my favour by punishing the child for refusing to succumb. His actions have left us all without a choice.'

'Do we have to stay here much longer?' croaked Peut. 'My bones are cracking.'

Beyond the door, Carapace's valet offered a solution. 'If I might be so very bold as to make the tiniest of minuscule suggestions,' he began, the servant deferring to nobility with the acquiescence of a whore collapsing into bed, 'why not perform a service for the princess and endear yourself to her by fulfilling her desires? She's locked away; there must be something she needs, and such an act will confirm your allegiance to her against the wishes of her stepfather.'

'Now I remember why I keep you on!' cried Carapace. 'For someone who lives in a world of socks and silver polish, you occasionally produce a superlative idea. I'll venture to her rooms at once.'

'He'll never be able to get her door open,' sniggered Spackle, hopping down. 'Come on, let's get there before him.'

As silent as a sunset, they entered the wet stone corridor running behind the panels of the fifth floor and made their way through the maze of dripping brick. It was within these walls that Suppurus, the disgraced Knave Of Chaucery, had avoided his scheduled beheading by remaining hidden for five days and surviving on his own regurgitated vomit. Although that was nearly a hundred years ago, his person, mummified by the crosswinds of the rumbling latrine flues, could still be found in the passageway with the index finger of its right hand wedged firmly in its throat.

The twins arrived minutes before the earl and secreted themselves in an alcove opposite Ginansia's room, behind a weevil-chewed tapestry celebrating one of Scarabold's most senseless massacres. Ginansia's door looked as if it would not be opened without the aid of a battering ram. Shortly, Carapace strode up, ran his tapering fingers across the pounded nailheads and brought his lips to the edge of the keyhole.

'Ginansia,' he called gently, 'I am mortified to find you imprisoned like this. Perhaps there is something I can do to secure your release.' The twins failed to discern the princess's reply as the draughts blowing along the corridor rattled and banged the tapestries, obscuring all sound from within her apartment. Peut peered out through a tangle of rotted stitches. Carapace seemed to have been granted an audience, for he was listening intently at the mortice and nodding to himself. He shifted position, listened some more, then wrinkled his forehead in alarm as a small sheet of folded paper was slipped to him from beneath the door. Gingerly, he unfolded the page and studied it with augmenting consternation.

'What you are asking is utterly impossible,' he cried, refolding the sheet. 'If the king found out he would have me killed in some brutal, lingering fashion.' He hunched against the door again.

'Of course I desire it, with all my heart, but how can I—? Yes, most certainly I wish to prove myself to you, but is there really no other way that I can help—'

A boot kicked at the door from within, sending Carapace reeling. It was clear that whether Ginansia's terms were met or not, she meant business. The earl deposited the slip of paper in his jerkin and set off at a lick.

* * *

Spackle and Peut were stumped. As spies, they had failed miserably. All they knew was that Carapace might or might not have agreed to aid the princess in some treasonable enterprise of her own devising. Asphyxia would be far from pleased by this incomplete bulletin. Spackle scraped a curtain of ragged black hair from his eyes and stared at his brother. Whatever Ginansia had requested of the Beetle Lord, it was sure to cause upset in the rest of the household.

'We'll have to follow him everywhere,' said Peut, 'use our initiative. Either he'll do as she requests and antagonise the crown, or he'll rat to the Great Wound and lose her for ever.'

'What about the princess?' asked Spackle.

'Forget about her,' came the reply. 'She's not going anywhere. Few would help her, and they dare not risk the anger of the king.'

'What about Leperdandy?'

'Pouting milksop!' Peut snorted derisvely.

'Wheedling catamite!' added his twin.

'Simpering sodomist!'

'Bulgy bilge bottom!'

How they laughed as they crept black into the brick-bound rookery that would lead them once more to Carapace's quarters.

Ginansia paced the floor, wringing a yard of olivine damask in her pallid hands. Outside, rain sprayed from the buttresses and leaked through the broken tracery of the stained-glass windows, discolouring the herringbone parquet upon which she stepped. To have defied her poisoned family and be rendered so completely powerless! Leperdandy meant well but could only fail her, and even the Beetle Lord had quailed at her demands. She had simply entreated Carapace to prove his love by visiting the dungeon chambers and arranging for the immediate release of all the prisoners held there. Was that too much to ask for? The family would be forced to curtail its cannibalistic behaviour, and in the ensuing aura of normalcy Ginansia would at last be heard. She would be a clear voice of reason, someone to lead the Baynes out into a bright new dawn.

Or so she thought.

In truth, Scarabold was not prepared to heed his errant stepdaughter, even if the direst of circumstances demanded it. Fate had always ruled the castle, her broad dark wings smoothing and combing out the terrible events of the years, and that was not about to change.

Fumblegut was pounding a mouse flat with an iron mallet. Two more and he would have enough for a hat. Too lazy to bother with skinning them, he simply smashed away at the pinioned rodents until their guts had departed their hides. He flicked the mouse innards from his pudgy fingers, then buried his hand down the back of his trousers and gave the sweating cleavage of his rump a good scratch.

As he rose and kicked the mallet aside, he decided that it must be time to eat again. Below ground there was no telling night from day. The only source of illumination came from flesh-tallow torches, and the only whisper of the outside world descended from the distant hissing of rain on tin gutters. Nobody bothered him down here. Nobody wanted to know what went on. Nobody dared to take even the smallest peek. And that suited the jailer down to the straw-strewn gore-soaked ground.

Fumblegut wondered about the boy in cell 71, a spirited young colt who had followed his father into pokey by admitting a minor act of vandalism against the Bayne escutcheon. A rowdy lad, he was, forever hammering his food plate against the bars, but of tender appeal. Fumblegut fancied burying his teeth into the child's plump buttocks but was forced to content himself with a cold tongue sandwich and a pot of porter. Although some dank recess of his mind had registered the increase in the number of cockroaches and stag beetles scuttling over the flagstone floor of the dungeons, Fumblegut failed to spot the spindly form of Carapace. The earl was sliding from shadow to shadow as he unlocked the prisoners' cells with the iron hoop of keys he had found tossed on a nearby table by the careless jailer.

Carapace had determined to do the bidding of his beloved; well versed in the ways of darkness, he slithered through the stinking cubicles like a passing eclipse, so that when the gloom lifted from each holding pen, the inmate within could discern a door now standing ajar.

Fumblegut had no idea he was being robbed of the castle's future meal supply. Ensconced in his private chamber, he focused only on the bottom of his draining pint pot.

Carapace could see that many of the dungeon's denizens would be unable to leave unaided. Some had been fattened up so much that they could barely raise themselves on their pustulant haunches. Crimson sores on the legs of others forced them to remain in strange static positions. Flesh had withered and rooted on arms too long chained together. Here were diseases and tortures beyond imagining, and the results of these twin horrors lay moaning in their own filth. But the earl had obeyed Ginansia's edict, and thus his mission could be counted a success.

A further torch-lit cell stood alone at the end of the muck-plastered corridor, separated from the rest. Carapace looked back anxiously at Fumblegut's closed door, convinced that any minute now all hell would break loose; the dazed prisoners were starting to emerge, and the sound of their shuffling movements would soon reach the jailer's ears. But curiosity had bettered him and, determined that his liberation would not be incomplete, Carapace approached the distant lone receptacle with key hoop cocked.

He reached the single jail room and read the notice pinned to the lock:

FEED BUT DO NOT TOUCH
By Order Of His Majesty The King

He tipped his ear and listened to a laboured wheezing then squinted inside. For a moment the cell's darkness refused to yield the figure within. But as the poor inmate's features clarified in torch light, everything became apparent.

What little colour there was in Carapace's face drained as he took a stammering step back. Someone clearly knew about this; someone would pay, and someone else would have to be told. He reached out to unlock the door but the keys jumbled themselves together in his hands, and then Fumblegut was emerging from his room to find himself jostled within a swirling cotillon of crazed inmates. It was clearly time to leave. Storing away the sights he had witnessed, Carapace searched for the entrance to the passageway that the princess had so carefully described. Ginansia possessed hand-drawn maps of almost every area in the castle, even though she had ventured to fewer than half of them herself, and had passed one to him beneath her bedroom door. Now he prayed that he could decipher it with enough speed to make good his escape. As he hunted the secret alcove, he forced himself to remember that any risk was worth taking for the warming glow of the princess's approval.

Imagine this: As Carapace was making his way back through the castle armed with his explosive nugget of hitherto hidden knowledge, Leperdandy was undertaking his own carefully plotted revenge for Ginansia's sake. Following a secret plan of his own devising, he first visited Dr Fangle's temporary office just beneath the leaking roof, then he crept unseen into the kitchen to fiddle about in the scullery, and finally he made his way to the Heart Of All Sorrow for a last-minute amelioration of the dining table. Satisfied with his arrangements, Leperdandy prepared himself for the evening meal.

For the past two hours, Spackle and Peut had been annoyed and confused. After trailing the Beetle Earl from Ginansia's apartment, they had lost him somewhere within the corridor walls. It was as if he had been provided with secret knowledge neither of them possessed, almost as if he'd been given a map. Peut slapped himself on the forehead; what about the paper that had passed beneath the bedroom door? It meant that Carapace was doing the princess's bidding, which somehow, obliquely, spelled trouble for them. And now he was back outside her chamber, angrily removing each of the forty nails with a hammer claw.

What in the name of Beelzebub Bayne was going on?

The Dining Hall was illuminated by forty-one tall candles, the number of days into the year. The candle boy dreaded December. Scarabold, always the first to table, was seated between Mater Moribund and Dwindoline. The Quaff had been sequestered in a poorly lit corner, the better to hide his bibulous demeanour. Aunt Asphyxia, unusually, had brought the twins to her side. They slouched to the left and right below her like a pair of badly potted ferns. Leperdandy, resplendent in a silken-starred waistcoat of midnight blue, touched his hair nervously as he watched and waited.

The Decrepend was droning on through the Blessing even though two further place settings had yet to be filled. He stopped so abruptly that everyone in the room looked up.

Ginansia was standing in the doorway on Carapace's arm.

Scarabold's mouth fell open. His stepdaughter was wearing a floor-length cream lace gown interwoven with honeysuckle buds. Their scent quickly filled the room, banishing the reek of candle tallow. The earl was bound into a corsetted leather military suit ornately knotted with lengths of polished steel, darts that had been removed from the bodies of his enemies.

As the couple took their seats, no one could think of a single thing to say. Scarabold's immediate reaction, to blaspheme foully and throw his fits about, quickly subsided. Mater Moribund's eyes settled on the couple and narrowed slightly before she turned her attention to the pouring of the soup. Leperdandy's, however, was shocked into another century. He had expected – counted on – Carapace to appear, but couldn't imagine what Ginansia thought she was doing. Ginansia knew very well what she was doing.

After he had removed the last of the nails, Carapace had informed the princess of his trip into the dungeons, and as he described his freeing of the prisoners she had seen a saviour's light aglow in his eyes. She felt sure that the mission she had given the earl had changed his nature, although she was a little surprised by the success of her pleas. And if she had not consented to marry him, she had at least agreed to go through with her Deflowering Ceremony.

But first there was a matter of proof. She had made Carapace promise that he would reveal his act of liberation to the Great Wound before announcing that he was now willing to form an alliance with the family Bayne. This way everyone would achieve a limited degree of happiness. Scarabold would have a strong new ally, Ginansia would have ended the castle's dependence on human livestock, and Carapace would have somewhere to bury his virtually permanent erection.

If only it had worked out that way.

At first, the only sound in the room was the clicking of spoons in bowls. The soup appeared to be cream of turnip, but Ginansia pushed hers to one side in case there was something of a more human nature lurking at the bottom. The Beetle Lord ate heartily, ignoring the fascinated stares of Asphyxia and Leperdandy, then smeared his napkin across his shovel beard, cracked his knuckles in a series of tiny pistol shots, and requested everyone's attention. A cockroach fell out of his tunic and was hastily flicked aside.

It was a moment upon which the future of the great and damned Bayne family hung. For Carapace was about to reveal the one discovery he had so far withheld from the princess – a discovery that would reshape the destiny of this dynasty.

Ginansia's worst fears were realised as the soup plates were efficiently replaced by steaming platters of grey stew. Nausea caressed her belly as she recalled uncaulking the steaming kitchen pots. Carapace, a lump of gristle already pendent from his fork, spoke out.

'My Lord, Ladies, Your Grace, you might well be wondering how I come to be seated here at table with the princess.' He lowered his fork in the ensuing uncomfortable silence. 'The fact is that Ginansia agreed to my terms on the fulfilment of a certain condition. Namely, that I should enter the dungeons below us –' a silence deeper and more horrible than the previous one ensued – 'and free the prisoners held therein.' He looked around the table, confronting a set of stony glares. 'You all know the purpose of penning up those poor unfortunates, even if you prefer to turn a blind eye.' He paused for dramatic effect before preparing to deliver his bombshell. Even now, those prisoners were presumably burrowing up towards the Dining Hall and were about to burst through the doors. He could not know that Fumblegut had successfully halted the mass escape by flooding a section of the dungeon passage. Carapace held the sweetness of the moment. 'But,' he was about to say, 'there is one prisoner kept in a solitary cell whose flesh is not for the delectation of his betters.' Indeed not, for at the far end of the dungeon he had discovered none other than Ginansia's real father, the Pater Moribund himself. Carapace slid the meat-laden fork into his mouth, savouring the taste of victory.

The earl was an amitious man. He had affected to enjoy Scarabold's company so that he might receive the attentions of his stepdaughter. But his discovery opened up another possibility; by revealing that the Great Wound had locked away his rival and lied to his family, he would earn Ginansia's gratitude and Scarabold's enmity, both of them desirable commodities. Better still, he would shatter the family Bayne for ever, watching as it descended into a bitter web of hatred, suspicion and treachery.

'Now I am able to reveal the truth,' boasted Carapace, chewing slowly. He took a sip of cloudy water, enjoying the looks of puzzlement that surrounded him. Revenge was truly a dish best served cold.

But not served as stew.

For suddenly he began to cough, then to choke, and then to scream out. And thick dark blood started to stream from his ears. Everyone watched in horror except Leperdandy, who stared down at his plate. The powder he had removed from Fangle's poison cabinet had been liberally shaken over Carapace's dinner plate. Poison dusted his cutlery and glittered at the rim of his water glass. And what an awful poison it was, capable of causing epilepsy in a month-old corpse as it dissolved each internal organ. Leperdandy had won a terrible, bloody revenge for himself and Ginansia. Now there would be no dynastic alliance, no Deflowering Ceremony, no reconciliation with his elders. Scarabold would no longer see him as an ineffectual fop but as a powerful political force to be reckoned with.

Things would have to change.

He smiled to himself as the earl sprayed gouts of blood about the place before vanishing backwards beneath the table with a disgusting gurgle. Silence fell once more as Ginansia gingerly raised the tablecloth and stared slack mouthed at the cascading blood fountain that had been the Beetle Lórd until a few seconds ago.

Leperdandy had prepared a short speech to explain Carapace's alarming demise. He caught Scarabold's good eye and was momentatily shaken by the Great Wound's odd reaction.

The king was smiling.

Then he lowered his fork once more, dug into a mound of streaky red meat and shovelled the lot into his mouth. 'Well,' he burbled, speaking through fat and gristle, 'it's a bloody shame the earl got too sick. I wouldn't touch his portion if I were you. S'pose we'll never know what he was going to talk to us about.'

Leperdandy sat back, appalled. What had he missed?

Where had he gone wrong? Scarabold was pleased to see the earl murdered and clearly wasn't prepared to be bothered with details. Slowly the suspicion dawned on him that someone else's plot had interfered with his own.

The Great Wound sat back and chewed happily. His kingdom was safe and sound once more. Carapace had discovered the truth about the pater, but fate had lowered her ebony wings across his path, bearing him away into a land of eternal night. There was no need for the others to know that the old king still lived. He glanced absently about the table, wondering which of them had done the murderous deed. But what did it matter, so long as life continued without change?

In Britannica Castle that terrible stormy night, Ginansia howled in rage and grief, Leperdandy was tangled in sheets of nightmare guilt, and the king slumbered peacefully on, his log-saw snores shattering the nerves of his two exhausted wives and just about everyone else within earshot.

Mother of the City

If my uncle Stanley hadn't passed out pornographic Polaroids of his second wife for the amusement of his football mates in the bar of the Skinner's Arms, I might have moved to London. But he did and I didn't, because his wife heard about it and threw him out on the street, and she offered the other half of her house to me.

My parents were in the throes of an ugly divorce and I was desperate to leave home. Aunt Sheila's house was just a few roads away. She wasn't asking much rent and she was good company, so I accepted her offer and never got around to moving further into town, and that's why I'll be dead by the time morning comes.

Fucking London, I hate it.

Here's a depressing thing to do. Grow up in the suburbs, watch your schoolfriends leave one by one for new lives in the city, then bump into them eleven years later in your local pub, on an evening when you're feeling miserable and you're wearing your oldest, most disgusting jumper. Listen to their tales of financial derring-do in the public sector. Admire their smart clothes and the photos of exotic love partners they keep in their bulging wallets, photos beside which your uncle

Stan's Polaroids pale into prudery. Try to make your own life sound interesting when they ask what *you've* been doing all this time, even though you know that the real answer is nothing. Don't tell them the truth. Don't say you've been marking time, you're working in the neighbourhood advice bureau, you drive a rusting Fiat Pipsqueak and there's a woman in Safeway you sometimes sleep with but you've no plans to marry.

Because they'll just look around at the pub's dingy flock wallpaper and the drunk kids in tracksuits and say, 'How can you stay here, Douglas? Don't you know what you've been missing in London all these years?'

I know what I've been missing all right. And while I'm thinking about that, my old school chums, my pals for life, my mates, my blood brothers will check their watches and drink up and shake my hand and leave me for the second time, unable to get away fast enough. And once again I stay behind.

You'll have to take my word for it when I say I didn't envy them. I really didn't. I'd been to London plenty of times, and I loathed the place. The streets were crowded and filthy and ripe with menace, the people self-obsessed and unfriendly. People are unfriendly around here as well, only you never see them except on Sunday mornings, when some kind of car-washing decathlon is staged throughout the estate. The rest of the time they're in their houses between the kettle and the TV set, keeping a sidelong watch on the street through spotless net curtains. You could have a massive coronary in the middle of the road and the curtains would twitch all around you, but no one would come out. They'll watch but they won't help. They'll say, 'We thought we shouldn't interfere.'

Fuck, I'm bleeding again.

Seeing as I'm about to die, it's important that you understand; where you live shapes your life. I'm told that the city makes you focus your ambitions. Suburbia drains them off. Move here and you'll soon pack your dreams away, stick them in a box with the Christmas decorations, meaning to return to them some day. You don't, of course. And you slowly become invisible, like the neighbours, numb and relaxed. It's a painless process. Eventually you perform all the functions of life without them meaning anything, and it's quite nice, like floating lightly in warm water. At least, that's what I used to think.

Around here the people have become unnaturally attached to the concept of shopping. They spend every weekend with their families scouring vast warehouses full of tat, looking for useless objects to acquire, shell-suited magpies feathering their nests with bright plastic objects. I shouldn't complain. I've always preferred things to people. Gadgets, landscapes, buildings. Especially buildings. As a child, I found my first visit to the British Museum more memorable than anything I'd seen before, not that I'd seen anything. I loved those infinite halls of waxed tiles, each sepulchral room with its own uniformed attendant. Smooth panes of light and dense silence, the exact opposite of my home life. My parents always spoke to me loudly and simultaneously. They complained about everything and fought all the time. I loved them, of course; you do. But they let us down too often, my sister and me, and after a while we didn't trust them any more.

I trusted the British Museum. Some of the exhibits frightened me; the glass box containing the leathery brown body of a cowering Pompeiian, the gilt-encased figures of vigilant guards protecting an Egyptian princess. Within its walls nothing ever changed, and I was safe and secure. I never had that feeling with my parents. Once my father drove us up from Meadow-fields (that's the name of the estate; suitably meaningless, as there isn't a meadow in sight and never was) to the West End to see some crummy Christmas lights and to visit my mum's hated relatives in Bayswater. When he told the story later, he managed to make it sound as if we had travelled from the steppes of Russia. He and my mother sat opposite my uncle Ernie and auntie Doreen on their red leather settee, teacups balanced on locked knees, reliving the high point of our trip, which was a near collision with a banana lorry bound for Covent Garden. I'd been given a sticky mug of fluorescent orange squash and sent to a corner to be seen and not heard. I was nine years old, and I understood a lot more than they realised. My uncle Ernie started talking about a woman who was strangled in the next street because she played the wireless too loudly, but my auntie Doreen gave him a warning look and he quickly shut up.

On the way home, as if to verify his words, we saw two Arab men having a fight at the entrance to Notting Hill tube station. Being impressionable and imaginative, from this moment on I assumed that London was entirely populated by murderers. A psychiatrist would say that's why I never left Meadowfields. In fact I longed to leave my parents' little house, where each room was filled with swirling floral wallpaper and the sound of Radio One filtered through the kitchen wall all day. All I had to do was get up and go, but I didn't. Inaction was easier. When I moved to Aunt Sheila's I finally saw how far my lead would reach; three roads away. I suppose I was scared of the city, and I felt protected in the suburbs. I've always settled for the safest option.

Look, I've taken a long time getting to the point and you've been very patient, so let me explain what happened last night. I just wanted you to understand me a little so you won't think I'm crazy when I explain the insane fix I'm in. It's hard to think clearly. I must put everything in order.

It began with a woman I met two months ago.

Her name is Michelle Davies and she works for an advertising agency in Soho. She's tall and slim, with deep-set brown eyes and masses of glossy dark hair the colour of a freshly creosoted fence. She always wears crimson lipstick, black jeans and a black furry coat. She looks like a page ripped from *Vanity Fair*. She's not like the women around here.

I met her because I was helping with a community project that's tied to a national children's charity, and the charity planned to mention our project in its local press ads, and Michelle was the account executive appointed to help me with the wording. The first time we met I was nearly an hour late for our appointment because I got lost on the Underground. Michelle was sitting at the end of a conference table, long legs crossed to one side, writing pages of notes, and never once caught my eye when she spoke. The second time, a week later, she seemed to notice me and was much friendlier. At the end of the meeting she caught my arm at the door and asked me to buy her a drink in the bar next to the agency and, utterly astonished, I agreed.

I'll spare you a description of the media types sandwiched between the blue slate walls of the brasserie. The tables were littered with *Time Outs* and transparencies, and everyone was talking loudly about their next production and how they all hated each other.

Listen, I have no illusions about myself. I'm twenty-eight, I don't dress fashionably and I'm already losing my hair. London doesn't suit me. I don't understand it, and I don't fit in. Michelle was seven years younger, and every inch of her matched the life that surrounded us. During a bottle of wine she told me about her father, a successful artist, her mother, a writer of romances, and her ex-boyfriend, some kind of experimental musician. I had no idea why I had been picked to hear these revelations. Her parents were divorced but still lived near each other in apartments just off Marylebone Road. She had grown up in a flat in Wigmore Street and lived in Praed Street. Her whole family had been raised in the centre of the city, generation upon generation. She was probably the last true Londoner. She was rooted right down into the place, and even though I hated being there, I had to admit it made her very urbane and glamorous, sophisticated far beyond her years. As she drained her glass she wondered if I would like to have dinner with her that night. Did I have to get up early in the morning?

I know what you're thinking – isn't this all a bit sudden? What could she see in me? Would the evening have some kind of humiliating resolution? Did she simply prefer plain men? Well, drinks turned to dinner and dinner turned to bed, and everything turned out to be great. I went back to her apartment and we spent the whole night gently making love, something I hadn't done since I was nineteen, and later she told me that she was attracted to me because I was clearly an honest man. She said all women are looking for honest men.

In the morning, we braved the rain-doused streets to visit a breakfast bar with steamy windows and tall chrome stools, and she ate honey-filled croissants and told me how much she loved the city, how private and protective it was, how she could never live anywhere else and didn't I feel the same way – and I had to tell her the truth. I said I fucking hated the place.

Yes, that was dumb. But it was honest. She was cooler

after that. Not much, but I noticed a definite change in her attitude. I tried to explain but I think I made everything worse. Finally she smiled and finished her coffee and slipped from her stool. She left with barely another word, her broad black coat swinging back and forth as she ran away through the drizzle. Kicking myself, I paid the bill and took the first of three trains home. At the station, a taxi nearly ran me down and a tramp became abusive when I wouldn't give him money.

On my way out of London I tried to understand what she loved so much about the litter-strewn streets, but the city's charms remained elusive. To me the place looked like a half-demolished fairground.

I couldn't get Michelle out of my mind.

Everything about her was attractive and exciting. It wasn't just that she had chosen me when she could have had any man she wanted. I called her at the agency and we talked about work. After the next meeting we went to dinner, and I stayed over again. We saw each other on three more occasions. She was always easy-going, relaxed. I was in knots. Each time she talked about the city she loved so much, I managed to keep my fat mouth shut. Then, on our last meeting, I did something really stupid.

I have a stubborn streak a mile wide and I know it, but knowing your faults doesn't make it any easier to control them. Each time we'd met, I had come up to town and we'd gone somewhere, for dinner, for drinks – it was fine, but Michelle always brought her friends from the agency along, and I would have preferred to see her alone. They sat on either side of her watching me, like bodyguards, ready to pounce at the first sign of an improper advance.

On this particular evening we were drinking in a small club in Beak Street with her usual crowd. She began talking about some new bar, and I asked her if she ever got tired of living right here, in the middle of so much noise and violence. In reply, she told me London was the safest place in the world. I pointed out that it was now considered to be the most crime-riddled city in Europe. She just stared at me blankly for a moment and turned to talk to someone else.

Her attitude pissed me off. She was living in a dream state, ignoring anything bad or even remotely realistic in life. I wouldn't let the subject go and tackled her again. She quoted Samuel Johnson, her friends nodded in agreement, I threw in some crime statistics and moments later we were having a heated, pointless row. What impressed me was the way in which she took everything to heart, as if by insulting London I was causing her personal injury. Finally she called me smug and small-minded and stormed out of the club.

One of her friends, an absurd young man with a ponytail, pushed me down in my seat as I rose to leave. 'You shouldn't have argued with her,' he said, shaking his head in admonishment. 'She loves this city, and she won't hear anyone criticising it.'

'You can't go on treating her like a child forever,' I complained. 'Someone has to tell her the truth.'

'That's what her last boyfriend did.'

'And what happened to him?'

'He got knocked off his bike by a bus.' Ponytail shrugged. 'He's never going to walk again.' He stared out of the window at the teeming night streets. 'This city. Either you're its friend or you're an enemy.'

After waiting for hours outside her darkened apartment, I returned home to Meadowfields in low spirits. I felt as though I had failed some kind of test. A few days later, Michelle reluctantly agreed to see me for dinner. This time there would be just the two of us. We arranged to meet in Dell' Ugo in Frith Street at 9 pm the next Friday evening.

I didn't get there until 10.30 pm.

It wasn't my fault. I allowed plenty of time for my rail connections, but one train wasn't running and the passengers were off-loaded onto buses that took the most circuitous route imaginable. By the time I reached the restaurant she had gone. The maître d' told me she had waited for forty minutes.

After that Michelle refused to take my calls, either at the agency or at her flat. I must have spoken to her answering machine a hundred times.

A week passed, the worst week of my life. At work, everything went wrong. The money for the charity ads fell through and the campaign was cancelled, so I had no reason to visit the agency again. Then Aunt Sheila asked me to help her sell the house because she had decided to move to Spain. I would have to find a new place to live. And all the time, Michelle's face was before me. I felt like following her ex-boyfriend under a bus.

It was Friday night, around 7 pm. I was standing in the front garden, breathing cool evening air scented with burning leaves and looking out at the lights of the estate, fifty-eight miles from the city and the woman. That's when it happened. Personal epiphany, collapse of inner belief system, whatever you want to call it. I suddenly saw how cocooned I'd been here in Legoland. I'd never had a chance to understand a woman like Michelle. She unnerved me, so I was backing away from the one thing I really wanted, which was to be with her. Now I could see that she was a lifeline, one final chance for me to escape. Okay, it may have been obvious to you but it came as a complete revelation to me.

I ran back into the house, past my Aunt Sheila who was in the kitchen doing something visceral in a pudding basin, and rang Michelle's apartment. And – there *was* a God – she answered the call. I told her exactly how I felt, begged absolution for my behaviour, explained how desperate I was to see her. For a few moments the line went silent as she thought things through. Once more, my honesty won the day.

'Tomorrow night,' she said. 'I've already made arrangements with friends, but come along.'

'I'll be there,' I replied, elated. 'When and where?'

She said she would be in a restaurant called the Palais du Jardin in Long Acre until 10.30 pm, then at a new club in Soho. She gave me the addresses. 'I warn you, Douglas,' she added. 'This is absolutely your last chance. If you don't show up, you can throw away my number because I'll never speak to you again.'

I swore to myself that nothing would go wrong. Nothing.

Saturday morning.

It feels like a lifetime has passed, but peering at the cracked glass of my watch I realise that it was just twenty hours ago.

I planned everything down to the last detail. I consulted the weather bureau, then rang all three stations and checked that the trains would be running. 'Only connect,' wrote E.M. Forster, but he obviously hadn't seen a British Rail timetable.

To be safe I left half-hour gaps between each train, so there would be no possibility of missing one of them. I bought a new suit, my first since wide lapels went out. I got a decent haircut from a new barber, one without faded photographs of people who looked like Val Doonican taped to his window. The day dragged past at a snail's pace, each minute lasting an hour. Finally it was time to leave Rosemount Crescent.

I made all my connections. Nothing went wrong until I reached Waterloo, where the Northern Line had been closed because of a bomb scare. It had begun to rain, a fine soaking drizzle. There were no cabs to be seen so I waited for a bus, safe in the knowledge that Michelle would be dining for a while yet. I felt that she had deliberately kept the arrangement casual to help me. She knew I had to make an awkward journey into town.

The first two buses were full, and the driver of the third wouldn't take Scottish pound notes, which for some reason I'd been given at the cash point. I was fine on the fourth, until I realised that it veered away from Covent Garden at precisely the moment when I needed it to turn left into the area. I walked back along the Strand with my jacket collar turned up against the rain. I hadn't thought to wear an overcoat. I was late, and it felt as if the city was deliberately keeping me away from her. I imagined Michelle at the restaurant table, lowering her wineglass and laughing with friends as she paused to check her watch. I examined my *A–Z* and turned up towards Long Acre, just in time for a cab to plough through a trough of kerbside water and soak my legs. Then I discovered that I'd lost the piece of paper bearing the name of the restaurant. It had been in the same pocket as the *A–Z* but must have fallen out. I had been so determined to memorise the name of the place, and now it completely eluded me. The harder I searched my mind, the less chance I had of remembering it. I had to explore every single restaurant in the damned street, and there were dozens of them.

I was just another guy on a date (admittedly the most important date I'd ever had) and it was turning into the quest for the Holy Grail. It took me over half an hour to cover the whole of Long Acre, only to find that the Palais du Jardin was the very last restaurant in the street, and that I had missed Michelle Davies's party by five minutes.

At least I remembered the name of the club and strode on to it, tense and determined. The bare grey building before me had an industrial steel door, above which hung a banner reading 'blUeTOPIA'. The bricks themselves were bleeding techno beat. In front of the door stood a large man in a tight black suit, white shirt, narrow black tie and sunglasses, a Cro-Magnon Blues Brother.

'Get back behind the rope.' He sounded bored. He kept his arms folded and stared straight ahead.

'How much is it to get in?' I asked.

'Depends which part you're going into.'

I tried to peer through the door's porthole, but he blocked my view. 'What's the difference?'

'You're not dressed for downstairs. Downstairs is rubber.'

'Ah. How much upstairs?' I felt for my wallet. The rain had begun to fall more heavily, coloured needles passing through neon.

'Fifteen pounds.'

'That's a lot.'

'Makes no difference. You can't come in.'

'Why not?'

'It's full up. Fire regulations.'

'But I have to meet someone.'

Just then two shaven-headed girls in stacked boots walked past me, and the bouncer held the door open for them. A wave of boiling air and scrambled music swept over us.

'Why did you let them in?' I asked as he resealed the door.

'They're members.'

'How much is it to be a member?'

'Membership's closed.'

'You told me the club was full.'

'Only to guests.'

'Could I come in if I was with a member?'

The doorman approximated an attitude of deep thought for a moment. 'Not without a guest pass.'

'What must I give you to get one of those?'

'Twenty-four hours' notice.'

'Look.' I spoke through gritted teeth. 'I can see we have to reach some kind of agreement here, because the rest of my life is dependent on me getting inside this club tonight.'

'You could try bribing me.' He spoke as if he was telling a child something very obvious. I shuffled some notes from my wallet and held them out. He glanced down briefly, then resumed his Easter Island pose. I added another ten. He palmed the stack without checking it.

'Now can I come in?'

'No.'

'You took a bribe. I'll call the police.'

'Suit yourself. Who are they going to believe?'

That was a good point. He probably knew all the officers in the area. I was just a hick hustling to gain entry to his club. 'I could make trouble for you,' I said unconvincingly.

'Oh, that's good.' He glanced down at me. 'Bouncers love trouble. Every night we pray for a good punch-up. When there's a fight we call each other from all the other clubs,' he indicated the doorways along the street, 'and have a big bundle.'

It was hopeless. My street etiquette was nonexistent. I simply didn't know what to do, so I asked him. 'This is incredibly important to me,' I explained. 'Just tell me how I can get in.'

I'd already guessed the reply. 'You can't.'

'Why not?'

'Because you had to ask.' He removed his glasses and studied me with tiny deep-set eyes. 'You're up from the sticks for your Big Night Out, but it's not in here, not for you. You don't fit.'

At least he was honest. I knew then that it wasn't just the club. I'd never be able to make the jump, even for a woman like her. Despondent, I walked to the side of the building and pressed my back against the wet brickwork, studying the sky. And I waited. I thought there might be a side exit I could slip through, but there wasn't. Everyone came and went through the front door. Soon my shirt was sticking to my skin and my shoes were filled with water, but I no longer cared. See Suburban Man attempt to leave his natural habitat! Watch as he enters the kingdom of Urbia and battles the mocking resident tribe! Well, this was one Suburban Man who wasn't going down without a fight.

But two hours later I was still there, shivering in the shadowed lea of the building, studying the lengthy queue of clubbers waiting to enter. When the steel door opened and she appeared with Ponytail and some black guy on her arm, I stepped forward into the light. One look at her face told me everything. I was sure now that she'd known I wouldn't get in and was having a laugh at my expense.

I'm not a violent man, but I found myself moving towards her with my arm raised and I think my hand connected, just a glancing blow. Then people from the queue were on me, someone's hand across my face, another pushing me backwards. There was some shouting, and I recall hearing Michelle call my name, something about not hurting me.

I remember being thrown into the alley and hitting the ground hard. In movies they always land on a neat pile of cardboard boxes. No such luck here, just piss-drenched concrete and drains. My face was hurting, and I could taste blood in my mouth. I unscrewed my eyes and saw Ponytail standing over me. The black guy was holding Michelle by the arm, talking fast. She looked really sorry and I think she wanted to help, but he wasn't about to allow her near me. I could barely hear what he was saying through the noise in my head.

'I told you this would happen. He got no roots, no family. He don't belong here. You know that.' He was talking too fast. I didn't understand. Then Ponytail was crouching low beside me.

'Big fucking mistake, man. You can't be near her. Don't you get it?' He was waving his hands at me, frustrated by his efforts to explain. 'She's part of this city. Do you see? I mean *really* part of it. You hurt her, you hurt – all of this.' He raised his arm at the buildings surrounding us.

I tried to talk but my tongue seemed to block my speech. Ponytail moved closer.

'Listen to me, you're cut but this is nothing. You must get up and run. It watches over her and now it'll fight you. Run back to your own world and you may be able to save yourself. That's all the advice I can give you, man.'

Then they were gone, the men on either side protecting her, swiftly bearing her away from harm, slaves guarding their queen. She stole a final glance back at me, regret filling her eyes.

For a few minutes I lay there. No one came forward to help. Eventually I found the strength to pull myself to my feet. It felt as if someone had stuck a penknife into my rib-cage. The first time I tried to leave the alley, the indignant crowd pushed me back. When I eventually managed to break through, the buildings ahead dazzled my eyes and I slipped on the wet kerb, falling heavily onto my shins. I knew that no one would ever come forward to help me now. The city had changed its face. As I stumbled on, blurs of angry people gesticulated and screeched, Hogarthian grotesques marauding across town and time. I milled through them in a maze of streets that turned me back towards the centre where I would be consumed and forgotten, another threat disposed of.

I feel dizzy, but I daren't risk lying down. There's a thick rope of blood running down my left leg, from an artery I think. I'm so vulnerable, just a sack of flesh and bone encircled by concrete and steel and iron railings and brittle panes. A few minutes ago I leaned against a shop window, trying to clear my stinging head, and the glass shattered, vitreous blades shafting deep into my back.

I can't last much longer without her protection.

The first car that hit me drove over my wrist and didn't stop. A fucking Fiat Panda. I think the second one broke a bone in my knee. Something is grinding and mashing when I bend the joint. He didn't stop, either. Perhaps I'm no longer visible. I can't tell if I'm walking in the road, because it keeps shifting beneath my feet. The buildings, too, trundle noisily back and forth, diverting and directing. I feel light-headed. All I know is, I won't survive until daybreak. No chance of reaching safety now. London has shut me out and trapped me in.

It's unfair; I don't think I should have to die. I suppose it's traditional when you screw around with the queen. As the pavement beneath my feet is heading slightly downhill, I think I'm being led towards the embankment. It will be a short drop to the sluggish river below, and merciful sleep beyond.

I wonder what her real age is, and if she even has a name. Or what would have happened had I learned to love her city and stay within the custody of her benevolent gaze. Does she look down with a tremor of compassion for those who fail to survive her kingdom, or does she stare in pitiless fascination at the mortals tumbling through her ancient, coiling street, while far away suburbia sleeps on?

Two Murders

1. *Normal Life*

I started when the doorbell rang. I'd been expecting it, but had dozed off momentarily in front of the television. I gave the lounge one more quick spray of lavender, walked into the hall and saw her silhouetted through the stained glass, her hand still hovering near the bell. I knew at that moment that she was perfect. A tiny waist, a dainty stance, girlish, shy, ash-blond hair swept up and held in place with a tortoiseshell slide, lustrous lashes, tipped-up nose, tight pink mouth, long neck; so perfect.

I opened the door with a friendly smile.

'You must be Isabel Lyons.' What can I say? She was everything I had hoped for, and more. Graceful, delicate, a miniature beauty, her turquoise eyes focused on distant thoughts, dressed in a navy wool coat and an orange hand-knitted scarf, dainty little brown-leather boots.

'I'm sorry I'm late,' she apologised. 'My last appointment overran.'

'That's quite all right. Please come in.' I held back the front door, bade her enter. Instead, she took a step back and tipped her head up. 'I love the outside mosaics. The little—' She twirled the fingers of her gloved right hand. Reluctantly, I stepped forward. I was wearing carpet slippers. I checked the street for inquisitive neighbours.

'The murals, yes, they're lovely, aren't they? The house is Victorian of course, but the murals look art nouveau, don't you think?'

'I don't know.' She tilted her head this way and that. 'I love them.'

She didn't know. Odd. On the phone she'd said she loved art nouveau.

'Won't you come in?' I beckoned once more.

'Of course.' She smiled and looked directly at me, into my eyes. Very unusual. People tend to talk to me indirectly, with their eyes slightly averted. And such a smile!

The sun was starting to set. I checked the street once more, and closed the front door. She was standing just behind me in the gloom.

I switched on the light and she gasped.

'People either love it or hate it,' I admitted. 'Let me take your coat.'

'I love it. Do you know the name of the artist?' She took a step closer, shucking off her raincoat as she examined the walls.

'No. I assume he was a minor pre-Raphaelite. The cherubs are rather poor, but the vines . . . the plaster needs some work. And this is the lounge.' I spoke quickly, displaying nervousness. I pushed open the door, wondering if she would like what she saw. Overstuffed armchairs, tasselled curtains, lincrusta wallpaper, copper coal-scuttle, Welsh dresser, shuttered windows. Deep greens, deep reds, dark corners. Some damp spots, unfortunately. I checked that the air-fresheners were still in place under the armchairs.

The last time someone came to the house – a young social worker named Michael – I invited him into the lounge and saw the leg, the bare leg, sticking out from behind the sofa. I had been planning to burn it days before, but had forgotten to do so. By this time, the flesh was green and purple. I had been forced to spray the ragged black thigh-stump in Calvin Klein because I had run out of lavender air-freshener. It's hard to tell if your own house smells; you only notice other people's. I wondered if mine smelled of death. It must have done that day, with parts of over ten bodies scattered around the place in various stages of decay. But Michael had taken his leave without noticing anything unusual. I had allowed him to leave. He didn't interest me.

Since then I had been getting rid of the body parts little by little, but my desires had overtaken my ability to destroy the evidence, and the backlog was a constant headache, which was why I had decided to rent out the house, and why Isabel was here to view the property. I couldn't go through an agent, you see. An agent would pry.

'I like the way you've kept the traditional style throughout. You can't beat a real fire, can you?' She smiled and turned about, almost too polite. There had to be something she didn't like.

'Would you like – a cup of tea?' I managed.

'That would be nice.' I showed her the scullery. I could never bring myself to call it the kitchen.

'So you live alone?' she asked, delicately blowing on the surface of her teacup.

'I prefer it,' I explained. 'I'm not one for company.'

'Shall we see upstairs?' she asked. I had assumed she would want to finish her tea first.

'Of course.' I led the way to the first-floor landing. The

street light had faded, and I turned on the lights as we ascended.

'These cupboards are beautiful.' Her outstretched hand caressed polish-darkened teak. 'Were they built by the architect of the house? They're so in keeping with the overall decorative design.'

I didn't fucking know, nor did I care. I have no eye for the beauty of objects that have never enjoyed life. Her endless questions were already starting to annoy me. She would be safe as long as she did not ask too many questions. I am not a man to be annoyed.

'I think they date from the time of the house,' I forced myself to reply.

'Do you know what year it was built? I can see the art nouveau influence again . . .' She trailed her hand across the inlaid irises on the banisters, following me as I continued upwards.

'And how many bedrooms do you have?' Questions, questions, as if she was frightened of leaving dead air between us.

'Three, but only one is decorated. The other two are just junk rooms at the moment. I've been meaning to clear them out.' Or rather, I had been meaning to clear out the remains of several itinerant youths and assorted bits of lonely young women who would not be missed. I pushed open the door of the master bedroom and flicked on the light, quickly checking that all was in order. I really should have done this earlier. I could tell from her face that this time she was clearly less taken with the surroundings. Had I forgotten something? The stench of damaged human flesh had been hidden beneath the pervasive smell of lavender.

'I did this room myself,' I said listlessly, wishing I hadn't agreed to show her around.

'Oh, I see.' She hated it. Well, it wasn't to everyone's taste. The purple geometries of seventies vinyl wallpaper. Hardboard walls coated in stained Marley-tiles. The gas cooker stuffed in an alcove, surrounded by suspiciously large metal cooking-pots. The foldaway divan and TV set buried beneath a mound of empty plastic snack-food cartons. This was the room in which I lived and strangers died. There were no dead people in here at the moment, except Mr Summerton, who was not dead, merely drugged and tightly tied up in the built-in wardrobe. Then again, I thought, he might be dead. I had been meaning to take care of him for three days now, but had been too busy at work to find the time.

'What's in there?' she asked stupidly, pointing to the fitted wardrobe.

'Just clothes.' I stood in front of the white laminated double-doors, surreptitiously pushing against them to make sure that they were shut.

'Because I thought someone might have built over the original fittings.'

'No. No, I don't think so.'

'Oh.' She looked disappointed.

I stepped away from the doors. 'Let's go back down.'

'Wait.' She hesitated, raising a forefinger. 'Because I keep—'

'What?'

'I keep thinking I can hear something.'

She was too quick for me. Reached behind my back and yanked at one of the handles. The door came flying open, and there was Mr Summerton screaming into the spittle-caked bin-liner knotted around his mouth, all rolling eyes and shitty trousers. The smell and the shock drove her back into my arms, good job too because I could lift her off the floor by her throat, squeezing hard and breaking the little bones in her neck. She died quickly and easily, and I threw her body on top of Mr Summerton, who '*mmmmggnnnmm*'ed even harder into his gag, gave them both a quick spray of lavender air-freshener and slammed the wardrobe door shut. I would clear them up tomorrow, or the next day.

In the hall I went through her coat pockets and found my ad ringed in Biro in her folded property paper. I also found her identity card, which said she was WPC Isabel Lyons. A policewoman. I had killed a policewoman. She must have told someone her suspicions. Someone would come looking for her. Perhaps they were already on their way here. Perhaps that was a good thing; I needed to be stopped.

It took me ten minutes to pack a bag. I walked to the station through fine night-drizzle, yellow needles in lamplight, steam-train breath, brisk hard steps, head lowered at the brown paving-stones falling away before my shoes. Caught a tube, then a main-line train to the coast, silver lines snaking into darkness, strobing sleepers shutting my eyes in the empty over-heated carriage. I reached the bleak grey-green seafront in under two hours. No one about. Houses dark. Wind rising. The black streets like those of a miniature village that had been unplugged for the night.

The Ocean Breeze Guest House was an end-of-terrace bed and breakfast place festooned with nylon curtains and china poodles. It smelled of damp and was run by a thin-lipped woman who was too busy watching me count money into her hand to take any notice of my face. The narrow bed and sixties wallpaper reminded me of childhood. They weren't pleasant memories. I lay on my back listening to the sinister susurrance of the sea. It was the first time I had been to the coast in years, the first time, in fact, that I had been out of the city in a decade. The next morning I consumed a grease-drenched breakfast, donned my raincoat and stepped out onto the rain-squalled promenade. There were few people outside. An elderly couple unwrapping sandwiches in a green wooden shelter. Two small boys running over the wet pebbles screaming obscenities into the angry sky. The pier looked as if it had surprised itself by bothering to open. I stood at the end of it, thirty feet above the heaving olive sea, and watched a melancholy young girl weave pink candy-floss beneath the rainbow lightbulbs of her little stall.

She was perfect.

Pink overalls, pink hair, pink lipstick, pink candy-floss. Round and round she rolled the stick, as if turning an invisible handle above the drum. I could smell the sticky sweetness through the rain. She looked at the cocoon of spun sugar she had gathered and tore off a chunk, like an angel ripping a piece out of a sunset cloud. But it was early, and I was in enough trouble. As I had told myself so many times before, I had to learn to fight the loneliness.

In town I bought two sticks of lavender air-freshener for my room, and glimpsed the front pages of the tabloids. Photographs of Miss Lyons stared back. None of me yet. I tried to think about her, how she had found me, who she had told, but the subject did not hold my interest. I am not really interested in other people because they do not do what you tell them to.

I thought about disguising my appearance, but I am unmemorable at the best of times. I removed my spectacles and bought a second-hand baseball cap, pulling it low on my forehead. Watched a movie in the town's only cinema, some rubbish about aliens. Picked yellow batter from fish and chips in an empty café. Took a bus to the end of the front and stood at the steel gates before a vast anonymous block of concrete, the area's power station, which hummed faintly in the silently falling rain, like radio waves, or wind in telegraph wires. Power stations make you feel lonely.

Back in the Ocean Breeze, an old man was dozing noisily in front of the evening news. I went to my room, feeling anticlimactic and empty.

The next morning the rain had stopped, but there was still no sun. I ventured back out on to the pier and watched the seagulls tumbling like scraps of litter. The candy-floss stand was inexplicably shut. I was disappointed not to see the girl standing there gathering her clouds. I bought a tea and locked my hands around the warm polystyrene, unable to decide on my next move.

She looked different from the other seaside people. Tall, freshly permed auburn hair, dressed in high heels and a glossy black fur coat, lightly leaning on the rail, looking out at the horizon. I stood a few feet further down and imitated her pose. She made a small gesture with her gold-bangled wrists that made me think for a moment that she was going to climb the railings and jump into the sea. Then she seemed lost in thought once more.

After a while her curiosity got the better of her, and she looked my way. Older than I first thought, forty-five perhaps, a little too made up, too many rings. She glanced at me with passing curiosity, then her gaze lingered. I moved a little closer, sipped some cooling tea.

'At least it's stopped raining.' I always speak first.

'Not for long. It never stops raining for long in this town.' She looked across. 'Do you have a cigarette?' As it happened I did, and matches, although I don't smoke. I carry them, you know, in case. I lit it for her. The smoke was taken by the wind from the sea.

'Do you live here?' I asked.

'God, is it that obvious?' She rested mink elbows back on the railing. 'Yes, at the edge of town. Just where the road runs out.'

'I'm visiting for a few days,' I volunteered. 'Sales conference.'

'Please don't tell me what you sell. My husband goes to sales conferences. He's at one now. Frankfurt, Birmingham, I don't know. As far as I can tell they're all the same.'

'They are,' I agreed, 'they're like towns. Quiet or busy, but the same wherever you go.'

To my surprise she laughed. 'Don't tell me I've met some-one even more depressed than me.'

I'd like to tell you what else we talked about, but I really don't remember. She was far from perfect. Not my type. Too dry, too knowing. But when she invited me back, I accepted.

I don't usually. They have to come to me. It's part of the whole thing, and easier too. But I was in a strange town, and she had a car, a silver Audi. The waxed interior made my clothes look very shabby. I had a hole in my shoe. The car shut out the sound of the world. She didn't offer her name, and I didn't ask. The sticks of lavender air-freshener were still in my overcoat pocket.

We pulled into a deserted close of new yellow-brick ranch-style houses, a suburban businessman's idea of sophisti-cation. I followed her inside, and seated myself on a white-leather sofa in the lounge. I thought she would offer me a drink, coffee at least. It was still only just past midday. Instead, she dropped her mink coat on the carpet and sat opposite me, in an armchair. She wore a two-piece knitted affair, too short in the skirt. She hiked the skirt even further when she sat. She was wearing red knickers.

'Does it look like anyone lives here?' she asked.

'What do you mean?'

'Well, Ilsa cleans every other day. My husband is away three weeks out of four. Does it look as if a human being inhabits this place?'

I looked about. The clean ashtrays. Neatly stacked magazines. Polished mirrors. Like the waiting room of a private surgery. 'No, not really.'

'You see,' she said after a long silence, 'we're not alive, not really. Do you know anyone who is? Honestly?'

'No.'

'I wonder how you want to do this.'

It didn't seem to me that she was talking about sex.

'Do what?' I asked, uncomfortable in surroundings that drew such attention to themselves.

'I mean, I don't know how you go about – what you do.'

I must have looked mystified. Her attitude changed. 'Oh come on, I know who you are. You only have to read a paper. Even the broadsheets are carrying your picture. You've sexually assaulted and murdered seventeen – or is it eighteen – women. Stabbed. Strangled. They're still looking for the parts. You're famous. So. How do you want to do it this time?'

I shifted uncomfortably. My buttocks were sticking to the leather seat. 'You want me to kill you?'

She rose and came closer. 'I'm living in hell here. I want to be at peace. That's all anybody wants, isn't it?'

'I— I can't kill you just because you're unhappy. Sort your life out. Get a divorce.'

'And what?' She dug a cigarette from an onyx box on the coffee table. 'Marry another career-blinded shit? Take more pills? Live in another luxury prison? I've tried killing myself before. I've used up all my cry-for-help credibility. I want you to treat me like you treated the others. Tell me if the sex part comes before or after.' She opened her legs lasciviously. 'What do you slide into me first?'

'I can't,' I replied slowly, rising to go.

'Why not?' Her eyes locked with mine. 'It's what you do. Why not?'

'Because this isn't about you. It's about me. My needs.'

'Oh of course, I forgot how selfish murderers are,' she spat, turning her back. If she wanted to rouse me to violence, she had failed. I walked out into the hall. She followed me, shouting. 'Don't think you're so different from other men. You just think about yourself. You're all the same. Gutless bastards.'

Shocked, I let myself out.

It had become overcast once more, and started to rain as I walked briskly away.

Two bus rides later I was back in town, passing truant children spray-painting the walls of a house with hieroglyphic filth, looking up at the eerie, humming power-station in the distance, watching the cars spraying along the seafront with their headlights on, the deserted bandstand with water sluicing from its gutters, the waitresses mechanically clearing tables in burger bars too brightly lit to hold secrets, the stooped women dragging plastic shopping-bags back and forth, the ancient couples seated silently chewing in parked cars, and knew that this was how it would always be until the end of time, millions of lives even shabbier and more revolting than mine had been, and I wondered.

What kind of world was it where a man who had cut a human body into pieces with a hacksaw and two bread-knives could be made to feel more normal than his surroundings?

There is a point in everybody's existence when the world is finally exposed, and you see life for what it really is. That is the moment when you have to decide if you can survive without hope.

I walked to the end of the low stone jetty, where the windswept waves washed the point, and cried, and cried.

When I had finished, I wiped the rain-tears from my face with a handkerchief and composed myself. I took the sticks of lavender air-freshener from my pocket and threw them into the heaving green sea.

Then I turned around, and walked back to the land.

2. *Home Again*

They keep asking me why I did it.

I try to tell them, but they're not listening.

They talk reasonably, pleasantly, and are politely silent as I reply. They hear, but they're not listening. The sheets of paper on the desk before me are filled with details of my case, but the wrong ones. They describe what happened, but not why. I stare at the words which form my admission of guilt. Oh, I'm guilty, I don't deny that. The boy was seventeen? eighteen? No, I had never seen him before. He was just passing me on the street, bouncing on his trainers with an angry swagger. I stuck the knife into his nylon jacket and he fell to his knees in shocked silence. I stabbed him over a hundred and seventy times. I stabbed him until there was nothing solid left to stab. Then, dripping from head to foot with his blood, I waited at the kerb until someone came to bring me here.

'Yes,' I agree, perusing the pages, 'this is exactly what happened.'

'You know what you did?' asks one of the incredulous cops.

'Certainly. And let me tell you why.' I'm handcuffed, so they can safely let me use the Biro. I want to write this down in my own hand.

A dead, hot day in mid-July. The air is countrified, dandelion spores rising gently on warm thermals, the lazy drone of a beetle alighting on dust-dulled hedge leaves. A suburban summertime, where the South London solstice settles in a sleepy yellow blanket over still front-gardens.

Westerdale Road has seashells cemented in its front-garden walls. It is the same as the other roads in the area, and yet each has a distinct identity. Farmdale Road houses a Victorian parish hall that provides a meeting place for scouts and cubs, and hosts Sunday School classes for reluctant children. Ormiston Crescent is a silent L-shaped street populated by elderly bad-tempered old widows who appear in their doorways at the sound of a football being kicked against a wall.

Like all of these streets, Westerdale Road has its characters. The deaf couple whose pond freezes over every winter, so that they have to thaw their goldfish from a block of ice in a tin bath beside the fire. The old lady who keeps stuffed cats on her sideboard. Some of the houses have Anderson shelters in their gardens, converted to tool-sheds in time of peace. Others are used to keep chickens, their distinctive sound and smell exciting the neighbourhood cats. Further along the street is a 'simple' man who sits on his front step smiling inanely in the bright sunlight.

The road backs on to Westcombe Hill. Odd how so many street names conjure pastoral imagery; 'Combedale Road', 'Mycenae Road'. Its houses form alleyways at their rear, a Victorian remnant my mother vaguely disapproves of, for here there is a subtle hierarchy. These backs of houses are populated by the shop owners of Westcombe Hill, and the cramped alley creates an enforced neighbourliness that she sees as 'common'. We at number 35 have a garden. We do not live above shops. The fact that we are relatively poor while they thrive (purchasing luxury items like television sets and cars) has nothing to do with it.

Noon. The silent sunlight scorches the streets, and everyone knows their place. Housewives are deep within their little terraced houses, polishing sideboards, making jellies, busying themselves in cool shadowed rooms. Their men are at work, mopping their brows in council offices, patrolling machine-room floors, filling out paperwork in dusty bank chambers. Their children are all at school reciting their tables, catching beanbags, and in the break following lunch there is a special treat; the teacher unlocks a paddock behind the playground of Invicta Infants, and here is a haven from the hot concrete, a small square meadow of cropped emerald grass hemmed in with chickenwire. Here we are allowed to lie on our stomachs reading comics, passing them between each other. It is peaceful, warm and quiet (the teachers do not tolerate the vulgarity of noise) and although we are in another suburban street, it feels like the heart of the countryside.

What was it this area possessed to make it so special, so irreplaceable and precious? A few roads, a pond behind a wall where sticklebacks were trapped in jars and dragonflies skimmed the oily water, a railway line with a narrow pedestrian tunnel beneath it, a station of nicotine-coloured wood and rows of green tin-lamps along the platform. Some odd shops; a perpetually deserted furniture showroom, damp and dark, its proprietor standing ever-hopefully at the door, a model railway centre with a brass-edged penny-slot cut in the window to make the trains go around, a tobacconist selling sweets from large jars, a rack of Ellisdons Jokes on a stand, none of them quite living up to their packet descriptions – what modern child would understand the pleasure of 'Fake Soot'? – a chemist with apothecary bottles filled with coloured water and a scale machine, green and chrome with a wicker weighing-basket, a bakery window filled with pink and white sugar mice, iced rounds, meringues and Battenburg cakes. An advertisement painted on a wall, for varnish remover of some kind, depicting a housewife happily pouring boiling water from a kettle on to a shiny dining-room table. Cinema posters under wire. A hardware shop with tin baths hanging either side of the door.

The confluence of roads and railway lines is bordered by an iron bridge and an embankment filled with white trumpet-flowered vines, and populated by families with forgotten children's names; Laurence, Janet, Percy, Pauline, Albert, Wendy, Sidney. No middle-class aspirations here, just the stillness of summer, the faint drone of insects, bees landing on flowerbeds in the police station garden, tortoises and chickens sheltering from the heat beneath bushes, cats asleep in shop windows with yellow acetate sunscreens, and life being lived, a dull, sensible kind of life, unfolding like a flower, the day loosening as slowly as a clock spring – an implacable state which we, as children, thought would never change, but which is now lost so totally, so far beyond reach that it might have occurred before Isis ruled the Nile. The sands have shifted now, hiding the contours of my happiness. I look for the patterns that shaped my life and find only tarmac, concrete and steel, the dead carapace of something lost to all but the mind's eye.

To look back on those times of sunset parklands, fathers carrying glasses of beer into the street on tin trays, mothers calling to one another across backyard fences, is to glimpse a world as yet unaltered by the spending power of teenagers. A post-war period that lasted less than fifteen years. Beeching closed the branch lines, road planners cut the street in half, smashed down the houses, constructed a vast swathe of concrete through the hill, the roads, the shops, the railway, the gardens, and like a bush cut through at the root, everything died.

Shops were boarded up. Families were relocated. Oil-drenched vibrations pulse the once-still air. Scraps remain; a few houses, a closed shop, a patch of pavement where once I stood with my face to the sun. The great motorway which replaced the area is virtually unused, a concrete landing-strip that lies across the land like the gravestone for a generation. Nostalgia sweetens the past, but this is how it really was. And so long as one person is alive to remember, how it remains. Life had been good and kind and constant.

I watched the destruction of everything I had faith in. The corruption of everything innocent. The tainting of everything pure. The degeneration into chaos of everything stable. This is how it is for most people of my age. My generation has seen more changes than any other. Most of its members never reveal their disgust, their horror, their misery at the shabby, trashy future. They brick it up, hide it away, lie down and die. I decided not to do that.

I didn't know the boy. I barely even saw his face. He was drunk, or drugged, there was no way to tell which. I only recognised him as part of a tide I cannot hold back. Adulthood asks us to store away the past and act with maturity, but the present is filled with chaos. I have had to grow up with the new. I am expected to fit into my time. I am a part of this unholy new anarchy, this ubiquitous coarseness, this cheapness of spirit, this destruction of human decency. I have to be a modern man. I am allowed to do anything. I can be sold to the highest bidder. There are no more rules. And if they say I am mad, even better; I can be a child again, like the children on the hoardings and the drunks in the street. Childhood has endless sparkling expectations and a smile as wide as a summer night.

This is what I write. I killed because I wanted something back. Memory recaptures the sensation, words hold it for ever on the page, but only the deed can restore it to life and lock it in place for ever.

Albert Camus said that a man's work is nothing but the long journey to recover the first two or three simple and great images which first gained access to his heart. My journey has ended. For me, the nightmare is over. I am home again.

Warner titles available by post:

❏	Darkest Day	Christopher Fowler	£6.99
❏	Disturbia	Christopher Fowler	£5.99
❏	Flesh Wounds	Christopher Fowler	£5.99
❏	Psychoville	Christopher Fowler	£5.99
❏	Roofworld	Christopher Fowler	£5.99
❏	Rune	Christopher Fowler	£5.99
❏	Soho Black	Christopher Fowler	£8.99
❏	Spanky	Christopher Fowler	£5.99

The prices shown above are correct at time of going to press. However, the publishers reserve the right to increase prices on covers from those previously advertised, without further notice.

WARNER BOOKS

WARNER BOOKS

Cash Sales Department, P.O. Box 11, Falmouth, Cornwall, TR10 9EN
Tel +44 (0) 1326 372400, Fax: +44 (0) 1326 374888
Email: books@barni.avel.co.uk

POST AND PACKING:

Payments can be made as follows: cheque, postal order (payable to Warner Books) or by credit cards. Do not send cash or currency.

U.K. orders under £10	£1.50
U.K. orders over £10	**FREE OF CHARGE**
E.C. & Overseas	25% of order value

Name (Block letters) ....

Address ....

....

Post/zip code: ....

☐ Please keep me in touch with future Warner Books

☐ I enclose my remittance £ ....

☐ I wish to pay by Visa/Access/Mastercard/Eurocard

Card Expiry Date
